Lady of the Sea

Kathy Keller

Kathy Keller
655 Tree Side Lane
Ponte Vedra, Florida 32081
www.kathykeller.com

Book Layout © 2017 BookDesignTemplates.com

Lady of the Sea/ Author Name. – 1st ed.
ISBN 978-1-7370503-5-3

*"A beautiful woman is a beautiful woman,
but a beautiful woman with a brain
is an absolutely lethal combination."*

—PRABAL GURUNG

CONTENTS

CHAPTER ONE

The Homecoming

April, 1795

Many a man has labored under the illusion that he is the master of his universe until a woman comes along to disabuse him of that notion. Captain Reese Thackeray, blissfully unaware of this human condition, stood imposingly on the quarter deck in full command, defiant of challenge as the *Sea Nymph* sailed gracefully into Boston Harbor.

Deckmen harbor furled the sails, and the first mate steered the tall ship into place along the Long Wharf.

"Drop anchors!" yelled the bosun.

Deckhands threw out hawsers to dock workers then who stood ready to secure the ship.

Thackeray stepped down to the main deck and a smile spread across his square-cut features as he gazed out over the controlled chaos of the busy harbor.

The air was rife with the shouts of the longshoremen and the noise of hoisting blocks as cargo was lifted onto and off of ships. Bales of cotton, hogsheads of tobacco, barrels of salted cod, and stacks of lumber and animal hides lined the piers for export. Vendors and importers ran hither and thither. Boston was no different from any other major harbor, but this was his home port and that made it unique to him.

As Thackeray continued to inventory the docks, he saw that new wharves had been added in his absence. Similarly, the counting houses and warehouses that lined the quay and piers had increased in number. Forever a man of consistency, he decided that these changes fell within the accepted parameters of his ordered world.

"The ship be moored, sir," announced the bosun.

Thackeray nodded and went to his quarters to finish the paperwork for the Customs Collector. When he completed the task, he returned to the main deck and summoned his first mate.

"Mr. Seaton, take this copy of the manifest to the Henshaw counting house and return with a voucher of payment for the goods, whilst I file the Entry of Merchandise form with Customs."

"Aye aye, sir," replied the first mate.

An hour later, the captain returned from the Customs House.

"Mr. White, where is Mr. Seaton?" he asked.

The bosun shrugged. "Ain't seen him since ye sent him off to the counting house, Captain."

Thackeray frowned. "He should have returned by now."

"Alex probably got his head turned by some pretty, little bird," said the bosun. "'Tis been a long time since last we was in port. You know how it is, sir."

Thackeray gave a slight smile. He did, indeed, know how it was. "Well then, the sooner Mr. Seaton arrives with a voucher, the sooner I can settle your accounts, and you may be off to satisfy whatever needs demand your attention. In the meantime, let us to the task of bringing up the cargo from below."

"Aye, sir."

Second mate Timothy Duncan approached then. "Captain, the Customs Inspector is here."

Thackeray nodded. "Send Mr. Seaton to me when he arrives."

Reese went to meet the inspector and escorted the man to his quarters.

The captain's living area was in the stern of the ship behind the double bulwark doors and four steps down. The area was spacious and divided into three main rooms—the parlor-dining area, the bed chamber, and a workroom, all well-lit from the band of windows that ran across the back and wrapped around the sides of the ship.

Thackeray led the inspector into the workroom. He had always maintained a good rapport with the Customs Inspectors, for they were charged with issuing the permits that allowed cargo to be unloaded. But Reese didn't know this one. The man appeared stern, humorless. He was all business as he carefully compared the entry form with the original invoices.

"I think you will find that all is in order," said Thackeray, impatient to begin the long, laborious work of unloading.

The stocky inspector peered over his glasses. "I shall be the judge of that, Captain."

After a painstaking examination, the man finally signed the permits.

As the inspector left the ship, Seaton was returning from his errand. "Where is the captain?" he asked the second mate.

"In his quarters," replied Duncan. "What took ye? The captain is gettin' mighty impatient—not to mention the rest of us."

The young officer shifted nervously. "I-ah-got delayed."

Duncan laughed. "Was she pretty?"

"Who?"

"The woman who delayed ye?"

"'Twas not a woman what delayed me," retorted Seaton indignantly.

Duncan caught a whiff of whiskey on the young man. "Bloody hell, ye stopped into a tavern for drink whilst the rest of us be waitin' for yer return to do the same."

"'Tis not as you think, Timothy.

"Did ye not stop at a tavern, Alex?"

"It was not for my own pleasure."

"Well, it certainly weren't for mine!"

The first mate hesitated. "I-I required fortification."

"For what?"

"The voucher from the counting house be a bit light."

The second mate's eyes narrowed. "How light?"

When told the difference, Duncan ran a hand across his face. "The captain ain't gonna like that."

"'Tis my thoughts as well, which is why I decided that you should be the one to give him the news."

The second mate raised his hands and backed away. "Oh no, not me, lad. I kenna run fast enough."

Bosun Andrew White walked up to them. "What're the two of ye jawin' about? Ye be lookin' a mite green, Mr. Seaton."

"The voucher from the counting house is light," said Duncan.

"Why?"

"Something about a breach of contract," replied Seaton.

White's bushy eye brows drew together in a frown. "The captain will not take kindly to this."

"Indeed. That is why I am charging you with the task of telling him."

The bosun balked. "You be the first mate, Alex. 'Tis your job."

"But you and Timothy have been sailing with the captain for a long time," argued Seaton. "He will take the news better from the likes of you."

Duncan gave a short laugh. "Aye, that we do know him, and 'tis why we ain't gonna be the ones to tell him."

White nodded in agreement. "Sorry, Alex. Best hand him the voucher and run. Two things you don't do with the captain—mess with his ship and mess with his vouchers."

At that moment, Thackeray appeared on deck and spied his first mate. "Mr. Seaton," he called. "There you are at last. Have you the voucher?"

With a last silent appeal to the first mate and bosun—to no avail—Seaton took a deep breath and walked over to break the news to the captain.

"A pity," remarked Duncan solemnly. "I rather liked the lad."

White nodded. "Lucky for Alex there be only sandbar sharks in the harbor."

The bosun and second mate grinned then as they watched the scene unfold. When they saw the dark expression sweep across the captain's face, they knew the eruption wasn't far behind.

Thackeray grabbed the voucher from his first mate to read it for himself. "Who the bloody hell is M. Sutton!" he bellowed, his deep voice carrying the length of the deck.

"The clerk said her to be the new manager," responded Seaton timorously.

The captain's brows shot up. "*Her*? A woman is managing the counting house?"

"Aye. Mrs. Sutton be her name."

"What does a woman know about trade!" thundered Thackeray.

The first mate cringed beneath the captain's glare. "I cannot say, sir."

Thackeray crushed the voucher in his hand. "I shall see to this myself."

As he stormed down the gangplank, the bosun remarked, "I should like to be a spider in that room."

Duncan nodded. "'Twill be a scene to behold."

"I'll wager a Spanish half dollar the captain will have this Mrs. Sutton seein' his side of it in a quarter hour," said White.

"Not if she is comely," countered Duncan. "Mrs. Hepplewaite had him wrapped around her finger and almost afore a preacher 'til he come to his senses. A pretty lady is used to advances and knows how to play a man. But a woman of plain countenance...she'll drop like a feather to flattery. Hey, Alex," he called out. "What say you? Is Mrs. Sutton a woman of pleasing or plain appearance?"

The first mate walked over to them, still feeling a bit shaky. "I-I did not make her acquaintance," he said. "But the clerk did relay to me that once her mind is made up to a matter, it is set hard and fast."

Duncan shook his head. "A woman of singular mind and stubborn disposition running a man's company—she must be plain. I'll wager she gives into the captain's charms *before* the quarter hour."

Reese Thackeray strode briskly down wharf and into the brick building of the Henshaw counting house.

The clerk looked up and smiled. "Captain Thackeray, welcome home, sir. I gave your officer the voucher. Did you not receive it?"

Thackeray threw the balled-up voucher on the clerk's desk.

"Oh, dear," said the clerk. "What happened to it? The bank will never accept this. I shall have to write you another."

"Please do, Mr. Phineas, but for the correct amount this time."

The clerk gave Thackeray a rueful smile. "Apologies, sir. I warned Mrs. Sutton there would be the piper to pay, but there was no changing her mind then, and I doubt she will change it now."

"Where is Benjamin Henshaw?" demanded Thackeray.

"Mr. Henshaw is retired from the company, sir...gout and other complaints," explained the clerk.

"Who is in authority then? I would speak with him."

"Uh, that would be Mrs. Sutton, sir."

"Did ye not hear me, Mr. Phineas? I would speak to the *man* in authority."

"Mrs. Sutton has the last word, Captain."

Thackeray struggled to control his temper. "I am quite certain that Benjamin Henshaw did not leave his company in the hands of a woman."

"Actually, sir, he did."

Thackeray looked at the clerk in disbelief. "Was the man feeble minded?"

"No, sir. Mrs. Sutton is Mr. Henshaw's daughter."

"I do not care who she is," snapped the captain. "A woman has not the mind for a man's business. There must be someone else with whom I can speak."

"If you wish to speak with someone in authority, sir, you *will* speak with me," said a feminine voice in a no-nonsense tone.

Thackeray spun around to view a striking, young woman standing in the doorway of the manager's office. She was tall for a woman—about five and a half feet, he gauged—but her frame was small making her appear more petite. Her hair, the color of winter wheat, was caught in loose curls at the back of her head. Short curls framed an oval-shaped face with sweet, pixie-like features, suggesting a young woman of some delicacy and naivety. Even more compelling were her startling green eyes set off by long, black lashes.

He walked over to her. "*You* are Mrs. Sutton?" he asked in surprise.

"I am," she replied. "And you are Captain Thackeray."

Thackeray may have imagined a far different picture of Mrs. Sutton, but apart from being taller, more powerfully built, and better looking than she had remembered, the captain was just as Marin had imagined him—full of himself.

His appreciation for the ladies and theirs for him was knowledge well-traveled. And she was hard pressed to keep from rolling her eyes as he ran a discerning gaze over her slender figure, the lines of which he found disappointingly obscured by the blue tunic she wore over her light-weight muslin dress.

She guessed he had come straight from the ship. His dark hair was in need of a cut, and he wore clothes more appropriate to a seaman— loose fitting tan breeches tucked into black boots and a loose-fitting white shirt open at the neck.

"What can I do for you, Captain?" she asked, striking her most businesslike manner.

"A mistake was made on my voucher, madam."

"There was no mistake, Captain."

"I had a contract with your father, Mrs. Sutton. My cargo includes spices and coffee from the Pacific, Chinese tea—for which I had to trade in Spanish bullion to good expense—and the best quality Chinese silks and porcelain to be found anywhere."

"That may be, Captain, but there is an over-abundance of Chinese porcelain and the value has decreased considerably. As to the rest of your cargo, three ships have preceded you. The warehouses are full of such goods. Surely, you have an understanding of the balance of trade, sir."

"Your pardon, madam, but what does a woman know of maritime trade, let alone one as young as you?"

Marin bristled at the patronizing tone in his deep-timbre voice. It wasn't the first time she had encountered such skepticism, and she found it galling to have her abilities questioned not just because of her gender, but also because people thought her younger than her years.

"Apparently, I know enough to keep a company from bankruptcy," she responded crisply. "I will remind you that my father's commission was for three years, not four."

"The extra year allowed me to turn over more cargo, Mrs. Sutton."

"To your benefit, Captain. Not to the benefit of Henshaw Import Company," she retorted. "When you failed to arrive at the expected time, we had not the goods to meet the demands of our retailers, which our competitors were only too happy to supply in our stead. We are a small company, sir, and only just recovering from the imbalance. Next time, stick to the contract, Captain, and you will get your price. Now, I have work to do. You may claim your voucher and redeem it at the bank or take your goods to another port."

Thackeray was speechless. By this point, he would have resorted to his infamous charm, but he found her so maddening he forgot to employ it.

"I cannot go to another port," he erupted angrily. "The cargo is being unloaded as we speak. I would have to reclaim the goods and go through customs again. Do you know how much time and paperwork that would require?"

Marin Sutton smiled sweetly. "Yes, Captain, I do.

She stepped back into her office and closed the door on him.

Thackeray's jaw dropped, and he turned to look at the clerk in astonishment. The clerk gave him another apologetic smile and held out a fresh voucher to him. Thackeray hesitated, torn between pride and practicality.

He had the option of trying to sell his cargo to other merchants in town, but if, as Mrs. Sutton had said, the warehouses were full, he would likely receive less money and more headache than the occasion warranted. After a few more moments of indecision, Thackeray snatched the paper from the clerk's hand and stormed out of the building, his ordered world turned upside down.

Seaton, Duncan, and White were supervising the daunting task of bringing the cargo from the hold of the ship to the deck when Thackeray returned from cashing the voucher. He strode briskly to his quarters, the scowl on his face a warning to everyone to stand clear for the time being.

White looked at Duncan. "Who do ye think won the bet?"

Duncan shrugged. "'Twould appear neither of us."

"I told you the clerk said Mrs. Sutton was tough," interjected Seaton.

The bosun shook his head in disbelief. "Never seen a female the captain ain't been able to win to his ways."

"Aye," agreed Duncan. "Mayhap Mrs. Sutton bears more consideration."

CHAPTER TWO

Still No Word

Over the next couple of weeks, the longshoremen saw to the transfer of the cargo from the ship to the wharf. Under the watchful eyes of the second mate and bosun, workers began to make the usual repairs of mending sails, repairing rigging, oiling the masts, scraping the hull, and caulking, tarring, and painting the ship.

Thackeray came on deck from his quarters. "How do we progress, Mr. Duncan?"

"Very well, sir."

"How long until the refitting is complete?"

"Andrew kept the ship in good order throughout the voyage. We should make done in six months' time, sir."

"Double the workers," ordered Thackeray. "I wish to leave as soon as I secure new contracts and commission enough cargo."

He was still fuming from his encounter with Marin Sutton and wasn't thrilled about having to deal with her again, perhaps all the more because he knew that she was right. He shouldn't have lingered so long in the Pacific Islands, but he didn't like being taken to task by a woman, particularly a woman in a world that was the purview of men.

Unfortunately, he had little choice but to deal with her. The larger merchants owned their own fleets of ships. Only the smaller importers contracted with independent ships, and competition was fierce. Thus, it behooved a captain such as himself to maintain a good relationship with the smaller merchants.

"What ports-of-call be ye thinkin', sir?" asked Duncan.

"England and France. If all goes well, perhaps a voyage to the Caribbean."

"'Tis ready we'll be then."

Reese was heading toward the bow, when he saw the subject of his ire walk up to the ship that had just docked—the *Eastern Hope*. Curious, he stopped to watch as Marin approached the crew members when they disembarked. Whatever question she had put to them, she didn't seem to receive any satisfaction from their answers.

When the captain of the ship debarked, she approached him in like manner. He shook his head and her shoulders drooped with disappointment. Gathering her emotions, Marin glanced up then to find Thackeray observing her. She glared back at him and turned to walk back to the counting house.

"Mr. Duncan, what do you know of the *Eastern Hope*?" asked Reese.

"She's just arrived from the Barbary Coast, sir. I talked to the second mate. He said they was almost taken by pirates. 'Tis glad I am we ain't tradin' there."

Thackeray furrowed his brows as he pondered the question. What interest could Mrs. Sutton possibly have in the dangerous coastal region of North Africa? Only the larger merchants dared to risk sailing there.

Benjamin Henshaw looked up from his newspaper when he heard the front door open and close. "Is that you, Marin?"

"Yes, Father, 'tis me."

"You are late," he remarked when she entered the parlor. She was downcast and that could mean only one thing. Henshaw sighed. "I gather another ship has come in from the Barbary Coast."

Marin nodded and sank into the wing chair next to the fireplace. "I questioned the captain and crew members to no avail."

He set aside the paper. "Marin, it has been over three years. I think you need to accept the inevitable."

"I cannot, Father, until I have proof of it." She paused for a moment. "I have been thinking about chartering a cargo ship to the Barbary Coast. It will bring a good profit."

Henshaw eyed her knowingly. "We both know that profit has nothing to do with it, daughter, and the risk is too great for a company of our size."

When she didn't argue the point, he considered the matter closed and broached another subject of more concern to him.

"I hear you burned a bridge."

Marin looked at her father in bewilderment. "How so?"

"I refer to your disagreement with Captain Thackeray."

"Who told you—Mr. Phineas?"

"You may manage the company, my dear, but I still maintain an interest."

"The captain is a bully," said Marin with a dismissive sniff. "He thinks a woman has no head for business. He actually stormed into the counting house a couple of weeks ago and demanded to speak with a *man* in authority about his voucher, which he found not at all to his liking."

"Perhaps with good reason. The captain did have a contract, Marin."

"Which he broke and did harm to our business," she countered. She gave a little giggle. "I think I rendered him quite speechless in the encounter."

"It is not wise to attack a man's ego, particularly in the presence of a witness," her father chided lightly.

Marin snorted. "He deserved it. You should have heard him, Father." She puffed herself up and mimicked Thackeray's condescending manner. "'A woman has not the mind for a man's business,' he said. 'What does a woman know of maritime trade?' he demanded to know. Then, Father, he had the audacity to question whether you were feeble-minded to have left your company in the hands of a female."

Ben Henshaw chuckled as he imagined the scene. "Be that as it may, Thackeray is a good captain with good instincts, Marin. He never has trouble raising a crew, his cargo always arrives in good order, and he is loyal. He was my first contract when I left the employ of John Barrell to open my own import business. Do not cut off your nose to spite your face," he warned. "Captain Thackeray is not forced to contract with you."

Marin waved off his concern. "The pool for an independent merchant captain is small, Father. And there are other captains with whom I can contract who do not have a problem with a woman being in a *man's* business." She stood up. "I shall see if Mrs. Cahill has supper ready."

As she walked out of the room, Henshaw shook his head. "Takes after her mother," he mumbled, picking up his newspaper.

CHAPTER THREE

A New Contract

Thackeray was in his quarters plotting his next voyage and figuring out the exports and imports for which he would seek contracts, when first mate Alex Seaton appeared in the doorway.

"Message for you, sir," the young man announced.

"From whom?" asked the captain, distracted by his task.

"Mrs. Sutton, sir."

Thackeray looked up sharply. "What does it say?"

Seaton opened the note and read it. "She wishes a meeting with you at the counting house, sir…three o'clock this afternoon."

Thackeray leaned back in his chair, and a smile slowly lifted the corners of his mouth. Her father must have taken her to task, for Henshaw was certain to have heard about their disagreement—retired or not—mused Reese.

"The clerk is waiting for your answer, sir," prodded Seaton.

"Tell Mr. Phineas that I shall attend."

"Yes, sir. I have another matter, Captain. Mr. White requests your permission to purchase a new figurehead. The present one took quite a beating this journey and he feels it beyond good repair."

"As he wishes," replied Thackeray, impatient to get back to his work.

"Very good, sir."

On his way to delivering the captain's response to the Henshaw clerk, Seaton waved down White and Duncan. "The captain has no objections to a new figurehead, Andrew. And...” The first mate looked around him and lowered his voice. “Mrs. Sutton has asked the captain for a meeting this afternoon,” he confided.

The second mate and bosun exchanged looks of surprise.

“What be yer bet, Timothy—the captain or the lady?” asked White.

Duncan shook his head uncertainly. “Mrs. Sutton did request the meeting. My wager is on the captain.”

At three o’clock, Reese walked into the Henshaw counting house.

“Good afternoon, Captain,” said the clerk. “Mrs. Sutton is waiting for you.”

At that moment, Marin called out from her office. “Mr. Phineas, has the captain arrived yet? He is late.”

Thackeray walked over to the door. “Perhaps you should consult your timepiece again, madam.”

Marin looked up from her desk. Her eyes widened in surprise, and the pen slipped from her fingers as she took in his appearance.

His dark hair was neatly cut and styled in the new fashion of the day—short in the back and on the sides with longer sideburns and the top left to a suitable length to wave across his forehead. He was dressed in gray tailored breeches, a double-breasted white waistcoat, and a dark green cutaway jacket that was well-fitted to his broad shoulders. As much as it pained her to do so, she had to admit that the man was most physically attractive, though she continued to question the reports of his reputed charm.

“Thank you for coming, Captain. Please sit down,” she said, quickly shuttering her thoughts.

But she hadn’t been quick enough, and Thackeray smiled to himself. Her reaction this time was one he was accustomed to receiving from women, and he sat down feeling smug and much more in control of the situation than at his last visit.

“Might I assume that you have reconsidered my payment, madam?”

"No, Captain, you may not. I have another contract to offer you."

The smile that played around the corners of his mouth disappeared. "I have been burned by one contract with you. Why would I consider another?"

"This would be a contract for a voyage of short duration," she explained. "You would not run the risk of price fluctuation. As you know, trade with the Chinese is one-sided. Outside of some furs and ginseng, the Hong merchants buy few American goods, limit trading ports to one, and charge ridiculous custom fees—not to mention the fact that they will trade their tea for only silver specie, of which there is a scarcity."

Thackeray was surprised by the breadth of her knowledge. Still, he was not comfortable talking business with a woman. "What is your contract...the Caribbean?" he asked, disinterestedly glancing around the office.

"No, Captain, 'tis for the Barbary Coast."

Thackeray swung his attention back to her. He could see by the steadiness of her gaze that she was serious. "I do not risk my crew on dubious profit, Mrs. Sutton."

"You would have a full cargo, and you know as well as I that the exports and imports bring a high value," she argued. "You could turn over your cargo three or four times, I should think."

"If one's ship isn't overtaken by pirates," he rejoined. "I have been away for four years, Mrs. Sutton, but I am hearing that Barbary corsairs still operate with impunity in the Mediterranean—as sanctioned by their states. Maritime insurance for ships trading in those waters is unsustainable, particularly for an independent ship as mine."

"The company will pay the insurance, Captain."

"'Tis not only the insurance that is cause for concern, madam. We are no longer British citizens and, as such, are not under British protection," Thackeray reminded her. "American merchant ships are sitting ducks for Barbary pirates, and apparently this government has no leverage to negotiate the release of those taken prisoner. There are sailors who have been held in captivity in Algiers for 10 years. Perhaps you remember accounts of the *Maria* and the *Dauphin*?"

"I am well aware, Captain," she replied stiffly. "There is negotiated peace now with Algiers."

Reese gave a sardonic laugh. "There has been 'negotiated peace' before with Algiers, Mrs. Sutton, but the dey seems to forget to convey it to his pirates. I had the misfortune of being on one such voyage where that was the case."

"Be that as it may, there are ships that have made the voyage without incident," Marin continued to argue. "The *Eastern Hope* has only just returned from the region."

"It was not without incident," countered Reese. "As I hear it, they were fortunate to have escaped."

"You may keep 60 percent of the profit in lieu of a contracted price—for hazard pay," she hastened to offer.

Thackeray's eyes narrowed. She was showing desperation. "Mrs. Sutton, I have the feeling that your quest is about something more than trade."

Marin looked away for a moment. "I seek answers, Captain."

"To what, Mrs. Sutton?"

She hesitated, reluctant to share any information of herself with this man, but she needed his help. "My husband was first mate on the *Clarabell* when the ship was taken by Algerine pirates three years ago," she began. "I have had no word of him or from him since. Every effort to discover his situation from sailors or released prisoners returning from the region has been to no avail. I must cast a wider net now."

Thackeray had not expected this, and he softened his manner. "My sympathies, madam, but I think you must make the assumption that your husband is deceased."

"I cannot, Captain...not without certainty."

"The leaders of these states use the crews of captured ships for slaves, sometimes selling them to other tribes. I suppose your husband could be among the latter. It would make it difficult to know of him, but I think it unlikely, Mrs. Sutton."

"Why is that?" questioned Marin.

"Officers are usually treated with more deference than crew members. They are given better quarters, more freedom, and are not worked at hard labor," explained Thackeray.

"Then how is it that he has not been seen, Captain? Why has he not written me of his circumstances?"

"You make my point, madam. There is a plague that occurs there every year in the month of May. If your husband has not been seen or heard from he most likely succumbed to it."

"Then someone would know of it," insisted Marin.

"Maybe, maybe not. Many things could have happened."

"You make *my* point, Captain. Not everything results in death."

Thackeray gave a sigh of impatience. "Mrs. Sutton, why do you think that I can determine the circumstances of your husband when others could not?"

"I am prepared to offer a ransom of $4,000," she replied. "I here tell that people have been able to free captured family members for thereabouts of that sum. If Nathaniel is alive, he will be brought to notice. Now, how soon can you sail? I can be ready in a fortnight."

Thackeray raised a brow. "I beg your pardon?"

"I am accompanying you, Captain. The situation has given rise to scammers who falsely promise to ransom families' loved ones if given the money. Thus, I would see to the ransoming myself instead of through an agent."

Reese overlooked what could have been perceived as an insult.

"Mrs. Sutton, were I even to agree to such a contract, I do not take women aboard my ship. It makes the crew nervous. They believe them to be a source of bad luck."

"I see. But your crewmen have no grievance with being on a ship named the *Sea Nymph*," retorted Marin.

She was quick and Thackeray had to allow a smile.

"Seamen believe sea nymphs to be the protector of sailors and fishermen. A ship named in their honor portends a safe journey, thereby ensuring me a better crew," he explained. "The only woman allowed on my ship is the figurehead at the prow."

Marin gave a huff of frustration. "Then enlighten me as to how a woman can be both a protector of seamen and a nod to ill fortune."

Thackeray shrugged. "There is no accounting for superstition, madam."

"You must carry women passengers upon occasion," she persisted.

"Not as common practice, Mrs. Sutton. Discomfort breeds complaints, and complaints spread disorder and resentment among my crew."

"I am no stranger to the rigors of sailing, Captain. I was born aboard my father's merchant ship, and my mother and I sailed with him in the years before and after the British siege until I was 12 years of age. I can stand a deck and steer a ship as well as any man."

"Be that as it may, you and I are not family, Mrs. Sutton, and your father did not sail in a sea as treacherous as the Mediterranean. Neither would you find quarters on my ship to be as comfortable as those aboard your father's, I can assure you."

"My passage is a condition of the contract, Captain. I can go as a supercargo representing the company and keep to my cabin however crude it may be."

Reese regarded her in amazement. Did the woman never take "no" for an answer? "Do you understand what happens to women captured by pirates, Mrs. Sutton?"

Marin hesitated. "I have heard tales. But from what I hear of your skills, I do not expect for us to be taken."

Thackeray couldn't decide if she had more guts than sense or just a high degree of naïveté. "While I appreciate your confidence, madam, I must decline your contract." He rose from his seat, his decision final. "Good day, Mrs. Sutton."

Marin said nothing as he walked out of the room. She could see that further argument was fruitless, and she refused to beg. She had figured he might balk at the idea but not in so definitive a manner. She had expected him to leave a little room for negotiation.

When she heard him leave the building, she stood up to gaze out the window. As he passed by, her eye followed his progress down the wharf. How, she wondered, did one change the mind of a blockhead?

A young man with a pleasant countenance, copper-colored hair, and dark brown eyes silently entered the room and stole up behind her. "Did you work your charm on the captain?" he asked.

Marin jumped and whirled about. "Thomas! We are no longer children," she chastised crossly. "Why must you persist in sneaking up on me?"

Undaunted by her show of temper, Thomas Langford laughed. "Because it is so easy to do, cousin. You are always deep in thought, consumed with business these days. You used to be more fun, Marin. Now you have the humor of a crotchety old woman. No one would guess we are of the same age."

"That is certainly true," she shot back. "You cannot seem to grow up. Honestly, I fail to see how you manage as a solicitor, Thomas. You need a wife to hold your feet to the ground. Nancy Guilford has expressed an interest, though I cannot think why."

Thomas gave a wistful sigh. "I should have married Susannah. We all used to have such fun together."

Marin rolled her eyes. "I fear you will never change."

"And I fear that you have," he replied soberly. "How went the meeting with Captain Thackeray?"

"Not well."

"Then choose another captain."

"You and Father said Mr. Thackeray is the best captain and has the fastest ship. I require both for, at long last, I would know the truth about Nathaniel."

"Thackeray is also a deliberative man. He does not take unnecessary risks. Hence his reputation. What did he say?"

"A lot of things. I cannot say if he objects more to the voyage or to having me on board," groused Marin.

Thomas looked at her in alarm. "Hold on there. You did not say anything about going as well. Uncle Ben will never countenance that; nor will I. 'Tis a fool's errand anyway. If Nathaniel were alive, there would have been some word from him. He was an officer. He would have been able to write you to ask for ransom. Barring that, he would have found some way to get word to you."

Marin gave a huff of impatience. "You sound like Father and the captain."

"Then we outvote you," said Thomas. "So get the idea of sailing to the Barbary Coast out of that pretty head. I would hate for anything to happen to you, dear cousin. Who else would I tease?"

"You mean torment. What are you doing here besides sticking your nose into my business?"

"I came to see if you and Uncle Ben require a ride to the Concert Hall tomorrow night."

Marin groaned. She had forgotten about the event. The concerts she enjoyed; the dancing and social time that usually followed, she did not.

"No excuses," warned Thomas. "You need to get out of this office for a bit of amusement."

"Listening to a group of gossipy matrons is not my idea of amusement," retorted Marin. "And I have no status, Thomas. I am neither widow nor wife. While women may show deference to my face, they pity my situation and are critical of my employment behind my back. Neither do gentlemen know how to approach me."

"Because your sharp tongue strikes terror in their hearts."

Marin glared at Thomas and continued on. "So I spend the evening alone fiddling my thumbs and trying not to look as awkward as I feel while everyone talks and dances around me."

Her cousin put a sympathetic arm around her. "I promise to save you from an evening of woe."

"That is what you said the last time until Elizabeth Clifton caught your eye."

Thomas gave her a rueful smile. "Apologies, cousin. I shall endeavor to redeem myself." He paused. "Seriously, Marin, you need to think about declaring Nathaniel. You are four and twenty. You still have time to make a life for yourself. No one would blame you."

"The law says seven years missing, Thomas. You know that."

"'Tis arbitrary. The judge has discretion, and I can make a credible case that you have exhausted all avenues to learn of his disposition."

Marin shook her head. "I cannot until I know for certain that Nathaniel is dead."

* * * * *

Thackeray entered the Bunch of Grapes Tavern on the wharf and started for a table, when he noticed Benjamin Henshaw motioning to him. The older man sat in a high back chair near the fireplace, and Reese walked over and sat down in the chair across from him. Henshaw signaled the barkeep for two drams of rum.

"I know you to favor this tavern," said Henshaw. "I was hoping you might appear."

"You had only to send word that you wished to see me, Benjamin. You appear hale. I heard you to be so much an invalid that you were forced to give over your business," remarked Thackeray with a touch of sarcasm.

Henshaw chuckled. "I fear reports of my poor state of health to be overstated. In truth, between you and me, my absence is temporary. My daughter needs something to occupy her time while she comes to terms with a personal matter. I believe you have made her acquaintance."

"I have," replied Reese dully.

Henshaw laughed. "No need to hedge, Captain. I know Marin can be willful. Her mother and I probably gave her her head too many times. But she has a good mind and a firm grasp of the business."

The barkeep came with their drinks and departed.

"I regret the disagreement over your contract," continued Henshaw, taking a sip of his rum. "You must admit, however, that my daughter does have a point. Your overlong voyage did put the company in some jeopardy," he chided lightly.

"Apologies, sir. It was not my intent to cause you injury."

"Duly noted, Captain. Now, I hope we can put this incident behind us and continue our business and our friendship."

"I take no exception to our friendship, sir. But I must confess that I do not relish conducting business with your daughter," said Thackeray. "I pray that your absence from the company is short."

Henshaw smiled. "As do I, Captain. As they say, idleness breeds vice. I am becoming overly fond of rum and hot chocolate, I fear."

Thackeray gave a snort of amusement. "Vices to be sure." He took a sip of his drink, thoughtful for a moment. "I wonder that your trade has not suffered more in the hands of your daughter than from my poor judgment, sir. A woman employed in a man's business cannot be looked upon with favor."

"Marin has shown herself to be capable. She learned to walk on a ship, and she cut her teeth on the mercantile business. Indeed, she can be quite winsome when she chooses to be," the older man added with a twinkle of amusement in his eye.

Thackeray ignored the jab. "It would appear that your daughter is aptly named then. 'Marin' means of the sea, I believe."

"It does. Her mother thought it fitting, and the child most certainly embodies it," replied Henshaw. "I dare say Marin would have her captain's license by now were she a man."

Thackeray grimaced at the thought. "How is her employment viewed otherwise? I cannot imagine it to be sanctioned by your social circle."

"There is ambivalence," admitted the older man. "But the law gives a widow license to be employed wherein her talents lie."

"How unfortunate that your daughter's talents lie in this direction," quipped Thackeray humorlessly.

Henshaw smiled again. "Indubitably so for you, sir, but it is to my good fortune."

"Mrs. Sutton does not view herself as a widow," pointed out Reese. "How is it that she is given the latitude of one?"

"Her cousin is a solicitor and secured the waiver for her," replied Henshaw. "'Tis of Thomas Langford I speak. I believe you know of him."

Thackeray nodded. "I have made his acquaintance a few times. We have similar pursuits. I found him to be an amiable fellow."

"Thomas has been trying to convince Marin to move on with her life. She usually takes his counsel, but on this she refuses until she knows the truth of the matter, and the truth of it, I fear, she will never know."

"I sympathize, sir, but if you are here to convince me to take a contract for the Barbary Coast, I have already refused your daughter."

"I would have assumed so, Captain. I know your feelings about trading in those waters. I must say I am surprised Marin approached you given the tenor of your initial encounter."

"As am I," replied Reese, tasting his rum again.

The older man sighed. "I had thought my daughter to abandon the idea after our talk. I should have known better. She is not one to give up easily once she gets something in her head."

"It is unlikely that I would find any information helpful to Mrs. Sutton anyway, if others have had no word of him to share," said Thackeray.

Henshaw was pensive for a few moments. "Yes, it would seem that Nathaniel has disappeared into thin air…. Well now, I have other business to be about as, I am sure, do you." He finished his drink and rose from the chair. "Good day to ye, sir. I am sure our paths will cross again before you leave port."

Thackeray nodded. "Indubitably so."

As Henshaw strode from the tavern, Reese noted with amusement that the older man made little use of his cane. His brow furrowed then as he considered the meeting. He had thought that the merchant was there to mend fences, but now he was beginning to wonder if there was more to the conversation than the older man's words had seemed to convey.

Reese shrugged off the thought and threw back the rest of his drink. He was reading too much into the matter, he decided. If Henshaw had been aware of his daughter's proposal, he was probably also aware of her harebrained idea to accompany the voyage and wanted to be certain that Thackeray would not give consideration to the contract. But then, there was nothing to prevent her from making the same offer to another captain.

It would appear that Mrs. Sutton was a bit of a handful, concluded Reese. He couldn't help wondering what manner of man her husband to be.

CHAPTER FOUR

The Concert

The Concert Hall, a venue for meetings, dinners, balls, and concerts, was a hubbub of noise and palpable excitement this night as people crowded into the large, three story brick building for a concert of works by Haydn.

The chairs were arranged in a semicircle, the seats in the front reserved for the privileged. The stage was lit with several large floor candelabras that had been wheeled into place to light the musicians' music; numerous sconces along the walls provided light to the floor.

Marin entered on the arm of her father with her cousin following behind, and they took seats on the right side of the stage. She slid the shawl off her shoulders and had just settled herself, when she looked over to lock eyes with Reese Thackeray, who was sitting in the same row on the left side of the semicircle. He nodded, and she quickly looked away. Thomas and Benjamin Henshaw noticed the captain as well and gave nods of acknowledgment.

In a short time, the orchestra and director, on loan from the theatre, appeared on stage and went to their places. The room quieted. Suddenly, the dramatic sound of horns split the air, followed by string instruments and a blend of oboes and a flute that never failed to send a thrill of excitement through Marin.

Joseph Haydn's Symphony No. 31, "Hornsignal," was one of her favorite pieces, but tonight she barely heard it. The captain's presence was an unsettling distraction. He seemed to sense when she glanced out the corner of her eye at him and turned his gaze to her. She inwardly chastised herself, at a loss to understand why he drew her eye at all.

She noticed that he sat between an older woman on his left and a younger, attractive woman on his right. He showed courtesy to both but appeared to have no allegiance to either. Was he alone? No, he was undoubtedly escorting the younger one, thought Marin, sneaking another look. A man as him would never attend a social event without a lovely, young lady on his arm.

Caught up in her musings, she was surprised when the concert ended. After the orchestra departed the stage, people began to make their way to another room for dancing and refreshments. This was the moment Marin had always dreaded, and she unenthusiastically followed the crowd with her father and cousin. She looked to see where the captain was and breathed a sigh of relief that he was nowhere in sight. He had probably departed, as she would desperately like to do.

When they entered the room, Marin heard her cousin, who was behind her, say: "Welcome home, sir. It is some time since last you were in port."

"Indeed, it is. Good evening, Mr. Langford. Good evening, Benjamin," came the reply.

Marin froze. She knew that baritone voice and whirled about to see Captain Thackeray looking quite dashing in wine-colored breeches and matching cut away coat, a double-breasted gray waistcoat, and snow-white shirt and cravat.

To Marin's great surprise, the older lady was on his arm. She was very attractive for a mature woman, petite and fashionably dressed with a stylish turban atop her still dark hair.

"Gentlemen, Mrs. Sutton, may I present to you my aunt Mrs. Caroline Billings. She is visiting from Newport," said Thackeray.

Marin's father smiled and immediately stepped forward to take her hand. "A pleasure, madam. Might I interest you in some refreshments, Mrs. Billings?"

The lady readily returned an engaging smile, her sparkling blue eyes suggesting one of good humor and a bright personality. "Why, yes, I should like that," she replied, taking his arm.

Her father handed his cane to Thomas. As he spryly led the lady off, Marin stared after the couple in astonishment.

"Well, Father seems to have recovered from his attack of gout," she remarked satirically.

Thomas grinned. "I hope your aunt is a widow, Captain."

"That she is," responded Thackeray, just as surprised by the sudden attraction between the two older people.

"I believe you have met my cousin Mrs. Sutton," said Thomas.

Thackeray turned to Marin and gave a slight bow. "Yes, I have had the pleasure," he replied, his tone suggesting otherwise.

"Have you found Boston much changed in your absence, Captain?" asked Thomas.

Reese looked at Marin pointedly. "I dare say that I have."

Marin bristled, knowing full well that he was alluding to her position at the trading house. "Things do change over time, Captain. It is called progress."

"Some progress is not always for the better, Mrs. Sutton."

Marin smiled tightly. "That depends upon one's perspective, sir. Perhaps, in the future, you should not stay away for so long. Then, change will not be so difficult for you to accept."

Thackeray raised a brow, momentarily taken aback.

"There is one change that I have found to my liking," he remarked, recovering himself.

Marin sighed, disinterested. "What is that, Captain?"

"Ladies' fashion," he replied.

Marin wore no tunic this time. The straight lines of her pink silk gown yielded a telling outline, and Reese's discerning eye took in her shapely curves beneath the thin fabric, as well as the appreciable cleavage revealed by the low, rounded neckline.

Thomas laughed. "I quite agree with you, sir. Now, a man knows exactly what he's getting. Corsets and hoops were quite tedious for a—for a woman," he quickly amended, catching Marin's glare on him. "Uh, perhaps you would care to dance, Captain. My cousin is an admirable dancer."

To the captain's amusement, a look of panic washed across Marin's face. And he allowed her to dangle a few moments longer before respectfully declining.

"I would be doing your cousin a disservice, sir. I have been so long from Boston I know not the latest dances. Your pardon, Mrs. Sutton."

Marin let out her breath in relief. "Of course, Captain."

"Well then, sir, let us enjoy a brandy," suggested Thomas.

Marin threw her cousin a look of reproach. "Thomas, you promised," she reminded him through clenched teeth. "I am sure the captain has plans of his own."

"Actually, Mrs. Sutton, I do not," interjected Reese.

"See there, cousin. I shall be back before the next round," he assured her. "I should like to hear the captain's stories. Perhaps I will accompany him on his next voyage to broaden my mind. Come along, Captain."

Reese gave Marin a slight bow. "A pleasant evening to you, madam."

As the men went off, Marin fumed. "Pleasant evening my foot!" she murmured and prepared herself to the contrary.

"I fear your cousin to be quite vexed with us," remarked Thackeray as the two men made their way to the bar. "Perhaps we should have been more discreet in our comments concerning ladies' dress."

"Yes, I do find myself sometimes lacking in propriety around Marin," admitted Thomas. "It is easy to forget that she is a lady and not one of the lads."

Reese looked at him in surprise. "She is quite comely. I think I would find it difficult to confuse the two."

Thomas laughed. "You did not grow up with her. She has a wit that is deliciously wicked when she chooses to employ it. She can be most unladylike…a bit of a rebel, you know. Great prankster. I shall have to tell you some stories sometime."

Reese regarded the young man in further disbelief. "We *are* talking about Mrs. Sutton, are we not? I have viewed no such humor in your cousin. She appears rather stiff to me."

Thomas laughed again. "The key word is 'appears.' Trust me, Captain. You have not been cussed until you have been cussed by Marin in Russian. Her tongue can be as sharp as a rapier sword."

"So I have occasioned, though not in Russian," responded Thackeray wryly.

At the bar, Langford ordered two drinks and handed one to Thackeray.

"Indeed, sir, a lesser man keeps his distance from my cousin," Thomas continued.

"I can see why," remarked Reese, taking a sip of the brandy. "How is it that she speaks Russian?"

"It was one of Uncle Ben's sailing routes. Marin seems to have an aptitude for languages. She speaks French and Swedish, too. Her mother was Swedish."

"I must confess, sir, I never imagined your cousin to be so interesting. She hides it so well."

Thomas tasted his drink. "Regrettably so. Nathaniel's disappearance has cast a shadow over her lighter side," he said with a sigh. "She is in danger of becoming quite dull, I fear, despite my best efforts. She would spend every waking moment in that bloody counting house if I did not drag her to these events."

"In the absence of any sightings or word of her husband these past years, I wonder that she does not take steps to declare him," commented Reese.

"With no proof of death, she views it a betrayal," replied Thomas. "For all of Marin's testing of conventions, she does have a streak of the traditionalist. And, over time, it is easy to credit noble traits to a person who did not possess them in the first place." Thomas paused. "She will not admit it, but I do believe there to be a sprinkling of guilt in the mix as well."

"How so?" inquired Reese curiously.

"She and Nathaniel quarreled on the day he left," explained Langford. "She hasn't quite forgiven herself for it and, on some level, feels responsible for whatever may have befallen him. 'Tis a ridiculous notion, I know, for such an intelligent woman as Marin, but guilt is the one thing all women seem to embrace so handily."

"You hold no fondness for her husband?" queried Reese.

"Suffice it to say I never believed him worthy of Marin."

"How so, if I may ask?'

Thomas hesitated. "Nathaniel did not show himself to be of noble character."

"He betrayed her trust?"

Thomas nodded. "On more than one occasion. I cannot say if she knew. Marin tends to keep her own counsel on personal matters."

"Do you think him to be alive?"

Thomas shrugged. "Nathaniel was always resourceful. It is hard to imagine that he would not find a way to survive. But I cannot believe that he would be so cruel as to not get word to Marin of his circumstances were he able."

Langford finished his drink. "Well, Captain, I promised to keep my cousin from an evening of misery, and she looks to be ready to burst. I fear I shall have to hear your stories another time."

"Indeed, sir, I would spare you the lady's sharp tongue."

Thomas gave him a wry smile. "I fear it is too late for that. Marin does not view patience as a virtue. A word of warning, Captain, she can be very determined when she feels the situation merits it."

As Thomas struck off across the room, Reese had a sense of déjà vu. The tenor of his conversation with Langford had seemed much like that of his meeting with Benjamin Henshaw in the tavern. In both instances, he had the feeling that a warning was being conveyed to him. Of what, he had no idea.

Reese looked over at Marin, still digesting Thomas' revelations of her. He hardly knew what to make of this woman. She was smart, beautiful, and bold—a rebel with a moral streak.

Reese could see the rebel side of her. As he looked around the room, he realized that many of the women still had yet to conform to the new freestyle dress inspired by the goddesses of Greek mythology and popularized by the French Revolution. Mrs. Sutton wasn't one of them. That he appreciated. That she had involved herself in a man's business, he distinctly did not. Without a doubt, she was uncommon from head to toe. He had yet to figure if he found that to be intriguing or exasperating.

CHAPTER FIVE

The Mission

M arin, I require your help," called out Benjamin Henshaw.

Marin entered her father's bedroom to find him fussing uselessly with his cravat. She shoved his hands aside and finished the task.

"Off again with Mrs. Billings?" she inquired with a hint of annoyance in her voice.

"I am escorting Caroline to the theatre," he replied.

"Caroline is it now?"

Henshaw sighed heavily. "Why are you so averse to her? She is a lovely woman, and I find her company enjoyable. Am I to deny myself so simple a pleasure?"

Marin regarded her father. At the age of 50, his reddish brown hair was graying and he was a bit heavier, but he still retained a trim enough appearance and was yet a vitally attractive man. Suddenly assailed with a sense of guilt, she gave him an affectionate hug. "No, Father, I do not expect you to deny yourself companionship. I know you have been lonely without Mother."

He placed his hands on her shoulders to command her full attention. "Marin, you must know that your mother will always hold a special place in my heart. I do not wish to forget her. And no one will displace my love for you."

Marin smiled. "I know that, Father. And you are right. Mrs. Billings is a lovely woman."

"What, then, is your complaint of her?"

Marin hesitated. "I find no fault with Mrs. Billings per se. But after all these years, must the first woman who draws your interest be Captain Thackeray's aunt?" she blurted out.

Henshaw dropped his hands from her shoulders and burst into laughter. "That is the basis of your complaint…her nephew?"

"I see no humor in the situation," said Marin. "Because of your friendship with Mrs. Billings, the captain and I are forced into close company when we can scarce abide each other. First, the picnic, then the dinner at the Concert Hall. I hardly think at your age that you and Mrs. Billings are in need of chaperones. The situation is awkward and most intolerable, Father…most intolerable."

"The captain is a charming man. I fail to see why he raises your ire so."

Marin gave a snort of irritation. "He is egotistical and dismissive of any woman who dares to dip so much as a toe into his *man's* world."

Henshaw chuckled. "Well, I am sure you can suffer the captain awhile longer until Caroline returns to Newport," he replied amusedly. "Consider yourself fortunate that we do not request the company of you and the captain this night." He put on his coat and kissed her on the cheek. "I shan't be late."

They descended the stairs together. Marin saw her father to the door and walked into the parlor where she dropped morosely into a chair, the captain dogging her thoughts. He seemed to be doing that too often of late, and it annoyed her to no end. It didn't help matters that he was provocatively handsome, and, as such, the topic of conversation among the ladies at social events.

Many men had attributes enough to be considered attractive but possessed some small physical flaw that prevented them from being deemed universally handsome—a nose a smidge too long, stature a few inches too short or too lean, eyes a bit too close together or too wide apart. But the captain seemed not to suffer such imperfections. Indeed, his mouth held a sensual quality that led one woman to shockingly confess that it invited imaginings of his lips caressing hers. His dark hair, cobalt blue gaze, and overall virile appearance prompted another to declare him an Adonis.

"An Adonis," scoffed Marin with the roll of her eyes. Well, the captain was not going to get swooning adoration from her! With such a man, it behooved a woman to look to his character flaws, which she concluded the captain had many.

"What are you sulking about?"

Marin started and looked up, surprised to see her cousin standing in the doorway. "Thomas…why are you here?"

"I came to see Uncle Ben. I have some papers for him to go over."

"Father went to the theatre with Mrs. Billings."

"Again?" Thomas chuckled. "They appear to be developing a rather close friendship."

"Indeed, it would seem so," remarked Marin, irritably.

"I sense you are finding that bothersome," observed Thomas.

She shot her cousin a look of annoyance. "I have no wish to deny my father happiness, if that is what you are inferring."

"What then? Mrs. Billings is a lovely lady."

"No doubt, but she is Captain Thackeray's aunt. I have no desire to cross paths with the captain more times than is absolutely necessary."

A smile spread across Thomas' features. "Oh, I see. Well, I suggest that you get used to crossing paths with him, dear cousin. You may have no say in the matter."

"Why is that?" she questioned sourly.

"Well, if Uncle Ben and Mrs. Billings were to marry, you and the captain would be family."

Marin shot upright in the chair. "Why did you say that! What have you heard!"

Thomas laughed. "Nothing. I'm just hypothesizing."

"Don't you even venture the thought," she admonished him. "'Tis too horrifying to consider."

* * * * *

The captain took his aunt and Benjamin Henshaw's friendship less seriously. He viewed it more as a temporary situation, though he wasn't any more thrilled than Marin at being thrown together with her in family social events. Even with his insights of her, Reese found her to be a challenge to his good nature.

At this point in time, however, he was more concerned about finding enough cargo. He sat at his desk going over the list. He had always carefully planned his trips so that he was in port at a time of fewer ships. The extra year he had taken in his last voyage had skewed the timing, and he was now having to compete for exports to Nova Scotia and England.

He had been putting off going to the Henshaw counting house to finalize a contract for goods to be brought back. He was not looking forward to negotiating with Marin. He had finally met a woman who, while equal to his wit, seemed to be immune to his charm and possessed a skilled knowledge of trade that he found damnably annoying. Going toe to toe with her on a social issue was one thing; on something that was his bailiwick was quite another matter.

He had thought about going directly to Benjamin Henshaw, then dismissed the idea when he recalled Thomas Langford's remark that men avoided his cousin because she could strike fear in their hearts. He was not about to be placed in that category.

"Captain?"

Thackeray looked up impatiently. "Yes, Mr. Seaton, what is it?"

"A note for you, sir."

"It isn't from Mrs. Sutton, is it?" Reese asked facetiously.

"No, sir. A lad brought it from a gentleman waiting in a coach on the wharf."

Reese took the note and read it, his brow furrowing in perplexity. "It comes from a Mr. Fielding, an emissary from the Secretary of State. He desires that I meet with him at the tavern this afternoon."

"What could he be wanting to talk to you about, sir?"

Thackeray looked at the note again. "I cannot say, Mr. Seaton. I suppose I shall have to attend the meeting to know. Tell the lad I will appear."

At the appointed time, Reese entered the tavern. The establishment was quiet with few patrons this time of the day, and he had no trouble spotting the emissary sitting at a table by a window that overlooked the wharf.

The man was busily writing and looked the part of a government envoy, thought Thackeray. He was middle-aged, slightly built, wore spectacles, and had not yet adapted to the more modern style, instead continuing to wear his thinning hair pulled back in a queue and keeping to the bicorn hat and fuller, longer coat.

Reese walked over to him. "Mr. Fielding?"

Engrossed in his task, the man looked up startled. "Yes?"

"I am Captain Thackeray."

"Oh, Captain, your pardon, sir," said the emissary, quickly collecting himself and closing a leather folder. "Please sit down. My thanks to you for coming. I know you to be a busy man."

Reese sat down and eyed the man guardedly. "Why does a government emissary seek a conference with me?"

Fielding chuckled. "I was told you were rather direct."

"You have made inquiry of me?"

"I have."

"To what purpose?" Reese demanded to know.

"As the captain of a merchant ship, I am sure that you are well aware of the importance of international commerce."

"Only as it pertains to my pockets, sir. I know nothing of the politics."

"Well then, allow me to broaden your horizons, Captain. International commerce is vitally important to America's pockets as well—indeed her very survival depends upon it," he said. "It enables the government to repay its war debt and to build a viable economy. And our ability to conduct trade with southern Europe is an important part of it."

The emissary paused to let that point sink in.

"Go on," prodded Thackeray, a note of suspicion in his tone.

Fielding took a deep breath. He could see that this was going to take all of his diplomatic training.

"When Mr. Jefferson was secretary of state," he continued, "he calculated that a quarter of New England's dried salt cod, a sixth of America's grain, and a significant amount of rice and lumber were being exported to that region of the world. Secretary Jefferson also calculated that more than a thousand seamen found employment on those merchant ships. Vice President Adams believes that those statistics can be twice that improved were our interests not being threatened in the region."

"I assume you are talking about the Barbary pirates," said Thackeray.

"I am, Captain. As you know, since the war, we no longer have the protection of British war ships. After the *Maria* and the *Dauphin* were taken in 1785, the Portuguese navy kept the pirates confined to their ports, thus allowing our merchant ships safe passage into the Mediterranean."

"I was away on a voyage to China for the past four years and have been largely unaware, Mr. Fielding. But I have since talked with the captain of a ship recently into port that narrowly escaped capture in that region. It would appear that circumstances have changed," noted Thackeray.

"Indeed they have, sir—three years ago to be exact. President Washington discovered that Portugal was negotiating a treaty with the dey of Algiers, and, in October of 1793, then Secretary Jefferson received the distressing news from our Consul in Lisbon that a large fleet of Algerine ships was once again preying upon American ships in the Atlantic. In that month alone, the pirates captured 10 ships and enslaved 110 crewmen and passengers."

"Was one of those ships the *Clarabell*?" asked Thackeray.

The emissary opened his folder and thumbed through the pages until he came to one in particular. "It was," he replied after scanning a list.

"Was there a first mate by name of Nathaniel Sutton aboard?"

The emissary consulted another list on a following page. "Yes. Do you know Mr. Sutton?"

"Not directly. I am acquainted with his wife. She has had no word of him. Do you know of his status?"

"No, I am sorry to say that I do not."

Thackeray regarded the man curiously. "You have come all this way to give me a history lesson, Mr. Fielding. Why? What does this matter have to do with me?"

"I shall get to that, but permit me to give you a little more history, Captain."

Reese sighed impatiently. "Proceed if you must."

The emissary gave him a smile of forbearance. "I shall make this as brief as possible, Captain," he replied. "It has always been Mr. Jefferson's position, both as minister to France and as Secretary of State that America must build a navy to deal with these pirates rather than pay tributes to the dey of Algiers," continued Fielding. "He argued his case so steadfastly that last year Congress finally passed the Act to Provide Naval Armament. It authorized the construction of six frigates. Work had just begun, when diplomats reached a treaty with the dey for a goodly sum to allow safe passage for American ships. Thus, Congress, in all of its wisdom, decided that a navy wasn't needed after all."

"Then your problem is solved," noted Thackeray.

Fielding shook his head. "No, Captain, it is not. It seems that the United States government has been too slow with its payments to the dey, angering him to the point that he has not only refused to release the crewmen taken prisoners, but he has also threatened war. Congress has ordered work to move forward once again for a navy, but it will be a few years until frigates can stand ready to convoy American merchant ships."

"Again, sir, I know not how this concerns me," reiterated Thackeray.

"I am coming to that, Captain. The current American minister to Portugal has been appointed minister to Spain," the emissary continued to explain. "His aid William Marsden is acting as interim minister until the new minister arrives in a year or two. Three months ago, a private charter from London was bringing Mr. Marsden's wife and six-year-old son to join him, when the ship went missing. The dey maintains that the ship sank during a storm, but we have reason to believe that it was, in fact, taken by his pirates."

"Why should the dey deny capturing the ship if he believes the American government to have violated the treaty by failing to provide him his contributions?" asked Reese. "He would feel justified."

"The government did not violate the agreement," corrected Fielding. "The dey received his contributions. It was just not with the speed that he expected, and, as punishment, he is now demanding an increased amount."

"Then there is a violation of the spirit of the treaty on both sides. So, why should the dey fear that the taking of this particular ship would place him in any jeopardy?" questioned Thackeray.

The emissary sighed. "It is one of those gray areas that only diplomats can argue, Captain. But suffice it to know, despite the circumstances, the diplomatic agreement yet remains in place, and, as such, this was not a merchant ship but a ship on a diplomatic mission in international waters during peace time. The taking of that ship is tantamount to a declaration of war. This is a line that even the dey does not dare to cross."

"But you said the dey already threatened war," Thackeray pointed out.

"The dey likes to saber-rattle, Captain."

"Still, Mr. Fielding, the United States has no navy as yet. What has he to fear?"

"The United States has signed alliances with Sweden and Portugal and is in the process of negotiating a treaty with Spain," explained Fielding. "I dare say the dey does not want to face the navies of four countries."

"How do you know the ship did not sink in a storm?" pressed Thackeray. "The winds are unpredictable there and the shoals difficult to navigate in a storm."

"Richard O'Bryen, captain of the *Dauphin*, yet remains a captive of the dey. Under heavy guard he is permitted to travel to certain countries to beg ransom money for his crew and other prisoners. On a trip to Lisbon, he slipped a message to Mr. Marsden that the dey's pirates had, indeed, taken the ship and all aboard are captives." Mr. Fielding leaned forward in his seat. "Quite simply, Captain Thackeray, we need for you to get them back, particularly Mrs. Marsden and the boy, before the dey sells them to be rid of the evidence."

Taken aback by the request, it was a moment before Thackeray responded. "What makes you think the dey has not already sold them?"

"We do not know definitively," admitted the emissary. "But the current Secretary of State Thomas Pickering has instructed all diplomats in Europe to give the appearance that the United States has accepted the dey's story of a storm. If the dey perceives no threat, it is hoped that he will keep Mrs. Marsden and the boy close in case he sees a way to use them as leverage."

"Mr. Fielding, I dare say that a government official would be the more appropriate choice to deliver a ransom," said Reese.

"There is no ransom," replied Fielding soberly. "Captain, the United States can scarcely meet the contributions demanded by the rulers of these Barbary states as it is. It most certainly cannot meet the ransom demands for dignitaries and their family members, nor do we wish to set a precedent for doing so."

Reese looked at him quizzically. "What is it you expect of me, then?"

"We want you to get Mrs. Marsden and her son out of Algiers by any means possible without triggering a war."

"I am not a diplomat, Mr. Fielding."

The emissary regarded Thackeray with a level eye. "This is not a matter for diplomacy, Captain."

Reese suddenly realized what the government wanted him to do, and he was silent for a long moment. "It is a tall order."

"This is why the secretary has sent me to you," said Fielding. "Captain, we are a new nation, and, in addition to commerce, our survival depends upon the treaties and alliances we are able to negotiate. At this point in time, we have exceedingly capable diplomats around the world working in the best interests of our country. Imagine, if you will, the attrition in their ranks if these dignitaries cannot enjoy the companionship of their wives and children while serving abroad out of fear for their safety? Who, then, would wish to serve at these vitally important posts?"

"I appreciate your situation, Mr. Fielding, but I have not sailed the waters of the Mediterranean in over 10 years. There are other captains just as capable who do conduct trade in the area. I advise you to seek out one of them."

"We have considered others, Captain. We feel that you are the only one who can handle a matter as delicate as this."

"Again, sir, while I sympathize with the plight of Mr. Marsden and his family, I cannot commit to such a mission," said Reese.

"I understand your reluctance, Captain. I know that a ship on which you were crewing some years ago was taken by Barbary pirates and that you were imprisoned in Algiers for several months before escaping."

Thackeray's features hardened. "Then you know that half the crew was lost in the escape, including the captain, whom I greatly valued as a friend and mentor."

"It was due to your courage and cunning that the ship and the others were not lost as well," said the emissary.

"'Tis of little consolation, Mr. Fielding. And I have determined not to lose another friend or crew member in that sea. You shall have to consider another captain," replied Thackeray on a note of finality.

As Reese stood to leave, the emissary raised a hand to stay him. "Captain, wait. There is another incentive that may hold more sway with you."

Reese sat down again and eyed the emissary closely. "What is that, sir?"

"The ship of which we speak is the *Neptune*. I believe your younger brother was serving as first mate."

Thackeray was taken aback. "I have not had recent word from Peter, but I know the *Neptune* to trade in northern Europe. You are persistent, sir, and if it is chicanery that you practice—"

"I promise you, Captain, I do not employ deception. The captain of the ship that had been chartered to deliver Marsden's family to him fell ill when he stopped in London to pick up supplies. The *Neptune* happened to be in port at the time, and her captain agreed to take up the contract and transport Mrs. Marsden and the boy to Lisbon. As there was a treaty in force with Algiers, no one expected piracy to be a danger."

"You are certain Peter was aboard?"

Fielding thumbed to another page and turned it around for Reese to read. "See for yourself, Captain."

Thackeray didn't have to look hard for his brother's name. It was just below the captain's name. He leaned back in his chair and ran a hand across his face feeling gut punched.

"I'm sorry, Captain."

Reese looked at the emissary, his features set, his tone resolute. "The government shall pay for the insurance, all supplies, and double pay for the crew—in silver specie. It will not be easy to find good, experienced men eager to crew a ship with such a mission."

"Silver specie is in scarce supply, but your demands will be met," Fielding promptly assured him. The emissary hesitated. "There is one other thing, Captain. Should you succeed in freeing Mrs. Marsden and her son, your deed must go unheralded. If the dey's deception is not publicly exposed, the president shall have leverage in future negotiations."

"And if I fail?" asked Reese.

"The government will disavow knowledge of your activities."

"It would seem that the odds are in my favor," quipped Reese sardonically.

Fielding gave a faint smile. "Take heart, sir. There is a man in Algiers who can be of help to you…an American prisoner who is in the dey's good graces. His name is James Cathcart."

"I will not go unarmed," said Thackeray. "I shall need funds for armaments as well."

"You cannot start a war, Captain."

Thackeray fixed hard blue eyes on the emissary. "There already is a war, Mr. Fielding, but no one speaks of it aloud or writes it in a declaration. In any case, as you pointed out, I do not represent the government. I serve my own interests."

CHAPTER SIX

Planning a Voyage

Reese called his officers and cook to his quarters.

First mate Alex Seaton was new to Thackeray's crew working his way toward the position of captain. But second mate Timothy Duncan, bosun Andrew White, and cook Daniel Potter, more commonly called Pots, were older and well-seasoned seamen. Thackeray held their trust and respect above any other captain they had served over the years so that they had come to pledge service only to him. Similarly, Reese trusted and valued the hardened sailors' loyalty and experience enough to hear their advice—solicited or not—for underlining their relationship was the bond of a shared experience. All had been aboard that ill-fated voyage with Thackeray over 10 years ago.

Thus, when he announced that his next voyage would be to the Barbary Coast, the second mate, the bosun, and the peg-legged cook looked at each other, surprised and alarmed.

"Captain," spoke up Duncan, "you said as how we was never to sail them waters again."

"'Tis opening old wounds to be be sure," admitted Thackeray. "But I have a personal interest and have been charged with an unsanctioned mission."

He explained about the taking of the *Neptune* by the Algerine pirates and that his brother was among the crew members imprisoned by the dey, as well as the wife and young son of the American consul to Portugal.

"Except for Mr. Seaton, you know what it is to tangle with these pirates," continued Reese. "You bear the scars from it—seen and unseen—and I will not ask you to risk yourselves again. I only require that you lend your experience to the refitting, crewing, and provisioning of the ship for the voyage. Time is of the essence."

There was silence.

Then Duncan stepped forward. "I be sailin' with you, Captain. Ye'll have need of a second mate ye can trust to have yer back."

"And a good bosun," added White. "Ye ain't sailin' without me."

"Aye, I be with ye, too, Captain," said Pots. "Ye looked out for us when we was in that hell hole. 'Tis our turn to look out for you."

"Mr. Seaton, how say you?" asked Duncan.

The young man hesitated, then nodded. "I have never sailed in the Mediterranean. 'Twill be a new experience."

"Are you all certain now?" asked Thackeray. "I will think no less of any man who—"

"We be certain," said Duncan. "'Tis time we have our revenge on those bastards."

Thackeray nodded, struggling to hold back the emotion he felt at their unquestioned loyalty. "I cannot ask for better officers. Mr. Duncan, how go the repairs? Can we sail in three weeks' time?"

"Aye, Captain. The major repairs should be done by then. The rest can be made on the voyage. The ship may be old, but she's sound."

"We are still putting into London port," said Reese. "You can finish more of the repairs there. Pots, begin the task of provisioning the ship."

"Aye, sir."

Reese looked at the bosun. "Mr. White, I leave to you the task of gathering a crew of 25."

"Twenty-five, sir? Your normal crew size is upwards of 10."

"Aye, Mr. White. I require a fighting force, and there may be attrition along the way. I need crew enough in place who can perform their tasks with precision as well as to fight. As it is, I fear that few experienced sailors of good character will care to apply when told the destination, but do the best you can. It may help that I am offering double the wages in silver specie. If you still come up short of men, you can recruit in London."

"What of the master surgeon?" asked Duncan. "Our last has signed on with another ship. For sure, we will have need of a surgeon on this journey."

"I am acquainted with one of good skill in Boston," replied Reese. "I shall approach him."

"Shall I disclose the mission to recruits, sir?" inquired White.

"Say only that they may be required to fight, which they should expect to do in those waters," replied Reese. "But assure them they will be well armed. And, Andrew, do not post for a crew. Quietly canvas the taverns in which sailors take their drink. I do not wish for word of my destination to get about any sooner than need be," he said, thinking of Marin. "That goes for all of you. Go about your business with a closed mouth."

"Aye, sir," the men replied.

Thackeray turned to his first mate. "Mr. Seaton, I would have you see to the collection of armaments—enough for every man."

"What of the cargo?" queried Duncan. "Half is already loaded, and we have not yet the contracts for a full hold."

"Proceed with loading the goods that we have," said Reese. "There is not the time to gather more. We shall unload the cargo in London, take on provisions, and refit the ship with cannons before sailing to the Mediterranean. Now to your tasks, mates. There is urgency in this matter."

As the others scattered, Duncan stayed back with a new concern. "There is danger that you may be recognized in Algiers, Captain."

"It has been over 10 years, Timothy. 'Tis unlikely."

"A Musselman does not forget an American prisoner upon whom he has sworn vengeance, sir. What of the peril to your brother?"

"Let us hope the connection between us is not made," replied Reese soberly.

* * * * *

Marin looked through the contracts on her desk, her brow puckered in bewilderment.

"Mr. Phineas," she called out.

The clerk quickly presented himself at her door. "Yes, Mrs. Sutton?"

"I do not see a contract from Captain Thackeray. Has he not presented one?"

"No, madam."

Marin regarded her clerk, further perplexed. "But I hear that he is preparing to sail sooner than expected."

"Yes, madam."

"Where is he going?"

"I have not heard, madam."

"Has he contracted with other importers?" she asked with some alarm.

"I cannot say," replied the clerk.

Marin thought for a minute. "Mr. Phineas, go quickly to the Customs House and inquire after Captain Thackeray. If he is preparing to depart, he will have a full cargo. There should be manifests filed and certificates and permits for loading issued. That should indicate his ports-of- call."

As the clerk hurried away on his errand, Marin rose from her chair and went to look out the window that overlooked the docks, but she couldn't get a clear view of Thackeray's ship.

"What is he up to?" she murmured.

An hour later, Mr. Phineas returned.

"Loading permits show that Captain Thackeray does not have a full load," he reported. "And the manifests he filed indicate that he is sailing to London."

Marin looked at her clerk in surprise. "The captain is sailing without a full load? How soon is he leaving?"

"I gather quite soon."

"Yet he has not contracted with us to bring back goods. Mr. Phineas, check with the other companies to see if the captain has contracted with any of them."

"Right away, madam."

Marin paced the floor of her office unable to put her mind at ease. Had she pushed the captain too far? In spite of her bravado, she really couldn't risk losing his business.

The clerk returned with a new report that both relieved and mystified her.

"I can find no company with which Captain Thackeray has contracted for imports," he said. "There are just the few contracts he has taken for exports."

"This makes no sense, Mr. Phineas." She picked up her shawl and flung it about her shoulders. "I shall get to the bottom of this."

"Where are you going, Mrs. Sutton?"

"To the wharf."

Marin walked briskly down to the end of Long Wharf where the *Sea Nymph* was anchored. It was a bright spring day, and she shielded her eyes from the sun as she looked up at the ship. Sailors scurried about the deck busily discharging their tasks.

She saw a man who appeared to be an officer and called up to him. "Ahoy there, sir."

Alex Seaton looked down at the pretty lady and smiled. "Good day, madam. How might I assist you?"

"Might the captain be aboard?" asked Marin.

"No, madam. He is finalizing some business."

"Are you soon to leave port, sir?"

"Aye, as soon as a crew is raised."

"It is my information that you sail to London."

"Aye."

"Why is the captain not returning with goods?" questioned Marin.

"Is he not?"

"No, sir, he is not."

"May I inquire as to the nature of your interest, madam?" asked Seaton, more guarded.

"The captain has not contracted with any importers. I wish to know the reason for it."

"Perhaps he has not gotten around to it yet."

"Apparently, he has not gotten around to gathering a full hold either," returned Marin with a touch of sarcasm. "Something else is afoot, sir, and I mean to know of it."

Seaton shifted uncomfortably. "I am only the first mate, madam. Perhaps you should talk to the captain."

"Oh yes, sir, I most assuredly will," replied Marin resolutely.

"Might I have your name, madam, so that I can relay to the captain who is inquiring?"

"Tell him Mrs. Sutton of the Henshaw Import Company," she said and marched off.

Seaton's jaw dropped. This was *the* Mrs. Sutton?

When Thackeray returned to the ship some time later, the first mate lost no time informing him of Marin's visit. "I fear she suspects something, sir."

"What did you tell her?" asked Reese.

"I pleaded ignorance and told her to talk to you. The lady was quite insistent. I knew not what else to say."

"You did well, Mr. Seaton. She can be a bit daunting."

"Indeed, sir. I was fortunate to have the separation of the ship between us," he replied in all seriousness.

Thackeray suppressed a chuckle at the young man's confession.

"I suppose I should have made a contract with her, false or not, but I had hoped to be away before she was aware."

"Begging your pardon, Captain, why do you not want Mrs. Sutton to know of your plans to sail to the Mediterranean?"

Briefly, Reese explained about Marin's husband being held prisoner in Algiers and of her attempt to charter the *Sea Nymph* to see to his ransom.

"I see. Perhaps now you will be able to accomplish the task for her," suggested Seaton.

"And I intend to if the man still lives," said Thackeray. "But she has had no word of him in over three years. I hold out little hope."

The first mate's brow furrowed in confusion. "Then why can she not be privy to your intentions to inquire on her behalf?"

"Because, Mr. Seaton, she will insist upon coming with us."

The young man looked at the captain in surprise. "Surely you are mistaken, sir."

"She had made it a condition of the charter, which is one reason why I refused her contract."

"But she cannot have meant it, Captain."

Thackeray gave him a smile of forbearance. "Mr. Seaton, I ask you to recall your encounter with Mrs. Sutton today."

"Yes, sir."

"What think you now?"

"I see your point, sir."

Something in the Wind

Marin sat at the table moodily staring at her breakfast of cold pork, baked beans, and pastry. With a sigh she pushed the plate away and picked up the mug of hot chocolate.

Her father peered over his spectacles at her. "Something wrong with your food, daughter?"

"No, I have not the appetite for it," she replied, taking a sip of her drink.

"Then what, pray tell, is ailing you? You have been in poor humor for the past several days. Is it because I am leaving to visit Caroline in Newport for a fortnight?"

Marin shook her head. "No. 'Tis her nephew."

"Captain Thackeray? What has he done now to spark your temper?"

"He has done nothing, Father, and that is the point."

Benjamin Henshaw looked at his daughter in confusion. "What is the point?"

"He is readying to sail to England and has not returned a contract to me."

"I see. I dare say I am not surprised. I warned you to curb your tongue, Marin."

"I hardly think the Captain is that thin-skinned, Father. And he was in the wrong. He cannot deny he was deserving of the consequences. Besides, he has not contracted with any other companies for imports that Mr. Phineas could find, and he is sailing with less than a full load.

No, there is another matter that occupies the Captain, of that I am certain. But I cannot fathom it."

Henshaw eyed his daughter curiously. "Again, I say that Captain Thackeray seems to have made quite an impression on you."

Marin stiffened. "And, again, I say to no good favor. The man is arrogant and, no doubt, a cad. I do not know why you hold him in such high regard."

"It is not without merit, daughter."

"Someday you shall have to convince me."

Her father frowned. "You have been working yourself too hard, Marin. I believe that you need some time away. Why not visit your friend Susannah in London? You can book passage on Captain Thackeray's ship."

Marin made a face. "The captain does not deign to have women aboard his ship. 'They are a bad omen and a distraction to his crew,'" she mimicked.

Her father chuckled. "I see. Well then, the *Olympia* is set to sail to London in a week or so."

Marin considered it for a moment. "It would be nice to see Susannah again. 'Tis been nigh on a year since last we saw each other. But I cannot leave the business, Father."

Henshaw smiled. "I believe I still remember how the job is done, daughter. And Mr. Phineas will suffice until I return from Newport."

"I will think on it," said Marin. She stood up and kissed her father on the cheek. "I must be off now."

On the way to the counting house, Marin picked up a copy of the *Boston Gazette*.

"Good morning, Mr. Phineas," she greeted the clerk upon entering the building. "Any news to report?"

"Good morning, Mrs. Sutton. No news."

She went into the office and hung her shawl on the hook, then sat down to scan the paper for mercantile news.

A boxed notice announcing the disappearance of a ship named the *Neptune* caught her eye. It was not known if the ship was captured by Barbary pirates or if it was lost in a storm. The home port was Salem. There was little chance she would know anyone, and Marin gave the names of the crew a cursory glance when one jumped out at her—Peter Thackeray, first mate.

"Mr. Phineas, come here at once!" she yelled excitedly.

Mrs. Sutton never yelled, and the clerk quickly appeared. "Yes, madam. What is amiss?" he asked in alarm.

"Mr. Phineas, you have known Captain Thackeray for many years. Has he a connection to a mariner by the name of Peter Thackeray?"

"I cannot say, but the captain does have a brother."

Marin jumped up from her seat. "I knew there was something in the wind."

"I beg your pardon, madam?"

"Captain Thackeray's voyage to England is not what it seems." Marin grabbed her shawl. "I am going out for awhile, Mr. Phineas."

The clerk stared after her nonplussed as she ran out of the building.

Reese was coming out of the tavern after finishing his midday meal, when he saw Marin hurrying up the wharf toward him. He uttered an oath and ducked back inside, but she had already sighted him.

"Captain Thackeray, do not try to evade me," she shouted. "If I must, I shall come in there after you."

He had little doubt that she would do just that, which could be highly embarrassing for the both of them, and, with a snort of exasperation, he walked outside.

"What is the nature of your urgency that you must accost me outside a tavern?" he demanded to know when she reached him. "Imagine how this must look."

Marin didn't care how it looked. "I know what you are about, Captain."

He coolly regarded her. "What is that, madam?"

"You are sailing to the Barbary Coast."

"I am sailing to England. Check the manifest."

"I did. I also checked with other merchants," said Marin. "You have not contracted with any of them for imports. You are dropping your cargo in England, picking up more provisions, and sailing to the Barbary Coast. It will do you no good to deny it. I saw the notice about the *Neptune* in the *Boston Gazette*. You are going there to learn about your brother."

Reese looked at her sharply. "There was a notice of the *Neptune* in the *Gazette*?"

"Yes, a short account of it."

"Bloody hell! Fielding said it would be kept quiet."

"Who is Fielding?" asked Marin.

"Never mind. The *Neptune* was lost in a storm, Mrs. Sutton."

"Do not play coy with me, Captain. According to the newspaper, some subscribe to the thought that the ship was taken by pirates. I suspect that is the one you embrace as well."

"You are not accompanying me," Reese replied firmly before she had the words out of her mouth.

"But, Captain, I know my way about a ship...I can take readings...I can tend to..."

Thackeray tuned her out; his thoughts were on his aunt. He couldn't allow her to learn about Peter in the newspaper. But if he told her the truth of the matter and of his rescue mission, she would worry herself sick over both her nephews.

"I know how to mend sails...I can help in the galley," Marin prattled on. "I can aid the surgeon—Captain, are you listening to me?"

"No, Mrs. Sutton, I am not," he responded impatiently. "The voyage is too dangerous. The crew may be forced to a fight, and I cannot have them distracted from defending their own lives to protect yours. I shall determine what I can about your husband and see to his release if possible."

"But you do not know him," persisted Marin.

Reese was not swayed. "I have his name, and you can provide me with a likeness of him if you have one. I cannot begin to fathom what your father and cousin would say about such lunacy."

"My father is soon to be in Newport, and I can handle Thomas."

Thackeray looked at her. "Your father is going to Newport?"

"Yes, to visit your aunt."

"Perhaps Benjamin can keep Aunt Caroline from learning about Peter," he said, thinking aloud.

Marin's chest heaved with frustration. "What are you talking about? Who is Mr. Fielding?"

"'Tis none of your concern."

"Captain—"

"You are not going, Mrs. Sutton, and that is my final word. If I must, I will post a guard at the gangplank to keep you away. Do not test me," he warned evenly.

As Reese walked away from her, he missed the determined glint in her eye.

CHAPTER EIGHT

Collecting the Crew

Thackeray looked down at the wharf from the main deck as activity swirled around his ship.

Wagons pulled up loaded with hogsheads of rum, beer, water and vinegar; barrels of salted meat, suet, and raisons; and bags of flour, bread, peas, and oatmeal.

Pots ranged from one wagon to the other on his peg leg, deaf to the complaints of victuallers, as he checked the flour for bugs and the bread for mold and opened barrels of salted beef and pork to make sure there were adequate levels of brine.

After much haggling, the requisite amount of rations was approved and the victuallers were paid. Then the work began to hoist the barrels and hogsheads onto the ship.

At the bottom of the gangplank, the bosun was logging in sailors who stood lined up on the pier with their canvas bags filled with clothes, bedding, and prized possessions.

"Next man up," he shouted. "Step lively, mate. Name?"

"Henry Shaw," answered the sailor in a raspy voice.

"Height?"

"Five plus five."

"Age?"

"Five and ten."

White looked up at the slightly built boy. He looked the part of a sailor with his slops, neckerchief, and flat-topped hat, but he didn't look near ready to cross that threshold into manhood.

"You sure ye be five and ten years?" he asked.

"Aye, sir," replied the sailor, keeping his eyes lowered.

"You ever crew on a ship before?"

"I sailed on my father's ship as a young lad. I am working my way to be captain of a merchant ship one day."

White studied the youth for a long moment. "Are ye afraid of heights?"

"No, sir."

"You do not look strong enough to handle rigging."

"I am stronger than I look, sir. I can do anything ye needs me to do."

The bosun looked dubious. "Do ye play an instrument?"

"No, sir."

"A pity. Musicians are held in high favor." The bosun looked the boy over again. "Mayhaps ye can lend the cook a hand. Can ye handle a pistol?"

"Ain't never tried, but I can learn."

"Do ye know where this ship is headin' upon leavin' London?"

The boy nodded. "Aye, sir."

"The danger gives you no pause? Ye may have to fight pirates."

The lad hesitated. "Every voyage presents a danger, sir. I'd just as soon sail a dangerous sea with a good captain than a safe one with a bad captain. Besides, I hear tell that Captain Thackeray be a cunning man. I am more confident of a battle of wits than of arms. The double pay don't hurt none neither," added the boy.

White burst out laughing. "By jiminy, I like your attitude, lad. Where was ye born?"

"In the middle of the Atlantic Ocean, sir."

"Ain't heard that one before."

"I was born on my father's ship, sir."

"Home port?"

"Boston."

"Family?"

"A cousin, sir."

"Name."

"Thomas Langford."

"Any weapons on your person? The captain don't allow them to be brought on board. Riggers will be issued rigging knives."

"I have no weapons, sir."

White finished writing the information in the log. "All right, take yerself over there to the master surgeon."

The sailor walked over to the surgeon.

The doctor was gruff and methodical. "Remove your hat. Any body lice?" he asked, making a check of the lad's hair and clothes."

"No, sir. My slops and bedding are new-purchased."

"That is certainly not often the case," remarked the surgeon dryly.

"I heard it said the captain keeps a clean ship, sir."

The surgeon opened the canvas bag and made a cursory check of the clothes and bedding. It was as the boy had said. Everything was new.

"Go aboard and stand with the others on the main deck," he directed.

Marin hefted the bag over her shoulder and smiled smugly as she climbed the gangplank. Her ruse had worked.

On deck, men were lined up shoulder to shoulder, and she took her place at the end, glad to be able to set the heavy bag down again. Four other sailors came on board then, followed by the officers.

Thackeray appeared from his quarters and began to walk down the line, reviewing each crew member. So far, they appeared robust. He could read the signs of experience and was heartened to find that most of them were not lacking in it. It had been a concern to him. Several of the sailors had sailed with him on the last voyage. When he came to Marin, he stopped. The sailor was shy of the average height of five feet six inches and looked young and untried.

"Mr. White, what recommends this one?" he questioned. "He hasn't muscle or experience as I can see."

"He's got heart, sir," replied the bosun. "He aims to work his way to captain."

After a heart-stopping moment for Marin, Thackeray nodded and moved on. He would put the lad ashore in London, he decided. In the meantime, the boy would be useful with the more menial tasks of a green hand.

When Reese came to the end of the line, he turned to the bosun. "Mr. White, show these sailors to their quarters. Then acquaint them with their positions and watches. Mr. Duncan, be prepared to set sail as soon as the wind favors us."

As the bosun led the sailors away, Thackeray walked over to his first mate. "Any sign of Mrs. Sutton?"

"No, sir," replied the officer.

"She must have taken my warning to heart then. Continue to keep a watch out for her until the ship leaves port, Mr. Seaton. It is my information and experience that she can be audacious."

"Yes, sir."

Marin's face fell as she followed the bosun below to the gun deck and forward the ship. She had never seen the crewmen's quarters on her father's ship, and she was shocked to see where she was expected to sleep. The area was cramped with the increased number of crew and dank with little light and no privacy.

Seeing the look of dismay on her face, a seasoned seaman smiled. "'Tis better than other ships I've sailed. It ain't the orlop deck."

There were three stacks of beds lined with straw three tiers high and rope hammocks slung in every nook and cranny.

"Choose bed or hammock," said the bosun. "Get yerselves settled, then return top side for yer orders. Quickly, lads, quickly."

The seaman nudged Marin. "The stacked beds sometimes collapse when the ship rolls. Take a hammock," he advised. "Claim that one. 'Tis farther from the hull and 'twill not be as damp."

Marin gave him a grateful smile and quickly claimed the hammock. She pulled out a thin mattress, blanket, and pillow from her sack and made up her bed.

The sailors returned to the main deck. Those deemed able-bodied seamen were assigned positions on the rigging and sails; less experienced sailors were dispatched below deck to man the bilges and anchor ropes. Marin was assigned to the cook.

The sails were unfurled and all waited for the winds that would move the ship out to sea. An hour later, the call went up. "Weigh anchors!"

Marin watched spellbound as the sails billowed in the wind. It was a sight that had never failed to thrill her when she departed ports on her father's ship.

When the bosun announced anchors aweigh, the *Sea Nymph* was slowly eased out of the harbor and headed out to sea. Thackeray returned to his quarters in the stern of the ship.

"Mr. Shaw!" bellowed Pots.

Marin jumped. "Yes, sir?"

"Why are ye standin' about? We have work to do."

"Aye, sir," she replied and followed the peg-legged cook below deck to the galley.

CHAPTER NINE

Adjusting to Life

Over the next three weeks, Marin adjusted to life on board a merchant ship, not as the pampered daughter of the captain accustomed to comfortable quarters and stewards to serve her, but as a crew member expected to do the hard, unenviable work of a lowly seaman.

The sailors had a language of their own, and, even with her aptitude for foreign tongues, it took awhile for Marin to grasp their lingo. Climbing ladders between decks while carrying heavy ropes and sail was also something she had to master. And she learned that the barrels placed around the main deck were for sailors to relieve themselves and knew now to avert her eyes when she saw a crewman heading for one.

A diet of hard biscuits, salted meat, and peas alternated with oatmeal and raisins was the menu; she missed her beloved pastries. Small beer and watered-down rum replaced her daily pleasures of hot chocolate and coffee.

Unaccustomed to alcohol, other than a fine wine, Marin didn't like the taste of the beer or grog or the way it made her feel until the effects wore off. But the drink was unavoidable with so much salted foods in the diet. Drinking water wasn't carried in great quantities; it became rank. And most of the water was reserved for the captain. The crew had to make due with rain water. It was small wonder that the crewmen were tipsy half the time, thought Marin, and marveled that they were able to execute their tasks as well as they did. She found it paradoxical that the captain forbade drunkenness.

It had rained a couple of times, filling the rain barrels, and one day the bosun called for all sailors to bathe themselves and wash their clothes. Marin was in a panic until she saw that it was the practice of most of the men to pour buckets of salt water over themselves in full dress, followed by buckets of rain water to get as much salt out of the clothes as possible to enable them to dry. She soon found, however, that clothes never fully dried in the salt air. Even the clothes in her bag were always damp. She didn't remember that being a problem on her father's ship.

Bathing was a regular regimen whether there was water in the rain barrels or not, as well as swabbing the decks. It seemed that the captain was a student of James Cook, a famous British explorer, navigator, and naval captain, who had written extensively about the benefits of keeping a clean ship from stem to stern.

The day was divided into five, four-hour watches and two, two-hour watches or dogwatches. The dogwatches made for a different schedule every day, which helped to relieve some of the tedium. It was during this time that the crew found the leisure to mend their clothes, do crafts, and make light with music.

Experienced seamen, referred to as able-bodied seamen or deck men, took turns manning the helm, keeping the watches, navigating, and trimming sails throughout the day and night. The green hands, those with little or no experience, worked below deck and were assigned the never-ending tasks of swabbing the decks, caulking, painting, and tarring.

Marin was surprised to find that, aside from the officers, social stratification did not stop at the shore. The experienced sailors were perceived to be of a higher class—the men working aloft in the rigging being the most elite. Only musicians transcended the lines. As a green hand, Marin normally would have found her status low, but assigned to Mr. Potter, she enjoyed some standing; the cook was considered to be as essential to the ship as the captain. Nevertheless, she was expected to do menial labor whenever necessary or free to do so.

Mr. Seaton, the only person besides the captain who might recognize her, took no notice of her. And it was easy for her to keep her distance from him. Like the captain, the first mate didn't associate with the sailors. The crewmen were under the authority of the bosun and the second mate. For added protection, she cultivated the raspy voice and kept her head down.

* * * * *

Marin had figured out that the best time to visit the latrines, located in the bow of the ship, was in the last half hour of a watch change. But one bodily function she had forgotten to consider was one unique to women. And on this day, she viewed the advent of it with alarm. Tearing one of her two extra shirts into strips, she fashioned a belt to hold the cloth that she stuffed inside her pants, praying all the while that her "affliction" wouldn't betray her.

The next day was no different than the others—long and tedious—and Marin was grateful when her duties were done. Her day ended with the second sitting of the last meal. Normally, she would leave the galley in the evening and make her way to the main deck. There were only the men of the watch and perhaps a few off duty crewmen present. It was quiet and easy to find a private spot, but this night she went straight to her quarters. Her back ached; she felt crampy; and her emotions were too close to the surface.

In her impulsiveness and determination to win a battle, she had never considered the hardships that she might encounter in her ruse, and she wondered if the captain would give her passenger quarters if she confessed the charade to him and threw herself on his mercy. She had never expected any of this, she thought miserably, as the swinging of the hammock lulled her to sleep.

There were no timepieces. The ringing of the ship's bell was the only way sailors had to tell time. The bell was rung every half hour with the turning of the hour glass marking the beginning and the end of the watches.

The next morning, Marin was awakened by eight bells—four o'clock—the ending of the middle watch and her time to rise. She climbed out of the hammock still half asleep and dragged herself to the galley to build the fire in the stove. Presently, the cook appeared, yawning and scratching his head.

"Mr. Potter, what manner of man is the captain?" Marin asked tentatively.

The cook shrugged. "The captain be a fair man, but he takes no nonsense. Keep yer head down, yer mouth shut, and yer nose to yer job, and ye'll be right with him. Iffen he catches ye stealin', fightin', or lyin', ye'll find yerself tied to the mast, flogged good, and put off at the next port."

"Oh," murmured Marin, disheartened. She knew the captain wouldn't flog a woman, but he would put her ashore.

The cook looked at her. "Why do ye want to know? You guilty of somethin'?"

"No, sir. I ain't guilty of nothin'," she quickly assured him.

"Then take these keys and go to the storeroom. Gather some biscuits for the crew and bread for the captain."

"Aye, sir."

Flour, bread, and biscuits were stored in the stern of the ship where it was dryer. This was also the area of the captain's quarters.

When she was devising her plan, Marin wasn't worried about Captain Thackeray discovering her. She knew that captains kept close to their quarters and didn't mingle with their crews, most times coming on deck just to take navigational readings or settle a dispute. But while Thackeray maintained a strict division, she soon discovered that he wasn't a traditional captain in every sense. At times, he unexpectedly surfaced and moved through the ship observing the activities of the crew with a keen eye. Praying this wouldn't be one of those times, Marin gathered the bread and biscuits from the storeroom and hurried back to the galley.

The ship's bell called the men to the first siting for breakfast. When all were served, Marin filled her plate and joined the others in a corner of the crew's quarters where they sat on crates or barrels to eat. One of the men tapped his hard biscuit on a makeshift table. When bugs ran out, Marin let out a cry.

"Looks like the green hand is afraid of bugs," jeered a sailor. "Hey, Pots, the tack is more weevil than biscuit."

The cook looked over unconcerned. "'Tis about that time. Count yourselves lucky that clean tack made it this far."

Still unnerved that there might be bugs in her biscuit, Marin set the hard tack away from her.

"Ain't no need to throw off yer biscuit, Shaw," said another sailor. "Just tap it and the bugs will leave." When Marin grimaced, he laughed. "Have a care, lad. A body might think ye was a lass."

"Sure got curls like one," teased a third man.

"Got them dark lashes, too," added a fourth.

Marin was floundering for a way to respond, when the bosun appeared.

"Finish up and be on your way, lads," he said. "There's work to be done."

With a bit of grumbling, the sailors finished up and made their way up the ladder to the main deck.

When the other half of the crew had eaten, Marin set to work cleaning up the galley in preparation for the midday meal.

"Shaw, take the captain his food. I have to make a check of the provisions," said Pots.

Marin felt the rise of panic that was always just below the surface. "I can check the provisions, sir," she quickly offered.

"Nay. We still be a fortnight from London port. The calm winds have put us off a few days. Mr. Duncan and I have to make a check of the supplies against the log to see how short we come. Go on with ye, lad. The captain don't like to be kept waitin'."

Marin looked at the tray of food. It looked more like the food she had been accustomed to eating on her father's ship. She wondered if the captain's bread had bugs in it. Somehow she doubted it.

She had cut her hair to shoulder length and kept it pulled back in a cue, but before leaving the galley, she took the neckerchief from around her neck and tied it around her head for further disguise, then buttoned her jacket to add more bulk to her figure. The captain seemed to have a discerning eye for feminine figures. As an added precaution, she smeared a little dirt across her face and donned her hat.

Marin's heart beat hard against her chest when she knocked on the captain's door. "The morning meal for ye, sir," she called out.

"Come in," he beckoned gruffly.

Marin opened the door and cautiously walked into the main room that was the parlor and dining area. It was handsomely paneled and comfortably furnished with various pieces of furniture from the colonies. Silk oriental rugs and exotic pieces from his ports-of-call in the Pacific Islands and China added splashes of red, gold, and yellow color to an otherwise masculine decor. Marin was surprised to see that the captain had an appreciation for the finer things. The luxury of the room reminded her of the quarters she had enjoyed aboard her father's ship, and she gave a sigh of envy.

Thackeray was bent over a table in the workroom with his back to her. "Put the tray on the dining table," he said.

Marin did as he ordered and started to leave.

"What is your name, lad?"

She stopped, her heart in her throat. "Henry Shaw, sir."

"How goes the galley, Mr. Shaw?"

"It goes well, sir."

"I see you up on deck quite often."

"Yes, sir. I am partial to sunlight and fresh air."

Thackeray ceased what he was doing and turned around. She didn't think it to be a flippant remark nor had she intended it to be, but he thought it impertinent, especially coming from a green hand.

"It would seem that you have a good deal of free time, Mr. Shaw."

His remark surprised and annoyed her. "Begging your pardon, sir, but I do not. When the cook does not require my services, I do my fair share of swabbing the decks and painting, and I help to repair cords and ropes, mend sails and to—"

"Do you make complaints, Mr. Shaw?"

"No, sir. I am here to learn."

"So you are." He picked up a couple pieces of twine from the worktable and threw them to her. "Show me some sailor knots."

Marin's fingers flew over the thin ropes as she quickly tied several knots from long practice. She wanted to throw the knots back at Thackeray, and it took a great deal of effort to control the impulse. Instead, she held them out to him and backed away, keeping a good distance between them and careful not to meet his eye.

Reese examined the knots. "They are adequate," he pronounced. In point of fact, they were quite good, and he was impressed by the lad's speed.

"Has fault been found with my work, sir?"

"No, Mr. Shaw—not that has come to my ears."

Thackeray's eyes narrowed as he considered the young seaman. The lad reminded him of someone, but he couldn't put his finger on it. The boy kept his head bowed in a deferential manner, but, in just this one exchange, Reese had deduced that the boy was bright, clever, and bold. He had been quick to challenge the captain's observation that he was a sluggard. He hadn't stepped over the line, but he had come bloody damn close to it, thought Thackeray, and it invited him to test the lad further.

"Since you are here to learn, I shall add one more task to your list," said Reese. "I would have you also act as as my steward, Mr. Shaw."

Marin stiffened. It was all she could do not to raise her eyes to him in dismay. "Yes, sir," she murmured.

"You may leave now, Mr. Shaw. And clean your face before next you come."

Marin quickly left his quarters angry and horrified. She wasn't sure what all the duties of a steward entailed, but she knew it would place her in closer contact with the captain. And how dare he infer that she wasn't busy enough! She scarce had time to sleep as it was. She worked as hard as any other crewman.

It had been a terrible day, and she wasn't feeling well in light of her "affliction." It left her bereft of energy to deal with problems of any size and, right now, they were all looking pretty big to her. She just wanted to curl up in her hammock and shut out the world for a few days.

When Marin walked into the galley, Pots regarded her closely. "Ye feelin' fit?"

"Aye," she replied dully.

"Ye don't 'pear to be. Go see Dr. Pennyman in sick bay."

"I'm well, Mr. Potter."

"That's an order, Shaw. I need ye to be on yer toes."

Sick bay was located in the forecastle of the ship. Marin knocked on the door, hoping that the surgeon might not be there. What could she possibly tell him? Certainly not the truth.

"Enter," called Pennyman.

Marin groaned. This was not going to be her day.

She opened the door. The room was a good size with four box hammocks, an examining table, a desk, and a cabinet. As she nervously hovered in the doorway, the doctor looked up from his desk and motioned her in. He was a little older than Thackeray, shorter in height with a less muscular build, but, like the captain, he exhibited a no-nonsense manner.

"What is the nature of your complaint—scurvy, lice, intestinal discomfort?" he inquired brusquely.

"No, sir. 'Tis-uh-a stomach upset," replied Marin haltingly. "Mr. Potter insisted I come. I told him that I require no treatment. 'Twill run its course. It always does."

"How often does this upset occur?" queried the surgeon, committing the information to his log.

Marin hesitated. "Just every now and then," she replied.

"Cramping?"

Again, Marin hesitated. "A little…sometimes."

When the surgeon finished the report, he studied her for a few moments, then stood up and went to the medicine chest. He took out a vial of sulfuric acid to mix up an elixir, reconsidered it and put it back. Instead, he mixed up the elixir with brandy, cinnamon, and ginger.

"Here, drink this," he said.

Marin took the cup and tentatively tasted the liquid. It sent a warmth through her, and the flavor wasn't bad, but she wasn't accustomed to the strong liquor. It brought tears to her eyes as she choked it down.

The doctor gave a slight smile. "An ale man, ay? How long has your voice been hoarse?"

"Hard to say, sir. A body tends to lose track of time on a ship."

"Since the beginning of the voyage would you say?"

"Aye, sir."

"You seem rather book learned for a sailor," he observed.

"'Tis necessary to becoming a captain, sir."

The surgeon regarded her again. "Return each day for the elixir while your ailment remains a problem."

"Yes, sir."

Marin went back to the galley with no intentions of returning to sick bay.

"Told ye the doc would fix ye up," said Pots, noting that she had some color in her cheeks.

Marin had to admit that the elixir did make her feel better but sleepy, and she sought out her hammock during a short respite from her duties.

She had just lain down, when the bosun hollered out: "Shaw, gather your belongings and take yourself to sick bay."

Marin sat up in alarm. "Why?"

"The surgeon wants to keep an eye on ye for a few days."

CHAPTER TEN

A Test of Character

The quarantine turned out to be an unexpected boon for Marin. As there were no other patients being confined, she had the room all to herself at night and reveled in the privacy of it. She was particularly grateful for the private latrine. These were also days that kept her away from the captain. It gave her the time she needed to rest, regroup, and regain her inner strength and determination to persevere.

For all of the gruffness the doctor projected, Marin found him to be approachable, a man of reason—unlike the captain—and instructive.

"If it is a captain you are intending to be, you shall have to know about the medicine box," he told her. "All ships must carry one, and it must be inspected before being taken on board as part of the customs permitting procedure for departure."

"Why must I know about it when there is a surgeon on board?" she asked.

"A surgeon is not always present either by choice or happenstance, in which case, the medicine box is the captain's responsibility," explained Pennyman.

"But how is a captain to know medicines when he is not a doctor?" she continued to question.

The surgeon opened a drawer and took out a pamphlet. "There is an instruction book…like this one. While you are here, I require that you acquaint yourself with it. I may have need of your assistance."

Marin took her assignment seriously. She passed the time reading the instruction booklet and familiarizing herself with the medicines in the box. Sometimes the surgeon allowed her to mix up tonics herself for ailing crewmen. And he taught her how to suture a wound.

On the fifth day, the surgeon declared Marin's confinement ended. She had mixed feelings about it. She was beginning to get cabin fever, but she liked having her own quarters and enjoyed helping the doctor. The privacy also had enabled her to let down her guard a bit and gain some relief at night from the uncomfortable binding of her breasts.

"Can I not be your steward instead of the captain's?" she asked hopefully.

The doctor looked at her in surprise. "The captain has instructed you to be his steward?"

Marin gave a snort of annoyance. "He thinks me not busy enough. Apparently, he does not expect me to sleep."

"I see. Well, take heart," replied the surgeon. "The captain is not demanding in this regard."

"I have aided you well, have I not, sir?"

"You have."

"Then perhaps you can tell the captain that you need my help more than he does."

"The captain has priority, Mr. Shaw. Off you go now. I dare say Pots has sorely missed your presence in the galley."

Marin unenthusiastically gathered her belongings. The surgeon watched her, his manner pensive, as she slung the canvas bag over her shoulder and trudged out of the cabin.

When Marin walked into the galley, as the surgeon had predicted, the cook was very pleased and relieved to see her.

"The green hand takin' yer place was all thumbs," he grumbled. "Couldn't turn me back once—not once. The fool nearly let the oatmeal burn. I ask ye, Shaw, who burns oatmeal?"

"Shall I help you prepare the midday meal, sir?" she asked, suppressing a giggle.

"Aye, but first take yourself to the captain to hear his preference for his supper. He tells me ye're to be his steward."

"Aye," replied Marin unenthused. "Can ye not say I am needed more in the galley, Mr. Potter?"

"Have no worries, Shaw. The captain assured me your new duties would not interfere. Now off with ye."

Never knowing what to expect from the captain, Marin struggled against a rising anxiety as she approached his quarters, and she stood outside for a few minutes to compose herself before rapping on the door. There was no answer. She hesitated, not sure what to do. She waited a few more seconds, then took a deep breath and opened the door.

"Captain," she called out cautiously. "Captain, 'tis Shaw. Mr. Potter wishes to know your preference for supper—"

"Mr. Shaw…how nice to see you."

Marin jumped and turned to see Thackeray emerge from the sleeping room. "Your pardon, sir. I knocked…Mr. Potter sent me to—"

"I heard you. Your voice sounds better," he remarked. "I presume you are cured of your complaints."

"Aye, sir."

"It was my thought that the doctor was being overly cautious, but he insisted his actions were prudent." Thackeray eyed her curiously. "Which would you say it was, Mr. Shaw?"

"I cannot say, sir. I am not a surgeon. But one cannot be over cautious with contagions on a ship…sir," she responded, consciously keeping her voice low and her head down.

"Indeed, Mr. Shaw. Dr. Pennyman said you were most helpful to him during the course of your confinement. In fact, it would seem that you have made yourself indispensable to a lot of people," continued Thackeray. "My second mate tells me you mend sails and ropes well. Mr. Potter maintains he cannot do without you in the galley, and now the surgeon sings your praises."

Although his manner and tone were off-hand, Marin sensed the same undercurrent that was present in their last exchange, and she struggled to keep her annoyance from showing.

"Begging your pardon, sir, but, as I have said, I am here to learn," she replied.

As Thackeray continued to regard his steward with interest, Marin shifted uncomfortably beneath his perusal.

"If there is nothing more, sir, I-I should take your meal request to Mr. Potter."

"Very well, Mr. Shaw. Tell Pots that I wish to have fresh fish."

Marin peered up at him in surprise. "Fresh fish, sir...from the ocean?"

"Yes, Mr. Shaw. I believe there is a sea full of them. You should be able to catch one."

"A dinghy put out in these waves will be swamped, sir. And a line will not reach the water from the deck."

"You are a clever lad. I am certain you will find a way," said Reese.

When Marin left the captain's quarters, as usual, she was furious. He was testing her but to what purpose? For a chilling moment, she wondered if he had discovered her identity, then dismissed the idea. He wouldn't be so subtle about it. He would be overtly enraged.

When Marin reported to the cook that the captain wanted fresh fish for his meal, Pots looked at her in astonishment.

"Today? The captain knows the boat cannot be put to sea in these waves. Are ye certain ye heard right, Shaw?"

"Aye."

"Well, there ain't no way. I'll go speak to him."

Marin was not about to concede defeat to the captain.

"No, wait, Mr. Potter. There must be a way," she said. A smile slowly lifted the corners of her mouth as one came to her.

Procuring a fishing pole and bait from the skeptical cook, she set off for a gun port portside. It should be just the right height from which to drop a line, she thought, pleased with herself.

It didn't prove to be quite so easy a task. Sprays of sea water hit her face and stung her eyes, and she had difficulty keeping her footing as the waves buffeted the ship. Water sloshed in, wetting her shoes and clothes. At times, she feared she might be pitched into the ocean as she leaned far out of the gun port to set her hook or play a fish, only to have it work lose from her line. Finally, she pulled in a good sized Haddock.

The cook's mouth dropped open when Marin plopped her catch on the table in front of him. The captain was just as dumbfounded when she presented it to him for his supper. The look on his face, she decided, had been worth every soggy, uncomfortable moment she had endured.

As the story circulated around the ship, the crew embraced it with great amusement. The captain did not, and he called her to account on the main deck before the entire crew.

"What did you think you were about, Mr. Shaw?" demanded Thackeray icily.

"I was following orders, sir," responded Marin.

"Following orders! Did I tell you to open a gun port in these waves, thereby risking this ship?" he barked.

"No, sir. You said that you wanted fresh fish for supper and for me to figure out how best to get it for you. Since the sea is too rough to put out a dinghy and the main deck too high to drop a line, fishing through a gun port was the best way I could figure," explained Marin, matter-of-factly.

Snickers sounded among the crew, increasing the captain's ire all the more.

"Some water came in," continued Marin, "but I swabbed it. I cannot see as how it was enough to put the crew or the ship at risk…" Her voice trailed off when she glanced up from under the brim of her hat to find him glowering down at her.

"Do not test my patience, Mr. Shaw," he warned, punctuating each word. "I should have you flogged for so reckless an act, but I will show leniency for your youth and inexperience. To the rest of you," boomed Thackeray addressing the crew, "no one shall open those gun ports for any reason. Now, get back to your positions."

Thackeray turned to his officers and saw the amusement on their faces. When he glared at them, the first mate and the bosun quickly went off to their tasks as well.

Thackeray looked at his second mate. "Well, what have you to say?"

"As an officer or as a friend?"

"Speak your mind, Timothy."

"You gave the lad an order, Reese—an impossible order."

Thackeray snorted. "Apparently, it was not so impossible."

"You cannot fault Shaw for his cleverness."

"He showed reckless disregard for ship and crew," argued Thackeray.

"The risk was of no consequence, Reese. Why give the order in the first place?"

"It was a test of character."

Duncan regarded the captain closely. "What angers you most…that the lad did not fail in his task or that he outsmarted you? Shaw is not a sluggard, Reese. He is clever, does what he is told, does not complain…the crew like him. What is your complaint of the lad?"

Thackeray was having difficulty figuring that himself and was slow to answer. "He strikes me as bold for his age and position and as one who will test the limits," he finally responded.

Duncan laughed. "Then I expect he will make a fine captain one day. He sounds like you."

CHAPTER ELEVEN

The Storm

At the noon sighting of the sun, Reese stood on deck with his log book prepared to record that hour's readings.

"Helmsman, report," he called out.

The crewman looked at the compass in the binnacle in front of the ship's wheel and relayed the course.

"Mr. Duncan, report."

"Log line says four knots, sir."

Reese jotted down the speed of the ship, noting any changes in the wind. He turned to his first mate who was peering through his sextant. "Mr. Seaton, report."

The first mate relayed the latitude and longitude.

Just then, the seaman in the crow's nest shouted down from his perch: "Storm on the horizon."

Thackeray frowned. Except for some rain along the way, the crossing had been uneventful. He didn't need a storm now to impede their progress.

"Mr. Duncan and Mr. White, prepare the ship for weather," he ordered.

For the next couple of hours, the crew scurried around securing the cargo and quarters and battening down everything that needed to be made fast.

As they headed into the storm, winds picked up and waves increased, and the seamen laboriously tacked back and forth. A huge wave hit the ship, and the vessel heeled to the port side and rolled.

Crewmen grabbed hold of rope and mast beams to keep from being washed overboard.

Marin had been making her way across the main deck, when she was knocked off her feet. Before she had time to react, she slid toward the starboard side, desperately grappling for something to hold on to. She was about to be thrown into the sea, when the captain grabbed hold of her. Another wave hit and water sloshed onto the main deck. The ship righted itself for the moment, and Reese pulled Marin to her feet.

"Get below," he shouted above the din, then disappeared into the melee.

The first mate manned the wheel. The second mate and bosun shouted orders as seamen scurried here and there. Gale winds buffeted the ship and driving rain drenched the deck; water poured down the hatches to the decks below.

Marin grabbed onto anything she could find to keep her footing as she struggled to get to a ladder to go below deck.

"Shaw!... Shaw!"

She stopped and saw a deck man waving to her.

"Fetch Mr. Duncan," he shouted urgently. "A sail broke loose on the mainmast. It has to be severed before it sends the spar through the deck. I cannot do it. Me arm is broke. Hurry, lad."

Marin looked around her. Neither the second mate nor the captain was in sight and everyone else had his hands full. She glanced up at the mast to see a sail flapping dangerously in the wind.

"There is no time," she said, making her way to him. "Give me your knife. I will do it."

"Ye've not the strength, lad."

"I will find it. Give me your knife."

"Have ye climbed a mast in a storm?"

"Yes," she lied.

He handed over his rigging knife. "Have a care, lad."

Marin tucked the knife in her rope belt and began to climb the rat-lines of the 80-foot-high mainmast. Luckily, she didn't have to go all the way to the top. Still, it was higher up than she thought. Her foot slipped once. She looked down and had to close her eyes for a moment to regain her equilibrium. She hadn't been entirely truthful with the bosun when she said she wasn't afraid of heights. At one point, she ducked just in time to keep from being hit with the unsecured part of the sail.

Thackeray glanced up, then, and saw the problem. A sailor was working to remedy it. It was a few minutes before Reese realized that it was Henry Shaw who clung precariously to the ratlines while struggling to cut the sail free.

"Mr. Duncan! Get a man up that mast to help Shaw," he yelled, pointing to the flapping sail.

Grasping the seriousness of the situation, Duncan quickly grabbed an experienced sailor and ordered him up the pole.

Marin had the rope cut halfway through and was grateful when the seaman arrived. Her arms were tiring and her strength was ebbing. With one fell swoop of his knife, the sailor finished the job, cutting loose the sail. Slowly, they descended. By the time she reached the deck, Marin was never so happy to have a firm foundation beneath her feet however much it swayed.

Finally, the ship sailed through the storm. The winds abated, the rain stopped, and the waves became calmer. When the sun broke through the clouds, morale rose among the exhausted crew.

Few escaped without some kind of injury and the surgeon triaged the victims, leaving those less seriously hurt on deck to await his attention and dispatching the more gravely wounded to sick bay for immediate treatment.

Now that the danger had passed and the adrenalin had run its course, Marin leaned over the side of the ship and heaved the contents of her stomach. Her legs were so wobbly they barely supported her.

The captain was making an assessment of the damage on deck and stopped when he saw her. "First time in a storm, Mr. Shaw?"

Marin cringed when she heard his voice—the voice that told her he was going to berate her for something. She slowly turned. "No, sir, but none such as this."

"Next time, find a seasoned sailor to attend a loose sail," he lectured. "I have lost four men to serious injury. I would not have desired to lose one to death."

"Everyone was busy and time was of the essence, sir."

"I applaud your courage, Mr. Shaw, but my order still stands. Have the surgeon look at your arm," he said and moved on.

Marin glanced down at her arm, shocked to see that the sleeve of her shirt was torn and blood stained and that there was a deep gash two inches long on the underside of her forearm. It hadn't really registered before, but now that the injury was pointed out to her, her arm was beginning to throb.

After attending the wounded in sickbay, the surgeon came up on deck to assess the rest of the sailors and spotted her. "Come with me to tend to the others," he said. He noticed her arm then, and Marin winced when he took hold of it and shoved back her tattered sleeve to examine the wound. "It appears we should start with you. That is going to require some stitching."

The surgeon took out a bottle of rum and poured some of it over the gash, then pulled out a needle and some catgut from a wood box. Marin sucked in her breath and felt a little woozy as he began to stitch the cut.

The surgeon chuckled. "If you are going to be a mariner, you will have to get used to this," he said. "Drink some rum. It will fortify you."

Marin didn't argue and took a sizable gulp of the liquor. She didn't care how it tasted as long as it dulled the pain.

"You know that was a foolish thing you did…brave but foolish," commented the doctor. "You could have been blown off the mast."

Marin snorted, growing annoyed with the criticism. "I have scaled many a tree and can climb as well as any other sailor."

"That may well be, but ratlines are not trees, Mr. Shaw. Experienced seamen have strength in their legs and arms from years of climbing masts, and they know how to protect themselves against the wind." The surgeon cut the suture thread and bandaged her arm. "There now, you can be of some assistance to me."

For the next couple of hours, Marin helped him tend to the rest of the wounded. Most had already tended to themselves with tankards of grog.

The deck was littered with debris, as well as bedding and clothes that had been laid out to dry in the remaining hours of sunshine. Inspection showed some damage to the keel and a weakening of one mast as well as the loss of the one sail. The rest of the day was given over to the repair of rigging and torn sails.

Marin had one remaining shirt, and, with the sailors busy, she found a private moment and a corner to change into it. She was on her way to the galley to help the cook, when the bosun waylaid her.

"Dr. Pennyman wants a word with you in his cabin, Mr. Shaw."

"Now, sir?"

"Aye."

Marin changed course and made her way to the surgeon's quarters, which was in the area of the officers' cabins directly beneath the captain's quarters.

The door was open, and she stood in the entrance. "You wish to see me, sir?"

"I do," said the surgeon. "Come in and close the door, Mr. Shaw."

Marin did as he ordered. "Is something amiss, sir?"

"I cannot say. Perhaps you should tell me," replied Pennyman. He folded his arms across his chest. His tone would suggest a certain casualness, but there was a sense of implacability and purpose in his manner.

She looked at him in bewilderment. "I beg your pardon, sir?"

"I should like to hear why a young woman is masquerading as a lad."

Marin's mouth fell open. Her first instinct was to deny it, but she realized how futile that would be, and her shoulders drooped in admission of the ruse.

"How long have you known?" she asked.

"I suspected for some time," admitted Pennyman. "I used the excuse of your voice to quarantine you to give you some privacy during your, shall we say, delicate time of the month."

Marin's face reddened. "Please do not tell the captain," she pleaded.

"Frankly, I am amazed that he hasn't figured it out for himself yet," said the surgeon. "A man likes to know when he is being deceived. Give me a good reason why I should hold my tongue."

Marin quickly explained about her husband's plight and her mission to discern his status. "When I heard that the captain was sailing to the Barbary Coast to learn of his brother's disappearance, I pleaded with him to allow me to accompany him. He steadfastly refused, and I had no choice but to conceive this charade."

The doctor unfolded his arms and looked at her in surprise, then burst out laughing. "You are the infamous Mrs. Sutton I heard so much about?"

Marin bristled. She didn't know whether to be flattered or insulted. "You will not tell Captain Thackeray, will you? 'Tis by his own stubbornness that I was forced to this deceit."

"I dare say 'twas by yours as well," pointed out the surgeon.

"Are you going to tell him?" she asked anxiously.

The doctor fell silent for a few minutes as he mulled over the situation, at great pains to conceal his amusement.

"This is a dangerous voyage, Mrs. Sutton—more than you know," he said at length.

"How so?"

"I am not at liberty to say. But suffice it to know you would be placing yourself in perilous circumstances. Why is it so important that you make this journey? Can you not leave it to the captain to determine the circumstances of your husband?"

"For more than three years, I have been living in limbo, Doctor. I must discern the situation for myself."

"I see. Well, even if I keep your secret, I must tell you that the captain is planning to leave you ashore in London when he sails for the Mediterranean."

Marin looked at the surgeon in alarm. "Why?"

The surgeon shrugged. "I suppose he does not wish to have a young boy's life on his hands. Much less will he want the life of a woman on his conscience."

"Ha. What makes you think that he has a conscience?" retorted Marin.

The surgeon smiled. "There are a lot of things about the captain that might surprise you."

"I doubt it. You can tell him that you will need me to assist you with the wounded in the event of a battle with the pirates," she suggested hopefully.

"Let us get through this part of the journey first and see what happens," replied Pennyman. "Upon my word, I will not disclose your secret—at least not before we come to London port. The captain does not tolerate chicanery. One storm is enough to weather on this voyage."

It was not the assurance Marin sought, but it would have to do for now.

CHAPTER TWELVE

London

L and ho."

The shout from the sailor in the crow's nest met with loud cheers from the seamen on the main deck.

Thackeray emerged from his quarters and peered through his telescope at the land mass that was Ireland.

Several days later, the first mate navigated the *Sea Nymph* through the English Channel to the Thames River and into the Pool of London—the stretch of river on the south side of the city where all shipping was handled.

Miles of wharves lined both banks. Hundreds of ships were moored in the river or along the quays and piers. From here, Seaton maneuvered the ship to a spot in the Legal Quays, the area between Billingsgate and the Tower of London where all imported cargos were held for inspection by the Customs Inspectors.

Behind the quays ran Thames Street, populated by warehouses, sugar refineries, and cooperages.

As the deckhands furled and secured the sails, the bosun shouted the order to drop anchors. Dock workers came forward then to moor the ship to the quay, and all hands moved quickly to dispatch their tasks, eager to go ashore.

The captain returned to his quarters to take care of the paperwork for customs. The bosun directed the crew to begin bringing the cargo from the hold to the main deck. And the cook began taking stock of the provisions he would need for the next leg of the voyage.

Marin had never liked the port of London. It was too busy, too clamorous. Neither did she find it colorful like Boston's Long Wharf. Perhaps it was the gray, dismal weather that seemed to dominate England that made the port appear dark, dirty, and somewhat ominous to her, but she was just as eager to go ashore as the others.

She was looking forward to seeing her friend and enjoying some female companionship for a change, not to mention privacy. The masquerade was growing wearisome for her. When they sailed from London and were far enough from port, Marin decided she would disclose her ruse to the captain.

It was two days before Reese received the license from the Customs Inspector to unload the cargo.

"Have a care at the unloading, Mr. Seaton. There is much thievery here," warned Reese. "Make certain the merchants take custody of their wares."

"Aye, sir."

Thackeray turned to his bosun. "Mr. White, Mr. Duncan and I are going ashore to the foundry and may be away for a few days. Mr. Seaton will be in command of the ship. The men are allowed their leave, but it is to be taken in shifts. Keep a tight rein. I can ill afford to lose crewmen to disorderly behavior." He turned to the surgeon. "How long is the recovery for the four men who suffered broken bones?" he asked.

"Three months," replied the doctor.

"We shall have to replace them then. Mr. White, see to the recruitment of eight more crewmen. Give preference to those who have military training in the use of the cannons." Thackeray looked at his cook. "Mr. Potter, as you will in the procurement of provisions. I want the ship ready to sail in two fortnights."

"Aye, sir."

Thackeray started to dismiss his officers, when another thought came to him. "Mr. White, send Mr. Shaw to me."

"Aye, sir."

When the bosun relayed to Marin that the captain wanted to see her, she felt the familiar sense of alarm. "Why?" she asked guardedly.

"He did not say. Did ye do somethin' to cross him?"

"Not that I can recall. Was he angry?"

"'Tis hard to know. The captain is always stern on board the ship. Me, Duncan, and Pots been speakin' up for ye, Shaw. Do not ye play us false. The captain ain't a forgivin' man when it comes to honor and order on his ship."

This didn't help to relieve Marin's anxiety. "I been mindful of my ways, sir. 'Tis on another matter that he orders me to him…of that I am sure," she added on a less certain note.

With the bosun's warning ringing in her ears, it was with some trepidation that she reported to the captain's quarters. She had been careful to stay out of his way. Beyond bringing him meals, straightening up his cabin, and laundering his clothes, she found him to be not demanding of his steward, as Dr. Pennyman had predicted. In fact, he seemed preoccupied with another weightier matter so that he took little notice of her as she quietly slipped in and out of his rooms. What complaint could he have of her now? she fretted. Or was he going to put her ashore?

When she arrived at the cabin, the door was open, and she hesitantly entered. He was in his workroom where he was most times, papers strewn across the table.

"You wished to see me, sir?"

He looked up at her. "I would have a bath before going ashore. Fill the tub with rain water. There should be plenty in the barrels from the storm."

Marin slowly let out her breath in relief. "Aye, sir."

Luckily, she didn't have to carry water far. Two rain barrels lay near the quarters on the main deck, but carrying the heavy buckets of water down the few stairs to the tub in the sleeping room was taking its toll on her.

She was pouring out the last bucket of water, when Reese walked in. He sat down on the edge of the bed and pulled off his boots and socks. Warily watching him out the corner of her eye, her eyes widened as he took off his breeches. When he stood up and stripped off the cover of his long shirt, she quickly averted her gaze.

He looked at her in amusement as he stepped into the tub and lowered himself. "Do not tell me that you are shy, Mr. Shaw, after quartering with a ship full of sailors for over a month."

"No, sir. But you are the captain."

Reese snorted. "We have the same anatomy—though perhaps with some degree of difference," he added, noting the slight build of his steward.

"Aye, sir. I shall leave you to your privacy, sir."

She hurried to the doorway.

"Mr. Shaw, you are not yet dismissed."

Marin stopped and slowly turned around. "Yes, sir?"

"I desire you to take that brush to my back."

Marin sucked in her breath and removed the brush from the hook. When he leaned forward, she dipped the brush in the water and began to scrub his back.

"Put some more vigor into it, Mr. Shaw."

"Aye, sir."

"So you wish to be a ship's captain one day?" he questioned rhetorically.

"Aye, sir."

"'Tis not for the faint of heart. Do you know what poses the greatest danger in such a profession, Mr. Shaw?"

"Storms, sir?"

"No."

"The crew, sir?"

"Not if you have a good cook and a competent second mate and bosun."

"What then, sir?"

"Women, Mr. Shaw. Have a care, particularly with those who hang around the port. They can leave their mark on a man if you get my meaning."

"Aye, sir."

"As for the others, they will either pick your pockets clean or march you before a preacher before your head stops spinning."

Marin raised a brow and scrubbed a little harder. "Indeed, sir?"

"Aye. Do not be fooled by a woman with a pleasing countenance, lad. It can mask a poor disposition, and a woman temperamental in nature can make a man's life a living hell," Reese continued to expound. He paused for a moment, reflecting. "I met such a woman in Boston this last time...as beautiful as a man could ever hope to find...but annoying as hell—God's blood, Mr. Shaw! Easy with that brush. I would have some skin left on my back."

"Your pardon, sir," replied Marin through clenched teeth. "Am I dismissed?"

"No. Lay out a suit of clothes from the trunk," he ordered.

Fuming, Marin put down the brush, resisting the impulse to hit him over the head with it, and went to the trunk. She took out the suit of clothes he had worn on his second visit to her office and laid them on the bed.

Reese stepped out of the tub. This time, Marin wasn't so quick to avert her eyes from the toned, muscular body, now that she was past the shock of it all. She noticed then a long, angry scar on his right thigh and wondered what had occasioned it.

"The towel, Mr. Shaw."

Marin roused and quickly grabbed the towel from the hook and handed it to him.

He wrapped it around his waist, eyeing her curiously. "You are as skittish as a cat."

"Apologies, sir. I am keen to go ashore...for a *short* while."

"All in good time, Mr. Shaw."

Reese walked over to the bed, and her eyes widened again when he let the towel fall. As he pulled on the long shirt, she leaned her head to the side to follow the drop of the apparel until it covered his buttocks. Marin sighed. As perfect a male specimen as a woman could ever hope to find, but annoying as hell.

CHAPTER THIRTEEN

An Old Friend

Marin was finally given leave to quit the ship for a few days. Quickly, she made her way to Trinity Square Gardens near the port. At the appointed place, she saw the cab and hurried up to it.

"Madam, may I accompany you?" she asked in a lowered voice.

A pretty, young woman with large brown eyes and chestnut colored hair glanced out the window. "Off with you. I have no truck with sailors, most certainly not with young lads."

Marin laughed. "Susannah, 'tis me."

The woman looked at her in astonishment. "Marin?"

"Aye,"

"Good heavens!" exclaimed Susannah. She quickly opened the door and gazed around the park. "Get in before someone sees you. The last thing I need is for my husband to hear that I was seen having an assignation—near the docks no less."

Marin climbed into the cab. "'Tis good to see you, dear friend. I was afraid you might not get my note. How well you look."

"Never mind that. Marin, I do not understand any of this. I received your letter that you were coming for a visit only a week ago. You should not be here for another month."

"I sent the letter by way of the *Olympia* and traveled on another ship that was leaving at the same time. I was only just released from my duties," said Marin.

"Duties...what duties? Why did you not travel on the *Olympia*? And why are you dressed that way?" Susannah wrinkled her nose. "You smell musty."

"'Tis the clothes. They do not dry well in the sea air."

When Marin removed her hat and the kerchief tied around her head, Susannah gasped. "What did you do to your beautiful hair? What in the name of heaven have you been up to?" she demanded to know.

"'Tis a long story, Susannah. I shall explain later."

"No, you will explain now, Marin Sutton."

Marin gave a sigh of resignation and told her friend the circumstances surrounding her odyssey. When she was finished, Susannah shook her head in disbelief.

"You have done some crazy things, Marin, but masquerading as a sailor on a merchant ship...this tips the scale. I cannot imagine your father and Thomas agreeing to this."

"Father was visiting a lady friend in Newport, and I left a note for him. As far as he and Thomas know, I sailed on the *Olympia* to visit with you—at Father's suggestion, I might add."

Susannah's face screwed up in bewilderment. "Then why did you not sail on the *Olympia*? If you had waited to board the *Sea Nymph* in London port, you would have needed to practice your ruse for only half the time."

"I feared the captain would already have his crew in place for the voyage to Algiers," replied Marin.

"How am I to smuggle you into the house past the servants as you are?"

Marin laughed. "If memory serves, you can be quite clever on occasion. I am sure you will think of something."

"Humph. You take much for granted. How is your cousin?"

"Annoying as usual. He hasn't changed a bit...always playing tricks."

Susannah shot her friend a pointed look. "Apparently, the apple falls not far from the tree."

"I dare say you have a mischievous side, too," Marin reminded the young woman. "Bye the bye, Thomas thinks he should have married you."

"There was a time when I thought so, too," replied Susannah. "Then I came to my senses when Richard came along. I will soon have one child to care for. I am not in need of another."

Marin looked at her in astonishment. "You are expecting a child?"

Susannah glowed with happiness. "I am."

"When?"

"Round about November."

"And you did not write me?"

"I wanted to be absolutely certain."

"I am so happy for you," said Marin. "I would hug you, but you don't appreciate the fine fragrance of my clothes."

"'Tis an acquired taste," admitted Susannah. "We shall hold the hug for later." She smiled wistfully. "I have missed you so, Marin. I have had little excitement in my life since Richard was sent here as part of Mr. Jay's diplomatic mission. He works all the time, and I am too often left to my own devices."

"Have you no friends?" asked Marin.

"Only among the American delegation. It is not easy to make friends in England since the War of Independence, you know. The British are rather unforgiving of us." Susannah grasped hold of her friend's hand. "Marin, you must promise me that you will allow me to aid you in your cause. I am with child, not an invalid, and I must have something delectably audacious to occupy me, or I shall surely go mad."

Marin laughed. "I knew the old Susannah was still in there. What of Richard?"

"I can handle Richard. He may be a diplomat, but I am a woman."

"Yes, men do seem to forget how clever a woman can be when the need arises," quipped Marin.

"Tell me how I can help," pressed Susannah.

"Very well. At times, I must go to the ship as Henry Shaw and will require some assistance to play both roles."

"Why? I thought you said the captain intends to leave you ashore."

"I am still part of the crew until the captain dismisses me," said Marin. "I cannot raise suspicion or incur his ire in case he can be persuaded to keep me on board when he sails for the Barbary Coast."

"But the surgeon knows who you are," Susannah reminded her. "He will expose your ruse."

"Perhaps I can appeal to Dr. Pennyman as well."

Susannah knit her brow in concern. "Marin, the Barbary Coast is dangerous. I hear Richard discussing it with other members of the diplomatic corps. Stay here and let this captain find out about Nathaniel. What information could you possibly gather that he cannot?"

"I cannot say," admitted Marin. "But I am driven by the need to go to Algiers myself."

Susannah sighed. "I shall do whatever you need me to do, though I do not agree with your decision. But you must not put me in a position where I must lie to Richard."

"I promise," said Marin.

When the hired carriage rolled up in front of a three-story Georgian-style townhouse three bays wide, Susannah opened the door and cautiously looked about. "Richard is at a meeting and the servants should be in the kitchen. It is their time of respite. I shall go first and make sure the way is clear."

The young woman stepped down from the carriage and quickly made her way to the front door. Quietly, she let herself in. Several minutes later, she poked her head out the door and motioned for Marin to come.

Marin got out of the cab and hurried up to the entrance, whereupon Susannah pulled her inside and whisked her up the stairs.

She showed Marin to a bed chamber at the end of the hall. "Stay here and be quiet until I come for you," she instructed.

Marin looked around her. The room was decorated in periwinkle blue and white and, although small, was inviting. Dreaming of sleeping once more in a real bed, she tested the mattress before settling herself in a comfortable wing chair.

An hour later, Susannah returned and quietly led Marin to her own chamber. At the sight of the bath that awaited her, Marin gave a squeal of delight.

"Hush," cautioned Susannah. "I told the maid the bath was for me."

Susannah rolled a screen in front of the tub to give her friend some privacy.

As Marin pitched out her kerchief, breeches, shirt, stockings, and shoes, Susannah regarded them with disdain. "What shall I do with these clothes?" she asked.

"Can you have them washed? I will have need of them again," replied Marin. She climbed into the hip tub and sank down into warm water. "A-a-h," she murmured, settling back against the tub. "I haven't had a proper bath since leaving Boston."

Susannah picked up the offending garments with two fingers and threw them into a basket. "How ever shall I explain these to the washer woman?" she murmured.

Aloud, she said, "I am laying out a proper change of clothes for you, Marin. 'Tis luck we are close enough in size. When you have finished with your bath and dress, you must present yourself at the front door as though you have only just arrived." Susannah frowned. "Alas, I know not what to do with your hair. Perhaps I can gather it in the back with combs and add a nosegay of flowers to disguise the short length."

At a sudden knock on the door, the girls froze.

"Madam," called the maid, "shall I assist you with your bath?"

"No, thank you. I can manage," replied Susannah. "I should like to be alone for awhile."

"As you wish, madam."

When Marin had finished with her bath and was dressed and coiffed, she followed Susannah quietly down the stairs. At the bottom, Susannah cautiously checked for any sign of the servants. Finding the area clear, she motioned to Marin.

Marin hurried down the rest of the stairs and across the foyer to position herself at the front door.

At the sound of the commotion, the housekeeper came running to the foyer to find the mistress excitedly greeting a strange woman.

"Your pardon, madam, I did not hear the knocker," she said.

"No matter, Mrs. Bennett, I was passing by. This is my very dear friend from Boston Mrs. Sutton," said Susannah. "Remember, I told you that she would be visiting. Has the room at the end of the hall been made ready for her?"

"I-I will see to it right away, madam," replied the older woman, flustered. "I had assumed it would be at best a month until your guest arrived."

She called for one of the two servant maids and gave the young woman instructions. When the maid hurried off, the housekeeper turned to Susannah. "Do you wish for tea and cakes to be brought, madam?"

"Yes," replied Susannah. "Please have a tray brought to the morning room."

"Very good, madam." The housekeeper quickly went off to the kitchen.

"How grand you live," remarked Marin.

"We are renting the house, and the servants came with it," explained Susannah. "It has taken some getting used to. The British are so prim and proper. 'Tis ghastly suffocating, not to mention expensive. The government gives us a stipend, which, of course, does not cover near the cost, but the Ministry feels the need to show the British that envoys from the United States can be just as civilized."

She led Marin into a bright, yellow room with floor to ceiling windows. Images of peacocks with plumes of green, turquoise, and blue decorated a sofa, and the seats of straight chairs were upholstered with a matching color of green. At the end of the sofa stood a floor loom with unfinished needlepoint.

"You are doing needlepoint?" questioned Marin in surprise.

Susannah laughed. "I told you I was desperate for something to do. It is progressing rather badly, I fear."

The housekeeper entered the room followed by a maid carrying a tray of pastries and a tea service; she set it on the table in front of the sofa.

"Shall she pour, madam?" asked the housekeeper.

"No, thank you, Mrs. Bennett. I shall attend it," replied Susannah.

"Very good, madam."

When the housekeeper and the maid left the room, Susannah gave a sigh of forbearance. "See what I mean—and I think they listen at the door," she added in a whisper. "I have to be mindful of my p's and q's at all times. Frankly, I should like to do something that shocks them all out of this dull complacency, but I shall play the role for Richard's sake."

Marin laughed. "I will endeavor not to compromise your good name."

The girls were reminiscing, when they heard Susannah's husband in the foyer.

"Richard," called out Susannah. "Come see who is here."

A lean man, taller than average, walked into the room, and a broad smile broke across his features. "Why, I must be dreaming. If it isn't Marin Sutton in the flesh looking lovely as always," he greeted. He walked over to her and kissed her on the cheek.

Marin smiled. "Hello, Richard. It is nice to see you again."

"You must have been divining my dear wife's thoughts from across the sea. I hear every day how much she misses you. I must confess, though, that I had thought your visit to be a month out," he said with some bewilderment.

"I fear that my letter was delayed," replied Marin. "I hope that my unexpected arrival does not inconvenience you."

"Most assuredly not. Whatever pleases my wife—and I can see that she is most pleased—pleases me. In truth, I am glad that you are here to keep Susannah out of trouble."

At this, Marin and Susannah exchanged conspiratorial smiles.

"Susannah has told me about the baby," said Marin. "My blessings to the three of you."

The young man beamed with pride. "Indeed, I am most fortunate."

"Will you join us for tea, darling?" asked Susannah.

"Regretfully, I must hurry back to the Ministry," replied Richard. "I came to retrieve some papers that Minister Pinkney is awaiting. I shall join you for dinner, and Marin can tell us all the news from Boston."

He kissed his wife on the cheek and bid the ladies a good day.

Marin and Susannah spent the rest of the afternoon relaxing and laughing as they further recalled their antics during their teen years in Boston. Her father was right, thought Marin. Seeing Susannah again was good for her psyche. Her state of mind had much improved in just these few hours.

At dinner that night, conversation was witty, cheeky, and political, and Marin felt very much at home in the company of her friends. As Richard regaled the women with stories about the vagaries of diplomats, she again found herself laughing without restraint. It had been a long time since she had felt this unfettered.

At first glance, Richard Greenfield was a plain-looking man. He had brown hair short on the sides and back and curly on top and long, narrow features, but he was one of those men who possessed traits that transcended ordinary looks to Marin's mind. His demeanor projected an air of calm and confidence and his dark brown eyes reflected a keen intelligence and clever wit. More importantly, he possessed the character of an honorable man. Marin liked him very much and thought him well suited to her friend. It was clear that he adored Susannah and she him, and Marin couldn't help feeling a measure of envy.

"What are your plans tomorrow, as if I couldn't guess?" asked Richard with a twinkle in his eye.

Susannah laughed. "Intuitive as always, my dear. Yes, I am taking Marin shopping but out of necessity. Her clothes were ruined when the ship encountered a storm." It wasn't a lie but more a qualified truth as she saw it.

"Indeed," replied Richard, amused. "I thought I recognized Marin's dress as being one of yours. Well, you have my blessing, ladies."

* * * * *

Over the next couple of weeks, Reese made trips to the foundry, plotted the tactical aspects of the voyage, and presented his letter of introduction as prepared by Mr. Fielding to the chief clerk of the Ministry.

Meanwhile, Marin continued to lead a double life with Susannah's help. With a long cloak covering her seamen's clothes, she left the house early in the morning for the ship, taking a cab to Trinity Square Gardens. There, she stashed her cloak underneath a bush and walked the rest of the way to the wharf. At the end of the day, Susannah arrived in a cab to pick her up in the park, whereupon Marin retrieved her cloak and returned to the townhouse as Mrs. Sutton.

Late one afternoon, Reese was in a cab returning to the ship from a visit to the foundry, when another cab leaving Trinity Square Gardens passed by him. He glanced at the occupants and did a double take. *It couldn't be.* He craned his neck to get another look, but the cab was far down the lane.

When Thackeray boarded his ship, his brow was furrowed with a disturbing thought.

"Is something amiss with the cannonades, sir?" asked his first mate.

"No." replied Thackeray, distracted. "Mr. Seaton, did you see Mrs. Sutton hereabouts?"

Seaton looked at the captain nonplussed. "No, sir. Why do you ask?"

"I…I thought I saw her in a cab leaving Trinity Square Gardens."

"I cannot imagine that to be the case, sir."

"Nor can I," responded the captain broodily.

"You know what they say, sir. Everyone has a double somewhere."

Thackeray grunted. "God help us if Mrs. Sutton has one."

Seaton snickered. "Just so, sir."

"Where is Mr. Duncan?"

"On the bow, sir, checking the rigging."

"And Mr. White?"

"Preparing the cannon carriages. He said we should be ready to receive the cannonades in a few days."

"Very good. Tell them I wish to hear their reports in my quarters."

"Aye, sir."

Thackeray went to his cabin and unlocked the door of a small room where weapons were being stored. He again took inventory of the swords and knives and was inspecting the pistols to make sure they were still in good working order, when his second mate and bosun arrived to give their reports. At the conclusion, Thackeray nodded, well pleased with the progress.

"Have you replaced the injured crew members?" he asked the bosun.

"Yes, sir. I found three amongst them who manned the cannons on a British naval warship. I would heartily recommend one of them, a Mr. Ferguson, to oversee the matter."

"Excellent. Proceed. Where is Mr. Shaw?" queried Reese. "I've scarce seen him about."

"He's been steady about, but he left for the day," replied the bosun. "I've given him his leave to come and go, seein' as how ye ain't keepin' him on and he ain't able to take a watch. Pots says there ain't much for him to do in the galley neither. The men are sick of ship food and have been takin' their meals at the tavern."

White laughed. "I seen the lad gettin' into a cab with a woman a few times at day's end and wearin' a smile the next day—not to mention a pleasant smell. 'Pears that Shaw has found himself a fine lady to keep him. Ain't surprisin' with them curls an' eyes he's got."

Duncan snickered. "Told ye he was clever. He ain't hardly wet behind the ears."

White shrugged. "Some women like that."

Duncan looked at the captain. "Shaw is a good worker. We could use a powder monkey if we have to fight."

"I will not bring a boy to battle. You know how ruthless Barbary pirates are," said Reese.

"Then you need to tell him now so he can find another ship to crew."

"If what Andrew says is true, the lad seems not to be in any strife," remarked Thackeray dryly. "But I will draw up his papers and pay. Andrew can give them to him tomorrow."

The next morning, the bosun gave Marin the news and surrendered her papers and the wages owed her. She had figured it likely, but it was still a gut punch. Each day that she wasn't dismissed had given her new hope.

"Is my work not satisfactory, Mr. White? I will do better," she promised.

"Nay, 'tis not your work, Shaw. 'Tis the captain's orders."

"I shall make a plea to him then," persisted Marin.

The bosun shook his head. "'Twill do ye no good. He says he'll not take a boy into battle with pirates. Sorry, lad. Ain't nothing for it. The captain's mind be set."

CHAPTER FOURTEEN

A Haunting Illusion

Susannah swept into Marin's room in a determined mood. "Come, we are going out."

Marin lay on a chaise longue staring morosely out the window. "I am sorry, Susannah, I do not feel up to it."

"Honestly, Marin, you must stop moping. 'Tis been nigh on a week since you were put ashore. Have you not thought of any recourse yet?"

Marin shook her head. "Nothing comes to mind. What am I to do? I cannot give up now."

"Perhaps it is for the best," said Susannah. "I shudder at the thought of you fighting pirates. I think you should leave the matter of Nathaniel in that captain's hands. At any rate, you will not come to a solution shut up here." She took Marin by the hands and pulled her to her feet. "Fetch your hat and shawl."

Marin groaned. "Where are we going?"

"Where every woman goes when she is feeling low."

"We just went shopping. I have everything I require, Susannah."

"Have you an evening gown?"

"Why should I have need of one?"

"Because we are going to a reception and dinner next week."

Marin balked. "I hate social occasions. You know that."

"This one will be different," promised Susannah. "'Tis the diplomatic corps. There will be talk of politics," she added as an extra enticement. "You shall find the ladies enlightened on the subject and the evening quite lively."

Marin perked up a bit. "The ladies are permitted their say in such matters?"

Susannah laughed. "Just try to stop them. 'Tis the legacy of Abigail Adams, I am told, from when Mr. Adams was Minister to St. James."

"Indeed," marveled Marin. "But a week is not time enough to construct a gown."

"There is a draper shop that keeps finished gowns on hand for occasions just as this. I am sure you will find something to suit."

The day turned out to be unexpectedly pleasant for Marin.

The draper's wife produced a dress that Marin found to her liking. Indeed, she was quite taken by the gown's cerulean blue color and the drape of the chiffon material. With a few nips and tucks, it would be a perfect fit. After that, she and Susannah progressed to the shoemaker, who promised to have the matching slippers made by the end of the week. Last, came the visit to the shop of the glove, stocking, and reticule maker. With these tasks dispatched, the ladies decided that such exhausting work deserved refreshment.

Reese was riding through the fashionable shopping district on Bond Street, idly glancing out the window of the cab, when two young women emerged from a tea house. They were laughing and looked to be having a grand time.

As the cab passed by them, one slightly turned his way. Reese went rigid. Much of her face had been shielded by the straw hat that she wore, but in the quick glimpse that he got, he could have sworn the woman was Mrs. Sutton. *It could not be…not again!*

He banged on the roof. "Driver stop!"

The conveyance stopped, and Thackeray jumped out and ran back to the spot, but the women had disappeared. He looked around for them, nonplussed. They must have caught a cab going in the other direction, he mused.

"Flowers for your lady, sir?" asked an old woman selling bouquets of jonquils and sweet William.

Reese shook his head and climbed back into the cab, disturbed and bewildered. What the bloody hell was wrong with him? He had managed to cross the Atlantic with not a single thought given to Marin Sutton, and now, all of a sudden, he was imagining that he saw her on two occasions!

When Thackeray returned to the ship, Seaton regarded him quizzically. "Captain, are ye feelin' fit, sir?"

Reese looked at his first mate. "No, Mr. Seaton, I am not," he snapped. "That woman is haunting me!"

"Who, sir?"

"Mrs. Sutton!"

As Thackeray stomped off to his cabin, Seaton stared after him in perplexity.

Duncan approached the first mate. "What's amiss with the captain?"

Seaton shook his head. "I cannot say. I think it has something to do with Mrs. Sutton."

"Mrs. Sutton…that woman in Boston who had him in such a dither?"

"Aye. 'Twould appear she still has him in a dither."

Duncan looked at Seaton in surprise. "How so? The woman is across the Atlantic."

Alex hesitated and lowered his voice. "The captain claims to have seen Mrs. Sutton in a passing cab," he confided to the second mate.

"Here…in London?"

"Aye. I told him that it must be another woman of her likeness, but the sighting seems to have unsettled him considerably. When he boarded just now, his exact words were: 'That woman is haunting me.'"

Duncan burst out laughing. "I must meet this lady whose arm has the stretch of an ocean."

"I do not believe that the captain finds it a laughing matter," responded Seaton, concerned. "I have not known him to be so distracted. I fear it may affect the mission."

The second mate clapped Seaton on the back. "No need to worry, Alex me lad. The captain will have his head on straight when the time comes. She ain't the first woman to unsettle him. 'Tis but a passin' fancy."

Alex glanced skeptically at his fellow officer. "You do not know Mrs. Sutton."

* * * * *

Reese had received a request by the Minister to appear before the diplomatic corps and was on his way to the American Ministry this morning.

As the cab wound its way through the busy city streets of London, he stared out the window scanning every woman he saw for any resemblance to Marin. He had had no further sightings of her, but he couldn't shake the idea that he had seen her. Why did this woman bedevil him so! he fumed. After awhile, with no questionable encounters, Reese settled back in his seat. He really had to get hold of himself.

Shortly thereafter, the driver pulled up to the northeast corner of Grosvenor Square in front of a modest, three-story brick house that housed the Chancery and the Minister to the Court of St. James. A butler answered his knock and ushered him down the hall to a large room where state business was conducted.

Paneled in cherry wood, it was a warm, attractive room. Candlelight from polished brass chandeliers and sconces alleviated the gloom of the gray day. Against one wall was a fireplace with a marble surround. Red drapes hung from floor-length windows, and a woven carpet of East India origin carpeted the pine floor. The only furniture was a desk in front of the windows and a long table in the center of the room for the purpose of conference. It gave one to know that serious affairs were discussed here, and upon entry, one was assailed with a sense of sobriety.

"Come in, Captain," greeted Minister Pinckney. He sat at the head of the rectangular table flanked by members of the diplomatic corps—three on each side. "Please sit down," he directed, motioning to the seat at the end of the table.

As Thackeray sat down, the Minister continued. "We have been discussing your mission, Captain. It comes at a rather delicate time. A treaty with England, which ties up loose ends from the negotiated peace of the War of Independence and which gives the United States important trade considerations, awaits ratification by Congress. And I am in the middle of securing an important trade and alliance treaty with Spain."

"I did not choose this time, sir," replied Reese. "Nor did I choose this mission. I was given no choice in the matter."

"Yes, Mr. Fielding explained in his letter that your brother is a captive as well," said the Minister. "Still, we cannot risk these agreements by provoking a war with the dey of Algeria."

"It is not my intention to provoke a war, sir."

"There is the report that you are arming your ship with cannons, Captain," spoke up one envoy. "It may not speak to an intent to provoke, but it does show intent to engage in battle rather than in diplomacy."

"As I understand it, sir, diplomacy is not an option in this case," replied Reese.

"Neither are hostilities," countered another diplomat. "You understand there is no formal declaration of war. It is a tightrope that you walk, Captain."

"Is that not always the case with these nation states?" questioned Thackeray.

A few men snickered.

"There is a new dey. Word has it that he is more reasonable than the last, whatever that means," offered one of the other diplomats.

"The rulers of these states all trend toward cruelty and childish games."

"There is another option," interjected Thackeray.

"What is that, Captain?"

"Trickery. But know this, gentlemen. If all else fails, I will defend my crew and ship against attack with every means at my disposal and leave diplomacy to others," said Reese, leveling an unwavering gaze on the delegation.

"What is your plan then?" asked the Minister.

"If I told you, sir, you would not be able to deny knowledge of it should it fail."

The Minister nodded. "I believe we understand one another. The Secretary of State has a high degree of confidence in Captain Thackeray, gentlemen. We can show no less."

The diplomats nodded in agreement.

The Minister turned to Reese again. "Word has come to us that Mrs. Marsden and her son are still being held in the dey's compound. I am hosting a reception and dinner. I should like for you to attend, Captain. I will have a map of the palace compound prepared for you to view then."

"Thank you, sir. I shall be honored to attend," replied Reese.

CHAPTER FIFTEEN

The Minister's Reception

Soft candlelight emanated from the windows of the Ministry extending a warm welcome to guests arriving for the Minister's reception and dinner.

Marin entered the Chancery with Susannah and Richard, and they were shown into a room that was once a family dining room under the first minister John Adams and was now a receiving room that connected to the room of business. Marin was dismayed to find that the guests numbered only 18, including her. A small group made it more difficult for her to hide, and when a servant offered her a glass of champagne, she readily accepted.

Susannah took Marin by the arm and introduced her to the other guests. Marin discovered that, as outcasts in a foreign land, the American diplomats and their wives had formed a close-knit group, and she soon relaxed as they made her feel welcome. Over the course of conversation, she had to grant that Susannah was right. The men in the corps were among the brightest in America, and their wives were just as witty, educated, and informed.

At that moment, Reese arrived. A servant ushered him down the hall to the business room. As they passed by the receiving room, he glanced inside to view a small but lively gathering of guests.

When he was shown into the large room with which he was familiar, he saw that a map of the dey's compound had been laid out on the conference table for him. Reese walked over to it and was studying it, when Minister Pinckney walked into the room.

"Good evening, Captain. How do you find the rendering?"

Thackeray looked at Pinckney, impressed. "From my memory, sir, it appears quite complete."

"You have been to the palace?" the Minister asked in surprise.

"It was over 10 years ago, but I still remember it well," replied Reese, a hard edge to his tone. "A ship I was crewing was the first to be taken by Barbary pirates after the War of Independence."

"You were a prisoner then?"

"For six months, until I and half the crew escaped, but each month seemed like a year. How did you come by this map?" inquired Thackeray.

"The dey has permitted the captain of the *Dauphin* to work in the British Consulate in Algiers. Captain O'Bryen managed to pass it to an envoy returning to England who, upon arrival, passed it to us," explained the Minister.

"I am surprised that we enjoy such good relations with the British," remarked Thackeray.

The Minister smiled. "The medicine is bitter, but John Jay's treaty helps it go down easier."

"Indeed. I should like to have a copy of this map if I may."

"Of course, Captain. I shall have my secretary draw one up for you. He is a meticulous copier. Is there anything else you require?"

"Perhaps an opinion, sir. Mr. Fielding advised me to seek the aid of an American prisoner named James Cathcart. Do you know of him?"

The Minister nodded. "Yes. Captain O'Bryen has made mention of him several times. It seems that the dey holds this man in such high regard he has appointed him Chief Clerk."

"Is Cathcart trustworthy?"

"I believe so. O'Bryen has spoken highly of him. If you have nothing more, Captain, I must play host now."

"Of course, Minister Pinckney. My apology for keeping you so long from your duties."

"None needed, sir. I am happy to oblige you in any way that I can."

Reese accompanied the Minister into the receiving room. He suddenly came to a dead stop and a look of incredulity flooded his features.

"Is something amiss?" inquired the Minister. "You look as though you've spied a ghost."

"That woman over there in the blue gown…do you know of her?"

The Minister followed Reese's gaze. "Why, yes. That is Mrs. Sutton. She is visiting the Greenfields. Lovely woman. Shall I introduce you?"

"That will not be necessary," replied Reese evenly. "I have made her acquaintance before. With your permission, sir, I should like to make it again."

The Minister smiled. "Of course, Captain."

Marin was engaged in spirited conversation, when she felt a presence behind her. She turned, and her jaw dropped when she saw Reese. She was so shocked to see him there and the fact that he now sported a closely trimmed mustache and beard made her question for a moment if it was really him.

Her failure to respond in time handed Reese the initiative, and he flashed his most charming smile. "Your pardon, ladies," he said in his deep timbre voice. "May I have a word with Mrs. Sutton?"

They nodded, staring agog at the mysterious, handsome gentleman.

Before Marin could gather herself, he put a hand beneath her elbow and led her away to a corner of the room.

"What are you doing here?" she demanded to know, disengaging herself from his grasp.

"I might ask the same of you?" he responded. "How did you get to London?"

"By way of the Atlantic Ocean," she replied flippantly.

Reese struggled to keep his temper in check. "You know what I mean. What ship?"

"The *Olympia* arrived last month, did she not?" questioned Marin. It was the truth. It just wasn't the whole truth.

Thackeray's eyes narrowed as he continued to regard her with suspicion. "*Why* are you here?"

"I am visiting an old friend."

"'Tis rather coincidental, don't you think?"

Marin shrugged. "Coincidences happen, Captain."

"Were it anyone but you, Mrs. Sutton, I might agree. How is it that you are here tonight?"

"My friend's husband is a member of the diplomatic corps. How is it that *you* are here?"

"You are not the only one with a friend in the Ministry," he returned.

She regarded him curiously. Why had he grown facial hair? It was not considered fashionable or a measure of honesty. Surely, he knew that; obviously, it didn't matter to him. Strangely, Marin didn't find the beard and mustache so off-putting. In truth, she thought it gave him a rather dashing appearance, if not a certain roguish appeal.

Marin turned her gaze on the guests. "When do you depart for the Mediterranean?" she inquired, trying to project a casual interest.

"'Tis of no concern to you," he replied. "When are you returning to Boston?"

"'Tis of no concern to you," she shot back.

They glared at each other. The stalemate was broken with the announcement of dinner. As everyone moved into the state dining room, Marin reluctantly accepted Reese's arm and escort.

The butler directed guests to their seats. His assistants seated the ladies. Marin was annoyed to find her place directly across the table from the captain. Reese was of a different mind about the arrangement. As long as she was in front of him, he could keep an eye on her. At least now he knew he wasn't delusional. He had actually seen her on those two occasions. But he couldn't say whether the discovery was a relief or a concern.

For Marin, the situation introduced more uncertainty into an already uncertain plan—and danger of a further unmasking. She had to keep a distance from him before he could put together the similarities between her and Henry Shaw. She still held out hope that the captain might change his mind about allowing Shaw to rejoin his crew.

As the first course was being served, Marin started to take off her gloves, when she realized that the condition of her hands and nails and the scar on her arm could give her away, and she quickly drew the gloves back on.

Dinner was slow and laborious. Course after course was served in seemingly endless service, and her charm and patience were wearing thin. It was dangerous to her interests to be so long in the captain's presence.

She looked up at one point to find Thackeray's gaze on her, studying her, before his attention was captured by a lady seated on his right. Marin knew then that her time was running out. The quizzical look on his face told her that he was already trying to put it together.

She cast around for a way to distract him; before long, he gave it to her.

"However does your business survive without your presence in Boston, Mrs. Sutton?" he asked.

Marin heard the smirk in his voice and knew that he was baiting her. "It survives temporarily in the hands of my clerk, Captain, while I attend to some business in London," she replied stiffly.

"Indeed. What business have you in London?" he continued to inquire.

"The business of imports, sir. I am acting as a supercargo as I am short a contract," she responded, giving him a pointed look. "In the meantime, I am visiting with a dear friend."

It sounded plausible enough, and it might account for why he had seen her leaving an area near the port that day. But Reese didn't believe her.

"You are the proprietor of a business, Mrs. Sutton?" asked a woman, overhearing the conversation.

Marin turned her attention to the older lady. "I am managing my father's import business until his health revives."

"How exciting. You must have quite a head for numbers," replied the woman admiringly.

Hearing a snort from Reese, Marin turned back to him. "Does the captain not approve of a woman being in business?"

"I do not approve of a woman trespassing into the domain of men, but I have no quarrel with a woman being in the business of women," responded Thackeray.

She bristled at his smug pomposity. "And what business would that be?" she questioned.

Reese shrugged. "Dressmaking, millinery…all such things as related to females."

"And men should be only in the business of men?"

"The same rule would apply, madam."

"Indeed." Marin glanced around the table. "Forgive me, ladies, if I misspeak, but do not men dominate the trades which fashion women's shoes, gloves, and stockings?"

"Why yes, and reticules, too," interjected one of the ladies.

Marin smiled. "Perhaps the Captain should inform these men that they are trespassing into the domains of women."

"Well done, Mrs. Sutton," declared a second woman stoutly. "What is good for the gander is good for the goose, I say."

"As do I," chimed in another female guest.

"Me as well," said a fourth woman.

"So you see, Captain, there are exceptions to every rule," Marin continued. "And, as long as there are exceptions, there are no hard and fast rules, except, perhaps, in the minds of some small-minded men."

As the women heartily agreed, Reese saw the quagmire he had just stepped into.

"You may as well concede, Captain," advised one husband. This is an argument that does not end well for men these days, and we are encouraged to avoid it. The ladies call this the Age of Enlightenment—freedom from bias and formality in thought as well as in dress."

"'Tis the age of audacity," grumbled another man. "And we have the uprising of the French peasants to thank for these outrageous ideas of free thinking and equality. It should not be encouraged."

This brought an uproar from the ladies.

The husband chuckled. "See what I mean, Captain? I fear Mrs. Sutton has opened Pandora's box."

"Yes, she is quite good at that," replied Reese.

Clearly, more had changed in the years that he had been away than women's fashion. When he looked over at Marin, she met his eye with a smile of sweet revenge, and he had the feeling that she had very cleverly led him into this patch of quicksand.

Susannah leaned across her husband to speak to Marin. "'Tis glad I am that you are friend and not foe," she whispered. "I had forgotten how devastating you can be in a debate. Do you know the captain? You seemed to engage him with an air of familiarity."

"He is the captain of the *Sea Nymph*," Marin whispered back.

"What!" Susannah regarded Reese closer. "I must say I imagined a much different person from your comments of him. You failed to mention that he is a rather intriguing man."

Marin glanced over at Thackeray. "I hadn't noticed," she responded.

Susannah laughed. "How could you not notice?"

"I am married, Susannah."

"It does not render a woman blind."

"If you knew the captain as I do, you would find that his arrogance negates any physical appeal he may have," countered Marin.

"Well, I dare say that Mr. Chumbley's sister does not seem to agree."

"Madam, shall I relinquish my seat to you?" quipped Richard to his wife. "I find it rather awkward to be in the center of a conversation to which I am clearly not an invited participant."

Susannah gave her husband a rueful smile. "Apologies, darling."

"Mrs. Sutton, how does your husband view the nature of your employment?" asked one of the ladies.

"I regret that I cannot say," replied Marin.

"You are a widow then?"

"That remains to be seen. My husband was on a ship overtaken by Barbary pirates some three years past, and I have had no word of him."

"How dreadful. It must be very difficult for you."

"Indeed. I have sought information but have gleaned none. I am seeking passage to Algiers to divine the situation for myself." She looked at Thackeray. "I understand that you are soon to sail to the Mediterranean."

"Is that true, Captain?" asked the woman.

"It is, madam."

"Well then, Mrs. Sutton can sail with you," the woman declared. "Surely, you must sympathize with her plight."

Thackeray blinked in surprise. He couldn't believe that he had been blindsided again. Seeing how neatly Marin was setting the table, he took a moment to regroup.

"I do sympathize, madam," he replied carefully. "But those waters are rife with pirates. 'Tis dangerous for American merchant ships to sail them—as evidenced by the loss of Mrs. Sutton's husband. An American woman is no less immune to capture. I will be happy to make inquiries on Mrs. Sutton's behalf."

The woman shuddered. "A female in the hands of pirates— 'tis not to be imagined."

"Quite right," agreed Reese. "And, in the case of the Barbary states, women also suffer great indignities at the hands of their rulers."

"How so, Captain?" inquired another lady.

"Piracy is an industry on the Barbary Coast," explained Thackeray. "Just as are men, captured women are regarded as bounty and treated as slaves. Some are sold to nomadic tribes. Those comely enough are added to the rulers' harems."

"Dear heaven!" exclaimed the lady, appalled.

Murmurs of similar sentiments erupted among the other women.

"Apologies, ladies, for being indelicate," said Reese, "but I believe the danger needs to be stressed to Mrs. Sutton."

"Perhaps the captain's suggestion that he make inquiries on your behalf would be the more prudent course, Mrs. Sutton," said the older woman to everyone's agreement.

He had turned the tables on her, and Marin inwardly fumed at the little smile of triumph he sent her.

"I have relied upon the promises of others to make inquiries of Mr. Sutton, but it has been to no avail," she responded. "I have come to the belief that, unless one has a personal interest in the matter, there is reason to question the depth of another party's inquiry or if that inquiry was even made at all."

"Even so, there is the matter of your safety," interjected another woman.

"I appreciate your concern, but I believe I would be safe enough," said Marin. "I have it on good authority that Captain Thackeray is quite resourceful. And it is my knowledge that his ship goes armed with cannons."

"Good gracious!" exclaimed the lady. "Surely, no trade is worth such a risk that cannons must be mounted, Captain."

"I beg to differ, my dear," interrupted her husband. "Since the end of the war and the loss of British convoys, the American economy has suffered greatly for its inability to freely conduct trade on the Barbary Coast. Some risk must be borne, but it shall not be for too much longer. Congress has given its blessing to raising a navy, and I dare say that warships are being built as we speak to convoy American merchant ships."

"I should think that it would behoove commerce to wait until a navy can provide safe passage then," the diplomat's wife continued to argue. "If so many merchant ships are being taken by these pirates, it is foolhardy for a captain to continue to sail there without protection."

"Not to worry, madam, Americans are a tough lot. We just fought a war to prove it. In time, these Barbary rogues will be brought to heel," the Minister assured her.

"Well, until then, I cannot see the benefit for the risk."

"Nor I," the other ladies repeated one by one.

The men exchanged uneasy glances, fearing the turn the conversation might take should it be allowed to continue, and they looked to the Minister for guidance. Minister Pinckney responded by announcing that it was time to move upstairs where the ladies would take their tea and dessert in the drawing room, and the men their brandy in the library.

The ending of the dinner had been handled with aplomb and diplomacy, but it seemed somewhat abrupt to Marin. She glanced around as people stood and began making their way to their assigned rooms. No one seemed to find the announcement strange, though some of the ladies remarked that it was unusual for them to take dessert in the drawing room rather than in the dining room. The matter was soon lost to other conversation, but Marin had the feeling that a nerve had been touched.

If Marin was curious about the moment, Reese was furious, more so at himself that he had underestimated her cleverness again. She had succeeded in maneuvering him into corners that had nearly caused the unraveling of a delicate mission. If it was her goal to cause trouble, she was achieving it. He had never encountered a woman before who was able to rain discomfort upon a corps of practiced diplomats.

* * * * *

"Marin, you are testing my limits," cried Susannah over breakfast in her room the next morning. "I told you. Richard has said nothing about Captain Thackeray or the Barbary Coast in recent days. And my answer will be the same no matter how many times you ask it."

"But you must have heard something," insisted Marin.

"Only that pirates are a concern in travel to and from the Portuguese Consulate."

Marin thought for a moment. "Have you heard mention of a ship named the *Neptune*?" she asked.

"Yes. Richard said it was lost in a storm. It was notable because the wife and son of the acting minister to the Portuguese Consulate were passengers."

Marin looked at her friend in surprise. "That is odd."

"What is?"

"Captain Thackeray's brother was the first mate on the *Neptune*."

"That is a coincidence," commented Susannah. "It was quite sad when the news came back to us. I had made the acquaintance of Mrs. Marsden and her son on several occasions. She was a lovely woman and the little boy was very sweet. It still saddens me to think about them."

"Susannah, Captain Thackeray is not sailing to the Barbary Coast to conduct trade."

Susannah sighed. "Another gut feeling? Why would he say that he was then?"

"He didn't," said Marin. "Everyone made that assumption, and he declined to deny it. 'Tis a ploy with which I am well acquainted."

"So I have had the occasion to observe," replied Susannah dryly. "What then is the captain's purpose for sailing to the Barbary Coast if not to trade?"

"He is going there to find his brother."

Susannah looked at her in bewilderment. "But the ship sank. Everyone was lost."

"I cannot say why, but the captain does not believe that."

Susannah's eyes widen. "What does he think happened?"

"Pirates."

"No, Richard would have told me," insisted Susannah. "He knows how upset I was over the loss. Besides, there has been no ransom demand."

Marin was pensive. "Mayhap the government or the ruler of Algeria does not want it known that the *Neptune* was taken by pirates," she conjectured.

"Why not?"

"I think it has something to do with Mrs. Marsden and her son."

"Marin, as much as I would like to believe that they may be alive, I fear your imagination is getting the better of you," declared Susannah. "You possess such a suspicious mind."

Marin sat up and perched on the edge of the chair. "Susannah, think about it. Reese Thackeray captains an ordinary merchant ship out of Boston. He holds no standing of importance of which I am aware. How, then, does he find himself a guest at the reception and dinner of the American Minister?"

"The same can be said of you," pointed out Susannah. "Perhaps the captain enjoys a friendship with a member of the corps as well. Not everything deserves scrutiny, Marin. Sometimes there is a simple answer."

Marin was resolute. "Not this time. For reasons with which I am unacquainted, the captain is known to refuse any contract for trade on the Barbary Coast. He would not be changing course now if he did not have good reason to believe that his brother is alive and being held prisoner."

"Good morning, ladies." Richard entered the room and walked over to kiss his wife on the cheek. "Are you feeling better this morning, dearest?"

Susannah looked up at her husband and smiled. "Yes, much better. Mrs. Townsley said the morning upset will soon pass."

Richard poured himself a cup of hot chocolate. "It gladdens me to hear it. I do not enjoy taking the morning meal alone. What are you ladies up to? You seem to have your heads together, which never bodes well for a man."

Susannah laughed. "You are as suspicious as Marin."

"Oh, and what has tweaked Marin's imagination and passion for intrigue now?" he teased.

"'Tis not my imagination," responded Marin stoutly.

"We were discussing Captain Thackeray," said Susannah. "Did you know that his brother was first mate on the *Neptune*?"

"Uh…yes…I believe he mentioned that," said Richard, taking a sip of the chocolate drink.

"It turns out that Marin is acquainted with the captain," continued Susannah.

"Indeed. He mentioned that as well," her husband replied wryly.

"Marin thinks the *Neptune* was not lost in a storm…that it was taken by pirates and that the captain is sailing to the Barbary Coast to find his brother."

Richard turned to Marin. "Did Captain Thackeray tell you this?"

"He tried to deny it until he couldn't," said Marin. "There was too much in evidence of it."

"How so?"

Briefly, Marin explained how she had come to her conclusions, beginning with the notice in the newspaper. When she had finished, Richard remained silent, astonished by her gathering of the facts.

"Richard, can this be true?" asked Susannah, finding her husband's reaction strange. "Is Marin right? Can Mrs. Marsden and her son be alive?"

Richard gave a sigh of resignation and set down his cup. "Thackeray said it might come to this." He went to the door and closed it before speaking. "Yes, it is true."

"Why did you not tell me?" asked Susannah. "You know how this tragedy has upset me."

"We did not know the truth of it for some time. I am sorry, darling. I could not tell you because it is a matter of great sensitivity. I cannot tell you anything more than this, and you must promise not to repeat any part of this conversation or share your thoughts on the matter with anyone. The lives of Mrs. Marsden and her son hang in the balance."

Susannah and Marin looked at him, their eyes wide at the disclosure and solemnly nodded.

"What of the captain?" asked Marin.

"The captain is working in the service of our government," replied Richard. "He has orders to gain the freedom of Mr. Marsden's family and as many of the crew of the *Neptune* as he can by whatever means possible."

Marin jumped to her feet. "What of the other prisoners?"

Richard shook his head. "I am sorry, Marin. Mrs. Marsden and the boy are the captain's first concern. The *Neptune's* crew are his second. But he has promised to find out what he can about your husband."

"That is not good enough, Richard."

"I am afraid that is the best we can offer, Marin. If the captain is successful, the Secretary of State can use the incident to perhaps force the release of the other prisoners that remain there."

"No…no, there is another way. There is always another way, Richard. And I will find it," she declared.

CHAPTER SIXTEEN

The Sea Nymph

r. Seaton, ahoy there," shouted Marin.

Alex looked down at the wharf from the deck of the ship in disbelief. He rubbed his eyes and looked again. "Bloody hell," he murmured under his breath. "Mrs. Sutton…is it really you?"

"It is. May I come aboard, Mr. Seaton?"

"Aye."

When Marin reached the deck, he stared at her in wonder. "Mrs. Sutton, what are you doing in London?"

"Visiting a friend," she replied.

"'Tis a relief to know that the captain is not losing his mind after all," remarked the first mate.

"I beg your pardon?"

"Nothing, madam."

"Where is the captain, Mr. Seaton? I require a word with him."

"He is in his quarters."

As Marin swiftly started off in the direction of the stairs that led to the cabin, the first mate knew that he should go after her and intercede with a warning to the captain first, but her brisk stride and determined manner gave him to know that it would be like trying to stop a stampeding horse. Truth be told, he feared her more than he did the captain.

Duncan walked up to him. "Who might the lady be?"

Seaton looked at the second mate still in a state of disbelief. "Mrs. Sutton," he replied.

Duncan raised a brow in astonishment. "That is Mrs. Sutton…here…in London?" He let out a low whistle. "Holy hell, wait until the captain sees her."

"I dare say he already has," said Seaton.

Marin burst into the cabin. "Captain Thackeray!"

Reese was sliding the blade of the razor along the edge of his beard and started at the sound of her voice, nicking himself. Uttering an expletive, he reached for a cloth and walked into the main room dabbing at the cut.

"What are you doing here, Mrs. Sutton?" he demanded to know, his tone fractious.

"I know all about your mission," she said.

Reese should have been surprised, but he wasn't. "So you have managed to breach the wall of silence of even a practiced diplomat."

"Richard had no choice. I had intuited most of the story."

"What do you want, Mrs. Sutton?"

"I want to go with you."

"No."

As he started to turn away from her, she grabbed hold of his arm. "I know what your orders are. If Nathaniel is there, I have to help him. He cannot be left behind. He may be sick or injured."

Reese removed her hand from his arm. "I told you before it is too dangerous, and you will get in the way. There is too much at stake."

She pursed her lips—another gesture of resolve that he had learned about her. When she glanced away, momentarily lost in thought, he could see the wheels turning in her head and cautioned himself to be on guard.

He could also see that she was upset about her husband and allowed her a measure of sympathy. "I remind you that, as an officer, your husband will be treated with more humanity, Mrs. Sutton. His plight is not as dire as you fear."

She looked at him. "Neither is your brother's, yet you go for him."

"The *Neptune* was a diplomatic ship, and her capture was a violation of American sovereignty. It is tantamount to a declaration of war, which is why the dey will never admit to the *Neptune's* existence."

"Yes, yes, Richard explained all that."

"Then you know that your husband cannot be part of the mission. It will be all I can do to free Marsden's family and perhaps some of the officers and crew."

"I know my way around a ship, Captain. I can be of help to your crew and to your plan," persisted Marin. "In the process, perhaps I can learn something about my husband."

Thackeray gave a sigh of impatience. "Mrs. Sutton, the closer we get to an encounter the more nervous the crew will become. They will start to look for signs of ill fortune, and they will come to view a woman on board as a bad omen. I cannot afford the distraction or the mutiny. The success of this mission depends upon every man knowing and performing his job without fear, thought, or question."

Marin made no response. Instead, she walked into the workroom and returned with a piece of cord. Quickly, she tied a bowline knot and tossed it to him, then walked out of the cabin.

Thackeray looked at the knot, not surprised that she would know the king of the sailor's knots given her sailing background, but it brought to mind a similar moment in time that raised the specter of Henry Shaw. Mrs. Sutton and the young green sailor were a lot alike. Reese snorted. It was amazing the degree of annoyance both could arouse in him.

He walked into the workroom and threw the knotted cord aside. He started to pick up a map, when he was again assailed with thoughts of Marin and Henry Shaw...how much alike they were. He knit his brows, nonplussed. Marin had never been in his quarters before. How would she know of his workroom and that she might find rope there? And how could she have known that he was arming his ship with cannons? Shaw...Henry...Henry Shaw...HENSHAW! It hit him like a thunderbolt.

Reese bolted out of his cabin and tore up to the main deck. "Where is Mrs. Sutton?" he bellowed.

Work came to a halt and a hush fell over the crew.

"The woman that was here…where is she?" he shouted impatiently.

"She went down the gangplank," said one seaman.

Everyone stared in wonder as the captain rushed down the gangplank, and they all ran to the port side of the ship to continue watching as he quickly made his way down the wharf to the woman in question.

When Reese grabbed hold of her, Marin gasped in astonishment.

"Let go of me!" she demanded. "What are you doing?"

Reese grasped her hands to examine them. They were work roughened and callused as a sailor's might be. As final proof, he shoved back the sleeve of her dress and saw the scar—the same scar Henry Shaw had as a result of his injury during the storm.

As bold as he knew her to be, the very idea that she would have the nerve to perpetrate such a deception had never entered his mind. That she had carried it off for the length of the voyage across the Atlantic without detection rendered him speechless.

Marin smiled smugly. "Perhaps you should reconsider your decision to deny me passage, Captain. It might prove embarrassing for you were your crew to learn the truth of Henry Shaw."

Thackeray's jaw clenched. "Do not overestimate a sailor's tolerance for deceit, madam."

He seized her by the upper arm and angrily propelled her down the quay to the ship.

The crewmen stared mystified when the captain brought the woman on deck.

"Summon all hands on deck," he shouted to the bosun.

Marin looked at him. When he was angry, he was unpredictable, and she was feeling less confidant of her bargaining power.

White rang the bell. Duncan and Seaton rushed up from below deck with Dr. Pennyman, Pots, and other seamen wondering at the urgency. The officers stopped short at the sight of Marin. The captain's expression was unusually stern, and they knew that he was at the boiling point.

Duncan looked at Seaton. "I thought you said Mrs. Sutton had left and all was quiet."

"She did leave," replied the first mate, bewildered.

When everyone had assembled, there was only the sound of the waves lapping against the side of the ship as the apprehensive crewmen waited for the captain to speak.

"Men, this is Mrs. Sutton," said Thackeray. "Mark her well. Some of you are new to this ship, but those of you who made the voyage from Boston on the *Sea Nymph* are familiar with seaman Henry Shaw. Take heed this day that Mrs. Sutton and Henry Shaw are—"

"What the captain is trying to tell you is that I have passed among you as Henry Shaw," cut in Marin, stealing the narrative.

Rumbles of disbelief, confusion, and anger rippled through the seamen, growing louder and more threatening.

Duncan turned to an equally astonished Seaton. "What the bloody hell—they'll tear the ship apart."

Reese himself was shocked by her confession. He hadn't been prepared to go that far, only to alert the crew that neither Mrs. Sutton nor Henry Shaw were to step foot on the ship again.

"What are you doing?" he murmured to her in alarm.

She ignored him and continued on, raising her voice above the din. "My name is Marin. It means 'of the sea.' I protected you through the storm."

A hush fell over the crew.

"She's a sea nymph!" a sailor suddenly blurted out.

More unrest rippled through the men, and Marin was beginning to question the wisdom of her actions.

Then a seaman near the bowsprit shouted excitedly: "Look! Look to the figurehead. 'Tis her... 'tis our lady of the sea!"

The crewmen rushed to the bow. Sailors could always find images or symbols that portended good or bad depending upon the circumstances; it was all a state of mind. And Thackeray strode angrily to the bow to firmly reassert his authority and dispense with this nonsense before it got out of hand any further. Duncan, White, Seaton, and Pennyman followed after the captain, curious.

All were brought up short, when they saw the figurehead. Marin pushed her way to the fore and drew in her breath sharply. The wood carving of the woman on the prow of Thackeray's ship bore a startling resemblance to her.

Reese and his officers watched in further amazement as sea hardened men dropped to their knees with cries of gratitude that the ruler of the seas had sent one of his daughters to protect them. Some had tears in their eyes. Not even Marin could have imagined such a scene or the effect that her brash declaration would have.

"Mr. White, disperse these men," Reese ordered tersely.

The bosun quickly moved to dispatch the crew to their tasks.

Reese then ordered his officers and Pots to his quarters. "You, too, Mrs. Sutton," he said, taking her by the arm.

Inside the captain's cabin, the air was tense. Reese sat at his grand, mahogany desk in the main room not unlike a headmaster glowering at wayward students. As everyone stood waiting for him to speak, the officers stole sidelong glances at Marin, still in a state of disbelief that this striking, young woman had crossed the Atlantic Ocean with them…eating, sleeping, working in their midst as the lad Henry Shaw. Maybe she was a sea nymph.

When the captain spoke, his voice was low and controlled, but everyone knew it was the calm before the storm and braced himself.

"This woman," began Reese, pointing to Marin, "masqueraded as a sailor for over a month and you mean to tell me that none of you took notice? Mr. White, she was under your supervision. What have you to say for yourself?"

"W-well, sir," stammered the bosun, "Shaw done his job, and some lads at that age still look like lasses until they get their first—" He stopped at a nudge from Duncan and looked at Marin. "Sorry, ma'am. I mean to say until they get more worldly experience."

Reese snorted and turned to the cook. "Mr. Potter, she was your assistant. What have you to say to this?" he demanded to know.

"Uh…what Andrew said, sir."

"Beggin' yer pardon, Captain, but Shaw was your steward," Duncan reminded him.

Thackeray glared at the second mate and quickly moved on. "Mr. White, what is the source of that bloody figurehead?"

"'Tis from the woodcarver Samuel Bottoms, sir. 'Twas the only carving that was finished and seein' as how you wanted to set sail so soon—"

"Were there no other wood carvers in Boston?" quizzed Reese, the aggravation building in his voice.

The bosun shifted uncomfortably. "I-I s'pose so, but…well, I liked this lady. She looked like a fittin' guardian for the *Sea Nymph*. Upon my word, Captain, I didna know she was in the image of Mrs. Sutton."

Reese turned a critical eye on Marin, who had remained remarkably silent. "Do you have any idea of the jeopardy you could have placed the ship and this mission in with that stunt, Mrs. Sutton?"

"Apologies, Captain, it was not my intention to—"

Thackeray pounded his fist on the desk. "What was your intention, madam?!"

The storm broke and everyone cringed.

"I warned you before about the dangers of playing fast and loose with sailors' superstitions," Reese thundered. "How is it that figurehead is in your likeness?"

"I-I cannot say," stammered Marin.

"Are you or are you not acquainted with that wood carver, Mrs. Sutton?"

"We are of the same social circle. But I had no hand in the matter of the carving," she hastened to say. "And Mr. Potter can tell you I had no hand in the procurement of it."

Silence fell, and Marin squirmed as Reese scrutinized her long and hard, his cobalt blue eyes seeming to bore straight into her. After what seemed like an eternity to her, he looked to his first mate.

"Mr. Seaton."

"Yes, sir?"

"Escort Mrs. Sutton off the ship and make certain she does not step foot on it again."

"Captain-uh-that may not sit well with the crew," ventured Duncan hesitantly. "The men think she has been sent to protect them on this voyage."

"They will have to be content with the figurehead as their protector," snapped Reese. "Now out, all of you!"

"But, Captain…" began Marin.

He turned a warning glare on her. "Out with you, Mrs. Sutton, before I do something we shall both regret."

Officers Duncan and White hustled Marin out the door with Seaton and Pots following close behind.

"And close the door!" shouted Reese.

Seaton quickly pulled the door shut.

Thackeray rose from his seat behind the desk and went to the liquor cabinet and poured himself a shot of whiskey. He downed it and poured another. Carrying the bottle with him, he sat down at the dining table to brood. A few minutes later there came a knock on the door.

"Who is it?" he growled.

"Pennyman."

"Enter at your peril."

The surgeon opened the door and strode into the room, a broad smile on his face. He pointed to the whiskey. "May I?"

Thackeray nodded.

Pennyman found a cup and sat down. "Mrs. Sutton is clever. You have to give her that," he remarked, pouring himself a drink.

"How the bloody hell could she have fooled everyone all that time!" erupted Reese.

The surgeon took a swig of his whiskey. "I would not say she fooled everyone."

Thackeray looked at the doctor sharply. "Are you saying that you knew?"

"I suspected for awhile before confronting her."

"How?"

"A doctor notices things a man might not, particularly if he isn't looking for them."

This was small consolation to Thackeray. "Why did you not tell me?" he demanded angrily.

"It was nearing the end of the voyage, Reese, and you were planning to put him—her—off in London anyway. I saw no point in needlessly causing a problem."

"And now, I have a bigger one."

Pennyman shrugged. "British officers are known to take their wives aboard warships and some even into battle. Mrs. Sutton is smart and knows her way around a ship. She may be of help to you in your plans."

"She is not going with us, William!"

"Why? Because she was able to fool you?"

The captain glowered at him. "I will not reward her for being headstrong, careless of her safety, and, by her acts, imperiling the lives of others." He started to take a drink and froze with a disturbing thought. "Dear God, I bathed in her company."

The surgeon burst out laughing, earning another glare from Thackeray.

"Well, I am glad to see that you find it so amusing, William."

"Come now, Reese, I have not known you to be shy in a lady's company. And I do not think you need to worry about Mrs. Sutton's sensibilities. She is, after all, a married woman, and she does not strike me as being a shrinking violet." The doctor finished his drink. "On that note, I must take my leave."

When the surgeon left, Thackeray poured himself another drink. He was not concerned about Mrs. Sutton's sensibilities. He was concerned about his own. The thought that he had been vulnerable to her in such a state without knowing it infuriated him. That it was to her of all people infuriated him even more.

How could he not have known she was Henry Shaw? he chided himself over and over. It was a colossal failure of his powers of observation on which he had always prided himself, and it shook him to the core.

Away from the captain's bluster and piercing glare, Marin found more humor in the matter. And upon her return to the Greenfield townhouse, she regaled Susannah with a full accounting of the unmasking.

Her friend stared at her in astonishment. "Without a doubt, posing as a sea nymph is positively the craziest thing you have ever done."

Marin laughed. "That is what you said about my disguise as Henry Shaw."

"No, I said that was bold. This is insane. And the figurehead being carved to your likeness…what are the chances of that?" questioned Susannah in wonderment.

"I take neither credit nor blame for it," said Marin.

"Still, Captain Thackeray must have been livid."

"He was a bit fearsome, I'll admit."

"'Tis a wonder he did not thrash you within an inch of your life."

"He probably would have but for the crew." Marin giggled. "I'll wager the captain regrets his choice of name for his ship now."

"Sea nymph or not, he has barred you—permanently," Susannah pointed out. "Even if you could convince Captain Thackeray to take you with him, the Minister would never sanction it. The captain is on a government mission."

"I did not come this far to fail, Susannah," replied Marin doggedly.

CHAPTER SEVENTEEN

In a Quandary

Thackeray stared at his officers when they brought him the news. He could scarce believe it.

"All of them?" he asked, incredulous.

"Aye, sir," they replied.

"Bloody hell!"

"Shall I fetch Mrs. Sutton, sir?" asked Seaton. "Perhaps she can bring some calm to the matter."

"Good God no!" exclaimed Thackeray. "I will not have that woman anywhere near this ship."

"What shall we do?" asked White.

Reese gave a deep sigh of frustration. "Mr. Seaton, carry a message to the Minister that I require an urgent meeting. Tell him…tell him certain circumstances have arisen."

There came an immediate reply, and Reese found himself once again before the delegation of diplomats. He had hoped it to be a more private meeting.

When he explained the situation to them, they were astounded, even as he withheld the story of Marin's charade as Henry Shaw.

"Am I to understand, Captain, that your entire crew is threatening to quit your ship if Mrs. Sutton does not accompany you on this mission?" asked a diplomat in amazement.

"Yes, sir."

"I am afraid that we cannot allow that," said the Minister. "It is too dangerous, and there is too much at stake."

"Your pardon, sir, but we have no choice in the matter unless I want to lose my crew," said Reese.

"These men actually believe Mrs. Sutton is a sea nymph?" asked another diplomat incredulously.

"Seamen are a superstitious lot," explained Thackeray.

"Indeed, and it seems that Mrs. Sutton is a very resourceful lady," remarked the Minister.

"Can you not gather another crew?" inquired a third diplomat.

"Members of this crew were chosen with great care and work in communion with each other. It would take some time to recruit another crew of equal trust and skill," replied Reese. "I remind you, gentlemen, that time is of the essence."

"The captain is right," said the Minister. "But the matter begs many questions. How did Mrs. Sutton come to know of the mission?"

"I am afraid the fault is mine, sir," said Richard Greenfield. "In innocent conversation with Mrs. Sutton, my wife mentioned the loss of Mrs. Marsden and her son on the *Neptune*, as she is still much distressed about it. Somehow, Mrs. Sutton managed to piece so much of the story together I could not credibly deny it. Upon the friendship of my wife, which Mrs. Sutton holds dear, she has pledged herself to secrecy."

"Richard, you are a diplomat. You could lose your position," the Minister chastised him.

"I ask your pardon and that of the corps, Minister Pinckney. I assure you that I take my duties and the trust placed in me most seriously, but, as you have heard, Mrs. Sutton is a force of nature not to be underestimated," replied Greenfield with a rueful smile.

"How did Mrs. Sutton come by her suspicions in the first place?" demanded another diplomat.

"She is quite adept at putting puzzles together," remarked Reese dryly.

"How so, Captain?"

"She saw the announcement about the disappearance of the *Neptune* in the *Boston Gazette* and the listing of my brother as an officer. When she learned that I was departing Boston earlier than expected, she deduced that I did not believe the story that the ship had sunk in a storm and that I was sailing to Algiers to find my brother. She pressed me to allow her to come along so that she could learn about her husband."

"Did you not refuse her in the strongest of terms?" asked a diplomat.

"Of course," responded Thackeray with a hint of annoyance. "But she followed me to England to plead her case once more. As you can see, Mrs. Sutton is a very determined woman."

"Indeed, it would seem so," commented the Minister humorlessly. "Still, I am at a loss to understand how your crew could so easily accept that she is a sea nymph, superstitious or not. Something else must have predicated it. And how is it, Captain, that at dinner the other night, Mrs. Sutton seemed to know so much about your preparations and plans? Did you tell her?"

"No, sir?"

"What then?"

Reese shifted uncomfortably in his seat. "'Tis a long story, sir."

"I should like to hear it, Captain. It behooves us to understand the workings of Mrs. Sutton's mind," said the Minister.

Thackeray hesitated, trying to find a way to tell the story of Henry Shaw that didn't make him look so ridiculous. There was none. As he gave the account of Marin's ruse in the best light possible, the secretary wrote feverishly. Members of the diplomatic corps leaned forward in their seats to catch every word as the tale only seemed to get more and more implausible. When Reese had finished, murmurs of amazement sounded around the room.

"This woman spent two fortnights at sea and nearly two fortnights in port on your ship masquerading as a sailor and no one took notice of it?" questioned the Minister.

Again, Reese shifted in his seat. He could well imagine the fool he must look. "The master surgeon made the discovery near the end of the voyage and provided cover for her to avoid disorder on the ship," he said.

The Minister leaned back in his chair in a state of wonderment. "It beggars the imagination, Captain. I scarce know what to say. Richard, were you aware of Mrs. Sutton's ruse?"

"No, sir. I was not," Greenfield assured the Minister, though he was certain that his wife did and resolved to have a talk with her on the matter.

"I cannot imagine how anyone mistakes Mrs. Sutton for a lad," continued the Minister. "It makes me wonder, Captain, if your crew has the acuity for this mission."

Reese stiffened. "I have a very able crew, sir, he responded levelly. "Mrs. Sutton knows her way around a ship. She did her job ably and was careful to draw no notice. Suffice it to say, she can be very cunning." He wasn't about to mention, at this point, that Henry Shaw had been his steward.

The Minister glanced over at his secretary who was agog at the revelations.

"Keep writing, George. Keep writing," he ordered.

"I have run out of ink, sir."

"Then get some more."

"Yes, sir."

The Minister sighed. "Well, Captain, it appears that we have no choice. Is Mrs. Sutton at home, Richard?"

"I believe so, sir."

The Minister addressed his secretary again. "George, dispatch a clerk to the Greenfield house with the message that we request an audience with Mrs. Sutton forthwith."

Susannah and Marin were in the morning room indulging their passion for hot chocolate, when the housekeeper entered.

"Madam, a clerk is here from the Ministry. The Minister wishes an audience with Mrs. Sutton."

"When?" asked Susannah.

"Now, madam. The clerk is waiting to escort her. He has a cab outside."

Susannah looked at Marin in bewilderment. "Why does the Minister wish an audience with you?"

Marin shook her head just as perplexed. "I cannot say."

"Mrs. Bennett, show the clerk to the drawing room and inform him that Mrs. Sutton needs some time to suitably present herself and will join him as soon as she is able," instructed Susannah.

"Yes, madam."

With the help of Susannah and a maid, Marin quickly changed into appropriate attire.

As she hurried off to meet the clerk, Susannah warned: "Behave yourself."

"Always," replied Marin with a twinkle in her eye.

As the clerk escorted Marin to the cab, he had difficulty keeping his gaze off her. He had heard she was pretty. The claims, he decided, were grossly underreported. When she smiled at him, his heart melted. By the time they arrived at the Chancery, he decided that he was very much in love with her.

He handed her out of the cab with great reverence and ushered her inside the dwelling and down the long hall to the room at the end. There, he tapped on the door and opened it. "Mrs. Sutton is arrived, sir," he announced.

Marin entered the room.

At that moment, the Minister's secretary came running down the hall with two bottles of ink.

"George, what goes on in there?" asked the clerk curiously.

"You cannot imagine it," the secretary responded, disappearing inside the room and closing the door.

At Marin's entrance, the members of the diplomatic corps stared at her in unabashed curiosity as they also tried to imagine her as the lad Henry Shaw.

Marin was at a loss to fathom their interest or the reason for the summons, but when their expressions turned stern and their demeanors stiff, she knew that the matter was serious. The presence of Thackeray sitting at the end of the table didn't help to ease her mounting ill ease. She looked to Richard, but the tepid smile he gave her was not reassuring.

"Mrs. Sutton, you have inserted yourself into a matter of great sensitivity and have managed to make a difficult situation more difficult," began the Minister. "As history would have it, you seem to have a penchant for stepping into places you have no business stepping into."

Marin's brow furrowed in bewilderment. "I beg your pardon, sir?"

"The captain has told us of your antics."

Marin glanced at Reese. "Oh. What did he tell you?" she asked with some hesitancy.

"Everything, Mrs. Sutton. And, as such, you have trespassed into the affairs of the United States government."

Now Marin understood the nature of the summons. "Your pardon, sir. It was not my intention to trespass into government affairs. Upon my word, I will not speak of the mission. I was merely seeking an acceptable means to find my husband."

"Forcing passage on a ship unavailable to you by assuming the identity of a sailor is not an acceptable means, Mrs. Sutton."

"I thought that Captain Thackeray was just being unreasonable. I did not know that he and his ship were operating under the government's authority, Mr. Minister."

"Ignorance is not a defense, madam. In perpetrating a fraud to get your way, you caused consequences. As though that were not audacious enough, you continued to show impetuosity and wanton disregard by passing yourself off as a...a sea nymph—" At the sound of snickers, the Minister broke off to send a quelling look around the table.

"I did not say that I was a sea nymph, sir. It was falsely assumed. I cannot control what people think," said Marin.

"Apparently, madam, you can when it serves your purpose. You seem to be quite adroit at making inferences that can be easily mistaken for truths, such as inferring to the captain that you had arrived in London on the *Olympia* when, in fact, you had arrived aboard his ship."

The sound of snickers was heard again, earning the offending diplomats another glare not only from the Minister but from Thackeray as well.

When all was quiet, the Minister continued sternly, "Your talent for the obfuscation of facts has put the American government in a quandary, Mrs. Sutton."

"It was not my intention, sir. Please accept my apologies," said Marin.

"I am afraid the matter has gone beyond apologies, madam. Captain Thackeray tells us that his crew is refusing to continue the voyage unless you are on board as well. You have left me with no choice but to instruct Captain Thackeray to give you passage to the Barbary Coast."

Marin blinked in surprise at the pronouncement and, for a minute, wondered if she had heard correctly. "You are allowing me passage on the captain's ship?"

"Against my better judgment," replied the Minister.

Marin's face lit up. "My thanks to you, sir. I was expecting to hear that you were sending me home to Boston."

The Minister snorted. "Would that I could. But I am not finished, young woman. Sea nymph or not, your status will be that of a crew member and, as such, you will be under the complete authority of Captain Thackeray."

Marin's smile faded as she glanced over at Reese and saw the humorless look on his face.

"If you fail to do his bidding and jeopardize this mission in any way, you will face severe consequences," warned the Minister. "Is that clear, Mrs. Sutton?"

When Marin didn't answer, the Minister repeated sternly, "Is that clear, Mrs. Sutton?"

"Yes, sir," she responded hesitantly.

"Well then, Captain, I command this woman to your authority," declared the Minister. "May God help you."

CHAPTER EIGHTEEN

Proper Respect

With the last of the provisions on board and the cannons and crew in place, the *Sea Nymph* departed the port of London. As the ship passed out of the Thames River and sailed into the Atlantic Ocean, Marin stood at the railing feeling a sense of déjà vu. Only this time, she wasn't stressed with hiding her identity or tasked with a job.

The first mate was passing by, and she called out to him. "Mr. Seaton."

He stopped. "Yes, mistress?"

"Would you please show me to my cabin?"

"Of course, mistress. This way."

He led her below deck to the stern and stopped before a door she knew to be a storage room. Marin looked at him in bewilderment.

"I believe you have misunderstood, Mr. Seaton. 'Tis a passenger cabin I seek."

"I am sorry, mistress, but the captain maintains only one passenger cabin and that has been set aside to accommodate Mrs. Marsden and her son. As space is limited by a larger crew, the need for more larder stores, and the addition of six cannons, this storage room is all that could be spared."

He opened the door, and Marin's face fell. The room was small and dark with no window. A platform bed had been constructed against one wall, and the only furnishings were a crude table, chair, and a washstand. As she looked about, she noticed something else.

"Mr. Seaton, I see only one trunk. Where are the others?"

The first mate shifted uneasily. "Perhaps you should talk to the captain, mistress."

"Indeed, I shall," she responded crisply.

At the set look on her face, Seaton hurried off in the opposite direction, endeavoring to be as far away as possible from the seismic clash that was sure to come.

Thackeray was entering information in the log book, when Marin burst into his cabin.

"Where are my other trunks?" she demanded to know.

"They were dispatched to the care of your friend Mrs. Greenfield," he replied continuing to work.

"How dare you! You had no right."

Reese looked up from his desk and coolly regarded her. "I am the captain, Mrs. Sutton, lest you forget. You are fortunate I allowed you one trunk. I chose what clothes I thought to be appropriate."

"You went through my trunks?" she cried indignantly.

"I found it a necessary exercise."

"I believe there to be enough room on this ship for four trunks," she retorted snidely.

"That is not the point."

"What is the point, Captain?"

"A sea nymph is mythological and has no possessions, Mrs. Sutton."

Marin was flabbergasted. "That is absurd. Are you telling me I can make no change of dress?"

"Perhaps you should have researched your roll better."

Marin let out a shriek and stormed out of the cabin.

"Next time knock before entering," he called after her.

Over the next couple of days, calmer winds prevailed literally and figuratively.

Marin was somewhat pacified when she discovered that the dresses left to her were similar in style and color and that if she wore the same straw hat and used the same shawl, a change of dress went unnoticed by the seamen. One gown, however, appeared to be an oversight. It was the pink gown she had worn to the concert in Boston at her first social encounter with the captain. She wondered how he had let it slip by and tucked it away under the others.

For the most part, her presence helped to dispel the fears or disgruntlement that might normally arise among a crew heading into dangerous circumstances. It amazed Thackeray the reverence they showed her as she moved among the hardened seamen, and, while he was pleased with the level of their cooperation, it rankled him that it was owing largely to her.

On the fourth day, his second mate and bosun came to his quarters with a complaint.

"State your business," he said, his manner surly. "I am busy."

"There is upset building amongst the crew," said Duncan. "Andrew and me been takin' notice of it…Pots, too."

Reese looked up from his desk, surprised and concerned. "I am unaware. What is the nature of it? It must be addressed immediately."

Duncan and White glanced at each other.

"Ye ain't gonna like it," warned White.

Thackeray glared at the bosun. "Out with it, Andrew. I have neither the time nor the temperament for games. What is the source of this unrest?"

"'Tis you, sir."

Reese was taken aback. "Explain your meaning," he ordered tersely.

"Well, sir, the men think ye not be showin' proper respect to Mistress Marin."

Thackeray stared at his officers, and the first mate and bosun shifted uncomfortably beneath the intensity of his gaze. "I hope you are not suggesting that I show deference to Mrs. Sutton," he responded in a tone that dared them to actually do so.

White took a deep breath. "If you do not, the men may lose their courage, sir. We will most likely be encountering pirates in a fortnight. Ye can ill afford to antagonize the crew now."

"I will not bow down to that woman!" exclaimed Thackeray, pounding his fist on the desk.

"I believe it would suffice if you invited Mistress Marin to dine with you," suggested Duncan.

"And not argue with her—at least, not in front of the crew," inserted White.

Reese looked at the bosun. "Shall I give her the wheel as well, Andrew?"

"Very good, sir. The crew will be much heartened to see Mistress Marin at the wheel now and again."

"I was joking!" exploded Thackeray.

"Actually, Captain, 'tis not a bad idea," interjected Duncan.

"Why the bloody hell would I do that, Timothy?"

Duncan hesitated, reluctant to raise the captain's ire further. "Because, sir, the men believe that Mistress Marin directs you."

It was the last straw. Reese rose from his chair and pointed to the door. "Out!" he ordered.

"One other thing, Captain, you should refer to Mrs. Sutton as Mistress Marin," White quickly added. "Calling her by her married name suggests an element of mortality and—"

"Get out!" roared Thackeray.

The two men hurriedly left the captain's quarters.

Outside, White wiped the sweat from his forehead. "He took that well, ay?"

Duncan shook his head. "'Tis never wise to back the captain into a corner. I would have some sympathy for Mistress Marin."

It took a few days for Reese to come around and begrudgingly embrace his officers' advice.

When the bosun carried the message to Marin that she was to take dinner with the captain that evening, she was surprised and clearly not pleased by the prospect either. She knew the captain to be still furious with her and kept her distance from him. She didn't want to give him an excuse to exercise any of his options of authority over her.

At six o'clock, she knocked firmly on his door. She had determined she would not show any signs of timidity. When Reese opened the door and waved her inside, however, her resolution faltered. His demeanor bespoke a contentious mood. He said not a word, instead motioning her to the chair to his left while he took his seat at the head of the table. It was on the tip of her tongue to remark that she hoped fresh fish to be on the menu but wisely refrained.

Pots arrived, then. He laid out the food on the table and poured the wine. "Anythin' else you require, Captain?" he asked.

Thackeray, his features still drawn into a scowl, mutely waved him off and the cook quickly departed.

The silence continued throughout the meal, broken only by the click of utensils against the plate as they ate. Occasionally, Marin glanced at him out the corner of her eye or over the rim of her glass as she sipped wine. If he noticed, he made no indication, choosing to remain aloof.

"I daresay I had more company alone in my cabin," she was finally moved to comment.

He leveled cold, blue eyes on her. "This is not about company, Mrs. Sutton."

"What is it about then?"

"The crew is desirous that their protector be shown more deference, such as having the honor of dining with their captain. So, you shall partake of supper here every evening. Like it or not, Mrs. Sutton, we are going to be spending more time together."

Marin was silent for a few minutes, then burst into laughter.

It was not the reaction he had expected, and it further increased his disgruntlement. "How do you find this amusing, madam?"

"Well, Captain, it would appear that I have the upper hand."

"Perhaps you should think again, Mrs. Sutton."

"Why is that?" she asked warily.

"Should unfortunate incidents befall the ship or the crew members, what do you think will happen?"

At the blank look on her face, Reese answered the question for her.

"The men will think their sea nymph to be not the protector they had thought. They will believe you to be bad luck now. Do you know what sailors do to talismans when they no longer bring them good fortune?"

Marin shook her head.

"They throw them overboard, Mrs. Sutton."

Alarm flashed across her face. "But incidents happened on the voyage to London. There was the storm with injuries to the men and damage to the ship. It was enough that they thought I had kept the ship from sinking."

"They knew not who you were then," Reese pointed out. "By walking amongst them in disguise, they think that you were evaluating their worth and, by keeping the ship from sinking, that you had deemed them worthy enough to save. Now that you have shown yourself to them on a voyage as dangerous this, they believe you are here to safekeep them from all harm. I will also be addressing you by your given name, as it appears that the use of your married name might invite question."

"How so?"

"Apparently, the idea of a 'Mrs. Sutton' does not correlate with the mythology of a maiden sea nymph. I would suggest that you not speak of your husband," said Reese. "I would also advise you not to become ill and to keep the scar on your arm covered. Such weaknesses suggest mortality. And to a mariner, madam, the only thing worse than a charm that goes bad is a trickster."

Marin dropped her fork and sat back in her chair, clearly concerned. She had never considered the possibility that she would have to appear immortal.

"I warned you before a mariner's belief in superstition is not to be taken lightly," continued Reese. "Most seamen are uneducated. They do not understand science. They only understand luck."

Marin considered her predicament for a moment. "Well then, Captain, I would advise you to do everything within your power to safeguard my status," she said.

Reese raised a brow in surprise. It was not the show of contrition and plea for help that he was expecting. "Under what consideration, madam?" he questioned coolly.

"Well, if the crew loses faith in me, it will endanger your mission. Hence it would seem that your success depends upon me being able to sustain my image as a good luck talisman," she explained.

Reese's sense of complacency deserted him. She was right. Their interests were not mutually exclusive but all too interdependent. The tug of war between them had just ended in a draw.

CHAPTER NINETEEN

Pirates!

There was the constant drilling of the crew in weaponry now as the *Sea Nymph* drew closer to the Portuguese coastline. When not on the watch or sleeping, the men practiced using swords, knives, and pistols. Ferguson, a new recruit who was once a sailor in the British navy, was experienced in the use of cannons and oversaw the instruction of those crewmen assigned to them. That they might have to fight for their lives was starting to become a reality to the men. That it would be against pirates was an even more frightening one.

Reese stood observing their progress this day from the quarter deck, his eye following Marin as she walked among the seamen easing their mounting anxieties. As much as he hated to admit it, she had a calming influence on the crew. But for how long would she be able to spin her magic? he wondered.

Marin glanced up to see him. When his eye met hers, she looked away.

The officers and the surgeon observed the scene with interest, and it wasn't for the first time over the past week that they had noticed the covert glances between the captain and the mistress.

"What do you think, Doc?" asked White.

"Difficult to say," replied Pennyman. "She is different."

White turned to the second mate. "Timothy, what say you…a quarter piece?"

Duncan shook his head, uncertain. "She has been a thorn in his side since they first crossed paths in Boston. The lass is spirited. The captain likes his women more agreeable. What say you, Mr. Seaton?"

"She most surely is fetching," said Alex, regarding Marin with a sigh of admiration. "But she has a husband, does she not?"

"Maybe, maybe not," replied Duncan.

As the captain turned a stern eye on them, the little group quickly dispersed.

At dinner that night, Marin seemed more withdrawn.

Reese regarded her with some concern. "Something amiss?" he asked. "You are not taking ill, are you? I do not need on the eve of battle for my crew to find that their good luck charm is fallible."

"No, of course not," replied Marin shortly. "Have you a plan?"

"I am coming to it," he responded. "I have a meeting of the officers tomorrow in the morn."

"I should be there, too."

He gave a sigh of annoyance. "Why is that, Mrs. Sutton?"

"Marin," she corrected him. "Perhaps I can be of help."

"How?"

"I cannot say as yet, but I am just as clever as you—more so I daresay—since I am a passenger on this ship against your objections. Besides, it will hearten the men to know that their protector stands by their captain in all matters."

Reese bristled at the reminder that she had out smarted him, and it still rankled him that his crew thought that he was under her guidance. But she was right. Appearances were important to keeping the crew focused.

"Very well—if you must," he responded curtly.

When Seaton, Duncan, and White arrived the next morning at the captain's quarters, they were surprised to find Marin present and looked questioningly at Reese.

"As you pointed out, the men believe her to direct me," Thackeray peevishly reminded them. "She should appear to be privy to the plan."

Reese spread out the map on the dining table, and his officers gathered around.

"The pirates are sailing farther afield from the Mediterranean into the Atlantic Ocean. The *Neptune* was taken around here," he said, pointing to a spot on the map off the coast of Portugal. "Thus, I predict we can expect an encounter in three or four days' time. Are the men ready to fight, Andrew?"

"As ready as they will ever be," replied the bosun.

"The pirates will come armed with scimitars. They can take off a man's head with one quick swipe of the blade. The crew have to strike from behind."

"They know, Captain."

"What about the cannons?" asked Reese.

"Ferguson has drilled the men good. They can load and fire the cannons in their sleep."

"Algerine corsairs prefer hand to hand combat. They are not known to be practiced with cannons. Tell Ferguson not to open the gun ports unless I give the command. I do not want to frighten them off."

"Aye aye, sir."

Reese looked at his second mate. "Timothy, instruct Samuels to raise the flag at my signal. Any questions?"

"No, sir," murmured the officers.

Reese turned his attention to Marin. "When the pirate ship is within range, you will go to your cabin."

"But I should be on deck when—"

"That is an order, madam. We have one chance to play our hand. I will not have you getting in the way."

Marin gave a huff of annoyance but didn't argue.

As the others filed out, Reese laid a hand on her arm to stay her. "You *will* follow my orders," he warned, "or suffer the consequences."

"What might those be, Captain?" she questioned.

He heard the challenge in her voice. At this point in time, they both knew she held all the cards, and he backed off.

"Circumstances can quickly change, madam," he cautioned.

Their eyes became locked in a battle of wills for several moments before Reese removed his hand from her arm. When she left the cabin, he had the distinct feeling that nothing had been settled.

* * * * *

Two days later, the sailor in the crow's nest shouted: "Ship ahoy!"

The crew came alert and the officers came running. Thackeray was already on deck peering through his spyglass.

"Is it them?" asked Seaton, taking the wheel.

"Aye, 'tis them," announced Thackeray. "They are farther north than expected. They are getting bolder. I sight close to 20 men; there may be more hiding below. 'Tis an old trick of pirates."

"How long until they are within distance, sir?"

"Three hours if they are traveling at five knots. I think that we shall help them close the distance. Full sail, Mr. Duncan," shouted Reese to his second mate.

"Aye aye, sir."

Thackeray turned to his bosun. "Mr. White, call the rest of the crew to arms," he ordered. "Keep half of them hidden below until the Algerines come aboard. We can play that game, too. Mr. Duncan will help you see to the distribution of weapons. Quickly now. They have spyglasses, as well. We must appear to be an unarmed merchant ship with a small crew."

Reese scanned the main deck to make sure the dummy cargo boxes were stacked around the deck in plain sight.

As the pirates came within distance, Thackeray ordered Seaton to turn the ship port side to them. "We want them to think we are inviting them aboard," he said.

White joined him then. "The men are armed and ready, sir."

Thackeray nodded.

When they were within earshot, Thackeray gave a friendly wave and shouted: "Ahoy, there."

The captain on the pirate ship waved back.

"Do you speak English?" asked Thackeray.

The captain pulled another man alongside him, whom Reese guessed to be a translator, and spoke to him for a few minutes.

"We come aboard?" asked the translator in broken English.

"Aye, four men—the captain, you, and two others," responded Thackeray. "No weapons."

"Seven men," countered the translator.

Reese shook his head. "Four men and no weapons," he repeated.

The man translated this to the Algerine captain, who then conferred with men whom Reese took to be his officers.

As Thackeray waited for a response, Marin came up to him, and he heaved a sigh of exasperation. "You are supposed to be in your cabin. Mr. White, escort her below."

"Captain, wait. I am their protector. The men will feel more reassured if they see me standing beside you," argued Marin. "And the pirates will be more inclined to believe that you are just a merchant ship if they see a woman on board. Look at them. They hesitate. They find something suspicious in your terms."

Reese could see that she was right. There was disagreement between the Algerine captain and his officers. When they looked over to see Marin, the officers seemed to relax their resistance.

The bosun waited for a decision. "Captain?"

"Let her stay," said Reese.

"Captain…five men," yelled the translator. "We traders like you…need supplies…pirates take."

"Come aboard," replied Thackeray. He turned to White. "Stand ready when they are on board."

"Aye aye, sir."

"Ship ahoy," the seaman in the crow's nest shouted out. "Starboard."

Thackeray swiveled around and trained his spyglass on the other ship. "I was afraid of this," he murmured. "They are flanking us. The first ship is a decoy. This other one flies the British flag, but I will bet my life they are Algerines, too. Andrew, as soon as the captain and his party are on board, tell Ferguson to open starboard gun ports. If that ship starts to turn, it means she has cannons aboard. Ferguson is to give the order to immediately commence firing then."

"Aye aye, Captain." The bosun hurried off.

Thackeray looked at Marin. "I have no time to argue with you. Remain on deck at your own peril and prepare to see some sights you may not want to see. At the first brandishing of weapons, find a place to hide. When the fighting starts, it will be fast and furious. Timothy," he shouted out to his second mate, "stand ready."

The smaller pirate ship moved within range, and the ships were lashed together with grappling hooks and ropes. A gangplank was laid, and the Algerine boarding party came aboard. Reese greeted his guests with easy affability; their captain returned the greeting, pretending friendship as well.

Used to European culture, Marin found the Algerine sailors strange and frightening. Their features and skin were darker, and, though medium in height, the men were well muscled. They wore loose pantaloons, short vests, and wide sashes around their waists. Beneath the low-crowned turbans, Marin could see that their heads were shaved, but they sported beards and bushy mustaches. In spite of their smiles, their black eyes seemed cold and expressionless to her, and she sensed a cruel side to them that sent a chill down her spine.

As Reese had predicted, the captain and the translator attempted to hold his attention, while the other members of the boarding party casually fanned off to distract the crewmen on deck. To their surprise, the corsairs quickly found themselves checked by sailors who had surreptitiously pulled pistols from hiding places.

Suddenly, the number of men visible on the deck of the pirate ship swelled. A shout went out from the bosun and the crewmen of the *Sea*

Nymph that were secreted below streamed on deck to meet the pirates swarming across the gangplank. Astounded by how fast everything was unfolding, Marin stood transfixed, unable to move, until Reese grabbed hold of her and shoved her behind some barrels.

"Stay put," he ordered.

The better marksmen in Reese's crew were supplied with the pistols and trained to shoot the pirates swinging the deadly scimitars, and the air was soon filled with smoke and the noise of gun fire and cries. Hand to hand combat with swords and knives quickly ensued.

There was no code of conduct. Every man fought for his life by whatever means. Blood was everywhere, and Marin watched in horror as men fell before her eyes, most of them mortally wounded. At one point, she saw Reese pick up a sword to protect the backs of some of his crewmen and lost sight of him. When she spotted him again, his shirt was so splattered with blood, she couldn't tell if he was hurt or not.

A couple of times, Reese glanced over to see Marin still crouched behind the barrels and decided that she was safe enough where she was.

"Ship on the starboard side is turning," shouted Seaton.

Marin jumped at the loud explosions as cannons below deck immediately took aim at the rigging and sails of the other pirate ship.

"Ship departing," reported Seaton. "

The sound of cannon shot and the first mate's pronouncement seemed to have a sobering effect on the Algerines. The pirates were in disarray now. Their captain and translator, held at gun point by Duncan, watched in shock as their fellow pirates were being subdued.

Reese made his way back to the corsairs' captain. "Tell your men to stand down," he ordered.

"What is the meaning of this?" the captain indignantly demanded to know through his translator. "We came in peace."

Reese pointed to fallen corsairs with scimitars still clutched in their hands. "It does not appear so."

"It was in the name of protection," the captain stoutly maintained, ignoring the fact that they had violated the boarding agreement. "I demand recompense."

"Strike the colors," shouted Thackeray.

Immediately, a flag bearing the signs of a pirate was raised.

"There is your recompense," said Reese.

The captain's and the translator's jaws dropped.

Reese looked at the translator. "Tell the captain to surrender his ship or my cannons will sink it in minutes."

The captain didn't need his translator to tell him anything now. He quite accurately assessed the situation and gave the order to the remaining crewmen to stand down. A dozen pirates were rounded up and quickly disarmed and, along with their captain and translator, were led below where they would be imprisoned in the cargo hold.

Marin emerged from her hiding place, shocked and sickened by the carnage, and turned to retch over the railing. She could never have imagined a scene so horrifying. She didn't know which way to turn. Bodies and pools of blood were everywhere, the shock and agony of death grotesquely reflected on the faces of the fallen.

Reese saw her and yelled to his bosun. "Mr. White, see to the cleansing of the deck straightaway and tell Mr. Seaton to carry Mistress Marin to her quarters."

"Aye aye, sir."

Pots and four men went to search the pirate ship for anything of use. They returned with baskets full of figs, dates, nuts, olives, pears, grapes and other fresh fruits.

"We're gonna eat well tonight, Captain," said Pots with a grin. "Those scalawags got a full larder, though you wouldna take kindly to their slovenly ways. Their decks could use a good swabbin'…food and whatnot all over them. Any special privileges for the captain?"

Reese shook his head. "He is a pirate."

The cook smiled. "'Tis just as I would have it."

Andrew White approached Thackeray. "What would ye have us do with the pirate ship, sir?"

"When everything of value is transferred, sink it," said Reese.

"Be ye sure, Captain? It would take only seven men to sail it, and it might make more of an impression on the dey if we was to enter the harbor with his ship under our flag."

"No doubt, but we are still several days from Gibraltar," replied Reese. "The ship we drove off may return with reinforcements. If we are forced to a fight, I have no wish to defend two ships, and the Algerine ship has no guns."

"I shall see to its sinking then," said White.

Reese walked over to Pennyman. "How did our crew fare?" he asked the surgeon.

"A few need stitches…nothing serious. We need to guard against infections though. The men fought well."

Reese nodded. "Perhaps you should look in on Marin. She was looking rather indisposed when she left the deck."

"I can imagine," replied the surgeon. "It must have been a hellish sight for her."

Reese was unsympathetic. "Maybe next time she will listen to me."

That evening, the crew was in high spirits, breaking into song and dance that could be heard throughout the ship.

Pots held to his promise and treated everyone to a fine meal from the exotic stores of food on the pirate ship. But Marin had difficulty enjoying the delicacies. She picked at her food and was notably quiet.

"The food is not to your liking?" inquired Reese.

"It is not the meal," she replied.

"What then?"

"You were right. I should have left the deck before the fighting…so much blood…so many bodies…" She looked at him. "How does one forget?"

"One doesn't forget," he responded. "Whatever the circumstance, every time a man is forced to fight…forced to kill, it scars the soul.

The best one can do is to try to bury the memory—until something forces him to remember again," he added with an edge to his tone. "Then the process begins anew."

"Was this the way it was when my husband was taken?" she asked.

"No. Merchant ships generally do not carry arms for fear of a mutiny. The captain would have surrendered his ship without a fight. It is more likely that the wounds your husband suffered were to his dignity."

Marin felt somewhat comforted. "Mr. Potter said you had dealings with pirates in these waters before. I presume it is how you were able to predict their movements so well. Is that why the government pressed you to take this mission?"

"I would have gone in search of my brother in any case," said Reese.

Marin fixed clear green eyes on him. "Then you should understand why I must go for my husband, Captain."

Thackeray didn't answer. It would only serve to anger her.

"How did your encounter come about?" she queried.

A dark shadow crossed Reese's features. "I was a seaman on a ship that was captured years ago. Duncan, White, and Pots were among the crew."

Marin looked at him in surprise. "What happened?"

"The ship that approached us seemed friendly and harmless enough—as did the one today," Thackeray recounted. "The captain said he needed information, so Captain Belmont invited a party on board. We thought it strange that there should be such a large crew on so small a ship, but we were supposed to be at peace with the Barbary states. The ruler of Tripoli was the first to recognize the United States as a nation." Reese gave a cynical laugh. "We did not know then that peace is always conditional with these leaders."

"Please, go on," prompted Marin when he fell silent.

Thackeray glanced at her, annoyed. "Why must you hear?"

"I need to know what Nathaniel may have experienced," she replied.

"Why...to feed your guilt?"

"No, Captain, in hopes of finding some release from it."

No stranger to guilt himself, Reese could sense her pain.

"The pirates came alongside," he continued. "The boarding party distracted us and before we knew it, the rest of their crew had swarmed onto the deck. They carried scimitars in their hands, swords in their sashes, and knives in their teeth. You could say quite literally that they were armed to the teeth; we were not. The captain had no choice but to surrender to them."

He paused for a few moments, struggling with the nightmare.

"They took our clothes and a crew of corsairs sailed us into the port of Algiers...marched us through the streets. People shouted and spat on us. We were locked in a pen and given bug infested rags to wear. Each night, we slept on a stone floor exposed to the elements. In the morning before the sun rose, we were taken into the mountains to break rocks until after dark. Every Friday, the Muslim holy day, Christian slaves were given the 'light' duty of dragging sleds full of dirt and stones to the harbor for a breakwater. We dragged those bloody sleds for two miles."

Thackeray poured another glass of wine and took a gulp.

"We were never given enough to eat," he went on. "One day, a prisoner was caught picking a persimmon from a tree and was beaten to death for it. The slightest infraction, real or imagined, brought about a beating." Reese looked at her. "Do you know how these guards administer a beating?"

Marin shook her head.

"They call it giving the bastinado. The prisoner is stripped and thrown face down on the ground with his hands tied behind him and his legs spread wide. Loops of cord at each end of a six-foot pole are secured around his ankles. Then the pole is lifted and the Guardian Basha and his guards take turns caning the soles of the prisoner's feet and posterior. The blows can count from a few dozen to 500 depending upon the mood of the Guardian Basha. Some prisoners die; some never walk the same again; some recover to endure more beatings."

If Reese was hoping to shock her, he succeeded. Seeing the look on her face, he added: "Your husband would not have been subjected to such punishment."

"Why must they take prisoners?" she asked. "Is not the cargo enough?"

"Prisoners are as much a commodity."

Marin's mouth twisted in disgust. "It is barbaric."

Thackeray shrugged. "Americans are not so different."

"How can you say that? We are civilized," she retorted.

Reese gave a short laugh. "Planters in the southern colonies enslave black people stolen from their lands by slavers; the dey enslaves white people stolen from their ships by pirates. The only difference is that in this land, madam, *we* are the inferior race. What is up is down; what is down is up."

Marin was taken aback by a perception she had never thought to consider, and she was beginning to see now the real dangers of this voyage.

"How long were you imprisoned?" she inquired.

"Six months."

"Were you ransomed?"

"I escaped," replied Reese.

"How?"

"After awhile, I was able to bribe my way to an assignment in the palace garden. A servant woman from the town brought her young daughter to play with the dey's children one day. The child wandered into the area of the dey's menagerie of animals at a time when they were released from their cages. She was in danger of being attacked by a tiger. I intervened."

"Is that how you got the scar on your thigh—" Marin stopped short when she drew his sharp gaze, and her face became flushed.

It came to him then how she would know of the mark, and Reese shifted uncomfortably in his seat. "The tiger swiped my side," he said, glossing over the awkward moment.

"What then?" she asked, also eager to move past her slip of the tongue.

"During the encounter, the uniform I was given to wear during the day was damaged, and I was beaten for it." Reese's features hardened. "I swore then that I was leaving that place one way or the other. The crew felt the same, and we laid plans at night when we were taken back to our pen."

"How did you escape?" quizzed Marin, when he seemed inclined to stop again.

Reese heaved a sigh of annoyance that bordered on anger. "Can the accounting thus far not suffice to satisfy your curiosity, madam?"

"'Tis not out of curiosity that I inquire, Captain, but out of hope. If you were able to escape, mayhap so was Nathaniel. It gives me more faith in the prospect to know of your means to that end."

Reese sighed again. He had no doubt that she was grasping at straws but humored her.

"I was able to get a note smuggled to Captain Belmont through the girl's mother to tell him of our intentions," he said. "Thereafter, she carried messages between us. Belmont and I decided that Holy Day was our best opportunity when most of the guards were at worship and our crewmen were together at work on the wharf. The captain and officers were permitted to go into the city at will, and at the appointed time, they made their way to the harbor. The girl's mother helped me slip out of the palace to join them. We overpowered the guards, grabbed their weapons, and fought our way to our ship at no small cost."

Thackeray's gaze took on a faraway look as he was pulled back into the moment, and he took another swig of wine.

"The ship was anchored in range of the cannons on the wharf," he continued. "To keep from being fired upon, Duncan and I set fire to the stores of gunpowder, while Andrew worked to get the ship under sail. Some of the sails were damaged by sparks from the explosion and a ship of corsairs gave chase, but we were able to get to safe harbor at Malaga."

Thackeray smiled wryly. "As it so happened, the Spanish had a great dislike for the British and held Americans in high esteem for defeating them in the war."

Marin understood now the comradery, the respect, and the loyalty that extended beyond duty that she had sensed between the captain and his older officers.

"Is that how Mr. Potter lost his leg…in the escape?" she asked.

Reese nodded, his blue eyes darkening. "Duncan and White still bear scars of the fight as well. Five members of the crew and Captain Belmont perished." He paused again. "Captain Belmont was a mentor to me. He is the reason I became a merchant captain."

Thackeray threw back the rest of his drink, his manner turning inward and broody. "I can blame no one but myself for the loss and have carried the guilt with me since." He looked at her. "So, you see, Mrs. Sutton—Marin—I understand something about the condition."

"Why should you blame yourself, Captain?"

"I was eight and ten years and thirsted for adventure. I convinced Captain Belmont to take the bloody contract."

"You were not the captain," said Marin. "The decision was his to sail there. He would not have made the journey based upon a young seaman's desire for adventure."

"How would you know that?" questioned Reese curtly.

"I know that my father never would have made such a call by that measure," she replied. "Would you as captain?"

Marin's point hit home. Of course he wouldn't. No good captain would be so capricious. The risks of every voyage, whatever the route, were carefully weighed against the rewards.

"Besides, the United States was thought to be at peace with the Barbary Coast then," Marin reminded him.

"Barring that, the escape was at my behest, madam. Had I not been so determined to take flight, perhaps Captain Belmont and the crew would have been ransomed and this day be alive or free of injury and scars."

"And perhaps not," she countered. "The captains and crews of the *Dauphin* and *Maria* are still imprisoned nine years later at the decrease of much of their crew through disease and cruel treatment. Your guilt is misspent, Captain, and I do not believe that it is the memorial that Captain Belmont would have wished from you."

That *she* should lecture *him* annoyed Reese to the point of anger, and he turned a sharp eye on her. "Mayhap you should take your own advice, madam. I dare say your guilt is misspent as well."

Marin blinked in surprise. "I beg your pardon?"

"What resolution do you really wish to find in regards to your husband?"

Marin stiffened. "What are you implying, Captain?"

"People can change in three years, Mrs. Sutton. Feelings can change. Perhaps your compulsion to find your husband is driven more by the guilt of ambivalent feelings you may hold for him."

Marin jumped up from her chair. "How dare you! You know nothing about me or my husband. And I do not believe that you are in a position to give advice on such matters," she replied icily.

Reese rose to face her. "Turnabout is fair play, madam."

"That is not fair play."

"Is it not?"

Marin's eyes flashed with fury, and she raised a hand to slap his face, but he caught her wrist in an iron grasp. Their gazes met again in a silent clash of tempers before she yanked her hand free and swept from the cabin.

Thackeray sat down at the table and moodily poured himself another glass of wine. Everything Marin had said was true. Events of that fateful voyage over 10 years ago had been due to no one's fault. Cerebrally, he had always known that, but he had felt the loss of his mentor so viscerally it had required someone to blame. To ascribe it to fate hadn't been good enough. And Reese had determined that the blame should be his to shoulder, perhaps as a self-punishment. It wasn't rational, he knew, but then grief never is, and one had to do what he needed to do to cope with the pain of such a loss.

Something else Marin had said struck him. Captain Belmont would not want a memorial built on a young lad's guilt.

CHAPTER TWENTY

Gibraltar

Marin stood at the railing, feeling the warmth of the sun and the salt spray upon her face and the sway of the ship beneath her feet, as the *Sea Nymph* sailed through calm waters.

Normally, it would bring her a measure of peace. But she felt unsettled this bright morning, and it had nothing to do with the danger and uncertainty that yet lay ahead. It had everything to do with the captain and his observations of the previous night. *How dare he intrude into her life?* she fumed, ignoring the fact that she had intruded into his first.

When it came time for supper, Marin sent her regrets citing a headache. She had no desire for the captain to intuit anything else about her.

Over the next few days, it did not go unnoticed by Thackeray that Marin was avoiding him. Absenting herself from the evening meal was becoming a habit with her. She had always relished crossing swords with him, pitting her intellect and cleverness against his, trying to outmaneuver him. Now, she shunned any interaction with him at all. He guessed the reason went back to his remarks about her marriage but decided her anger should have passed by now.

After glancing at her empty chair for a third night, Reese determined that he couldn't have her calling the shots. The next morning, he summoned Dr. Pennyman to his cabin.

"Has Mrs. Sutton expressed an illness to you?" he asked.

The surgeon looked at Reese in bewilderment. "She has made no complaint to me. I dare say she appears the picture of good health when I see her on deck. Why do you ask?"

"She has been choosing to take her evening meal in her room. Each night, she sends a different excuse."

Pennyman cocked his head. "As I recall, you felt quite put upon when it was suggested that Marin dine with you. I should think ye to be gladdened by her absence."

"I believe it was brought home to me that her presence is mandated for the sake of the morale of the crew," Thackeray responded crisply.

"Are you sure there is not another reason, Captain?"

Reese eyed the doctor closely. "What are you inferring, William?"

The surgeon shrugged. "A few of us have noticed an exchange of glances between you and the lady, though admittedly when one thought the other wasn't looking."

Reese snorted. "I know not her motive, but speaking for myself, I seek only to gauge how she is affecting the crew. As such, relay to Mrs. Sutton that I *will* expect her for dinner tonight."

Pennyman smiled. "I shall tell her."

Marin was not surprised when the doctor brought the captain's message to her. More surprising to her was that it hadn't come sooner, but it annoyed her just the same. Though the surgeon presented the message in a more diplomatic tone, Marin clearly heard the order behind it, and she presented herself at the captain's quarters that evening in a contentious mood.

"You are late, madam. I feared I might have to personally inquire after you," Reese remarked lightly when he opened the door to her.

Marin stiffened but made no reply.

He walked her to her seat at the table and held the chair for her. It was something he hadn't done before, and she glanced curiously at him as he took his own seat, her guard up.

"I trust you are feeling better," he said, pouring wine for them.

"Would it have made any difference? One does not ignore a summons from the captain," she replied brusquely.

"You set the table, madam, now you must dine at it."

His tone was such that it was not a cutting putdown but a casual statement of fact. Either way, it struck a sour note with her and she glared at him.

"Captain, I would settle a matter straight off," she informed him crisply.

"What is that, madam?"

"I hold my husband in goodly affection. The other night you suggested otherwise."

"Apologies, madam. As you pointed out, I do not know you or your husband."

Marin was taken aback. This was not the contentious, taciturn captain of her daily acquaintance.

"Why are you being so...so unobjectionable?" she demanded to know.

"I prefer to call it accommodating," replied Reese. "We have reached a point in this journey when we must all work together as one if we are to survive this mission. There can be no conflict, no disaffection among the crew, and that includes between you and me. Now, more than ever, the crew will be taking their cues from us."

"In other words, I must pretend to tolerate you," quipped Marin.

"And I you," he returned.

"It shall be a stretch of my acting ability," she mumbled under her breath as she reached for her wine.

For the days that followed, Reese was less restrained and more obliging towards her as he kept a tight lid on any conflict on the ship. Though the reason was abundantly clear to her, Marin didn't appreciate the captain's conciliatory manner. She would much rather cross swords with him. It kept boundaries in place.

* * * * *

First mate Alex Seaton steered the *Sea Nymph* through the Strait of Gibraltar, a nine-mile swath of ocean that separated Europe from North Africa and was the entrance into the Mediterranean Sea.

Marin watched from the main deck in amazement as massive rocks jutted up from the sea in breathtaking wonder to dwarf the tall ship on both sides. The fluffy white clouds against the bright blue sky and the azure tinted water created a panoply of color that was jaw-dropping. But the crew noticed little of the scenic wonder. They were on full alert as they neared the pirates' lair.

Thackeray stood on the quarter deck scanning the area through his spyglass for any sign of trouble. When he saw no evidence of danger, he called out for the American stars and stripes to be struck in place of the pirate flag. With that done, he ordered his first mate to put into the port of Gibraltar.

When Reese came down to the main deck, Marin walked over to him. "Why are we putting into port, Captain?"

"We need to take on supplies," he replied.

"How long will we be here?"

"Two days."

"Can we not leave tomorrow?"

"No, madam, we cannot. We are five days from Algiers, and I aspire to arrive on Friday when—"

"It is their Holy Day and fewer guards will be on post," she finished.

"You were listening," he noted. "This is also a chance to gather information if any is to be had. It behooves us to be as well armed in knowledge as we are in weapons."

The British port of Gibraltar was a garrison town. Two British frigates and a Swedish brig were at anchor. It was chiefly a supply point and safe haven for ships trading in the Mediterranean. So the American tall ship raised no suspicion when it dropped anchor in the bay as well.

The captain of the port, who was also the commander of Gibraltar, was rowed out to the ship and came on board. Middle-aged and portly, Commander Walter Teaberry took out a handkerchief and wiped the perspiration from his face, out of breath from the exertion of climbing the rope ladder.

"Getting too bloody old for this," he grumbled, out of sorts. He looked at Reese. "You are the captain?"

"I am, sir...Captain Thackeray of the *Sea Nymph* out of Boston Harbor."

"I enjoy no good memories of Boston Harbor, Captain," the British commander continued to grouse. "State your business, sir."

"We seek supplies on our way to Algiers to pay ransom for American seamen," explained Thackeray. "We carry no cargo."

"The American problem with the Barbary states is one well known to me. I do not doubt your quest," said Teaberry. "Still, I am required to make search of the vessel for contraband as piracy and smuggling abound. I shall begin in the hull."

Duncan, White, and Reese looked at each other. The commander was not in good humor. What would his reaction be when he saw the Algerine prisoners? Would he compromise the mission? Marin had been hanging back unnoticed, wondering the same thing.

As Teaberry was about to go below, she walked over to him. "Commander, I have not made your acquaintance."

Teaberry stopped and turned, and an appreciative smile immediately spread across his jowly features. "Indeed, madam, how could I have been remiss to overlook so lovely a lady. You must excuse my poor manners. I am Commander Teaberry at your service," he said with a courtly bow. He took her hand and brought it to his thick lips. "And how might I address you, fair lady?"

"Everyone calls me Mistress Marin, sir."

"It is my honor to make your acquaintance, Mistress. How do you find yourself in waters so dangerous to Americans?" he asked, reluctant to release her hand.

"It is a long story, sir. I am sure you are far too busy to be burdened at the moment."

"'Tis never a burden for one as beauteous as you, Mistress Marin, but I fear that you are correct. With the governor not in residence, my time is short at the moment." He paused with a thought. "Perhaps you will be my guest at dinner tonight and recount your story."

Marin smiled coyly. "I should be ever so honored, Commander."

At this, Thackeray loudly cleared his throat, and she glanced over at him.

"Uh, Commander, may I have the captain accompany me? I believe he could benefit from your insight on matters in the region. You strike me as a man who is quite knowledgeable."

Teaberry hesitated, flattered but clearly not thrilled by the suggestion. "Of course, dear lady. Captain Thackeray, you are welcome to join us—if you like," he offered half-heartedly.

"You are too kind, sir," responded Reese.

The commander took a cursory look about the deck. "Well, Captain, everything appears to be in good order."

"Do you not wish to survey the hull?" asked Reese.

"You look to be an honest chap, and I must be off to tell the cook that there will be guests this evening." Teaberry smiled and took Marin's hand again. "I shall see you at eight o'clock. Until then, dear lady."

The commander left the ship and quickly climbed down the ladder to his boat. When he was rowed out of earshot, Seaton, Duncan, and White snickered, then burst into laughter.

"Well done, Mistress Marin," said Duncan.

"It was like you was never there, Captain," added White, still chuckling. "We are in your debt, mistress."

"Aye," agreed Seaton. "We would have had the devil's own time of it explaining the prisoners below deck were it not for you, madam."

Marin smiled, pleased with the compliments. "Thank you, gentlemen. It is heartening that some men can acknowledge there are things a woman can handle better," she replied, looking pointedly at Reese.

Thackeray bristled. "Now that you all have had your merriment, there are tasks to be done," he said brusquely.

After spending so much time at sea and not under the most comfortable circumstances even now, Marin was excited about leaving the ship and going into a new town. She was also tired of her plain dress. This night called for something special, she decided, sea nymph or not, and she pulled out the pink silk gown. If comment were to be made, she would simply say it was within her powers to change her appearance to match the occasion.

At half past seven, her face flushed with excitement, Marin made her way to the main deck. The captain was already there waiting for her.

He looked quite dashing. His dark hair and beard were trimmed, and he was neatly attired in fawn-colored breeches and waist-coat and a dark brown jacket, instead of the loose-fitting pantaloons and shirt that he wore day-to-day about the ship. And she sucked in her breath at the strange, little flutter she suddenly felt in the pit of her stomach.

"Good evening, Captain, she greeted."

"Mistress." The corner of his mouth turned up in a slight smile as his eyes took in every curve of her figure silhouetted beneath the silk garment, just as that night in Boston. "May I say you look quite fetching, madam."

Marin was surprised. "You have no complaints about my dress?"

"I find no fault."

"What about the mythology?"

"The dress serves a purpose, and I am sure you will figure an explanation for the crew if need be," he replied.

As he walked her to the dinghy that hung suspended at the level of the deck, she glanced at him, bemused. Just when she thought she knew what to expect from him, he proved her wrong.

Two crewmen stood waiting to ferry them ashore, and they stared at Marin in awe.

"'Ain't never seen a sea nymph as pretty as you, Mistress," said one shyly.

The other seaman snorted. "Ye ain't never seen one afore, Freddie."

"Well, if I did, Isaiah, she wouldna be as pretty as Mistress Marin," Freddie retorted indignantly.

"Aye, I expect so," agreed Isaiah.

Marin smiled self-consciously, feeling undeserving of their praise when she was endeavoring to trick them all. "Thank you, gentlemen. You are too kind."

They returned shy, silly grins and nudged each other. "She called us gentlemen," they murmured to each other.

Reese gave a snort of impatience. "*Gentlemen,* may we proceed? I should like to arrive to port this night."

The sailors looked at the captain's stern features and jumped to attention. "Aye aye, sir."

They scrambled into the boat and took up their positions. When Reese took Marin's hand to help her in, she felt that funny, little flutter again. He stepped in and sat down next to her, and the small boat was slowly lowered to the water. The sailors rowed with alacrity to make up for having incurred the captain's displeasure, and they quickly reached shore.

A carriage was waiting to transport Reese and Marin to the commander's house. As they rode through the street, the excitement on Marin's face faded. Gibraltar was a small town—largely a frontier outpost—with no outward sign of culture or sophistication. But most disturbing was the degree of destruction. Everywhere she looked were charred buildings and piles of rubble with little evidence of rebuilding.

"This is not what I had expected to see," remarked Marin, disappointed.

"Nor I," said Reese.

The carriage soon arrived at the commander's house. It was a modest dwelling built of limestone. A female servant opened the door to Marin and Reese and showed them into a small, equally modest parlor with Moorish influences. Commander Teaberry shortly appeared from another room to welcome them and escorted them into the dining room. There appeared to be little formality in this outpost, and Marin was surprised to see that the table was well set with linen, china, and silver.

The commander's seat was at the head of the rectangular table. He sat Marin next to him on his right and placed the captain at the other end of the table, a gesture not lost on Reese. When Marin removed her shawl to lay it on her lap, the commander's eyes bulged at the cleavage exposed by the low neck of her gown. It was well within acceptable boundaries, but apparently the commander had not enjoyed such a sight in a long while, thought Reese suppressing a chuckle.

Two servants of foreign birth, a man and a woman, entered and served a course of mutton and fresh vegetables and discreetly withdrew.

"There is much destruction in the town, Commander," noted Reese. "Was there a storm?"

Teaberry shook his head. "It comes from the war with Spain. People call it the Great Siege."

"If I remember correctly, that ended over 10 years ago," said Reese.

"Twelve years ago, to be precise," replied the commander, hard pressed to drag his eyes from Marin even to eat. "The only buildings not destroyed were the troops' barracks and the Convent on the south side where the governor takes up residence. The rest of us have been confined to this western half." He sighed. "As you can see, recovery has been slow."

"Why is that if the war is over?" asked Marin.

"The economy was destroyed," the commander explained. "With no business opportunities, the merchants left and the civilian population declined. But what one war takes away, another restores," he added wryly.

"How so?" questioned Reese.

"England has been at war these past two years with France and nearly all of Europe. It seems we are at war with everyone. Please tell me, Captain Thackeray, that the United States has not entered the fray, as well," pleaded Teaberry, half joking. "We have not quite forgiven the American colonists for the last war."

"Not to worry, sir. A new treaty between the United States and Great Britain is being ratified by Congress as we speak," said Reese.

The commander nodded. "As I was saying, it can be said that these wars are having one good aside. The port has become a stopping off point for troops and naval ships. Merchants are beginning to return, as well as tradesmen and laborers, most of whom are immigrants looking for opportunity. But the resurgence introduces a new set of problems."

"Overcrowding, I presume," remarked Thackeray.

"Yes. Gibraltar is but two and a half square miles of surface, most of which is still to be rebuilt. Along with the civilian population, there are 4,000 troops encamped here—much more when the naval fleet is in port."

Teaberry turned to Marin. "I ask your pardon for subjecting you to such humble offerings, my dear. I must confess to being motivated by self-interest. Alas, I am surrounded by devastation, drunken soldiers, and immigrants. I miss the refinements of England, the conversation of gentlemen, the company of lovely ladies as you."

"Take heart, sir," replied Marin. "The fortunes of Gibraltar appear to be turning for the better in spite of what other problems that might occasion."

The commander sighed deeply, his eyes falling once again on her décolletage. "Aye, but they turn slowly."

Reese grinned when the commander refilled Marin's wine glass and set it farther from her reach, forcing her to lean forward for it. It was an old trick of young lads.

"And now, Mistress Marin, I would have your story," said Teaberry.

Before Marin could answer, Reese interjected: "Miss Marin's brother was an officer on a ship captured by Algerine pirates some time ago."

Her brother? Marin looked at Reese in bewilderment but followed his cue. "Uh…yes, and I have had no word of him in three years," she continued. "When I heard that Captain Thackeray's ship had been chartered to ransom prisoners, I insisted upon sailing with him to determine my 'brother's' fate and to hopefully secure his release."

"You are very brave, my dear," replied Teaberry admiringly. "Those devils can be a treacherous lot. The dey may not be at the wheel of the ship, but he commands the pirates just the same."

"You have met him, then?" questioned Reese.

"I have."

"They say he is of a more even temperament than his predecessor."

Teaberry snorted. "Perhaps, but that is not saying much, Captain. The difference is he will chop off a man's head after hearing his defense rather than before it."

"But is he more given to negotiations?" asked Marin anxiously. "That is our information."

"It depends upon his mood," said the commander. "The rulers of these states are all childishly mercurial. But two things they do respond to are riches and flattery."

Two more courses of food were served along with a prodigious amount of wine as Reese learned all that he could about the Algerine dey from the commander, though it wasn't an easy task to hold the man's attention with Marin in the room, he noted dryly.

"My dear, have you no husband to accompany you on your quest or to go in your stead?" questioned Teaberry with great interest.

The inquiry took her by surprise, and she looked at Reese for guidance.

"Mistress Marin is a widow," Thackeray interjected.

Marin glared at him, fearing it would embolden the tipsy commander. Her fears were well founded as the man became more forward in his advances—taking her hand, patting her arm, winking at her. And though he was subtle at first, Marin was all too conscious now of his ogling so that she draped her shawl around her shoulders, crossing it in front of her to cover her décolletage. Now she understood what the captain had meant when he said the dress served a purpose.

Reese could tell by the increasingly desperate looks she sent him that it was time to bring the evening to a close before she said or did something to dampen the commander's good will towards them.

"It is easy to see that Gibraltar is in capable hands, sir," remarked Thackeray, when the commander had finished with one of his stories. "Many thanks to you for the bounty of your generosity, but, alas, the evening grows late and Mistress Marin and I must return to the ship."

Teaberry smiled at Marin and laid a hand over hers. "Ah, but the evening never grows too late in the Mediterranean, Captain, whilst in the company of a beautiful woman."

Marin pulled her hand free and abruptly rose from her chair. "Your pardon, Commander. I feel a frightful headache coming on." She looked at Reese, a warning glint in her eye. "If you please, Captain…"

Reese stood up. "I fear the lady doth speak, sir," he said with an apologetic smile.

The disappointed commander got unsteadily to his feet. When he tried to take Marin's arm, she sidestepped him and preceded him into the entranceway. At the front door, she bid the commander a brisk farewell and rushed down the path to the carriage, not stopping to wait for Reese.

When Thackeray arrived and got into the conveyance beside her, he didn't say a word. She didn't care if he was angry with her or not.

As the carriage pulled away from the commander's house, she braced herself for a lecture. Instead, she heard him chuckle.

Marin looked at him in surprise. "You find something humorous?"

"I thought you were going to break into a run down that path. Whatever must the commander think?"

Marin gave a derisive snort. "The commander was so full of drink I doubt he thought anything."

"Perhaps, but he did comment on how fleet of foot you are."

"That man was shameless," she huffed. "Why did you not come to my defense? He was clearly untoward."

"Your cousin Thomas told me that you are quite adept at handling men. I believe his words were that your tongue is as sharp as the blade of a sword."

Marin glared at him. "It was my impression that I did not have that weapon at my disposal."

"It was just as well that you restrained yourself, madam."

"Why did you let Commander Teaberry think that I was a widow and that I was seeking to ransom my brother instead of my husband?" she demanded to know. "You placed me in an untenable situation."

"'Tis only for another day."

"Another day—oh, no, Captain, I will not abide that man for another hour let alone another day."

"I am afraid you shall have to," said Reese. "Teaberry is quite taken with you and has invited us to dine again. We require his help. He might not be so obliging if he knew that you were married."

"You are using me as bait?! You are unconscionable! I give you fair warning, Captain, should the commander get out of hand again, I will not hesitate to use another weapon at my disposal."

"What is that, madam?"

"Did not Thomas tell you that I have a wicked right cross?"

Thackeray raised a brow. "He failed to mention that fact. Might I suggest, then, that you invest in some lessons in the art of diplomacy?"

He smiled as Marin huffed with exasperation and settled back against the seat muttering to herself.

CHAPTER TWENTY-ONE

Algiers

The next evening when Marin met Reese at the dinghy, he noted that she was wearing one of her plain gowns with a higher neck and long sleeves.

Noting the disappointment on his face, she remarked: "I do not make the same mistake twice, Captain."

"A pity," he replied, handing her into the boat.

Commander Teaberry had much the same reaction as did Reese to her dress this night. His disappointment, however, was a little less subtle. But Marin had steeped herself in charm and managed to override it. She also kept the conversation near and dear to his heart—himself—and diverted the commander's attention from her by encouraging him to talk about his campaigns and "daring military exploits." In addition, she created opportunities for Reese to ask more questions.

Reese silently marveled at her handling of the commander. He shouldn't be surprised, he thought. He had witnessed her talent for manipulation enough times. Still, he found her ability to enchant fascinating. Never having been on the receiving end of her charm, he wondered fleetingly what it might be like to be in her good graces.

When the *Sea Nymph* weighed anchor on the third day, Marin breathed a deep sigh of relief. She stood at the railing on the main deck, her favorite place to be upon departing a port, and watched as they sailed out of the bay into the Mediterranean Sea, leaving behind Gibraltar—and Captain Teaberry.

Supper was of no concern to Marin this night. After dealing with Commander Teaberry, she decided that the captain was no problem at all to handle. She didn't need to exert herself in conversation or charm. She didn't care in the least if he was entertained or impressed, and that silly flutter of attraction seemed to have passed. Thus, when she sat down at the table this evening, she was in a good mood and feeling more in control.

Reese's manner, however, was ponderous. He poured glasses of wine for them and settled back in his chair pensively fingering his beard, leaving his food largely untouched.

Marin glanced over at him a few times as she ate.

"Is something amiss, Captain?" she finally asked.

He looked at her and roused himself.

"The commander imparted some news that gives me pause for consideration," he replied.

"Is it important to the mission?"

"That remains to be seen."

He lapsed back into silence.

"Well, I dare say you could show me some gratitude," she remarked, somewhat perturbed.

"For what, madam?"

"For engaging Commander Teaberry to your benefit, of course."

Reese turned his gaze to her again. "As I see it, madam, you were employing your talents to perform a duty as a member of the crew to everyone's benefit."

Marin laid down her fork, indignant. "Do you think it was easy putting up with…with that man's attentions?"

"You seemed adept enough," Reese carelessly responded.

"You clod!"

She angrily rose from her chair, letting loose with a string of foreign words that he easily deduced were not complimentary to him.

Her cousin's words suddenly came to mind. *You have not been cussed until you have been cussed by Marin in Russian.* And despite his heavy mood, Reese couldn't help laughing.

Marin halted her tirade in mid-sentence and stared at him, stupefied.

"Your pardon, madam," said Reese, bringing himself under control. "I was reminded of something your cousin once said. Do sit down and finish your dinner."

"I am quite finished," she replied icily.

As she stormed out of the cabin for yet another time, Reese sighed wearily. What was he to do about her?

The next morning, Thackeray was on deck early.

A chain of mountains rose up along the North African coast, and a thin strip of beach ran parallel to it as they neared Algiers.

"Take frequent soundings, Mr. White," he shouted to his bosun. "There are shoals through here."

"Aye, sir."

Duncan walked up to him. "I just saw Mistress Marin. She ain't too happy 'bout you."

"It takes little effort to incur Mistress Marin's disapproval," responded Thackeray.

"Ye been verily hard on her, Reese. Seaton, White, Pots, and me been takin' notice of it. 'Twill not be long 'til the crew takes notice of it, too."

"She is entirely too smug about her sense of importance on this ship and to this mission, Timothy. It can lead to mistakes when I can afford not one."

"So can antagonizing her further," pointed out Duncan. "Whether you want to admit it or not, she is important to the success of this mission, Captain. Andrew and I ain't had a more manageable crew. And she kept the Gibraltar port commander from searching the ship and finding the prisoners. The British are still bloody unhappy about the

American uprising. Would you have had the commander's cooperation without her help?" questioned Duncan. "You need to make peace with her, Reese. You may have need of her again. As she said, there are some things a woman can do better."

Thackeray knew that his second mate was right, but it galled him to have to admit it.

"All right, I shall make amends," he grumbled. "Where is she?"

"When last I saw her she was headed to her cabin."

As Thackeray strode off in that direction, Duncan sighed, doubtful of a positive outcome. In spite of his edict that a temperate mood be maintained among the crew, the captain's disposition at the moment was not that.

Reese's mood was not uplifted when Marin answered his knock and immediately slammed the door in his face.

"Madam, open this portal or I shall break it down!" he roared. "You have five seconds. Do you hear me? Five seconds!"

At the very end of her time limit, Marin opened the door a few inches. He shoved it open the rest of the way and stormed into the room.

"Ignoring an order is a punishable offense, madam. And make no mistake, you are under my command," he railed.

"Ha! What shall you do...flog me before the crew?" she questioned flippantly.

His nostrils flared. "A hand taken to your backside, I can promise you, will be sore punishment enough."

"You would not dare."

"Do not test me," he said, in the low, level tone that boded ill for the subject of his anger.

When he advanced on her, Marin knew that she had pushed him too far. "Stop!" she cried. "I shall concede it was ill-advised of me to shut the door on you."

"And you are under my command. Say it!" he ordered.

"Yes, yes, I am under your command," she repeated begrudgingly. To have to make such a declaration was humiliating, but a paddling, she had deduced, would have been more so. She glared at him. "Please have the good grace to leave my cabin now."

"My business is not yet finished. Mr. Duncan has relayed to me that you appear to have another complaint. What is the nature of it now?"

"What does it matter, Captain? 'Tis a fool who tries to break through an impenetrable wall. Nothing is gained."

"Madam, I remind you that you forced your way into this business and on this journey. I warned you before you will get no special consideration."

"I am not asking for special consideration, just an acknowledgment that I have made contributions of value."

Thackeray took a deep breath to hold his temper in check. "Very well. I shall concede that you have been helpful, but I give you fair warning. There is only one captain on this ship. Do I make myself clear?"

"Quite," she replied.

"Now that we understand each other, no more of your excuses. I shall expect you for supper tonight."

"No, sir, you shall not," said Marin.

Reese's eyes narrowed. "I thought we had come to terms."

"We have. Dr. Pennyman has invited me to sup with him."

For one of the few times in his life, Thackeray was at a loss for words and most of those times had been with her.

For the rest of the day, the word went out. Stay out of the captain's way. He is not in good humor.

Thackeray's mood did not improve when he sat down that evening to eat alone. Glancing at Marin's empty seat, Reese drummed his fingers on the table before jumping up from his chair to pace the floor. It irritated him that he was irritated she was having dinner with his surgeon. He could make no sense of it. Meals with her usually ended with her storming out the door anyway. Only once had he found the experience to be remotely positive.

Pots arrived to gather up the dishes and remains of the meal only to find the food barely touched. "The meal ain't to yer likin', Captain?" he asked concernedly. He shook his head. "The green sailor helpin' me ain't no help at all. The man is all thumbs. I sure am missin' Henry Shaw."

Thackeray glared at him. "The meal was acceptable. I am not hungry. Take it away…leave the wine."

Later, White joined Duncan on deck as the sun set. "Any change in the captain's mood?" he asked.

The second mate shook his head. "Pots says 'no.'"

"What do ye s'pose the doc is about invitin' Mistress Marin to supper?" asked White.

"I suspect he is stirrin' the pot," replied Duncan.

The bosun looked at his fellow officer in perplexity. "To what purpose?"

"Think on it, Andrew. A man don't always know that he wants somethin' 'til he thinks another values it, too."

* * * * *

Weather and winds were with them. Marin looked through a spyglass as the *Sea Nymph* sailed into view of Algiers.

A wall of stone flanked by towers and bastions rose up from the semi-circular harbor to form an impressive fortress cut into the mountain. There was a wall some 30 feet high on the land side and another about 40 feet high on the sea side built to keep out intruders. Within the stone walls were dense clusters of multi-tiered white, square-shaped dwellings that brought to mind cubes of sugar fixed on the side of a hill.

The harbor was not a natural harbor. A causeway or mole connected islands and a castle-like fortress with a lantern to the city, giving the harbor its semi-circular shape and providing a wharf for loading and unloading ships. Inside the harbor, other vessels were moored some 15 yards from shore and secured by cables lashed to cannons on the walkway.

They were just outside the harbor when Thackeray ordered his bosun to drop anchor and to replace the American flag with the pirate flag. At the same time, the gun ports were opened and the cannonades brought forth. The Algerine prisoners were brought up on deck, then, and placed in full view of the guards at the gate. All was in place; all knew their tasks.

The appearance of such a ship caused an uproar among the guards of the port. And Thackeray observed through his spyglass a frenzy of activity on the wharf. He smiled. It was as he had hoped.

An hour later, the captain of the port was rowed out to them waving a white flag of truce and parlee.

Marin stayed off to the side to watch the drama unfold.

When the boat was within distance, Thackeray had the translator and the Algerine captain brought forth.

"Tell him to come aboard," Reese ordered the translator. "Tell him his safety is assured."

The translator relayed the message. The port captain hesitated, then instructed the boat to row closer. One of Thackeray's crewmen dropped the ladder, and the captain came aboard.

The translator introduced Thackeray as the captain of the ship. The harbor captain looked at Reese closely. He was not as swarthy, but the American with his beard and dark features didn't look so different from his fellow Arabs. Only the blue eyes and his height gave him away.

"What do you want?" he asked warily through the translator.

"I wish an audience with the dey," replied Thackeray "I have contribution."

"What contribution?"

"His pirates and their bounty."

The port captain was taken aback when the translator relayed Reese's response. "You make an offering of the dey's own goods to him?" he asked, incredulous.

The audacity of the proposal was mind boggling to him, and he was not pleased to have to take such a proposal to his mercurial leader, whose temper was known to be explosive and sometimes misplaced. That he was essentially admitting that the dey was engaged in piracy had escaped the port captain in the moment.

He perused Reese's ship and crew. The seamen bore arms and looked to be a blood thirsty group. "The dey is observing Holy Day," he said. "Effendi transacts no business today. Tomorrow he may see you. I will pilot your ship to the inner harbor."

"The ship will remain anchored here," said Reese.

"It is the custom for the harbor captain of any port to steer a foreign ship into port and take custody of its cargo," persisted the captain through the translator.

"Perhaps, but this is not any port, and I shall not surrender my ship under any circumstances," countered Reese.

In truth, Commander Teaberry had warned him not to accept the gesture. Too many unsuspecting captains had found that their ships had been anchored at the far end of the wharf beneath the guns of the fortress, thus preventing their departures until the dey decreed it. And the release usually came with a high price.

When the translator relayed Thackeray's answer, the harbor captain wasn't happy about it, but he didn't have a choice.

The captain of the pirate ship noticed Marin then and spoke excitedly to the port captain. The port captain looked over at her. She was tall, slender, and beautiful—more so than the other women captives they had taken. She wasn't dark featured like the Arabs from the interior parts of the country but resembled more the blonde and red-haired women of fair complexion from the areas around the sea coast.

Marin returned his gaze with no hint of the fear and uncertainty she was feeling.

As the sun embraced her with an aura-like effect, a babble of voices broke out among the prisoners, and one of them cried out: "Ibna az-Zahra."

Reese looked questioningly at Duncan and Seaton, but they were just as bewildered as he was.

The port captain hesitantly approached Marin and stared into her eyes. Uttering something in Arabic, he took a step back. He turned and spoke to the translator, his manner urgent.

"We go speak with Dey Hassan Bashaw. We come back tomorrow," the translator relayed to Thackeray with the same sense of urgency.

Before Reese could question the man further, the translator hurried after the port captain who was hastily departing the ship.

Seaton and Duncan walked over to Reese.

"Why was they jabberin' about the Mistress?" asked Duncan.

Reese glanced over at Marin. "I cannot say," he replied, more concerned than he let on. "Strike the pirate flag and raise the American flag. I see foreign ships in the harbor. There may be dignitaries in port, and I wish not to raise questions."

The next morning the port captain and the translator returned.

"The dey wishes to see 'daughter of light,'" said the translator.

"Who is that?" questioned Reese, though he had a sinking feeling he already knew.

"Her," replied the translator, pointing to Marin as she walked up on deck.

Reese shook his head. "No. She remains on the ship."

The translator and the port captain conversed for a few minutes.

"The dey demands to see her…only her," insisted the translator. When the port captain moved toward Marin, crewmen blocked his way.

"Does the dey not wish his men returned?" asked Reese.

"He does not care. They are shamed," replied the translator.

Marin observed the tense conversation between Thackeray and the Algerines, as well as the protective stance of the crewmen toward her, and suspected that she was the subject. She sidestepped the seamen and walked over to Reese. "What is amiss?" she asked.

"Apparently, the dey does not care about the return of his men or their bounty," said Thackeray.

"What does he want?"

"You. He wishes you to take an audience with him—alone."

Marin looked at Reese in surprise. "Why?"

"I would venture to say that you are thought to bring good fortune," he replied.

"How? I have done nothing to put forth the suggestion."

"Tales carry, madam. I suspect the translator overheard the crew making such reference to you and relayed their stories to his captain, who then passed them on to the port captain. Whatever appearance you presented yesterday gave flight to their fancies all the way to the dey."

"They did act strange when they saw me," recalled Marin. "But I did nothing."

"Apparently, you did something whether you are aware of it or not," said Reese.

"Well then, I shall go to see the dey," she declared.

Reese looked at her as though she had lost her mind. "No, madam, you will not. For once, stop and think how your actions may result."

"I am, Captain. The prisoners are no longer leverage," she said in a lowered voice. "I have to go if you hope to get an audience with the dey and proceed as planned."

"Perhaps, but you are now *my* leverage. If you go there alone, I will have none at all."

Marin walked over to the translator and the port captain who were still being corralled by the seamen and pointed to Thackeray. "He must come with me," she stated firmly.

The two men hesitated, then conferred again. The port captain finally nodded. "We shall let the dey deal with this dog," he spat in Arabic.

The translator turned back to Thackeray. "You may go," he said, omitting the port captain's slur.

Still, Thackeray had caught the insult. He had been called it enough times by the guards during his imprisonment.

"Captain, ye kenna mean to let Mistress Marin go ashore. Ye know they kenna be trusted," said Duncan. "Besides, the crew will not permit their talisman to be taken from them. They will not allow her leave the ship."

Reese looked around him. The entire crew was on deck now watching the situation closely. Some had assumed a belligerent stance, and there was a tenseness in the air.

Marin looked up at the cloud that was blocking the sun. Gauging the moment of its passing, she walked to the center of the deck, raised her hands above her head, pressed her fingertips together, then slowly lowered her arms as though placing an arc of protection over the ship just as the sun broke through the cloud.

Awed murmurs sounded among the crew and the Algerines.

Marin turned to address the astounded seamen. "I must go ashore, but understand this. In my absence, I have placed this ship under my protection." At this, she looked meaningfully at the port captain who was staring at her with open-mouthed wonder.

Reese and his officers were no less impressed by her performance.

"I am going, too," declared Duncan. "After what the commander at Gibraltar told ye, ye need someone to watch your back, Captain."

"One more man is not going to make the difference, Timothy, and I need you here. I will find James Cathcart."

"You will not be permitted to go armed, sir. How do ye expect to match them?"

"My wits shall have to be my sword, and I dare say Mistress Marin will be armament enough," responded Reese dryly. "Watch the harbor closely for any untoward movement. If Marin and I do not return or send a signal in two days' time that all is well, set sail immediately."

"But, Captain—"

"That is an order, Mr. Duncan." Thackeray walked away then to give the rest of his officers their orders.

Duncan approached Marin. "Watch the captain's back," he said. "He has an enemy among the dey's soldiers."

Marin regarded him with consternation. "Who? How know you this?"

"During our escape years ago, the captain killed the nephew of the previous dey," explained Duncan. "The man's brother hates Americans and has sworn vengeance against the one who killed his brother."

"Dear God. Does this man know that it is the captain he seeks?" asked Marin in alarm.

"If not by name, he might by sight. 'Tis why the captain grew the beard."

"Perhaps the man is dead," suggested Marin hopefully.

Duncan shook his head. "Commander Teaberry told the captain that the man heads the Janissaries now."

"What are the Janissaries?"

"The dey's soldiers. Have a care. His name is Ahmet."

CHAPTER TWENTY-TWO

Into the Lion's Den

When Marin stepped onto the causeway at the foot of the mole head near the castle of the lantern, she felt more than a passing fear in this foreign land. As a child sailing on her father's merchant ship, she had embraced foreign ports, eager to meet people of different cultures and customs. These experiences had enriched her life. But this place, these people were so different from Europe. She didn't understand their culture or their religion.

Reese came alongside her. "Whatever the American or British custom or your thought, assume it is the opposite here," he counseled her. "Observe and keep your wits about you. Be respectful, but do not show fear."

Marin nodded.

Reese started to take her arm, when the translator stopped him. "You must not touch 'daughter of light,'" he warned.

They followed the port captain along the mole or causeway and passed through a large, intimidating gate and down a passageway that ran underneath the wall to inside the fortress. Marin was led to an ass whereupon a box was placed on the ground to aid her in mounting the animal. When her seat was secure, a boxlike canopy with curtains was placed over her and the curtains drawn closed.

The party started off. The morning was warm, and it felt stuffy inside the box. Marin could hear the sounds of a marketplace which grew fainter as they traveled farther from the port on the main highway towards the city center.

The dirt road was uneven and so narrow they had to travel single file. People stood along the street to glimpse the curious new foreigners. They had heard about the pirate ship and the special lady. Reese noted with wry amusement the vastly different treatment. The first time he had been paraded through the street as a prisoner it was to the jeers and spittle of the public.

It seemed a long distance before they came to another center of commercial activity. Marin peeked through an opening in the curtain. The Souk el-Kebir, the principal market street, crossed the sector, and the air was filled with the sights and sounds of the bazaar and the pungent aroma of spices and coffee. People busily moved about the streets and sat in cafes. She was surprised to see that women were similarly dressed as men in baggy pantaloons and robes of fine silk and that many of them wore veils across their faces.

The donkey was brought to a stop, and the canopy box was removed. Marin slid off the animal and looked about her. There was a fountain in the middle of a square, and next to an open area or maydan, she saw a building that seemed remarkable only for its size.

It was three stories high with four wings. Except for the marble benches outside and two fierce looking Turkish guards wearing bejeweled turbans and threatening swords tucked into sashes around their waists, there was little to suggest that this was the grand palace of the dey. As were the privileged populace, the guards were dressed in fine silk pantaloons, shirts and vests but wore shiny, black leather boots instead of slippers.

Adjacent to the maydan were two mosques—one a magnificent multiple domed structure in the Turkish design, the other a smaller one. Marin was awed by everything around her; Reese saw only the danger and bitter memories.

The harbor captain led them past the heavily armed Janissaries into the compound. Marin gaped in amazement as the vaulted entrance gave way to an open courtyard with a large fountain. Surrounding the courtyard were two tiers of balconies with intricate fretwork supported by twisted marble columns. Another guard came forward then to escort them the rest of the way, and the port captain fell back to return to his duties at the harbor.

Marin and Reese followed the guard along the portico and into a section of the building. As they walked down a corridor, Marin took note of the distinctive décor of twisted columns and ceramic tiled walls of various designs and hues. She had found the Russian Byzantine architecture to be unusual and exotic, but the mix of Moorish, Ottoman, Persian, and European influence inherent here was unlike anything she had ever seen.

They passed mysterious hidden stairs and several rooms before stopping outside of one.

The guard left when a young man about Thackeray's age approached them. He was standard in height with fair coloring, a round face, high brows and forehead, and deep set eyes.

"Captain Thackeray?" he inquired.

"Aye," replied Reese guardedly. "Who might you be?"

"I am James Cathcart."

Reese visibly relaxed. "This is Marin Sutton."

Cathcart smiled. "I am pleased to make your acquaintance, madam. When I was told to expect you, Captain, I must confess that I had not expected you to arrive in such a fashion. The pirate and 'the special lady' have created quite an uproar."

"I am at a loss to understand what interest I should hold beyond that of a slave, sir," said Marin.

"Stories have preceded you, mistress. You are a lady who brings good fortune."

"But that was for the benefit of Captain Thackeray's crew," she explained.

"The dey does not believe your powers limited to them," replied Cathcart. "Come now, the dey is not a patient man. As Chief Clerk and Regency of Algiers, I shall make the introductions and translate.

Do not portray yourself as a soothsayer, mistress. The Qur'an does not look with favor upon fortunetellers."

For the first time, Marin was seeing a serious consequence to her actions, and her anxiety rose as she and Reese followed Cathcart through the door. An impetuous ruse to gain her passage on a ship was catapulting her into dangerous uncharted territory.

The room was large and decorated with delft tiles and elegant Turkish carpets scattered over marble floors. The dey sat cross-legged on a seat draped with a predominantly blue tapestry, and he held a fan of ostrich plumes in his hand.

Even seated, he presented an imposing figure. He was dressed in a long gown of blue silk and wore a jeweled turban upon his shaven head. A long black beard threaded with gray covered much of his face. Marin thought him to be the age of her father.

The dey silently regarded his visitors for several minutes—his black eyes hard, cold, and assessing. His attention fell on Marin as Cathcart read off in Turkish the accounts of the port captain and the claims the translator had overheard from the crew of the *Sea Nymph*. The dey asked a few questions to which Cathcart replied.

Then, the ruler did something quite rare in the course of an audience. He set down his fan, rose from his seat, and walked over to Marin. He was surprisingly tall—the height of Thackeray—and lean. She willed herself to remain steady as he gazed into her eyes, just as the port captain had done. And like him, the dey reacted with the same degree of astonishment.

He clapped his hands and barked orders to a servant boy who jumped to attention and left the room. Then, the dey motioned Marin to a three-foot high slab of marble that projected from the wall topped with an elegant cushion.

"Effendi wishes for you to sit," instructed Cathcart.

When Marin sat down, the ruler returned to his seat. A short time later, the slave reappeared with a tray and served them coffee.

"It is a gesture of great honor that the dey bestows upon you in offering you this drink," Cathcart explained to Marin.

The dey spoke then in Turkish.

"He says that you are very beautiful, that you must be a daughter of Fatimah," relayed Cathcart. "Fatimah was the daughter of the prophet Mohammed. She was very beautiful as well. People revered her and called her 'lady of light.'"

Marin's brow furrowed in perplexity. "How odd. The translator called me a 'daughter of light.'"

"The port captain and the translator both reported that they saw an aura surround you on the ship."

"'Twas but a trick of the sun and clouds," confided Marin.

"That may be, mistress, but your eyes are not."

"I beg your pardon?"

"Your eyes are very green. You are thought to be blessed," said Cathcart.

Marin regarded him in confusion. "I do not understand."

"It is a color so rarely seen in eyes some people consider it magical. In the Musselman religion, the color of green is sacred. The marabouts or monks as you might call them wear green gowns. It was the favorite color of Mohammed. He is said to have worn a green cloak and turban. And the Qur'an talks of a paradise where people wear green garments of fine silk."

Now Reese understood why the Algerine pirates, the port captain, and the translator had reacted the way they did.

The dey turned his attention to Reese.

"Cathcart, why is she in the company of this pirate dog who dares to offer me the recompense of my own men and bounty?" he spat scornfully.

When Cathcart put the question to Marin, he warned: "Be careful how you answer."

Reese was apprehensive as well about how she might respond. There had been no rehearsal; there was no book of instruction. She was not supposed to be part of this plan.

Marin keenly felt the pressure. Instincts told her not to disclose that she was with the captain for the purpose of learning about her husband, and she couldn't compromise Reese's cover as a pirate. In the end, she decided that she had no choice but to play out the scenario she, herself, had set into motion.

"The captain took me from another ship, your grace. Seamen believe I bring them good fortune," she said.

When Cathcart relayed this back to the dey, the ruler responded: "And now you shall bring good fortune to me, for in my presence you will remain, daughter of light. Or do you favor only Americans?" he asked with some suspicion.

"I am a child of the sea. I favor no country," said Marin. She proceeded to speak in French, Swedish, and Russian to illustrate her point.

The dey was clearly impressed and pleased, and the relief in the room was palpable.

The ruler looked at Reese, then. "Cathcart, tell me why I should not put this dog down."

The clerk quickly translated the dey's sentiments to Reese, praying that the captain had a good answer as well.

"Tell the dey I can claim more riches for him than can his pirates who are now imprisoned on my ship," replied Reese.

When Cathcart translated, the dey bristled. "How?" he demanded to know.

"Tell him I am not bound by treaties and recompense from other countries as is he. I am free to plunder any country's merchant ships at will," said Reese.

The dey stroked his beard, thoughtful, after the captain's response was conveyed. "If I grant you my protection, I shall surely invite these nations to war with me."

"Tell him they will not know we are aligned," countered Reese when it came back to him. "I shall not come into port."

"How then shall I receive my reward?" questioned the dey, growing irritated again.

"Tell the dey that I will appear to stop his ships as well. In truth, it will be a rendezvous to transfer his part of the wealth," answered Reese.

As Cathcart relayed this, the dey gave an impatient wave of his arm. "Bah! You are a Christian. How am I to trust you? You hold your ship off shore. Perhaps I should ransom you. How much would your crew pay for you?"

"Nothing," said Reese. "They do not need me to sail the ship. And if they see movements they deem threatening, they will leave. You will get no ransom or spoils. You know the nature of pirates."

The dey gave an ill-humored laugh. "How bold and sure this man is of himself, Cathcart. Perhaps I shall hold him as a slave, and he can still serve me."

Cathcart scrambled to keep up with the translation of the brisk back and forth, becoming more and more concerned by the dey's rising contentiousness. He tried to send a warning to Reese, but Reese paid him no mind.

Marin was becoming concerned as well at the tenor of the exchange between two strong men. She hoped Thackeray would keep sight of the fact that he was the one in the lion's den.

Reese, however, was taking a calculated risk. Men like the dey despised weakness, while, at the same time, they resented any show of strength that could be seen as a defiance to their power. Thackeray was betting his life that greed trumped all.

"Perhaps you might do well to hear him out, effendi," ventured Cathcart diplomatically. "If you imprison the captain, his crew will depart. Neither will the United States ransom a pirate, citizen or not. What have you to gain by holding him?"

"Satisfaction that I can put a collar on this cur and whip him at my pleasure," spat the dey. "Ask him why it pleases him to serve me?"

When Cathcart put the question to him, Reese readily replied: "I need assurance that your pirates will not attack my ship. In return, I shall increase both our riches while yet they can be made before this age of piracy ends—and with it your contributions."

At the translation of Reese's response, the dey gave a derisive laugh. "Piracy shall never end."

Thackeray looked at Cathcart. "Tell the dey that its demise is on the horizon."

When Cathcart relayed the prediction, the dey regarded Reese with a piercing dark gaze, and he spoke with growing agitation to his clerk.

"Effendi wants you to explain," said Cathcart.

"The European countries have navies now pledged to the protection of their merchant ships against piracy," replied Reese.

The dey scoffed. "They are all too busy fighting wars with each other. Why should I worry?"

"Wars end. And America is not waging war anywhere," said Reese.

The dey laughed. "What have I to fear from America? The government can barely pay its tributes. Perhaps that is not such a bad thing, ay Cathcart? Its merchant ships are rich plunder."

"The government is well engaged in the building of a navy with the express purpose of convoying its ships to the Barbary Coast," interjected Reese. "Americans have an expertise in ship building. Permit me to say, your grace, your ships are few and of an inferior construction."

The dey again fixed a sharp gaze on Thackeray after Cathcart's translation. "America is building a navy? Why have I not heard of this?"

"I have it on good authority as well," continued Reese, "that the American government has completed negotiations for treaties with England and Spain and, as you know, is already aligned with Sweden and Portugal. I dare say the Americans will be a force to fear within a few years' time."

The dey again stroked his beard, clearly disturbed when all this had been conveyed to him. He motioned Cathcart to him, and they spoke quietly for several minutes. When they were finished, Cathcart approached Reese.

"The dey wishes to think on the matter. In the meantime, I convinced him to commend you to my oversight. Hence, you shall be my houseguest. The young lady will remain here in the seraglio, an apartment in the women's area of the palace. Do not worry. She holds a position of honor and will be well attended."

Cathcart relayed the arrangement to Marin. Glancing uncertainly at Reese, she stood and followed the slave from the room. Thackeray mentally castigated himself. The dey's adoption of Marin had not been one of Reese's calculations. Now, he had to rescue two women and a child—and there was no longer a plan in place.

CHAPTER TWENTY-THREE

Time Is of the Essence

Cathcart led Reese to his house not far from the palace.

The residence was not what Thackeray had expected to see and was surprised that it was located in the upper-class quarter where the ground was more level between the shore and the hill. It followed the same architectural style of all the other residential dwellings—a central courtyard surrounded by a veranda and a roof top terrace—but it was much larger than the more modest homes and had a fountain in the center of a more spacious courtyard. Thackeray knew this to be the home of a privileged man.

They walked across the courtyard into one of several apartments. It was cool and quiet, and light filtered in from the yard and from small windows set high in the thick exterior walls. The chamber was richly embellished with horseshoe arches, twisted columns, and Tunisian tiles and held the usual furnishings of a Turkish carpet, sofa, and a low marble table around which cushions were arranged on the floor.

Reese regarded Cathcart with some confusion. "Are you not a prisoner?"

"I am."

"How is it you roam the streets so freely and enjoy a life of privilege?"

"I am a private slave, not a public one, but a slave nonetheless with all the feelings of degradation that accompany such a mark," replied Cathcart with a measure of resentment.

"What is the difference?" asked Reese. "I am unaware of this distinction."

"Public slaves are dispatched to hard labor. Private slaves are dispatched to the palace and are able to purchase certain positions of power," explained Cathcart.

"How?"

"It depends on how well one plays the game. Everything in Algiers operates on a system of bribery."

"I remember, but with what did you have to bargain?" queried Reese. "The bloody bastards took everything I and my crew had when we were captured. I was lucky enough to gather a few coins through trickery."

"It is easier to come by coin now," said Cathcart. "Countries, including the United States, periodically send small allowances for their prisoners, and the money is divided up and distributed once a year. Also, prisoners are allowed to beg alms from visiting caliphs, sheiks, and dignitaries. If one is thrifty and smart enough to learn the system, he can bribe his way to more advantageous positions."

"Even so you have acquired all of this?" questioned Reese skeptically.

"It took years," replied Cathcart. "But there was much luck amongst the hardship and scheming."

"How so?"

"The dey has first pick of the prisoners when they come in. I was fortunate to be among the five he chose from the *Maria* to work in the palace. I eventually bribed my way to a position at the marine and, thanks to the plague, I advanced to clerk of the marine. The Neapolitan prisoner next in line for that position had died of the disease." Cathcart gave a cynical laugh. "One develops a macabre view of what 'good fortune' means here. It is usually predicated upon someone's demise."

A dark shadow crossed Reese's face. "In spite of the sweet smell of spices, Algiers reeks with the odor of death."

"Aye, but death creates opportunity," said Cathcart. "I came to the dey's attention with my work at the marine. When his clerk died last year, he offered me this position. But that was merely the first step."

"And what was the second?" questioned Reese.

"Procurement of specie," replied Cathcart. "As I said, everything comes at a price, and this promotion came with a particularly steep cost. But I knew it to be too strategically important to pass up."

"Where would you have gathered such a purse?" asked Thackeray.

"I begged and borrowed money from agents of Scotland to meet the demand."

Thackeray looked at Cathcart in surprise. "Scotland gave you a loan?"

The dey's clerk smiled. "I can be quite persuasive."

"It would seem so. But how do you repay it?"

"The position carries with it a handsome stipend, and visiting dignitaries are only too happy to present me with gifts for influence."

"To what purpose?"

"'Tis the Chief Clerk that determines who receives an audience with the dey, and my services do not come cheap," responded Cathcart with a twinkle in his eye. "The dey also gave me a tavern from which I am allowed a share of the liquor duties. I have three taverns now and purchased this house with the revenues."

Reese laughed appreciably. "You are, indeed, a clever man, sir."

From what I have heard about you, Captain Thackeray, I dare say you would have mastered the system quite handily yourself in time."

"I did not care to stay around long enough to learn it," said Reese with tinge of bitterness in his voice.

"Yes, I know," replied Cathcart. "We crew members of the *Maria* were brought into harbor just after you and your men escaped, and I dare say we paid the price for it. The dey at that time was especially unforgiving," he added with a wry smile. "Prisoners have tried to escape since then but none ever succeeded, and they met their ends in a most brutal fashion. The Turks are very good at that.

"For myself," he continued, "I decided to learn the game, bide my time, and hopefully live long enough to be released. In the meantime, as there is no consulate to work on their behalf, I do what I can in my position to ease the plight of the American prisoners. The Turks seem to dislike them the most."

"Your pardon, sir. I meant no disrespect."

Cathcart smiled. "None taken, Captain. We all have different means and instincts for self-preservation."

He spoke to a young slave who quickly returned with a bottle of wine and cups and disappeared. The host motioned Reese to a seat on the cushion and sat down cross-legged on the other side of the low table.

"The Algerines make excellent wine," said Cathcart, filling their cups.

"I thought the Qur'an forbids the use of liquors," remarked Thackeray.

"It does, but the Algerines are hugely fond of wine and managed to discover two passages in the book that finds moderate use acceptable."

"How convenient," remarked Reese dryly.

Cathcart chuckled. "Oh, the convenience does not end there, my friend."

"How so?"

"In the instance of tobacco use, those addicted to it claim that it is the saying of their prophet that men who bear the name Mussulmen should smoke this weed called tobacco. There is also the question of whether coffee is forbidden by the Qur'an due to its intoxicating qualities, yet it is the drink of choice—even for the dey."

Thackeray snorted. "It would appear that Christianity is not alone in its hypocrisies."

"Just so. Where there is a will, one will find a passage to support it in the sacred books."

Reese tasted his drink. "It is good wine. I can understand why the allowance was sought."

"Even so, do not approach the dey with fumes upon your breath," warned Cathcart. "Though once a prodigious user himself, since ascending to the position of ruler he has taken on the yoke of those who rigidly deem it unlawful to taste, make, or maintain oneself with the use of liquor."

"Pardon my confusion, sir, but did not the dey reward you with taverns?" questioned Reese.

Cathcart chuckled again. "I am a Christian."

"Well then, it would appear the stigma does have its advantage here after all," remarked Thackeray.

"Perhaps a few, one of which I dare say you made use of once yourself."

"To what do you make reference?" asked Reese.

"It was smart of you to have chosen the Holy Day for your escape when Christian prisoners are detailed to the harbor and most lightly guarded."

"It was not my plan alone."

"You are too modest, Captain. I know you to have been the mastermind."

"How so?"

"I learned of it from Captain O'Bryen of the *Dauphin*. He and his crew were captured soon after you."

"I never encountered the captain or his crew. They must have been held in another pen," surmised Reese.

Cathcart nodded. "They were held in the bagnio with the Neapolitans. There is yet talk of your escape among those who still live, you know. The explosion was heard all over Algiers. O'Bryen and I still wonder how you gained access to the powder stores. All but two of the dey's ships were destroyed."

"That shall have to remain my secret," replied Reese. "I will tell you that the destruction of the dey's ships was an unintended benefit. I had meant only to distract." Reese paused. "If you know the story, then you know we paid a heavy price."

Cathcart shrugged. "Freedom always costs more, but one's internal compass points in the direction of it anyway. As an American, you should know that. I believe you lost your father at Bunker Hill in the War of Independence."

Reese looked at Cathcart in surprise. "How do you know so much about me?"

"Suffice it to say, O'Bryen and I have developed lines of communication that are far reaching, Captain."

"How? O'Bryen is a prisoner, too, is he not?"

"Richard enjoys wide latitude and travels under guard to raise ransom money for other prisoners," explained Cathcart. "He puts the opportunity to good use."

"Is my name known here?" asked Reese.

"If it were, you would be dead by now. Guards take little notice of the names of the rank and file prisoners. They die too quickly. O'Bryen and I have held your name close."

"Did your lines of communication tell you that it was I who killed the former dey's nephew during the escape?" queried Thackeray.

Cathcart looked at him in alarm. "It was you? The man's brother is a captain in the Janissaries now."

"So I have heard. He swore vengeance. I know not if he will recognize me, so I shall have to keep from his notice."

"Just so. As you go about, you must also have a care of the lisberos," warned Cathcart. "They are the dey's spies about the city. Trust no one. I should caution you as well that the Algerine women are rather forward and have a particular fondness for Christian men. I dare say that their eye will soon find you. Ignore their overtures and do not complicate yourself. It is an offense punishable by death for a Christian man to engage in relations with a Moorish woman."

Reese nodded. "Tell me, sir, do you know of an American prisoner named Nathaniel Sutton? He was first mate on a ship taken some three years ago—the *Clarabell*."

"I know the ship, and I know most of the American prisoners. The name is not familiar to me. Why do you wish to know?"

"He is Marin's husband. 'Tis why she is on this voyage."

Cathcart was taken aback for a moment, then became concerned. "Make no mention of this," he counseled. "The dey will not take kindly to her having a husband about. It diminishes her aura of mysticism and will bode ill for Mr. Sutton, should he be alive. I will make discreet inquiry."

Reese nodded. "Are Mrs. Marsden and her son well and at hand?"

"Yes. They are kept in an apartment in the seraglios in the northwest wing of the palace. The harem is above the Diwan and treasury." Cathcart frowned. "But, the dey is getting increasingly anxious to send them off to the interior lest the American government discover that they are alive and held captive. Even more does he fear that they should be found to have died while in his custody. With the news that the United States is building a navy, he will be even more impatient to act."

"Then time is of the essence," said Reese. "Are you able to get word to my brother that I am in Algiers?"

Cathcart nodded. "He resides in an apartment in the palace on the second floor of the northeast wing. The captain and second mate have died of the plague. It was particularly virulent this spring. His name will be known to the dey. I would advise you not to use it. I shall call you Captain Reese."

Cathcart thought for a moment. "Perhaps Mistress Marin can be of help in making contact with Mrs. Marsden. She appears to be a clever lady."

"That, sir, is an understatement," replied Thackeray dryly.

"Oh, how so?"

Reluctantly, Reese gave an accounting of her escapades to gain passage on the journey.

Cathcart laughed uproariously. "You could not discern that she was Henry Shaw?"

"Suffice it to say that she hid her identity well," replied Thackeray, still finding little humor in the matter.

"She must have special abilities indeed to be so convincing to your crew and the dey."

Reese snorted. "She acts upon their superstitions. 'Tis a dangerous game she plays."

"Indeed," agreed Cathcart. "You must work quickly. If the dey accepts your proposal, and I am certain that he will, he will wish you to sail in a few days to avoid any suspicion of an alliance with you."

"Tell him that I require at least a week to make repairs," said Thackeray. "Is my brother free to move about?"

"He is permitted no communication with foreign dignitaries. But he is free to seek out a tavern for food and drink and is watched when he leaves his apartment."

"Can you arrange for him to meet me at one of your taverns tomorrow evening?" asked Reese.

"I can, but you must return to the house before the city and neighborhood gates are closed at sunset. Flutists move about playing a Turkish melody to signal curfew. Do you remember much of the city?"

"Only the way from the bagnio to the palace and the marine."

Cathcart called out something in Arabic, and a large black man entered the room and handed him a folded parchment.

"This is Kendzu, my manservant. He will see to your needs. He understands English. You can trust him."

Cathcart unfolded a map of Algiers on the table. "Thank heavens for high windows," he remarked. "Lisberos lurk around every corner and listen outside every window. Now to business. There are five city gates," he said and pointed to their locations on the map. "The roads leading from the gates divide the city and meet in front of the Ketch-aoua Mosque. There are two major regions: the lower plains area of the elite and the upper mountainous area of the more modest and poorer populations. The higher up the hill, the more reduced the circumstances. Each one of these regions is divided into harahs, ethnic quarters separated by gates."

Cathcart paused. "I should think you would limit your concern to the lower city and port area. Bab-Djezira is the main road leading from the city to the port. Running parallel to the port is the Souk el-Kebir, the grand market street. The mercantile area below it near the port gates is of a lower status. The consulates, more highly regarded artisans and markets, and the residences of the wealthier merchants, dignitaries, and government officials are located closer to the center of the city where streets from the port meet the Souk el-Kebir."

Cathcart pointed to another spot on the map. "This is where we are now, and there is the dey's palace. This is the mosque he attends. Down here near the port commercial activity is the Street of Seven Taverns where my taverns are located. Have a care. It is also the quarter of the corsairs, and you are not a popular person with them. Do you know French or Spanish?"

"I know French and some passable Spanish," said Reese.

"In the city, Mahometans and Christians speak a language that is a mixture of Spanish, Portuguese, Italian, and French. 'Tis a tongue understood by natives and has a universality in this part of the world."

Reese nodded. "I recall some of the language."

"Good. So that you do not draw undue attention, I will leave you with two changes of dress: one of silk to move through the higher status marketplaces; another of coarser threads for moving among the common people. Now tell me, what is your plan so that I might better aid you?" asked Cathcart expectantly. "It will not be easy to abscond with Mrs. Marsden and her son, your brother—and, most assuredly, not with the dey's newfound 'daughter of light.'"

When Reese didn't answer, Cathcart glanced quizzically at him. "You do have a plan, do you not, Captain?"

"I did have," replied Reese with some annoyance. "But, as so often happens when Marin inserts herself, it went awry."

Cathcart frowned. He did not find this comforting.

CHAPTER TWENTY-FOUR

The Hand of Fatima

Marin was shown to a large apartment with the traditional embellishments of curved arches, twisted columns, and a cluster of lamps suspended from a high ceiling.

It was furnished with a green upholstered sofa and a low marble table around which gold fringed cushions embroidered with flowers were arranged for seating on the floor. Rich Turkish carpets covered blue tile floors; a mosaic of green and blue tiles decorated the walls. The bed was a raised platform that was separated from the rest of the room by a large wood panel intricately carved with images of birds and fauna.

A eunuch brought her a tray of various fruits and nuts along with a vessel of cool water. Marin hadn't eaten since leaving the ship in the morning. In all the uncertainty and drama, she hadn't realized how hungry and thirsty she was, and she sat down at the table to gladly partake of the offering.

When she had taken her fill, the slave beckoned her to follow him.

"Hammam," he said.

He led her from the apartment, down some narrow stairs, and through a long corridor with vaulted arches. Marin could hear the echo of women laughing and talking in Arabic. They came to a cavernous, humid area, then, that opened to two very large pools of water, one of which had steam rising from it.

The pools were surrounded by cubicles with stone sofas and tables. A woman was lying on one table receiving a massage from a eunuch slave. Several women frolicked in the water, while others relaxed on sofas and conversed. To Marin's shock, the women were all either nude or partially clad in a thin cloth that covered them from their waists to their knees.

Marin looked across the steaming pool and saw an attractive lady with fair hair and features who held a young boy close to her. The child was unclothed, but, unlike the other women, this lady wore a shift and stood as though to shield the boy from the sight of the naked concubines. She guessed this was Mrs. Marsden. What luck! thought Marin. Perhaps she did attract good fortune after all.

When she advanced into the hammam, all eyes swiveled to her and everyone went still for a few minutes. Word had spread of her like wildfire throughout the seraglio. The dey had 30 jealous concubines, and it was their assumption that Marin was the latest. A couple of the women spoke to each other in Arabic and laughed. Marin didn't need to understand the language to know that it was a derisive remark.

The black slave clapped. "Hand of Fatima," he admonished them, pointing to Marin.

The women regarded the eunuch with confusion. The Hand of Fatima was an amulet, a talisman to ward off the evil eye and misfortune, not a person. One of them came forward to question the slave further. His reply brought gasps and loud murmurings. Five of the ladies pressed closer to look at the color of her eyes. When they fell back, a babble of voices broke out among them.

What had started out as a bit of chicanery to secure passage on a ship was no longer a joke. Marin was fully aware that her value and safety, as well as that of others, now depended upon the color of her eyes and her ability to deceive. And she was trying to figure the best response.

Should she pretend to invoke a protection shield over them as she had done with the crew of the *Sea Nymph*? It had worked with them because they had fancied that they had experienced her protection during the storm. But with these women, Marin sensed an ambivalence, a feeling of distrust prompted by jealousy. If any of the concubines made the determination that she had fallen victim to misfortune—however loosely defined—in spite of the shield, Marin could find herself in grave danger. She was under no illusions that she had yet to prove herself to the dey.

The women watched curiously as Marin stripped down to her shift, stepped into the pool of warm water, and walked over to Mrs. Marsden. She placed one hand on Mrs. Marsden's head and one on the boy's head as though to bless them. The woman had no idea what was occurring, and she started to shrink away, drawing the boy to her.

"Do not be afraid," said Marin in a low, quiet voice.

The little boy looked up at her and smiled. "She is an angel, Mama."

Her months in captivity had taught Mrs. Marsden all about palace intrigue, and she had learned to trust no one. Her policy was to never speak; her only goal was to keep her son by her side at all times. Luckily, young boys were allowed in the baths with their mothers until the age of seven.

"Who are you?" she asked fearfully.

"I am a friend," replied Marin.

Mrs. Marsden nervously observed the attention they were receiving from the concubines. "You must not show me favoritism," she said under her breath. "I am much resented by the others. Treachery abounds. They will take my son."

"Please do not worry yourself."

Marin turned to the other women and eyed each one of them, stopping for a moment longer to mark the leaders, then lifted her gaze to the heavens. The movement caused much disconcertion among the concubines. They didn't know if they were being blessed or cursed, and they grabbed their robes and ran from the hammam.

Marin smiled to herself and dipped down into the steam pool. When she was done, the slave motioned her to the cool water pool for refreshment. After a suitable amount of time in the latter pool, she gracefully stepped out of the water, whereupon the eunuch met her with a blue silk robe fit for the anointed. Marin slipped it on. The slave picked up her discarded gown and led her from the hammam.

Mrs. Marsden watched in wide-eyed astonishment. Who was this woman that she was treated with such high regard? Why did the concubines flee in fear of her? And was she really a friend?

* * * * *

The next morning, Marin was summoned to the dey's public room to find the ruler in the midst of an uproar. The concubines were present all trying to talk at once. When she entered, a hush fell over the room. The dey sat upon his chair unsure of how to react to the women's charges. He didn't want to upset his talisman; he didn't yet know the full power of her charm. But neither did he wish for his harem to be unhappy.

Cathcart walked in then, summoned to translate, and he looked at Marin questioningly. "You called for me, effendi?" he asked. "How may I be of service to you?"

The dey recounted the incident as told by the concubines and demanded to know the meaning of it.

Cathcart made the translation to Marin. "I hope you have a good answer," he added under his breath.

"It was the only way I could think of to talk with Mrs. Marsden," replied Marin.

"You shall have to do better, mistress. The concubines told him that you favored the woman with the boy. He fears you work to their benefit instead of his."

Marin's mind raced for a response. "Tell the dey that I must know wherein negative emotions and forces may lie as they restrict my ability to attract good fortune."

Cathcart regarded her with a measure of uncertainty before translating her answer to the ruler.

"The dey is not yet satisfied," Cathcart reported back. "He wants you to explain."

"Tell him that I was testing the woman and the boy," she said.

When Cathcart translated her answer to the dey, the ruler looked at him in alarm. "If the woman and the boy herald ill fortune, I shall send them to the interior," he said.

Cathcart quickly relayed this to Marin, fearing that she may have overplayed her hand.

Marin knew her own moment of ill ease as she again searched for an answer to satisfy the dey.

"Mr. Cathcart, please tell effendi that I sensed no ill winds surrounding the woman and the boy, only fear, which I can easily remedy with time in their presence. But tell him that I did feel much antipathy among the women of his harem—not directed at him, but directed at each other," she said, in an effort to divert the focus. "It must cease or the enmity shall most certainly obstruct my power to draw good fortune to the dey."

When Cathcart conveyed this to the dey, he stiffened and his features darkened as he passed an eye over his concubines. The women sucked in their breaths and quickly promised him that they would mend their ways.

Cathcart gave Marin a smile and a nod of acknowledgment. Her quick wit had not only brought the haughty concubines to heel, but it had also gained her unfettered access to Mrs. Marsden and her son.

Later that day, Cathcart went in search of Reese and found him in one of his taverns.

"The dey has commanded another audience with you," he informed Thackeray.

"To what end?"

"I cannot say."

"Mayhap he is accepting the proposal," surmised Reese.

"I would not presume so without you being put to further test," said Cathcart.

Reese was thoughtful for a moment. "Perhaps the delay shall work to my advantage. I have yet to figure a meeting with Mrs. Marsden."

"I dare say Mistress Marin is ahead of you."

Reese sighed heavily. "What has she done now?"

Cathcart told Reese what had transpired at the women's hammam and of Marin's quick-witted response when called to account by the dey.

"Word has spread of her status so that the guards give her a wide berth for fear she might sense an aura of negativity about them. I dare say we are fortunate to have her on our side. She is a clever lady." Cathcart chuckled. "She had the harem in quite an uproar."

"I can well imagine," replied Reese, not so amused. "She knows not the word 'subtle.'"

Cathcart chuckled again. "In any case, she now freely roams the palace, but she is not permitted to leave the grounds as long as you remain in port."

Reese frowned. It would make his job more difficult, but it was as he would have expected. "Marin is well then?"

"Quite, but I fear she soon will be in need of a deed to prove her power. Everyone in the palace resents her because of the influence she has over the dey, yet they are too afraid to plot against her. They will be looking for any sign they can point to that may show her to be a trickster."

"We must prod the dey to accept the proposal then, so that I can go back and forth to the ship to lay plans and so my crew can come ashore for supplies," said Reese.

"Have you a plan?"

"'Tis coming. Have you taken word to my brother to come to the tavern?"

"I have. I did not tell him that it is you he comes to meet."

Reese nodded. In their youth, they were both known to be quite reckless. How deliberative was Peter now? he wondered. "James, I have not seen my brother in five years. What manner of man is he?"

"By all accounts, he comports himself well and is a man of integrity," replied Cathcart. "Captain O'Bryen has taken him under his wing." Cathcart paused with a sudden thought. "It occurs to me that, after seeing the both of you, there is much physical resemblance. You must avoid being seen together."

A group of soldiers swaggered into the tavern, then, demanding food.

Cathcart made a face of disgust. "Janissaries."

"Ahmet is among them," observed Reese, pulling the hood over his head.

"Bloody hell," murmured Cathcart. "He is coming this way. Let me handle this."

The soldier stopped at the table and picked up Reese's plate of food and began eating it, deliberately trying to provoke a challenge, but Reese kept his head down.

"Who is your friend, Cathcart?" he inquired in Turkish.

"A friend, Captain."

The soldier glanced at Reese closer. "This is the pirate who brought insult to the dey. You welcome a dog to your tavern in friendship?" he questioned angrily.

"He is a man with whom the dey seeks to do business," Cathcart responded levelly.

"What kind of business?"

"That is for the dey to say, but 'tis important enough for the dey to make him my guest. Go on your way, sir."

The soldier wavered. As the dey's Chief Clerk and Regency of Algiers, Cathcart had a protected status. Ahmet grunted, dropped the plate on the table, and returned to his group.

"The bloody bastards," muttered Cathcart. "Keep a wide berth, Captain. They are as hated and feared by the townspeople as the lisberos. They do what they want and take whatever they like, of which women are no exclusion. They walk into houses and strut around the markets stealing at will. In their hearts, the Moors are kind, honest people. It is the lisberos and these soldiers who encourage their jealousies and back biting."

Reese noticed Ahmet's eyes on him. He had obviously aroused the man's curiosity.

After leaving Cathcart, Reese went back to the house and changed into the clothes of the upper class. He spent the day familiarizing himself with the area, walking the warren of streets that wound between the mud-brick and stucco houses and often ended in steep stairways; and he followed the twisting alleys crowded with cafes, shops, and market stalls that intersected with the Souk el-Kebir. Small houses with shops built into vestibules lined the Souk el-Kebir. The street was so narrow that in some places roofs overhung the road.

Reese returned to Cathcart's house and exchanged the silk clothes for the dress of the common people—linen pantaloons and shirt and a loose, white hooded jacket—and followed the Souk el-Kebir to a street that led to the port.

Here, he watched the activity and observed the points of congestion around the wharf, making a mental note of the time of day. The lisberos were easy to spot, and he was careful to avoid their notice.

Late in the afternoon, Thackeray pulled the hood over his head and casually made his way back to Cathcart's tavern.

An hour later, a man entered the establishment. He was close to the same height and build and possessed the same dark good looks and blue eyes as Reese, but he was clean shaven, thinner and bore the wearied look of one losing hope.

As instructed, the young man casually made his way to a table in a darkened corner and sat down on a cushion next to the other occupant. When Reese shoved back his hood, his brother smiled, the strain in his face relaxing.

"It is good to see you," said Peter. "I knew you would come whatever the story put around. Mrs. Marsden aside, I would not have faulted you if you hadn't. I have a better idea now of what you endured, though I have been fortunate enough not to experience it." His features hardened. "I have seen men bastinadoed half to death over the most ridiculously imagined infractions."

"Mrs. Marsden aside, nothing would have kept me from knowing the truth of your circumstance. It has been too long, Peter," said Reese, his voice gruff with emotion. Mindful of the lisberos and customs, it was all he could do to restrain himself from clasping his brother to him in a more heartfelt greeting.

Peter surreptitiously glanced around the tavern. "It is dangerous for you to be here, Reese. The brother of that soldier you killed—"

"I know about Ahmet," said Reese. "Have you crossed paths with him?"

"A few times after I was brought here."

"Has he made the connection?"

"My name seemed to bear no recognition for him. But it was clear that I reminded him of someone. You are well served by the beard, I dare say." Peter gave a humorless laugh. "Such tricks we once played using our likeness to advantage."

Reese saw the irony in it as well. That same similarity now played to their detriment. "We must keep a distance between us and avoid Ahmet, Peter. I cannot have the Janissary's memory jogged at this point. Henceforth, all communications must come through Cathcart."

Peter nodded. "How do you come by the dey's protection?"

Over wine and a meal of boiled mutton and couscous, Reese explained about Marin, the circumstances of the audience with the dey, and the proposal he had presented to the ruler.

"'Tis bold," remarked Peter with admiration. "There was much talk among the servants in the palace about a pirate sailing into port and challenging the dey. I should have known it was you. Do you think the dey will accept your proposal?"

"Though he is reputed to be more reasonable, his greed is just as voracious as the one he succeeds. He will accept," replied Reese.

"Have a care. These bastards are not to be trusted." Peter eyed his older brother curiously. "Tell me more about Mistress Marin. She sounds intriguing and seems to have caught your interest."

"'Tis not an interest that brings good humor," returned Reese shortly. "She upends my plans at every opportunity with her proclivity to act with no reasonable thought put to it."

Peter smiled with amusement. "I must meet this woman who can visit such disorder upon my brother."

Reese snorted. "I would have a care with that desire."

"In any case, it would appear that the lady's ingenuity has brought her a presence in the seraglio and access to those of interest," noted Peter. "How else might you have accomplished the task?"

"Let us hope it is to a deliberative end," replied Reese. "With that woman, one never knows."

Peter chuckled. "Methinks thou doth protest too much, brother." He sobered then. "I know the priority of your mission, Reese, and I shall work to that end. If I am not able to leave with you, I will survive. The lot of an officer is not so dire. I am sure you heard that I am captain now by virtue of attrition. That bloody plague has wiped out most of the crew of the *Neptune*."

Reese looked at his brother. "I have two missions, Peter—one is the government's; the other is mine. Upon my word, we shall leave this place together."

CHAPTER TWENTY-FIVE

A Fight to the Death

Cathcart had been gently and diplomatically pushing the dey to accept Reese's proposal. But the next afternoon when Reese was called to appear before the ruler, the Chief Clerk felt a measure of ill ease. The dey was in a prickly mood, and, as capricious as the ruler could be, that was when he was the most dangerous.

"Tread lightly," warned Cathcart. "He has something up his sleeve. While he favors your proposal, he is still angered by your audacity."

"I had to get his attention," said Reese.

"I dare say you got it. While effendi admires strength and cunning, he does not like it waged against him."

The dey motioned for Cathcart and spoke to him. At that moment, an Algerine man was led into the room by a guard. Reese instantly recognized him as the captain of the pirate ship he had captured. The man approached the dey, bowed, and kissed his hand. When he stepped back, he glowered at Thackeray.

Cathcart returned to Reese. "Effendi says the captain seeks to restore his honor. You are to fight this afternoon in the courtyard outside the east wing of the palace. Do not dispatch your opponent too quickly. Effendi seeks to see you taken down a peg or two."

Reese glanced over at the pirate. "Have no worry on that score," he remarked dryly. "Though less in stature, the man is young, well-muscled, and fit."

"Add to that, he is fighting for his life."

Reese looked at Cathcart sharply. "'Tis a fight to the death?"

Cathcart nodded. "If he does not kill you, the dey will have him put to death for losing his honor yet a second time. There is no greater crime here for a man than to be shamed. Of course, there is also the risk that the dey will not spare him anyway if, by his killing you, effendi decides that it has cost him too great a financial reward."

"Bloody hell," murmured Reese, trying to follow the labyrinth of the dey's mind. "So in winning, one still loses."

Cathcart smiled. "Such is the paradox of life here, my friend. Watch your back. It will not be a fair fight. The dey wants to see how much, if any, good fortune graces you."

"So I am to take enough blows to appease the dey's ego, but not so many as to make it appear that fortune does not smile upon me. I shall try to remember that as I fight for my life," quipped Reese humorlessly. "If I prevail, what then is to be my reward?"

"The dey will agree to your proposal."

"What are the rules?"

Cathcart looked at him. "There are none. Do not mistake your opponent for a man of honor, Reese. He will not hesitate to strike the fatal blow however way he can. Neither must you."

Marin ran down the corridor to the courtyard, the sun high in the sky. She could hear the cheering of the soldiers as she neared. At the opening to the courtyard, she saw the dey's clerk and called out to him.

Cathcart turned, surprised to see her. "Mistress Marin, what are you doing here?"

"I heard about the fight."

"Do not go out there, Mistress. Women do not attend such events."

"I am not just any woman, Mr. Cathcart."

"I am inclined to agree with you, madam. But you will incur the displeasure of the dey and may be a source of distraction for the captain when most he needs to stay focused. 'Tis a fight to the death."

Marin looked at him, horrified. "You must stop it."

"I cannot."

"Then I will. I will speak with the dey. I shall tell him that the captain is tied to his good fortune."

"In which case, the dey will expect the captain to prevail," said Cathcart. "Do not you see, Mistress? This is a test of not only the captain but also of you."

The air went out of Marin. "This is all my fault. The captain is right. I act without thought to the consequences. And now, he may pay the price and the mission will fail." She looked at the dey's clerk with tears in her eyes. "What have I wrought?"

Cathcart gave her a sympathetic smile. "You must not be so hard on yourself, Mistress. I dare say the captain overstepped himself as well. Take heart. All is not lost until it is, and Captain Thackeray is a resourceful man. Return to your apartment. I will send word when all is done."

"Please, sir," pleaded Marin, "I cannot leave until I know that the captain has prevailed and is not seriously injured."

Cathcart hesitated for a moment. "There is a balcony from which you can observe. But if you avail yourself of it, you must do nothing that brings notice of you—whatever happens," he counseled her sternly. "Or all shall be surely lost."

Marin nodded. "I will be most discreet. My thanks to you, sir."

The combatants were already engaged when Marin reached the balcony.

Reese had allowed the captain to get in a few punches, mindful of Cathcart's warning. He had a bruise on his cheek and a cut above his eye before he began to fight back, landing some punishing blows. When his opponent finally stumbled, Reese saw Ahmet hand a knife to the Algerine captain. When no one offered him a weapon, Reese immediately understood what Cathcart meant when he said that it would not be a fair fight.

A grin stretched across the pirate's face as he slowly advanced on Thackeray, waving the weapon. He jabbed at Reese, but Reese quickly sidestepped him and shoved him from the back to throw him off balance. The corsair turned and lunged again, and the blade sliced into Reese's upper left arm.

Watching from above, Marin clamped a hand over her mouth to keep from crying out when she saw blood staining his sleeve.

Reese winced and staggered. The pirate captain threw dirt in his face to further disorient him and, as he came at Thackeray again with the knife raised to stab him in the chest, it was all Marin could do to keep from shouting out a warning.

Reese wiped his eyes and recovered just in time to deflect the man's arm, and the two fell grappling on the ground. Hampered by his injury, he lost momentum enough to give the pirate the advantage, and the pirate was poised to plunge the knife into Reese's heart, when Reese sent a fist crashing into the man's jaw, knocking him backwards. The men quickly scrambled to their feet.

Marin anxiously clasped her hands together and bit her lip.

"Worry not. Reese is no stranger to fights," said a male voice behind her.

Marin started and quickly turned to see a tall, young man.

He came to stand beside her and gazed down into the courtyard. "Reese will prevail."

"I fear you may be over confident," said Marin. "Pirates are no stranger to fights either, and Reese is bleeding. He will lose strength sooner."

"'Tis a flesh wound perhaps requiring some stitching. I would venture to say he no longer feels it. His opponent is still at a greater disadvantage."

Marin looked at the man as though he were crazy. "How can you say that? The captain is wounded and the Algerine has the knife."

"The corsair also has a weakness in his right shoulder—probably from an old injury—that Reese has noticed and is exploiting. Luckily, it is his dominant side."

"How do you know?"

"See how the pirate captain favors it now? He is losing strength and mobility the more Reese forces him to jab. I dare say the man is feeling the pain of it. Soon, he will have to switch the knife to his left hand with which he has less force and accuracy."

Marin saw that the man was right when a short time later the pirate switched hands, but still the brutal fight continued.

Reese grabbed the man's wrist, the knife inches from his chest again, and for a long hair-raising, nail-biting minute, both struggled to get the upper hand. In a final match of strength, Reese turned the knife to plunge it into the pirate's heart. Blood spurted out, and the man staggered for a few moments before dropping to the ground.

There was no cheering for the victorious American; just shocked silence among the observers. The dey nodded and left the dais to return inside the palace. It was difficult to know if he was pleased or not.

Reese was bloodied, his eye swollen, and he swayed from exhaustion and loss of blood as the adrenalin ebbed from his body. Cathcart came forward to help him inside the palace.

Marin wanted to go to Reese to be certain that he wasn't seriously injured, but, for once, she thought through her impulse and realized that it would be detrimental to both of them. He was in good hands with Cathcart.

She turned her attention to the young man standing beside her and saw the resemblance now. He was thinner than the captain, but he had the same dark hair and similarly handsome features.

"You are Peter Thackeray," she said.

"And you are the infamous Mistress Marin."

"Why do people always say that?" she grumbled. "How do you know me?"

"Aside from the fact that you are the talk of the palace, my brother was quite descriptive of you."

"Oh. Well, I can quite imagine the captain's comments," she responded dryly.

Peter smiled. "He neglected to say how comely you are. You must have indeed ruffled his feathers."

Marin snorted. "'Tis not difficult. The man is as prickly as a hawthorn bush, not to mention insufferably—" she stopped. "Your pardon, sir. I speak of your brother."

Peter grinned. "I have heard women speak worse of him."

"Humph. I am not surprised. When did you see the captain?"

"Cathcart managed a meeting between us," replied Peter. "I dare say that seeing him was a balm for my tried soul."

Marin hesitated. "Mr. Thackeray, have you…have you knowledge of a prisoner named Nathaniel Sutton…of the ship *Clarabell*? He was an officer like yourself."

Peter shook his head. "I regret to say that I have not. Reese told me your story. Every year, the plague runs through the city. It was especially bad this year. The captain, second mate, and most of the crewmen from my own ship have perished. I am very sorry to say that it is more than likely that your husband succumbed to the disease as well at some point. But perhaps you can take comfort that, as an officer, he was treated much better than his crew."

Marin smiled half-heartedly. "Yes…thank you."

She knew he meant well, but she was tired of being given this assurance. If she heard it one more time or was told about the plague again, she would scream. In the absence of concrete information, it felt like a pat on the head, a patronizing nod to a foolish woman in a vain search for her husband.

There suddenly came the sound of guards coming down the corridor, and Peter pulled her into a dark corner behind a column until they passed.

"We should not be seen together," he said. "Take that corridor. It leads to the women's quarters. If you are challenged, say you became lost. It is easy to do in this place."

Marin nodded. When she looked again, Peter had already slipped away.

CHAPTER TWENTY-SIX

Running Out of Time

Reese came awake and looked around him in confusion for a moment before realizing that he was in Cathcart's house.

"Good. You are awake now," said Cathcart entering the room. "How are you feeling?"

"Like I was keelhauled." Everything hurt from his jaw to his ribs. His shirt had been removed and Reese looked at his bandaged arm in surprise before remembering the knife wound. "How long was I asleep?"

For the better part of a day. The physician to the dey tended you and gave you a powder."

"I remember. How does Marin fare?"

"She was quite beset with worry about you. She had wanted to prevail upon the dey to cancel the fight when first she heard of the challenge."

Reese winced as he raised himself up on one arm in alarm. "You did not let her, did you?"

"I convinced her of the merits of not interfering in the matter, though I believe she was at great pains to heed it. She watched the fight from afar."

Reese lay back on the bed. "She shouldn't have. Already, she was witness to a bloody battle with the dey's pirates, the sight of which she cannot forget. Could you not keep her from it?"

"Could you not keep her from your ship?" countered Cathcart.

Thackeray sighed resignedly. "Point taken. Just the same, keep a close eye on her, James. One can never be sure of what she may do."

"So far she has played her hand well."

"Do not be lulled," warned Reese.

"I bow to your experience, sir," said Cathcart, suppressing a chuckle. "If you are up to it, Captain, I bid you come to the apartment for supper this night. We have much to discuss. The dey has accepted your proposal. He is giving you a week to refit and provision your ship."

Reese nodded. "I shall be present."

"Then, I will leave you to your rest now." Cathcart started to leave when he turned back with an afterthought. "By the way, I would keep a wider berth from Ahmet if I were you. You turned his knife on your opponent."

Reese groaned. "Do not tell me he would seek to avenge his honor as well."

Cathcart smiled. "Not as yet. But his dislike of you is tenfold now."

Thackeray took supper with Cathcart sitting on the sofa. Negotiating the stairs from his second floor apartment had been difficult enough with his bruised ribs. Assuming the position on the floor was out of the question. Afterwards, he and Cathcart discussed strategy quietly and in darkness. Cathcart's trusted manservant Kendzu kept watch for any lisberos lurking about.

"If 'our people' can get safely to the harbor, members of my crew can be waiting beneath the quay to row them back to the ship under cover of darkness," said Reese.

"They won't be able to get through to the wharf then. The city gates close at sunset," Cathcart reminded him.

Of course. He knew that! Reese put a hand to his forehead and closed his eyes for a moment to clear his mind. He had to stay sharp. He winced with pain as he shifted his weight on the sofa.

"You took quite a beating," said Cathcart watching him closely. "You need more rest. Perhaps we should take up this matter in the morning."

"No," said Reese. "We have not the luxury of time. What about bribing the guards?"

"They will take your money, but you cannot trust them. They know the dey will have their heads if they allow the gate to be breached," replied Cathcart.

"Then everyone will have to be in place just before sunset."

"Marin is forbidden to leave the palace, and Mrs. Marsden and her son are forbidden to leave the women's quarters. How do you propose that we get them to the harbor?"

"I shall have to figure that later," said Reese.

"Assuming that you can get them there, how are they to get past the guards at the gate?" asked Cathcart.

Thackeray thought for a moment. "A diversion will have to be created to draw the guards away before they can seal the city."

"I shall leave that to you, Captain. In any case, I would say you would do better to direct everyone to the Bab el-Hout gate. It opens to the mole on the east and is accessed from a secondary road off the main road," said Cathcart. "It is used by fishermen and local traders. It would be easy for Peter, Marin, and Mrs. Marsden and the boy to become lost among them."

"I remember the gate," said Reese. "The fishermen pull their boats up on a sandy shore. I can make use of one of the boats to transport everyone to the ship."

Cathcart shook his head. "You shall have to make other arrangements. Prisoners attempted an escape once by rowing a fishing boat to a departing ship. After that, an ordinance was passed that fishermen must remove their oars when they leave their boats."

Reese gave an impatient sigh, tired of being stymied at every turn. "My crew shall have to have the jolly boat waiting then. I have been observing the fortifications," he said, moving on. "The castle of Sardinia and the castle of the lantern have two and three tiers of cannon respectively. I know that Barbary pirates are not adept at handling cannons on ships. How are the guards on land?"

Cathcart laughed. "Not much better. Most of the cannons were taken from the Tunisians in 1617. The lower tier at the castle of the Lantern has 32 pounders, but they are not kept in preparation for defense. The compartments are full of lumber, ships' stores, and pirates' cargo instead of supplies of powder. The powder was moved away from the wharf after your escape. An enemy could destroy the city before the guards could bring those cannons into play.

"But beware," he cautioned. "There is another battery of some 80 cannons that are kept at the ready—12, 18, and 36 pounders pointing from north to south at the entrance to the harbor on the other side of the mole."

They talked long into the night. Slowly, a plan began to form, and the next day Reese returned to his ship.

* * * * *

Thackeray and his officers immediately began their preparations. Each man had his task.

For the next two days, bosun Andrew White surveyed the ship with a sharp eye making sure all the rigging and sails were in good order and all other necessary repairs were made. First mate Alex Seaton marked the winds. Ferguson looked after the cannons and powder, continuing to drill his men on the procedure. Reese, Duncan, Pots, and a green sailor the cook had tapped to be his aide rowed ashore.

While the cook and his helper went to the markets to collect stores of food and drink, Reese took Duncan to the wharf to familiarize him with the plan and the avenue of escape. Just before sunset, they rowed back to the ship with Reese and Duncan marking the traffic at Bab el-Hout or Fisher's gate, as the prisoner's had come to know it, and the moment at which the gates were closed.

Reese also kept track of the number of Algerine ships tied up at the wharf. Of the six ships from the day before, four remained. Thackeray hoped that one or two more might depart before he had to put the plan into operation in case they gave chase. One problem that continued to bedevil him was how to get Marin, Mrs. Marsden, and the boy out of the palace and to the gate.

The third day rolled around with still no answer.

"You need to rest…give your body time to heal from that fight," Pennyman admonished him, rebandaging Reese's arm. "There is still the danger of infection from the knife wound."

Thackeray winced when the doctor examined his ribs. "Did Duncan set you upon me?" he quizzed shortly.

"He is worried," replied Pennyman. "He said you have been in much discomfort on your forays. You should not be going into Algiers today."

Reese snorted. "Timothy is given to exaggeration, and I have a troublesome detail to attend with very little time left to me. I am well enough."

As Thackeray painfully moved off the table and struggled to put on his shirt, the doctor regarded him skeptically. "You need to rest," he repeated. "The solution to your problem is not going to show itself to a mind clouded with pain, and you are only delaying the healing process."

"I will rest tonight," said Reese.

Pennyman shook his head at his patient's stubbornness and helped Thackeray put on his shirt. "Timothy said he is not accompanying you today," he remarked.

"I have another chore for him to do."

"Is a crewman to row you ashore then?"

"Everyone has a task, William."

"Damn it, man!" thundered the doctor. "If I must, I shall row you myself. I know when someone is pushing the limits, and I give you warning, Captain. Your strength will not hold when most you need it."

Reese heaved a sigh of annoyance. "All right. If it will silence your wagging tongue, I shall press a crewman into service."

Under Pennyman's watchful eye, Thackeray commandeered Pot's helper to row him across the harbor.

When Reese was put ashore, he cut through alleyways to the Souk el-Kebir. As he walked through the bazaar, he was conscious of a young girl watching him from the doorway of the shop in her house. He had noticed her interest in him before when he passed by, but he had chalked it up to Cathcart's warning that the Moorish women were drawn to Christian men. Ever conscious of the lisberos lurking around every corner, he didn't engage her and kept his distance.

He heard a commotion then. Soldiers on horseback came galloping down the narrow street, and people screamed and scurried to get out of their way, pressing themselves against the side of buildings to provide the soldiers room enough to pass.

The soldiers led by Ahmet reined in their horses, dismounted, and began to plunder the stalls. Reese casually turned to move away, but Ahmet spotted him and yelled to him.

Reese stopped and waited as the brutish man approached. The soldier said something in Turkish. When Reese shook his head and shrugged to indicate that he didn't understand, animosity emanated from the Janissary's gaze, intensified by his inability to question or to goad Reese with disparaging remarks.

The Turk suddenly furrowed his brow with a nagging sense that he had met this American before. Unable to recall such a meeting, he roughly pushed Thackeray aside. Reese winced with pain, catching himself, and stared after the Janissary as he moved on. Thackeray frowned. He had seen the elusive recognition on Ahmet's face. It was only a matter of time before the man placed him.

CHAPTER TWENTY-SEVEN

Renegade

Marin was climbing the stairs to the seraglio, when a group of men spilled into the courtyard from the public room where day-to-day business was conducted. She glanced down at them and froze for a moment, then ran back down the stairs to the courtyard as the men were exiting the compound.

He looked different dressed in native garb. He had a bushy moustache that extended long on the sides, and she could see that his head was shaved in spite of the turban, but Marin was certain it was him.

"Nathaniel!" she called out. "Nathaniel!"

The man in question stopped and glanced back at her for a second, then continued on.

Marin ran to the vaulted entrance but was barred by the guards. "Let me pass!" she shouted, struggling to get past them. "Let me pass!"

Cathcart came upon the commotion and hurried over to the guards. He said something in Turkish, then took Marin by the arm and led her away. "Do not make a fuss," he warned when she started to balk.

When they were in the privacy of the corridor that led to the garden, he unhanded her.

"Why did the guards stop me?" she angrily demanded to know.

"The dey has given them orders that you are not to leave the palace until after the *Sea Nymph* sails."

Marin looked at Cathcart in alarm. "Why?"

"The dey fears that the American pirate captain will try to kidnap you."

"How am I to leave here then?"

"It does make matters difficult," admitted Cathcart. "The captain is putting his mind to it."

Marin sighed dismally. "I fear the captain has the fate of too many people resting upon his shoulders."

The clerk gave her a smile of reassurance. "His shoulders are broad. He will find a way. Why were you so determined to leave the palace?"

"Mr. Cathcart, those men who just left…I think one of them was my husband."

Cathcart started to laugh and caught himself. "Your pardon, Mistress Marin, I do not mean to discount you on a matter of such importance to you, but it is highly unlikely that your husband would be among that group."

"How can you know?" asked Marin.

"They are corsairs, Mistress. They just sailed a Russian ship into the harbor loaded with furs and another crew of prisoners."

Marin's shoulders drooped. She could have sworn that she had detected a flicker of recognition in that man's eyes when he saw her, but Nathaniel most certainly was not a corsair.

Cathcart took her hand and patted it comfortingly. "I will continue to inquire after your husband," he promised.

The next afternoon, Cathcart went looking for Reese. It was an hour before he spotted Thackeray at the wharf. "Come to the tavern," he said in passing.

Reese nodded, his brow furrowing with concern. Something must have happened. He quickly finished his transaction and made his way to the tavern. Once inside, he went to the usual table in the corner and ordered food and drink. Cathcart arrived soon after and joined him.

"What's amiss?" asked Thackeray anxiously.

"You must get Mistress Marin out of Algiers sooner than you might be planning," said Cathcart.

"Why? What has happened? Is she in danger?"

"Possibly. I found out something about her husband."

Thackeray looked at him in surprise. "How when no one else has met with any success?"

"She thought she saw him yesterday at the palace with a group of men come to make an accounting to the dey. It made me wonder about something—"

"Bloody hell, James, is Nathaniel Sutton dead or does he live?"

"He lives."

Reese looked away not sure how he felt about the news. "Did you tell Marin?"

"No."

"Why not?"

"He is the captain that brought in the Russian ship."

Thackeray swung an incredulous gaze on Cathcart. "Sutton is a corsair?"

Cathcart nodded.

"How? He is a prisoner, a Christian, worse yet an American—the three most despicable traits in the eyes of the Turks," said Reese.

"The man is a renegade."

"What is that?"

"A Christian who becomes a Musselman," explained Cathcart. "As the story goes, Marin's husband was caught in a Moorish woman's bed, which, if you remember, carries the penalty of death unless the culprit denies his Christian faith and embraces the Muslim faith. He goes by the name Abdul Azeez now, 'servant of the most powerful.'"

Thackeray ran a hand across his beard trying to figure all the problems that could come from this development. "No wonder Marin could gather no news of him. Did he see her?"

"Yes, and he knows that she saw him," replied Cathcart. "There is no telling what course of action he may take." Cathcart paused. "There is more, Captain."

Reese sighed heavily. "What more, pray tell, could there be?"

"Sutton is married to the Moorish woman."

The news landed with a thud. "Are you certain?" asked Thackeray dumbfounded.

"Quite. Should I tell Mistress Marin about her husband?"

"No. She will insist upon confronting him, and it could imperil the mission."

Cathcart nodded. "I have convinced her for now that the man she saw was not her husband, but if she has another encounter with him, I know not what will happen."

"You shall have to be vigilant that she does not have another sighting until all is made ready to leave," said Thackeray.

"How soon will that be, Captain? Do you have a plan to get everyone to the gate?"

"Nothing has presented itself as yet," admitted Reese. "But even were there a plan, the winds have not favored us. I can do nothing until they do. In the meantime, you must keep an eye on Sutton that he does not get in our way."

"With the bounty of the Russian ship, Marin remains in high favor with the dey. I should not think that her husband would dare to compromise her," remarked Cathcart.

"Maybe not, but he will try to find a way to use her to advantage himself. I have it on good authority that Sutton is a conniver."

Cathcart sighed. "I fear you swim against the tide, my friend. I pray your stroke is strong."

Thackeray left the tavern in a heavy mood. With the added variable of Nathaniel Sutton, time had just run out.

He was walking up the Souk el-Kebrik when soldiers on horses came barreling down the narrow road again. It seemed to be a frequent occurrence. At the head was Ahmet wielding a club at anyone too slow to clear his path.

Reese was looking for a place to escape the cruel Turk's notice, when he felt a tug on his arm. He looked down to see a young woman 17 or 18 years of age, pretty, with dark hair and dark eyes. It was the girl who had watched him with such interest when he passed by her shop.

She spoke in the common Algerine dialect—the combination of French, Spanish, Italian and Portuguese. But he understood her well enough to know that she was directing him to come into her shop. He hesitated before deciding that Ahmet posed more of a danger to him than did the lisberos and this young girl at the moment, and he ducked inside the building just as the soldiers rode by. The Janissaries didn't go far before they dismounted and began to rifle through merchants' wares.

The girl directed Reese to the stairs.

Again, Thackeray hesitated. Was she inviting him to take part in a sexual encounter? She saw his reluctance and shook her head, guessing the nature of his ill ease.

"Roof," she said.

Reese could hear the soldiers moving closer, and he quickly followed her up the stone steps to the terrace-like roof. As she led him across the terraces of other houses, he realized that the flat roofs actually provided a walkway, an alternative to the road. The two-foot high wall served to protect walkers from falling off.

Reese was wondering how they were to descend, when she stopped at a dwelling and called down below. He understood that she was asking permission to enter the house. A woman's voice answered, and the young girl descended the stairs, waving for him to follow her.

Downstairs an older woman regarded him curiously as the girl led him through the room and outside to the street well ahead of the soldiers. He saw that he had only to cross to another street and follow it to Cathcart's harah or neighborhood.

Reese turned to thank her, but she had disappeared inside the house. His brow furrowed in perplexity. She had known that he was in danger and had led him to safety. Why had she helped him? Why had the older woman regarded him so strangely? He didn't have time to think about it. There was much to do. Thanks to this young woman, he now had a plan to get everyone to the gate—if the Algerine lass was willing to help him again.

He made his way to Cathcart's house and slipped inside to leave a message and instructions with the trusted manservant. When he left to return to his ship, he heard the Muezzin calling out the Adhan from the minaret summoning Musselmen to prayer.

CHAPTER TWENTY-EIGHT

Risks

Two days later, Thackeray awoke to find that the winds had finally changed in his favor. Cathcart had felt the change as well and watched for Reese's signal—the flash of a mirror. When it came, he quickly moved into action.

Thackeray called his officers together for a final review in his quarters. At the conclusion of the meeting, he looked around the table. "Everyone knows his task?"

The officers nodded soberly.

"In the event that things go awry tomorrow, you are to set sail and save yourselves," said Reese.

The plan was subject to failure on many levels—human error, weather, miscommunication—and the officers looked at each other.

"We ain't leavin' ye behind, Captain," declared White.

The others agreed.

Thackeray swept them with a steady gaze. "It is not up for debate, gentlemen. It is an order."

"But, Captain, much depends on the Algerine lass. How can ye be sure that she will ally herself with us?" asked Duncan.

"She helped me to escape the notice of Ahmet and the soldiers once before unbidden," replied Reese. "I believe she will be disposed to do so again when Cathcart approaches her."

"How so?" the second mate continued to question. "There is much peril to her."

"She will be well compensated…and the Algerines hate the soldiers, Timothy."

White shook his head, unconvinced. "Is that reason enough to trust her, Captain?"

"Do not underestimate the power of coin and retribution," said Reese. "Are they not why you risk all for this mission?"

"No, Captain— 'tis out of loyalty to you," replied Duncan.

As the others nodded, Reese was humbled and, again, passed an eye over his officers. "I do not make light of your allegiance, gentlemen. Indeed, I value it more than I can say. But even more do I value your lives and those of the rest of crew. The order still stands. Is that clear?"

Duncan, White, and Seaton regarded each other for a long moment before reluctantly agreeing.

Thackeray rowed ashore later that morning to set everything in motion. He entered the city through the trade and fishermen's gate and walked down the secondary road to the main street. Kendzu, Cathcart's servant, passed close to him and covertly slipped him a note. Reese gave a slight nod and continued on. When he was far enough away, he looked at the note. It was directing him to a new meeting place.

Reese made his way southwest to the Bab Azoun gate. Activity was brisk. It was the major marketplace for the sale of meat and olive oil and the industrial center of the city, where animals were butchered, hides were tanned, and fabrics were dyed. Traders from other regions gathered here to hawk their wares, and day laborers waited outside the city gate seeking employment.

Reese found Cathcart waiting for him near the inn. "Could you not have found a more disagreeable place to meet?" he questioned dryly.

Cathcart laughed. "It has its purpose. The dey's spies avoid it for the foul smells, and we are not likely to be noticed here among all the outsiders. When are you to sail?"

"Tomorrow," replied Reese. "Has the girl been approached?"

"Yes. She is eager to help," Cathcart assured him. "As luck would have it, her mother works in the palace and will also be of service to us."

"You are sure they can be trusted?"

Cathcart nodded. "The girl says she owes you a debt, and I can tell you Algerines always pay their debts."

Thackeray looked at him nonplussed. "What debt?"

Cathcart smiled. "You did not recognize her?"

"No. Why should I?"

"She is the little girl you saved from the tiger in the palace garden. She recognized you when she saw you pass through the market."

Reese was stunned. "It has been over 10 years."

"She remembered you."

"James, you must tell her that her debt was paid. It was her mother who had provided me access to the powder store that day."

"Her mother paid her debt to you, Captain. The child is now paying hers to you."

"Is it not the same debt?" asked Reese.

"No, not to them. I told you that the Algerines are, at heart, honorable people."

Reese was moved by the sentimentality. "We must take great care not to expose them."

"Women in this culture are very clever at not being seen when they do not wish to be," said Cathcart. "Godspeed, my friend."

"Thank you for your help, James. I shall see to it that the government does not forget you."

They clasped hands and departed for the last time.

Cathcart returned to the palace and encountered Marin on her way out to the garden.

"Mr. Cathcart, I have been looking for you," she cried. "The winds are changing—"

He put a finger to his lips and motioned her to a dark, isolated area of the corridor.

"Have you word from the captain?" she asked anxiously.

"I have. Be prepared to leave on the morrow."

Marin looked at him in surprise. "How?"

"The clothes of a fisherman and the robe and headscarf of a Musselman woman will be left for you and Mrs. Marsden. You are to dress in both in that order," instructed Cathcart. "When it is time, a servant woman will come for you and Mrs. Marsden and the boy, and you will all leave with the day servants from the city."

Cathcart paused to look around them to make sure they were not being overheard. "Stay with the servant woman. She will lead you safely to a city gate that opens to the harbor. There you will discard your robes and become local fishermen. The captain will be waiting outside the Bab el-Hout gate— 'tis the fishermen's gate—with a boat to row everyone out to the ship."

"Won't we be noticeable with the boy?" asked Marin.

"Servants often bring their children to play with the royal children, and he will be suitably attired."

"What about the guards outside the apartments?"

"They will be taken care of. Can you relay this information to Mrs. Marsden?"

Marin nodded. "I am sure to see her at the hammam. What about Peter?"

"I shall get word to him, and he will make his own way to the gate. Unfortunately, what is left of his crew will not be returned in time to their pens. I will look after them until they can be ransomed." He took her hand. "Farewell, dear lady. It has been my pleasure to know you. You truly are most clever."

Marin smiled. "'Tis high praise indeed from a man who raised himself up from prisoner to the Regent of Algiers and Clerk to the dey. May our paths cross again, Mr. Cathcart."

When Marin entered the hammam later that day, the animated chatter of the concubines ceased and an awkward tenseness invaded the chamber. They immediately became guarded and began to gather their robes and vacate the baths.

Over the past days, Marin had tried to gain Mrs. Marsden's trust, but the woman remained suspicious of her, fearing her to be a spy of the dey. With the concubines' hasty departure at Marin's entrance, Mrs. Marsden gathered her son and moved to leave as well.

"Mrs. Marsden, please wait," said Marin. As the woman shrank from her, Marin struggled to contain her frustration. "Please, Mrs. Marsden, you must trust me."

"Who are you? Why do the concubines fear you?" the woman asked warily.

"I do not have time to explain," replied Marin. "If you wish to leave here with your son, you shall have to trust me. Listen closely. I know not when we will be able to speak again. There are people here who will help you to escape this place."

Mrs. Marsden looked at her with a mixture of surprise and uncertainty. "When? How?"

Marin explained the plan. When the lady still appeared skeptical, Marin fixed an unwavering eye on her. "Mrs. Marsden, this is your one and only chance for freedom. There is no ransom coming. The dey has told the story that your ship was sunk in a storm and that all aboard perished."

Mrs. Marsden's wariness gave way to shock. "No—oh dear God, my poor husband. What must he be feeling?"

"The United States government knows the story to be false but cannot acknowledge it," said Marin.

"I do not understand."

"I shall explain later, but know this. To keep the truth from becoming known, it is feared that the dey may soon sell you and your son to a tribe of nomads in the interior."

Mrs. Marsden put a hand to her mouth, horrified. "What must I do?"

"Watch for instruction but have a care to raise no suspicion," said Marin. "Now take the boy and return to your apartment."

Mrs. Marsden nodded. She quickly gathered her son and left the hammam.

Marin spent much of the night in wakeful preparation and the next day in tense vigilance, her nerves strained, watchful of any sign lest she should miss it. The dey had summoned her, desiring to have her in his presence before entertaining trade negotiations with the French ambassador. The slave served coffee and brought in a tray of fruit and a bowl of figs. There was no translator; the dey seemed content with silence, and Marin was happy to oblige. When they had finished, the dey dismissed her with the wave of his hand.

Marin returned to her apartment and found a hijab—a head scarf—and robe on her bed. Folded up inside of them were the other articles of clothing. She quickly discarded her shift and dress and donned the male peasant costume of baggy linen drawers, shirt, and jacket, then pulled on the robe to cover them. Lastly, she tied back her hair and put on the head scarf. She hoped Mrs. Marsden was doing the same.

A glance out the window told her that it was a few hours before sunset. Cathcart had told her that everything was being planned around the closing of the gates. She paced the apartment, her nervousness increasing with the lengthening of the shadows.

At the sound of a loud thud outside, Marin ran to the door and opened it. She jumped aside as a large black man quickly dragged the unconscious guards inside. A woman dressed in a hijab and robe stood behind him and motioned for Marin to follow her. They moved down the gallery to Mrs. Marsden's apartment, where she and her son awaited them outside the door appropriately dressed in like fashion. The woman motioned for Marin and Mrs. Marsden to draw the veils across their faces and to follow her to the stairs.

As they descended to the courtyard, other servants from the city were departing, and they smoothly blended into the group. Mrs.

Marsden held on tightly to her son. Marin could see that the little boy was frightened but was putting on a brave front, and she took hold of his other hand and gave it a squeeze of reassurance. When they came to the exit, Marin held her breath and averted her eyes as they passed by the guards and through the vaulted arch, seemingly without notice.

They continued to follow the women across the square to the road. Dressed in robes and veiled head scarfs, one woman was indistinguishable from another, and Marin felt a wave of panic when she lost sight of her guide. She didn't know her way around the port city and had no idea where the fishermen's gate was. Not knowing what else to do, she continued to lead Mrs. Marsden and her son down the dusty, narrow street, frantically scanning the group for anyone who might stand out to her.

As they came closer to the wharf, women began to peel off and turn down side streets.

"Where are we to go?" whispered Mrs. Marsden.

Marin could hear the anxiety in Mrs. Marsden's voice and struggled to tamp down her own fears. Her pace slowed as she tried to figure out what to do. It was a frightening feeling to know that people were counting on her, and, for a moment, she considered the weight the captain carried on his shoulders. The crew depended upon him everyday at sea for their lives, and Mrs. Marsden and her son were depending upon her now for theirs.

She felt a nudge against her shoulder and glanced at the woman who had come up next to her. The woman inclined her head toward another side road and veered off in that direction.

Marin hesitated, plagued with indecision. She didn't know if it was the same woman who had led them out of the palace. Maybe the bump wasn't intentional and she was misinterpreting it as a signal, the woman's actions had been that subtle.

When the woman stopped and turned to them and again motioned with her head, Marin nudged Mrs. Marsden. "Follow her," she said.

They walked down alleyways to the Souk el-Kebrik, moving as quickly as they could without attracting attention. Here, the woman turned and led them down the twisting, winding market road that paralleled the port. She stopped in front of a house and waved everyone inside. The woman dropped the veil from her face, then, and Marin could see that she was younger than the woman who had led them out of the palace.

Suddenly, they heard the pounding of horses and men shouting at the women on the road.

"Soldats!" exclaimed the young woman.

She spoke in a curious dialect that Marin realized was a mixture of languages, and Marin was able to pick out the French words to gain enough of an understanding.

"Viens."

Marin nodded, and the young woman led her charges up the stairs to the terrace roof. They could hear the cries of women on the street below as soldiers tore off their veils.

"They are searching for us," said Marin. "They must have discovered that we are missing."

"Dear God in Heaven," murmured Mrs. Marsden, fearfully drawing her son closer.

"Par ici," said the young woman. "Vite!"

"She wants us to follow her," said Marin.

"Where?" asked Mrs. Marsden in alarm.

As did Reese, Marin saw that the flat roofs of the dwellings connected and understood that they acted as a foot path. "Across the roofs," she said.

They hurried after the young woman. She stopped at one of the houses and waved Marin, Mrs. Marsden, and the boy down the stairs. At the bottom, they encountered the older woman who had helped them to escape the palace.

"Mama, soldats," the younger woman whispered.

The older woman's brow creased with concern, and she looked at Marin and Mrs. Marsden and motioned for them to discard their robes and head scarfs. She then handed them low flat turbans. They put on the hats and stuffed their hair underneath.

The older woman fastened the veil across her face, opened the door, and cautiously peeked out. She motioned for Marin, Mrs. Marsden, and the little boy to follow her outside.

"Pas anglais," she warned, putting a finger to her lips.

"She is telling us not to speak," Marin whispered to Mrs. Marsden.

The woman walked ahead of them careful to keep just enough distance between them, and Marin realized that she didn't want to appear to be in their company. When they came to another road, the woman pointed to it and walked on.

Left on their own, Marin felt uneasy as they started down the road. She breathed easier when she saw the gate. Fishermen sat in rows selling their fish. Up ahead, she saw Peter. He saw them as well.

Then, someone else caught her eye.

Reese anxiously awaited everyone at the jolly boat. The melody of a flute began to signal curfew. They were running out of time.

When the little group finally appeared, he breathed a sigh of relief. He waved, and they hurried up to him.

"Where is Marin?" he asked tensely.

Peter looked around him. "She was behind us."

Reese uttered an oath. "Leave with the explosion even if I do not return," he ordered the oarsmen.

"But captain—"

"That is an order." Thackeray turned to his brother. "Make sure Mrs. Marsden and her son get to the ship."

Peter nodded, his brow furrowed in concern. "Have a care, Reese."

They clasped each other by the shoulders.

"I look forward to beating you in arm wrestling," added Peter.

Reese smiled. "Wishful thinking."

He set off then and disappeared through the gate.

Threading his way through the thinning crowd at the fish market, Reese searched for Marin. She was dressed to fit in with the common man on the street, and he was at a loss as to how to pick her out. He concentrated on men of her height looking for one with a more feminine walk.

The street and alleys were crowded with people returning to their harahs before the neighborhood gates were closed, and Marin hurried down the road along the wharf trying to catch up with the man ahead of her—the man she had seen at the palace. She was certain it was Nathaniel, and she couldn't leave Algiers without knowing for sure. The captain had his mission; she had hers.

Suddenly, there was an explosion. Soldiers came running from everywhere to the wharf. Minutes later, there came a second explosion and, shortly thereafter, a third and fourth. People screamed and began running. In the midst of the confusion, Marin felt someone grab her. She gasped and turned.

"Reese!" she exclaimed, surprised and relieved to see him. "What has happened?"

"'Tis our cue to get out of here," he said, his manner tense.

"I cannot leave yet. I am sure I saw Nathaniel. I have to know if it is him."

"There is no time for that. The boat is departing."

"Then leave me."

"Do not be ridiculous."

He took hold of her and pulled her toward the road to Fisher's gate. She resisted but was no match for his strength. The man she had been following turned and watched as Thackeray propelled her along with him.

They were nearing the gate, when a horse came thundering down the street to corral them. Ahmet jumped off and pulled a scimitar from his girdle. His features were arranged in a dark scowl, and Reese could see the blood lust in his eyes.

Reese pushed Marin aside and jumped out of the way as Ahmet lunged forward swinging the curved sword. The force of the lunge without making physical contact threw the Turk off balance for a moment. He turned, enraged, and prepared to charge again.

Reese cursed. He didn't have time for this, and his body was still recovering from the earlier fight with the corsair captain. He took out a concealed pistol and fired. Ahmet staggered, a look of surprise on his face, and fell to the ground. Marin stared at the lifeless body, shocked and paralyzed by the chaos around her.

Reese grabbed hold of her and forced her into a run with him down to the gate. The guards had been drawn away by the explosions, and the heavy doors stood half closed. Reese quickly pushed Marin through the opening and followed after her.

Peter came running to meet them. "Thank God. I feared you were not coming."

"We were confronted by Ahmet," said Reese.

"Ahmet—how did you escape?"

"I shot him."

"Dead?"

"I assume so. I did not stay around to check. Did the boat leave?"

"It did."

"Why the bloody hell are you still here?" questioned Reese angrily. "You had your orders."

"Your crewmen are quite capable of getting Mrs. Marsden and the boy to the ship, and I am not leaving my brother behind—orders be damned," retorted Peter. "We can take one of the fishing boats on shore."

"Look again," said Reese. "There are no oars. There is an ordinance against leaving them behind." He gazed across the harbor. "Our boat is about 30 feet offshore."

"It is not sitting still," pointed out Peter, following his train of thought.

"Aye, but we should be able to get close enough to get their attention. Come, our time is near passed," said Reese.

The men quickly stripped down to their breeches.

"What about Marin?" asked Peter.

Reese glanced at her. "Can you swim?"

Marin looked at him still in a daze. "What?"

"We're wasting time. Peter, grab hold."

Marin gasped as Reese and Peter hooked a hand under her arms and pulled her backwards into the water with them. The brothers were strong swimmers, having learned the necessity of it in their profession, and they swam on their sides towing Marin on her back between them. Flotsam from the explosions fell all around them; smoke filled the air.

They finally pulled within 10 feet of the jolly boat. With Reese holding Marin afloat, Peter shouted and waved. A crewman spotted them and brought the rowing to a halt. When the brothers swam up to the boat, one of the crewmen reached over the side to pull in a sputtering Marin. Reese and Peter climbed in beside her, taking a moment to catch their breaths.

"Captain, thank the stars," cried a sailor. "We wasn't keen to leave ye, but Mr. Peter said as how Mistress Marin would protect ye."

"You did right," replied Reese. "Now row. Peter, take up an oar."

Thackeray picked up another oar. Both men were tired from the swim, but their adrenalin had kicked into high gear, and they rowed hard along with the crew.

Having recovered her wits, Marin moved to sit beside Mrs. Marsden and her son, and they watched in awe as the wind picked up the flames and carried them to the buildings along the wharf, further adding to the pandemonium.

Crews of the foreign ships frantically sought to distance their ships. The corsairs desperately worked to save their plunder stored in the warehouses. The guards had their hands full with rebellious prisoners returning from their day of labor on the harbor who sought to take advantage of the chaos. In all the bedlam, only one man noticed the jolly boat skimming across the water to the American pirate ship.

When the boat came alongside the *Sea Nymph*, a crew was waiting. They dropped ropes over the side. The jolly boat crew quickly attached them, and the crew on deck hoisted the boat. When it came level, Seaton helped the boy and the women step onto the deck of the ship.

When Reese stepped out of the jolly boat, the first mate said, "You gave us quite a turn when we saw that you, Mistress Marin, and your brother had missed the boat, Captain. Then we saw you swimming for it. What happened?"

"I will explain later. Are Duncan and his men aboard?" asked Reese.

"Aye, that we are," answered Duncan, coming from the bow. "Ain't never rowed that dinghy so fast."

"Any injuries?"

"None. All went as planned. Providence was with us, Captain."

"Andrew, are the jolly boat and dinghy secured?" called out Reese.

"Aye, sir."

"On with it, then." Reese didn't have to issue the order twice. The crew executed their duties with practiced speed and precision. The sails were unfurled and the anchors lifted. In a short time, the wind launched them on their way.

As the ship sailed out of the marine, the last hurdle was the battery of cannon on the north end around the castle lantern. The shoals would force them within range of the big guns, which did have a store of gunpowder, and Reese held his breath as he trained his spyglass on the battery. But the guards posted there had no idea what had occasioned the blasts and assumed that the ship was leaving to escape damage, presenting no threat. Reese lowered the spyglass and smiled as the *Sea Nymph* glided unmolested from the harbor into the Mediterranean Sea.

Mrs. Marsden hugged her son and wept that her ordeal was over. "How can I ever thank you, Captain?" she asked, wiping tears from her eyes.

"No need, madam," replied Reese. He motioned for the bosun. "Mr. White will show you and your son to your quarters. You could probably do with some rest before dinner."

As the bosun led mother and son away, Peter walked up to him. "I echo Mrs. Marsden's sentiment. My thanks to you, brother. I was not relishing years of exile there. I have not Cathcart's cunning nor appreciation for the place."

"It cuts both ways, Peter. You have my gratitude as well for waiting behind, but, next time, follow my orders. I would not see your life forfeited over the folly of another. In any case, do not celebrate yet. We have no way of telling how many of the dey's ships were lost. There is the possibility that we still might be pursued."

Marin walked past then, dripping wet and bedraggled, on her way to her cabin, and shot Reese a withering glare.

"Uh oh. I suppose we should have given her fair warning before dragging her into the water," said Peter.

"She is angered on another matter," replied Reese.

Peter chuckled. "You do have a way with women. What offense did you commit this time?"

Reese glared at him. "How you presume, brother. The truth of the matter is that Marin had turned back at the gate to give chase to a man who bore likeness to her husband. Before she could make certain his identity, I caught up with her to force her back."

Peter sobered. "I sympathize with Marin, but I weigh on your side, brother. I shudder to ponder your fates had you and Marin been stranded in Algiers for the sake of a man who most likely is dead."

Reese was silent for a long moment. "She might not have been mistaken in her sighting," he said at length.

Peter regarded his brother with astonishment. "Sutton is alive?"

Reese nodded and relayed some of what Cathcart had discovered about Nathaniel Sutton, that he was a renegade and a corsair, omitting the rest of the story for the time being.

Peter shook his head in disbelief. "Did you tell Marin?"

"No. She would not have believed me, and I needed her to stay focused on the mission at hand. As it was, she jeopardized it twice when she thought she saw him."

"She has been looking for her husband for over three years, Reese. You need to tell her the truth."

"I will when the time is right."

Peter looked at his brother skeptically. "When will that be?"

"When she is too far away to do anything foolish," replied Reese. He clasped a hand on his brother's shoulder. "Come, let us to the task now of finding some clothes."

"Aye. Clad only in wet breeches, I fear we are a bit underdressed for the ladies."

After changing into dry clothes, Reese introduced his brother to his officers and left Peter swapping stories with them. Marin came on deck then and went to the bow to watch the waning sunset. Reese saw her and hesitated for a moment before following after her.

"Feeling better?" he asked, coming to stand beside her.

Marin didn't answer and continued to train her eyes on the distant horizon.

"How long will you continue to lay blame to me, madam?"

"Most likely forever, Captain."

"That is a long time," he quipped.

When Marin remained silent, Reese sighed resignedly. "What would you have had me do? Leave you behind to answer to the dey? How long do you think your tricks would have served you?"

She turned to him, her eyes flashing with anger. "I would have had you give me time to know if that man was Nathaniel."

"There was no time, Marin. We had already missed the boat. We were fortunate it was still within swimming distance."

She turned away from him. Rationally, she knew he was right; emotionally she couldn't embrace it. She had never been this close to resolution only to have it so rudely snatched away.

Reese studied her for a few moments. He was not going to get through to her this way, he decided, and took a different tact.

"Marin, the man you pursued this day and imagined to have been your husband on another day was a Musselman and a corsair. Can you conceive of your husband being either?"

It was a few minutes before she responded. "No, I cannot fathom how it could be the case," she grudgingly admitted.

"Then what more is to be said?"

When put to her this way, Marin felt a little foolish.

"If you are so inclined, perhaps you will favor us with your presence at supper at half past the hour," continued Reese. "Mrs. Marsden would most likely enjoy the company of another woman who has an understanding of her experience. In the meantime, remember that you still have a role to play with the sailors. Now is not the time to show displeasure with their captain."

Marin looked at him. "Perhaps I am tired of being an object of good fortune," she responded crisply.

Reese was unsympathetic. "You made your bed, madam."

As he walked away, Marin turned her gaze back to the sea. However much it rankled, the captain was right. Her job wasn't done, and, at the very least, Mrs. Marsden didn't deserve to be caught in the middle of another conflict.

Marin forced herself to a more amicable mood and presented herself at the captain's quarters for supper, a shade late as usual. Peter, Mrs. Marsden and her son were already seated. Reese rose from the table and guided her to her usual chair to his left.

The cook and his helper bustled in with trays of food and laid out tantalizing dishes of fruits and vegetables. When Pots set down a platter of fresh fish before them, he winked at Marin. Thackeray shot her a warning glance when he heard her snicker.

"We can serve ourselves, Mr. Potter," said Reese.

"Very good, sir. May I say, sir, 'tis happy we all are to have Mistress Marin back in our midst again. We was sorely missin' ye, Mistress. Had a bit of the bad luck we did. Tyler had the runs and Green hurt his leg and—"

"I believe we get the idea, Mr. Potter," interrupted Reese.

"Aye, sir."

"Thank you, Mr. Potter," said Marin, smothering a giggle.

When the cook and his aide departed, Reese explained Marin's position on the ship. "So, it behooves us to refer to her absent a second name as it might infer mortality," he finished dryly.

"It would seem that you are a special lady, Mistress Marin," said Peter.

"I can see why," interjected Mrs. Marsden. "There is a light about her. My Randall thought her an angel upon first sight, didn't you darling?"

The little boy nodded. "She is pretty, mama," he whispered shyly.

"Indeed she is," his mother agreed. "And quite brave. I was rather panicked when I thought we had lost our guide on the street, but Marin remained settled. And her handling of those nasty concubines was most clever."

"Yes, Mistress Marin can be quite resourceful," remarked Reese.

Marin glanced at him, surprised. His tone was not sarcastic and his features held no sign of annoyance this time. He had actually paid her a compliment. Her mood further lightened, and she took it upon herself to play hostess while Reese saw to the wine.

Whether it was the aftereffect of a harrowing escape or the calming influence of the ruby red drink, the air in the room was relaxed, pleasant, and jocular and, for the time being, Marin forgot that she was angry.

"Tell me, Reese, how did you manage the explosions?" asked Peter.

"I was wondering that myself," said Mrs. Marsden.

Thackeray explained how Duncan and three crewmen rowed under cover of darkness to the Algerine ships, that were moored closely together in the harbor, and strapped barrels of gun powder to the backs of a couple of them. The next day, they joined the fishing boats returning to the harbor before sunset and ignited the fuses at the sounding of curfew.

"How very daring, Captain," remarked Mrs. Marsden, awed by the feat.

Marin herself was astounded by the sheer magnitude of the plan, by how just one wrong move or action not executed in time could have brought disaster. And she became painfully aware that she was the only one who hadn't seen her part through. Her thoughtless defection at the gate had put many at risk.

"Reese always did take to challenges…sometimes creating them," Peter was saying. "Aunt Caroline had her hands full with the two of us. Our parents died when we were young, and the dear woman, just widowed herself, took over raising us," he explained. "Reese nearly gave her a heart attack one day when she saw him jump off the roof. She didn't see that it was into a pile of hay. It was after that trick that she hauled him down to the wharf and signed him on with Captain Belmont, an old friend of hers." Peter laughed. "I believe it was a matter of divide and conquer."

"As it turned out, Aunt Caroline made a sound decision. I made my career at sea because of Captain Belmont," said Reese. "He was a good man and a good captain."

"That he was," agreed Peter. "I should like to have sailed under him as well."

"So you followed your brother to sea, then," said Mrs. Marsden.

"Aye. Reese would return home from a voyage and recount such tales of the places he had seen that I was bitten by the bug for adventure as well." Peter looked at Marin. "Reese tells me you have had quite the adventurous life of sail yourself, Mistress."

"Only as a child," replied Marin. "I must confess that I have missed it."

"Mama, I should like to be a sailor, too," announced the little boy.

Reese smiled. "To be a seaman you must learn to tie sailors' knots."

"How can I learn that?"

"I shall have one of the sailors teach you tomorrow."

The little boy nodded excitedly. "I should like that, sir."

"Well now, I think it time for you to be abed, young man," declared Mrs. Marsden. "It has been a lovely evening, Captain, after a most harrowing day. I shall sleep well tonight."

"I will escort you and Master Randall, Mrs. Marsden, as I find myself rather done in as well," said Peter.

They rose from their seats and departed the cabin. Reese was surprised that Marin didn't leave with them but remained seated at the table.

"Something on your mind?" he asked, refilling her wine glass.

She shook her head. "I think I should just like to be drunk."

The corner of Reese's mouth turned up in a half smile of amusement. "I can oblige you, but I have not seen it reported where sea nymphs have been observed in such a state. Perhaps conversation might serve you better."

"I do not want to talk, Captain. I do not want to think."

Silence lapsed between them as she drank the wine, quiet and introspective.

"I must extend my apologies," she said at length. "You would be right to be angry with me."

Reese regarded her, surprised. "I beg your pardon?"

"As you have often charged, I cared only about my own interest and, in so doing, endangered the lives of everyone—Mrs. Marsden and Randall, Peter, Mr. Cathcart, the Algerine women who helped us, the ship's crew—and you—for a fool's errand. If Ahmet had prevailed in visiting his revenge upon you because I mistook a stranger for Nathaniel…well, I could not have borne the burden of it."

Reese was hard pressed to hide his astonishment. He couldn't have done a better job of admonishing her than she was doing herself. She looked so miserable that he debated whether to tell her the truth about her husband. After a moment's consideration, he decided against it.

"Marin, I see no probability that your husband will return to you. Declare him and move on with your life," he counseled.

"It is not that easy, Captain. You have never been married."

"No, but I was once betrothed."

Marin looked at him in surprise. "What went awry? What did you do?"

Thackeray gave a snort of annoyance. "You sound like my brother. I did not do anything. She could not accept the long absences of a mariner, and I could not give up the sea."

"Why did she not sail with you? My mother and I were happiest when on a ship with my father."

"Your father was fortunate. My lady was not so inclined."

Marin sighed. "I had hoped for such a life with Nathaniel when one day he captained his own ship. But I fear a life at sea was not in his plans either."

"What were his plans?" asked Reese.

"To assume control of my father's company," she replied with an edge to her tone. She paused. "I have sometimes wondered if that was the reason he married me." Marin put a hand to her head feeling dizzy. "I think it time I seek my bed, Captain."

She stood up and swayed, suddenly hit by the full effects of the alcohol.

Reese rose to take her arm. "I shall see you to your room."

He stood so close to her. Marin closed her eyes, her senses heightened by the feel of his hand on her bare skin, the sensual scent of sandalwood about him. He was so strong a presence at a time when she needed a safe haven. It would be so easy to…she pulled her arm free.

"I can see myself to my cabin, Captain."

She started unsteadily toward the door, when the ship heaved and rolled and her feet went out from under her. Reese caught her as she was about to hit the floor. She was struggling to regain her balance when another wave hit.

"We must be sailing into rough waters," said Reese. "I think you would be well advised to let me help you to your cabin."

This time, Marin didn't argue as he half carried her to her door. When they entered the cabin, he helped her to the bed and lit the lantern.

Marin groaned as the ship continued to roll. "Fetch the bucket!" she cried.

Reese quickly obliged. She set the bucket on her lap and retched. Between moans and the rolling of the ship, Marin continued to throw up.

Feeling a moment of calm, she set the bucket aside. "Help me out of my dress," she said.

Reese raised a brow wondering if Marin was sober enough to know what she was doing. "Are you certain of this?" he asked.

"Yes, yes!" she snapped. "Get me out of this bloody dress!" She was so miserable that any discomfort at all only added to her distress.

With a shrug, he untied the sash and raised the dress over her head. He hesitated at the demi corset.

"Yes, that, too," she ordered. "Hurry!"

When he had the garment off her, she grabbed the bucket and wretched again, then fell back against the bed in her shift moaning. "Can you not do something to stop the roll of this bloody ship?"

"Sorry, madam. The next time I suggest that you eat more food and drink less wine," replied Reese.

When there came no retort, he saw that she had fallen asleep. He removed her shoes. As he pulled a cover over her, he looked down at her for a long moment, at last glimpsing the vulnerability she kept well-shielded by a keen wit and a sharp tongue. He started to reach out a hand to stroke her cheek but pulled it back and left the cabin cursing Nathaniel Sutton.

The next morning, Marin awoke with a headache and slowly sat up in bed. Her mind was woozy, and she put a hand to her head trying to remember. When her eye went to her gown and corset laid over a chair, her eyes widened in mortification as it came to her how they had gotten there. Oh dear Lord, how could she ever face the captain again? She moaned and lay back down on the bed, hit by another wave of nausea. She would worry about the captain later, she decided.

There was a quiet knock and the door opened slightly. "Marin?" called the surgeon. "The captain said you are under the weather and asked me to look in on you."

"Come in, Dr. Pennyman."

The surgeon entered the cabin. "I have a tonic that might help you to feel better. I also brought you coffee, water, and bread with honey. Your stomach must be pretty empty by now."

Marin grimaced at the thought of eating or drinking anything.

The doctor set the tray on the table and smiled. "Wine and a rough sea do not mix well," he said, pouring the medicine into a cup and holding it out to her.

"What is it?" she asked suspiciously.

"Surfeit water."

"What is that?"

"It is aqua vitae with damask rose water, sugar, and raisins."

She sat up, took the cup, and slowly sipped the liquid.

"The tonic will help you to sleep off the effects of the hangover," said the doctor. He neglected to tell her that the aqua vitae was brandy. He moved the tray to the bed. "Be sure to eat and drink water before you go back to sleep. Later, I would suggest a walk around the deck."

Marin did as the doctor directed.

When she awoke again, it was evening. Feeling much better, she dressed and hesitantly ventured out of her cabin, hoping against hope not to encounter the captain. She didn't know what she would ever say to him to explain away her conduct of the previous evening. The very thought of it made her cringe.

Marin climbed the stairs to the main deck and breathed a sigh of relief when there was no sight of the captain. It was quiet. Only the working crewmen were on deck. The others were either eating or sleeping. The seas were calm. There was a light breeze, and she took a deep breath feeling more invigorated. She walked over to the railing of the ship and gazed up in wonder at the broad strokes of pink and purple color splashed across the sky with the waning of the sun.

"Sunsets in the Mediterranean are quite notable," remarked Reese coming up behind her.

Marin started and inwardly groaned. "Yes, they are," she replied woodenly.

"You were missed at dinner tonight. Might I assume you are recovered now?"

Marin nodded, training her gaze on the horizon. "I shall never drink wine again," she declared stoutly.

Reese gave a light laugh. "That is what everyone says the next day. In a week or so, you will forget all about your resolution."

He moved to stand next to her, showing no inclination to leave, and she debated whether to address her indiscretion or to ignore it. In the end, she decided to take the bull by the horns

"Captain, about last night…it was most unlike me," she said, continuing to avoid his eye. "I hope you do not think that I am…well, that I am in a habit of making immodest requests of men."

"In truth, madam, nothing you do surprises me anymore," he replied.

Marin glanced at him not sure how to take that remark, but she wasn't up to arguing.

"I have few gowns at my disposal and must share them with Mrs. Marsden, you see," she went on to explain. "It was a matter of practicality. It shan't happen again I can assure you."

"Of course."

"I trust the matter will stay between us, Captain."

"I am a gentleman, madam."

She regarded him dubiously. "I cannot say that I am comforted by your assessment."

"I guess you shall have to settle for my word, then."

"Neither am I assured by that, but it shall have to suffice, I suppose," she replied primly.

Silence fell between them.

"What will you do about your husband?" asked Reese at length.

Marin sighed wearily. "Although the facts seem to say one thing, my instincts tell me another. Thus, I feel duty bound to continue to seek word of him."

"Perhaps it is not your instincts that are speaking," suggested Reese.

Marin stiffened. "I believe we had this conversation before, Captain."

"Mayhap we need to have it again, Mistress."

"It does not matter how many times we have it," retorted Marin. "You are wrong. You know nothing of me, and I think it impertinent of you to suggest that you do."

"I beg to differ, madam. I think we have come to know each other fairly well these past months—perhaps more than either of us had intended," Thackeray added wryly, thinking of her days as his steward. "I submit we are not so different."

Marin gave a derisive laugh. "On what basis, Captain?"

"We both have used guilt to punish ourselves."

"Our stories are not the same, and, under the circumstances, I will not abandon Nathaniel," she stated firmly.

Reese hesitated. "What if he has abandoned you?"

Marin looked at him sharply. "What is your meaning?"

"If you are so certain that your husband is alive, perhaps you need to consider that his disappearance might be at his own behest."

Reese hit a nerve and tears glistened in her eyes. "Can you not leave me with some dignity, Captain. Must you shred all?"

"Madam, I do not lay the blame at your feet but at his if such be the case," he replied, taken aback.

"Why can you not let the matter rest?" she lashed out angrily.

"Because I do not wish for you to waste more years on a futile, perhaps undeserving vigil."

"It is not your concern, Captain."

"I am making it my concern, madam."

"Why?"

His large hands cupped her face and his mouth closed on hers in a kiss that was neither aggressive nor hesitant but commanding and sure.

"That is why," he said, releasing her.

Marin looked at Reese, stunned, and hurried off to her cabin.

It was a sleepless night.

The line had been breached. Marin was furious. If she was conflicted before, she was doubly so now. The captain's kiss hadn't lasted long, but it was long enough to have awakened sensations that she hadn't felt in a very long time. The woman in Boston who dreamed of a kiss from him would not have been disappointed.

Even more grievous to Marin was that the captain was right. Her odyssey was about trying to resolve the guilt she had assumed for a failed marriage, and his suggestion that Nathaniel's disappearance might be by his own volition tore at her self-esteem.

The sailor who was assisting the cook came with her breakfast.

"Is the captain on deck?" she asked.

"Aye, Mistress. Watchin' fer pirates after us."

Marin ate her meal and finished dressing. She twisted her hair into a knot and pinned it in place at the back of her head, then donned her straw hat. Try as she might, she knew there was no avoiding the captain in the face of yet another awkward moment between them, and she prepared herself as best she could.

When she stepped onto the main deck, the seamen doffed their hats and shouted greetings to her, raising her spirits.

The Marsden lad came running up to her. "Miss Marin, look what I did," he said, proudly showing her a length of knotted rope. "I made them. Joseph showed me how to make sailor knots."

Marin smiled. "And how well you learned. They are perfect."

The little boy beamed with pleasure. "The captain and Mr. Seaton are going to let me steer the ship now."

He ran off then in high excitement.

Mrs. Marsden hurried up to Marin. "Oh dear, I do hope Randall wasn't bothering you. He seems to be rather unchained, I fear. He has been too long without the hand of his father."

"Please do not concern yourself. It heartens me to see a child so happy." said Marin. "You must be excited at the prospect of being reunited with your husband."

"Decidedly so," she responded with a twinkle in her eye. "I cannot thank you and the captain enough for rescuing Randall and me from that terrible place. I shall always be in your debt."

"I believe your praise should be directed more toward the captain," replied Marin.

"Oh, no. Captain Thackeray told me that you deserve much of the credit."

Marin blinked in surprise. "He did?"

"Yes, indeed he did. Marin, I must offer you my apologies," said Mrs. Marsden, contrite. "You were risking your life to help Randall and me, and I fear that I made matters quite difficult for you."

Marin smiled. "Under the circumstances, it was understandable," she replied. "I regret that I could not be more forthcoming with you in the days before the escape. The important thing is that you and your son are away from Algiers."

Mrs. Marsden gave her a hug. "Thank you. You truly are an angel. Well, I must be after Randall before he tries to take over the ship," she said with a laugh and dashed off.

Marin glanced up to find the captain watching her from the quarter deck. She quickly looked away and returned to her cabin. She wasn't as prepared as she had thought to face him.

When evening fell, she was still in turmoil, but Marin knew she couldn't excuse herself from supper. The captain had warned her to keep up appearances.

She felt more unsure of herself than ever before, and her manner was reserved when she sat down at the table next to Reese. Luckily, the little boy's excited chatter about his day and Peter's humorous discourse provided cover for her.

Reese, on the other hand, was relaxed and affable. He noted with amusement that Marin didn't touch her wine. He also noticed that she kept her eyes averted from him, and it was not lost on him when she left in the company of the others at the end of the evening.

He had resolved not to press her, but he wondered how long it would be until she accepted a new reality. She was stubborn, but she was also a woman, and there was a familiarity growing between them that would not go unaddressed.

Without a window in her cabin, Marin depended on the bells to tell the time. But the next morning, she was awakened from a deep sleep by a knocking on the door. Groggily, she got out of bed.

"Apologies, Mistress," said the first mate when she opened the door. "The captain wishes for you to accompany him to a meeting."

Marin yawned. "What meeting?"

"With Commander Teaberry."

It was like being doused with a bucket of cold water, and Marin instantly came awake. "You must be mistaken, Mr. Seaton. We are at sea."

"No, Mistress. We have put into the port of Gibraltar."

Marin quickly dressed and stormed on deck. Thackeray was waiting for her.

"Why have you put into Gibraltar?" she demanded to know.

"Because, madam, an Algerine ship has been spotted, and we are safe here," he calmly explained.

"Can we not outrun it?"

"Perhaps, but if there is another ship of corsairs in the Atlantic, we could be caught between them."

"But we have cannons," she argued.

"So might the corsairs, and I cannot risk the lives of Mrs. Marsden and her son."

Marin let out a huff of frustration and uttered some words in Russian.

"Careful, madam, the deck has eyes and ears," he cautioned, suppressing a grin.

She glanced around her and forced a tight smile. "I see no reason why I must accompany you to meet with Commander Teaberry."

"I have a favor to ask, and you have the power to convince him," responded Reese. "As you have said, women are better at some things. Now, may we proceed?"

Marin's chest heaved. She was beginning to wish she had never said those words. "Very well. Let us to it then and be done."

As she peevishly marched off to the dinghy, Reese fervently hoped that her mood would improve by the time they reached shore. In addition to being stubborn, she was unpredictable, which made for a combustible combination.

When they arrived at the wharf, a soldier ushered them to the commander's office.

Reese leaned down and whispered: "Smile. Be charming."

Marin glared at him and gritted her teeth as they walked into the little room.

A broad smile stretched across Teaberry's heavy jowls, and the rotund captain of the port practically tripped over his feet in his eagerness to greet her.

"My dear Mistress Marin, I had hoped for these poor eyes to feast upon your beauty once again. When it was brought to me that the *Sea Nymph* had dropped anchor in my harbor, I rejoiced that my prayers were answered. May I say that I have missed your company beyond measure, mistress."

Marin had forgotten how annoying she found the man as his eyes roved over her, and it was all she could do to keep from pulling her hand free when he took it and pressed his thick lips to it in a lingering caress. It sent a shiver through her that most certainly was not of a pleasant nature.

At a nudge from Reese, she smiled tightly. "Thank you, Commander. It is my pleasure to see you again as well."

"Please, dear lady, be seated," directed Teaberry. Continuing to keep hold of her hand, he wrapped his other arm around her waist and guided her to a chair before taking his seat behind a desk.

"Thank you for seeing us, Commander," said Marin.

"Tch tch, 'tis Walter, remember?" admonished Teaberry with the playful wag of his finger.

She smiled again. "Walter, I know how busy an important man as you are."

"I am never too busy to see you, my dear," Teaberry assured her. "Did you find word of your brother in Algiers?"

Marin shook her head and took out a lace handkerchief to dab at her eyes. "I regret to say that I did not."

"Such a pity," he clucked sympathetically. "What matter requires you to grace this wretched port with your presence once more, though it gladdens me much that you do so?"

Marin looked questioningly at Reese. She had no idea why they were there. "Perhaps I should let Captain Thackeray explain."

The commander glanced at Reese. "Oh, yes, Captain Thackeray…welcome back to Gibraltar, sir," he greeted with less enthusiasm. "Please be seated, Captain. You crane my neck, and it is of a sore disposition this day."

Reese sat down in a chair next to Marin.

"Now, how might I be of assistance?" he asked, his eye returning to Marin.

"We are in need of a favor, sir," said Reese.

"What sort of favor?"

"We require a convoy to Lisbon."

Teaberry's attention swiveled back to Reese. "A convoy? I doubt my superiors in London would be too pleased to have the British navy escorting an American merchant ship, Captain."

"If you remember, sir, Great Britain just signed another treaty with the United States. I do not believe there would be an objection in the interest of diplomacy and friendship."

The commander looked skeptical. "Perhaps. What occasions this favor, Captain Thackeray?"

"While seeking information about her brother in Algiers, Mistress Marin caught the interest of the dey," explained Reese. "He sought to keep her prisoner and add her to his harem. I was able to free her, but we are being chased by one of his pirate ships, undoubtedly under orders to reclaim Mistress Marin."

Teaberry was aghast. "The devil you say!" He looked at Marin appalled at the very idea of her being held captive in a Musselman harem. "But why a convoy to Lisbon?" he asked.

"I also succeeded in freeing the wife and son of a diplomat who oversees the American consulate there and must see to their reunion. I am sure the Portuguese navy will see us to safe waters upon our departure from that port," said Reese.

Teaberry drummed his fingers on the desk top as he considered the matter. "Yes, I can see that the dey would go to great lengths to recapture a woman of such rare beauty as Mistress Marin, but I am not sure that I have the authority to grant your request. I shall have to make a plea to my superiors."

"It could take weeks to receive a reply, Commander," pointed out Reese.

"Yes, I am afraid so," agreed Teaberry, smiling at Marin.

Marin shifted uneasily sensing a sudden wiliness in the commander's manner.

Reese felt it, too. "I cannot be so long in port, sir, as this has become a diplomatic mission to deliver Mrs. Marsden and her son to her husband," he said.

"Well then, if Mistress Marin is the treasure the pirates seek, I would suggest that you leave the lady in this safe harbor and see your mission completed. I will administer to Mistress Marin's every need—until such time as a transport can be arranged to England for her."

Marin was inwardly alarmed. "That is too kind of you, sir, but I have been so long from home and miss my family." She took out her handkerchief again and began to cry. It wasn't hard to fake tears this time.

Clearly flustered, Commander Teaberry cast around for a way to console her. Each assurance that he would take care of her brought louder sobs.

"Please, Mistress Marin, take hold of yourself," he pleaded.

In desperation, he looked to the captain, but Reese shrugged helplessly. "I have not the way with the ladies as you, sir."

The commander waffled. "Perhaps, in light of this new treaty and as yours is a diplomatic mission, I might find my way clear to oblige your request, Captain. But I do so in the interest of this dear lady."

Marin stopped crying. Tears shimmered in her eyes, and she gave him a winsome smile. "My thanks to you, Walter. You are indeed a man of honor and courage. I shall sing your praises to both the British ministry and the American government."

The commander gave a wistful sigh. "Such praise from your lips is sweet indeed, my dear, though I shall regret your absence. When do you wish to sail, Captain?"

"As soon as you can have a convoy ready. I should like to have two ships, sir."

"As luck would have it, there are frigates readying to leave port on the morrow. I shall place three at your disposal. Mistress Marin is too valuable an asset to risk," declared the commander.

"I am in your debt, sir," said Marin.

The commander smiled craftily. "In that case, Mistress Marin, I shall collect payment in the form of supper this evening so that I might gaze upon your beauty one more time."

Marin suppressed a groan. "It is small recompense, indeed, sir. What time shall Captain Thackeray and I arrive?"

It was clear by the look on Commander Teaberry's face that his invitation had not included Reese. "Uh, Captain, I can imagine you have much to attend. I assure you I shall not consider it ill-mannered of you to decline the invitation."

Reese appeared to consider the matter, and Marin gave him a surreptitious kick.

"Thank you, Commander. I assure you it is not an inconvenience. My crew has everything in hand," he replied, holding back a grin.

"Well then, shall we say eight o'clock as before?" asked Marin brightly.

"Aye...eight o'clock," the commander responded dully.

As Reese walked Marin to the boat, he remarked, "That was quite a performance you gave. 'Such praise from your lips is sweet indeed,'" he recited, mimicking the commander with a mirthful chuckle.

"Well, you got your convoy with no small sacrifice on my part and no help from you—again," she returned crisply.

As she charged on ahead, Reese strode after her.

"Hold on," he said. "There is another matter I wish for us to consider."

She stopped and turned with an impatient sigh. "What is that?"

"The other night—"

"There is nothing to discuss, Captain."

"What complaint do you make, madam…that I kissed you or that you liked it?"

Marin blushed and marched on to the dinghy.

Reese smiled. At least she hadn't denied anything.

When they returned to the ship, Mrs. Marsden was taking refreshment on the deck. Chairs and a small table had been brought out for her, and she hailed Marin. "Mistress, come join me," she called. "My son seems to have abandoned me for the helm and Mr. Seaton."

Marin smiled and walked over to her. "You look much heartened," she remarked, taking Randall's chair. "It gladdens me that one of us is knowing a good day. What occasions yours? Perhaps it will be contagious."

Mrs. Marsden laughed. "My cup of blessings runneth over. 'Tis a glorious day, indeed. Randall and I are freed from that horrible place, and time draws near when I shall be with my husband and my son with his father." She stopped, suddenly mindful. "Apologies, Mistress. Forgive me."

"Please call me Marin. For what must I forgive you?"

Mrs. Marsden hesitated. "I hope you do not mind, but Peter told me about your husband. It was thoughtless of me to prattle on so about my happiness when you have been thwarted in yours."

"No, no, I take much pleasure in your happiness and in that of your son," Marin assured her. "Please do not shade it in my presence." She sighed. "I know not what to do. I have been counseled to move on, but I find it a difficult task."

Mrs. Marsden regarded Marin for a long moment. "May I offer a pearl of wisdom?"

"Please do. I seem to be lacking in them these days."

"It is my belief that life is meant to be a book of many chapters, Marin, the number being different for everyone, for it depends upon how many a person is willing to open."

Marin considered this for a few moments, then glanced over at Reese who was conversing with his second mate. "How does one know when to open a new chapter?" she asked.

Mrs. Marsden followed Marin's eye to the captain and smiled. "Your desire to do so must be stronger than your fear."

Marin spent the rest of the afternoon pondering Mrs. Marsden's "pearl of wisdom." It made sense in an ordered life, she concluded, but hers was not that. Her life was marked by uncertainty and riddled with complications that would not allow for the easy closure of this "chapter." Fear had nothing to do with it, she decided. But even as she thought it, the captain rose to mind. He was not making the situation any easier with his insights and kiss, and her annoyance with him sprang anew.

She turned her thoughts to the evening ahead then. In her present state of mind, she simply could not endure another dinner with Commander Teaberry. Much against character, she was about to slip into self-pity, when it suddenly came to her how she might regain some control—at least in regards to this one aspect of her life.

At the appointed time, Marin appeared on deck for the row over to shore.

"Good evening, Captain," she greeted pleasantly.

"Mistress."

As she struck off for the dinghy, he stared after her in surprise. This was not the thorny Marin of the last few days.

"Come along, Captain. We must not be late," she called.

Reese raised a brow and followed after her.

On the trip to the commander's house, Thackeray wondered at the change in her demeanor. He was loath to question it for fear of having her revert to a less cooperative mood.

Supper proved to be no less curious to him. In spite of the commander's overt, annoying attention, Marin did not find it difficult to enjoy her meal this time. Knowing how she had dreaded the event, Reese was surprised by her easy amiability and appetite. She exhibited none of the tenseness or strained forbearance when last they had dined with Commander Teaberry. Indeed, Reese had been prepared to step in this time, but she didn't seem to require or ask for his help. She appeared to be in complete control.

"Oh, dear," said Marin. "I seem to have dropped my napkin. Would you mind, Walter?" she asked, kicking it further under the table.

"Of course, dear lady."

When the commander leaned down to retrieve the napkin, finally having to get off the chair and crawl underneath the table, Marin discreetly took out a vial from her reticule and poured the contents into the commander's half empty glass of wine.

Reese's brow shot up in alarm. "Madam?"

"I have the matter in hand, Captain," she quietly assured him.

Teaberry suddenly let out a howl of pain and popped his head up from under the table, rubbing his forehead.

"Oh, was that you I kicked, Walter? I am so sorry," said Marin. "I felt something touch my leg. I thought it a spider."

"Quite alright, Mistress," the commander assured her with a sheepish smile.

Huffing and puffing with the exertion, he climbed out from under the table and got back into his chair, the wayward napkin in his hand looking slightly the worse for wear.

Reese viewed the farcical scene in amazement and with some trepidation, debating whether he should intervene. He had no idea what she had put into the commander's drink and what the consequences of her action might be this time.

Marin reclaimed her limp napkin and gave the commander a disarming smile. "How very chivalrous you are, sir. I dare say you are in need of refreshment," she said, pouring a little more wine into the commander's glass.

Teaberry drank deeply of the liquor, and Marin and Reese leaned forward in their seats, watching closely for a reaction. When Teaberry set the glass down and began to expand on the hardship of his duties there, showing no apparent effect from the drink, Reese glanced questioningly at Marin. She shrugged, mystified. The commander leaned toward Marin, then, his finger in the air to make a point, and fell face down on the table, narrowly missing his plate of food.

Marin blinked in surprise. "Commander?" She gingerly poked at him, but he didn't move.

She and Reese were staring at the comatose Teaberry, wondering what to do about him, when a servant woman entered the room.

"I-I fear the commander has consumed too much wine," said Marin.

The servant snorted. "Wouldn't be the first time, madam."

"Indeed. Well then, Captain Thackeray and I shall take our leave and let the commander to his sleep. Please relay our thanks and appreciation for a lovely dinner."

"Yes, madam."

As they quickly left the house, Reese whispered: "What did you put in that poor man's wine? You did not kill him, did you?"

"Of course not," scoffed Marin. "It was a sleeping potion that Dr. Pennyman gave me."

"Were you supposed to use all of it?"

Marin looked at him with a measure of uncertainty. "I assumed so. Dr. Pennyman did not say otherwise. What difference does it make?"

"The difference is whether or not we have a convoy tomorrow. Let us hope Teaberry has already arranged for it, for I doubt he will be early to rise in the morning—if at all. I must remember not to turn my back on you," remarked Reese soberly.

During the carriage ride back to the wharf, Marin was silent, having taken Reese's comment to heart and overcome with fear that she might have killed the commander. England hanged murderers, and she had no doubt that her gender would earn her little sympathy. Dear God, what had she done? Every time she tried to take control, she seemed only to make matters worse.

As the two crewmen rowed them back to the ship, Marin glanced at Reese a few times wondering if he was angry with her. He was his usual stern self when in the presence of his crew, so it was difficult for her to tell. She couldn't blame him if he was. When they reached the ship and stepped onto the deck, she hastily retreated to her cabin.

Pennyman emerged from sick bay. He spotted Thackeray and walked up to him. "How went your evening?" he asked.

"It was…irregular," remarked Reese.

When he recounted the night's events, Pennyman burst out laughing.

"Not to worry," the surgeon assured him. "Marin did not administer an overdose."

"Next time, warn me when you arm her," said Thackeray, unamused.

CHAPTER TWENTY-NINE

Truce

To Marin's immense relief, the commander was standing on the wharf the next morning, looking the worse for wear but alive just the same, as the Sea *Nymph* sailed out of the bay of Gibraltar accompanied by three British navy frigates. Dr. Pennyman had tried to calm her fears, but until she saw for herself that she had brought no lasting harm to the commander, she could not be reassured.

The next several days enjoyed good weather. The pirate ship had disappeared from view, and the tenseness that had earlier permeated the ship now gave way to a light, festive mood. Those musically inclined took out their instruments and played jigs while others sang and danced.

Little Randall had become a mascot of the ship and was rather attached to Reese and Peter as they took turns teaching him some skills. Marin was amazed by Reese's patience with the boy when he taught Randall how to take sightings with the sextant. She hadn't imagined the captain to have more than an ounce of patience in his makeup.

Marin liked Mrs. Marsden, and they struck up a close friendship. She also got to know Reese's brother better. Though Peter's demeanor was more relaxed, it was easy to see that he and Reese shared the bond of brotherhood. Aside from their physical similarities, they possessed the same sense of honor, integrity, and commitment to duty. They were both solid men as her father would say. One could always count on them.

When the *Sea Nymph* finally sailed into the port of Lisbon, there was much excitement. The crew was looking forward to some relaxation on shore.

Mr. Marsden stood on the wharf, and his wife and son excitedly waved and shouted to him. When the ship was moored and the gangplank lowered, she and the little boy ran down into his arms. The emotion of the reunion was such it could be felt on the ship, bringing a tear to even the most hardened sailor.

"It makes a man think," remarked Peter as he and Reese watched the scene.

"About what?"

"Having a wife to come home to…a son to teach his craft to."

"I tried that once if you remember," said Reese. "There are not many women who want to share a man's life at sea."

"I can think of one," replied Peter.

Reese followed Peter's eye to Marin who was standing at the railing waving to Mrs. Marsden as the family drove off from the wharf in an open carriage.

"Are you going to tell her about her husband?" asked Peter.

Reese shook his head. "What is the sense of causing her more hurt? It will be easier for her if she thinks him dead."

"If she finds out about him and that you kept the truth from her, she will never trust you again."

"Keep your own counsel, Peter. Only you, James Cathcart, and I know the story. Let us keep it that way."

"As you wish, brother, but I think it to be a mistake." Peter paused. "Marin is a singular woman. I believe I should like to get to know her better," he commented casually.

Reese turned a startled gaze on Peter that quickly turned to disapproval. "I do not think her to be your type."

Peter laughed. "I knew it. You have feelings for her. Admit it."

Reese snorted. "I have work to do." As he walked away, he could hear his brother's laughter.

For the next two days, the *Sea Nymph* took on more provisions, the crew were allowed some shore time, and Reese and Marin were feted by the American consulate and entertained by the Marsdens. On the third day, the ship departed accompanied by four ships from the Portuguese navy and carrying a diplomatic pouch of letters and reports to the president and secretary of state.

Peter had conveniently absented himself, and Reese and Marin were alone this night for dinner for the first time in a long while. It felt strange but not altogether uncomfortable, at least from Reese's point of view now that her attitude towards him had seemed to temper.

"You are not eating," he observed, taking a bite of his food.

"I am not hungry," she replied.

"You did not eat last night either."

"I think events have conspired to unsettle me. Perhaps I need to spend more time in my cabin and rest," said Marin.

Reese laid down his fork and knife and leaned back in his chair to consider her more closely. He could see that she was bothered by something. Something had been disturbing her since they departed Gibraltar.

"Pennyman told me that you had taken my comment seriously about Commander Teaberry. It was not my intention to cause you the undue stress of thinking that you may have killed the man," he said.

"It matters not. It was all my doing," Marin replied in a low, quiet tone. She paused. "I should have told you of my plan to give the commander a sleeping potion. I had not considered that he might not have arranged for the convoy beforehand and probably wouldn't be in any condition to do so the next morning."

"Then, I dare say we are even in our transgressions," said Reese, surprised that she was taking the matter so much to heart.

Marin gave him a faint smile. She fell silent again, and he glanced at her quizzically. She was in a strange mood.

"Is there something else at work here, madam?" he asked.

Marin hesitated. She seemed about to say something then changed her mind. "No. I think I shall retire now."

As she rose from her chair, he stood up.

"Good night, Captain."

"Good night, madam."

Reese watched her walk to the door. "You may try, but you cannot ignore them, Marin," he called out.

Marin turned to him. "Ignore what?"

He moved closer to her. "Unspoken thoughts and feelings do not go away, Marin. I have learned from my own experience that they only get louder and more persistent the further you try to run from them."

Marin stiffened. "If you are talking about Nathaniel—"

"I am talking about us."

His voice was low and hypnotic. He put an arm around her waist and lowered his head to press his lips against hers. She was hesitant at first, then responded with a passion that surprised him. When her lips parted and her arms went around his neck, he moved to take full advantage of the moment.

He deepened his kiss and slipped his hands beneath her dress and shift. The feel of his fingers on her bare flesh moving up her thigh to cup her buttocks sent an unexpected and incalculable thrill through her. When he brought her tighter against him, Marin knew what the next step would be, what she wanted it to be. And in those split seconds, a war waged within.

She suddenly went still and pushed his hands away. "I cannot," she said, pulling back from him and rearranging her dress.

"Do you not wish to?" asked Reese, certain that he had read her correctly.

"Until I know of Nathaniel's status for certain, I cannot betray my vows."

"Marin—"

"Please do not make this more difficult than it is," she pleaded and hurried from the cabin.

Reese stood motionless for a minute, then gave a short, humorless laugh. Marin's cousin had warned him that beneath Marin's rebellious nature lurked the heart of a conformist.

If he told her the truth about her husband now, she wouldn't believe him, particularly after what had just happened—or nearly happened—between them. She would think he was trying to create opportunity for himself.

Reese raked a hand through his hair, angry with himself. Peter was right. He should have told her as soon as they had left Algiers and let the chips fall where they may, but he hadn't wanted to chance a wider divide between them than already existed. The longer she was allowed her false narratives, though, the harder it was going to be to convince her of the truth without tangible proof. So, what the hell was he to do now? He risked losing her either way.

For the duration of the voyage, Marin and Reese agreed to an uneasy truce, trying to ignore and grapple with the attraction that had been growing between them for longer than either had realized. Marin spent much of her time helping Dr. Pennyman in sick bay and Pots in the galley. And Reese kept to his cabin busy with paperwork and updating log records. The only time he came on deck was to gather the readings of their position and speed.

On one day, Marin appeared on deck from her cabin to find Reese recording the noon position of the sun with his sextant. Both stopped and gazed at each other for a moment before Marin hurried past him to go to sick bay.

The scene did not go unnoticed.

Peter looked at the bosun. "Looks like you lost your bet, Andrew. I fear you owe Doc and Timothy some specie."

"The journey ain't over yet," replied White. He let out a snort of annoyance. "Ain't never seen a man and a woman tryin' so hard to disregard what's in front of their noses. Mayhap you need to do some more pot stirring, Doc."

"As I recall, that did not sit well with the captain the first time," interjected Duncan.

Dr. Pennyman took a puff on his pipe. "To be sure, love is a tortuous route that runs between head and heart."

Duncan shook his head. "Ain't never gonna be a way clear for them two. They be too much alike."

"Perhaps that is the tie that binds," commented Peter.

CHAPTER THIRTY

Going Home

Sailing against headwinds, Reese had planned a more southerly route across the Atlantic that took them up the coast from Charleston. And in early October, beneath sunny skies, the *Sea Nymph* sailed into Boston Harbor.

When the ship was anchored and moored, Marin bid a farewell to the sailors and wished them well on their next voyages. They mournfully watched her debark then, wearing her straw hat, and seemingly disappear into the crowd on the wharf. Seaton and Duncan were waiting out of sight to whisk her to a hired carriage that would take her home.

At the prearranged signal, a splash was heard and White, standing at the bow, shouted: "Look here! Mistress Marin has returned to the sea."

The crewmen rushed to the bow to see ripples in the water and her straw hat floating on top. It was all carefully choreographed so that Marin's charade as a sea nymph vanished with her.

As the carriage bore Marin away from the port, the stern lecture Reese had given her rang in her ears. She was prohibited from coming anywhere near Boston Harbor until *all* the crewmen had departed on other ships. That could be months, she fumed. What was she to do with herself if she could not work at the counting house?

Marin looked out the window at the familiar sights. She hadn't realized how much she had missed Boston, her family, her home. Her mind turned to her homecoming then, and she wondered how to explain her adventure to her father. Technically, she hadn't lied to him in her note. She did sail to England to visit Susannah. She had just neglected to tell him her other intentions.

The carriage drew up in front of her father's house. She stepped down from the conveyance and gazed at the neat, clapboard dwelling for a few moments. Everything looked the same, she thought with a smile.

Mrs. Cahill came running out the door. "My stars in heaven, I could scarce believe me eyes when I looked out the window," she cried, clasping Marin to her bosom. "'Tis been four months and nary a word from ye. Mr. Ben missed ye terrible and been most worried about ye."

Marin stepped out of the housekeeper's enthusiastic embrace. "I am sorry, Mrs. Cahill. It was most thoughtless of me not to write."

"Did ye have a merry visit with yer friend?"

"I did…most merry. Is my father at home?"

"He is at the counting house. Shall I get you something to eat? You could do with some meat on those bones," said the woman, looking Marin over with a critical eye.

Marin laughed. "No, I am not hungry, but you could help me prepare a bath. I have been so long at sea I should like to have a proper soaking."

"Of course, madam. Where are your trunks?"

In truth, Marin was forced to leave her possessions behind when she departed the ship, for, as Reese pointed out, a sea nymph has no possessions, but she couldn't very well tell that to the housekeeper.

"I-uh-I was in such a hurry to arrive home, I left my trunk on the ship for later transport," she replied. "I suspect it will appear in time."

"You have one trunk?" questioned Mrs. Cahill in surprise. "You were months in London and you return with just one trunk?"

"There was a storm," said Marin, letting the housekeeper assume the rest.

"Well, no matter," declared the woman. "You have plenty of clothes upstairs."

Mrs. Cahill hustled her inside the house and, in short time between the two of them, Marin sat luxuriating in a bath of salts and lavender scented soap until the water cooled to an uncomfortable temperature.

She had just stepped out of the tub when she heard her father come in. She quickly put on her robe and hurried from the bathing room off the kitchen.

"Father!" she cried, running into the parlor.

The older man's face lit up, and he gathered her in his arms. "Daughter, I feared ye to have forgotten your way home."

"Never, Father. I have missed you so."

She rested her head against his shoulder, enjoying the warmth of his embrace, in need of a parent's comfort.

Henshaw furrowed his brow. "What is it, Marin? You seem unsettled."

"It is just good to be home again, Father."

"It is good to have you home again," he responded. "How is Susannah?"

Marin smiled and stepped away from him. "Quite well. In fact, she is expecting a child next month."

"Well, that is good news. You must have found much in London to please you to be gone so long with nary a word."

"I am sorry, Father. The days slipped past me. It was rather a busy time."

"Indeed, I expect that it was."

"What news here?" she asked, eager to change the subject.

"Well, most notably for me, Caroline has moved her residence to Boston."

Marin's smile wavered. "Oh…how nice."

"On what ship did you arrive?" her father asked off handedly.

Marin wracked her brain for a way to answer without really answering.

Henshaw snorted. "Before you dig yourself deeper into that hole, daughter, I should tell you that I saw Captain Thackeray at the wharf and had quite a long and illuminating conversation with him."

Given the more serious tenor of her father's voice now, Marin knew that the cat was out of the bag.

"Father, I-I did not lie to you," she stammered. "I did go to visit Susannah and—"

"I know. You just omitted your other intentions."

"Truth by omission and assumption is something she is quite adept at," commented a familiar deep voice.

Marin whirled about to see Reese standing in the doorway. "What are you doing here?" she demanded to know.

"I brought your trunk from the ship."

When she made no response, her father looked at her. "Marin...?"

Marin rolled her eyes and huffed. "My thanks to you, Captain."

"You must excuse my daughter," said Henshaw. "She seems to have forgotten her manners."

"It can happen when too long at sea," replied Reese, a smile playing at the corners of his mouth when he saw Marin bristle. "I shall see you this evening then, Benjamin."

Henshaw nodded. "I look forward to it, Captain."

As Reese left the house, Marin turned to her father. "What is happening this evening?"

"I invited Caroline, the captain, and his brother to take supper with us," he replied.

Marin felt her stomach drop. "Father, I-I should like to be excused. The journey was overlong and I feel a malady—"

"None of your excuses, Marin. I shall expect you and your good manners to be present."

His tone was firm and his features set, and she knew there was no getting out of the engagement.

Marin put her best foot forward when the time came and warmly greeted Mrs. Billings and Peter. With Reese, the best she could manage was a stiff acknowledgment.

"What did you tell my father?" she asked, taking him aside.

"Everything," he replied.

Marin looked at him, mortified. "Everything?"

"Benjamin already knew most of the story. He had sent a letter to your friend inquiring after you when he had had no word, and she confessed that you had sailed to Algiers on my ship." Reese chuckled. "Even as your father, he had not figured you to go to such lengths. I dare say he was rather taken aback by the audacity of Henry Shaw."

"Did you tell him of Henry Shaw's stewardship to you?" she questioned archly.

Reese shifted uncomfortably. "I did not…out of consideration."

"For you or for me?"

"I determined that it served neither of our reputations."

Marin gave a derisive snort. "Indeed."

Mrs. Cahill rang the dinner bell.

Reese offered his arm. Marin hesitated then took it. Even beneath the fabric of the coat, she could feel the strength in his arm—and that annoying flutter in her stomach—as they moved into the dining room.

Marin and Reese were seated next to each other on one side of the table with Peter and Caroline on the other side and Ben at the head of the table. Mrs. Cahill bustled in with a light repast of baked beans, codfish cakes, cheese, and coarse dark bread made from rye and maize.

When the wine glasses were filled and the food passed, Henshaw cleared his throat. "If you please, I have something to say."

Everyone fell silent.

"Now that we are all together by the grace of God, I wish to announce that I have asked Caroline to marry me," he said. He reached over and took her hand, and they smiled at each other. "And I am very happy to report that she has done me the honor of accepting. We ask all of you for your blessings."

Marin's mouth dropped open, and the fork slipped through her fingers to clatter on her plate. Peter and Reese were the first to recover from the surprise announcement and were pleased to give their consent to the union.

"Marin, have we your blessing?" asked her father.

Reese nudged her, and Marin realized that all eyes were on her.

"Uh…certainly, Father. I-I hope that you and Mrs. Billings will be very happy," she stammered.

"I know this may seem sudden to everyone, but Ben and I have been discussing the matter for quite some time," said Caroline. "We wanted to wait for all of you to return so you could share in our happy day. How coincidental that you should return at the same time and on the same ship," she added with the lift of her brow. "No doubt there is more to the story to which I have not been privy. I seem to have been kept in a state of ignorance." At this, she directed a look of reproof to her husband-to-be.

"We meant only to keep you from worry, my dear," said Henshaw.

"Do not blame Benjamin for his silence, Aunt Caroline. He was complicit at my behest," intervened Reese.

Caroline turned an eye to her nephew. "I appreciate your concern, but I will not be kept in the dark on matters—particularly as regards my family."

"Be careful what you wish for, my dear," advised Henshaw wryly. "It has been my experience that sometimes ignorance is bliss, as they say."

When he looked pointedly at his daughter, Marin lowered her gaze and shifted guiltily in her seat, to the brothers' amusement.

Reese stood and raised his glass. "To Aunt Caroline and Ben, may you know a long, happy, and peaceful life together." Even as he uttered the words, he had his doubts about the latter sentiment with Marin in the family.

CHAPTER THIRTY-ONE

Nowhere to Run

It was a bright, fall day seasonably cool. Foliage colors were at their peak, and a brisk wind blew off the ocean. Inside the Henshaw home, a fire burned warm in the parlor, and there was an air of excitement and good cheer as Marin stood up for her father and Peter and Reese stood up for their aunt as witnesses to the couple's marriage.

Marin was torn. She liked Caroline Billings, and she was glad that her father had found new happiness. But why did fate have to decree that it be with the captain's aunt and at a time when she most needed space from the man? In a short period of time, he would be sailing off on another voyage, and she would be returning to her duties at the counting house. Normalcy would reign once again. But until then, how were they to avoid each other?

During the blessing, she glanced over at Reese. He looked very handsome in his ivory vest and claret coat. He was clean shaven and his dark hair was neatly trimmed, but she found, with some surprise, that she actually missed the roguish appeal of his beard.

He turned his head and caught her eye on him. When she blushed and looked away, the corner of Reese's mouth curled up in a knowing smile. He still held her interest.

After the ceremony, the family, the magistrate, and some friends enjoyed refreshments in the parlor.

Thomas sidled up to Marin. "Smile, you look as though you are attending a funeral, cousin."

"I need some time to adjust is all," she replied shortly. "This came as rather a surprise."

Thomas chuckled. "I did warn you. Let's see. What relation does this make you and Reese now?"

"Go away, Thomas. I am in no mood for your jests."

"Still prickly, I see. I would have thought you to have bridged your divide with Reese by now."

"Why would you think that?"

"Uncle Ben told me about your little adventure." He laughed mirthfully. "I should like to have been there when Reese discovered that you were Henry Shaw. The two of you together on a ship for months in such close quarters…it strains credulity and quite fires the imagination."

"You are a dunderhead, Thomas!"

As Marin stormed off, Thomas grinned. He glanced over at Reese, and his brow furrowed in bemusement. He had noticed the captain's eye drifting to his cousin more than once and hers to him, and given the raw nerve he had just tapped in her…he stroked his chin, thoughtful.

Caroline, too, observed her nephew and stepdaughter but with more concern. She had been conscious of an indifference between them at the onset of her relationship with Marin's father but was certain that, in time, it would pass. Instead, it seemed to have heightened and morphed into something she couldn't explain.

She approached her youngest nephew. "Peter, did something occur between Reese and Marin on the voyage?"

"Why do you ask, Aunt?"

"They are…well, they appear strained to be in each other's company—more so than before."

Peter hesitated. "I believe there was some disagreement on a matter."

"Oh dear," murmured Caroline worriedly.

"Do not concern yourself, Aunt. They will resolve the problem in due time," he assured her.

Having watched the body language of her stepdaughter and nephew this day, Caroline wasn't so sure.

* * * * *

Marin had temporarily moved in with Thomas to give her father and Caroline some privacy, which was partly true. The larger truth was that she didn't want to encounter Reese should he come to visit his aunt.

This morning, she restlessly paced the floor until Thomas glanced up from the task on his desk and protested. "For heaven's sake, Marin, you are going to wear a hole in the rug. You have not left the house for days. Take yourself out and leave me to my peace."

She flounced on the sofa, disquieted. "What am I to do? I cannot go to the counting house. I am barred from the wharf indefinitely."

"'Tis your own fault," Thomas reminded her, going back to his work.

Marin stuck out her tongue at him. "How long is Captain Thackeray in port?" she asked.

"He said to be about a year."

Marin bolted upright. "A year! That will never do."

Thomas looked up at her, surprised by the outburst. "It takes that amount of time to refit a ship after so long a voyage. You know that. Thackeray was not able to properly complete the task upon his return from China before having to dash off on that mission to Algiers."

He put down his pen and regarded her closer. "I must say, Marin, you have been acting quite odd since your return to Boston. You are as skittish as a colt. And you work overly hard to avoid Reese. I know the two of you have had your disagreements, but I sense there is another matter between you that requires settling."

Marin gave a snort of impatience. "'Tis your imagination at work, Thomas."

Thomas stood up and walked over to her. "No, I do not believe so. I dismissed the idea once. Now I am inclined to entertain it again. Could it be that you and Thackeray—"

"No!" snapped Marin. "I told you before nothing happened."

Thomas smiled. "Something must have happened. Is that not why you moved in here and hold yourself prisoner? You are afraid to encounter him."

"I am not. If you must know, we had a disagreeable parting and agreed to keep a distance between us, which Father and Caroline have now made quite difficult to do."

"Indeed. Well, I am afraid you shall have to bury the hatchet again for the evening."

Marin looked at him guardedly. "Why? What is occurring this evening?"

"Caroline invited us all to supper."

A look of panic flitted across Marin's face. "I received no word of it. Surely, she means for only you to attend."

"A message came this morning while you were still abed. It was most explicitly an invitation for the both of us. And do not try to plead illness. I will not allow it."

Marin stamped her foot. "Why do the fates conspire to make my life so difficult!"

"Perhaps because you work so hard to defy them," said Thomas.

Marin's mood had not much improved when she and Thomas arrived at the Henshaw house that evening. Marin could see through the window that Reese and Peter were already there, and she took a deep breath to brace herself.

"Reese is not going to bite, you know," said Thomas.

"Oh, do shut up, Thomas," she responded shortly.

Her cousin laughed and took her by the arm to pull her to the door.

Caroline greeted them warmly. Marin exchanged greetings with her father and Peter and gave a stilted nod to Reese. After a few minutes of conversation, Caroline directed everyone into the dining room. This time, Marin was seated next to Thomas and across the table from Reese. It wasn't any more comforting. Several times she glanced up to find his gaze on her.

She paid scant attention to her food. She ate little and tasted nothing. As tense as she was, the captain was that much more composed. It only served to disquiet her more, and she made no objection to Thomas refilling her wine glass.

"'Tis luck you are not on a rolling ship," quipped Reese, the corner of his mouth curling up in amusement.

"How is that?" asked Thomas.

"'Tis of no interest," replied Marin, kicking the captain under the table.

"Reese, do tell us some stories of your adventure," encouraged Caroline.

Reese thought for a moment, then launched into an account of Commander Teaberry's infatuation with Marin. Much to Marin's chagrin, the captain turned out to be quite the raconteur. Before long, he had everyone in stitches, particularly upon hearing how she had drugged the commander.

"That sounds like my cousin," said Thomas through his laughter. "Marin is not one to easily give up control in any situation."

"Yes, I have had occasion to notice," replied Reese dryly. "But I managed to assert some authority nonetheless."

Marin glared at him, the arrogance in his tone rankling her. "Indeed, Captain, I seem to remember the crew believing that you acted under my direction and as such you were obliged to dance to my tune."

She turned to Peter. "Your brother is not one to so easily relinquish control either, but I managed to assert some authority nonetheless." She smiled smugly when she saw Reese bristle.

Peter chuckled. "It would appear that there were two captains on the voyage."

This did not go over well with Reese either.

The light mood fell flat and the rest of the dinner was constrained, dashing Caroline's hopes for a pleasant evening that would help to bring them all together into a happy family unit.

* * * * *

Another week passed before Marin was found to be of a cheery disposition.

She went shopping, received a letter from Susannah, and was given notice that her banishment from the wharf had been lifted. It had been a good day—until Thomas informed her she would be dining alone this evening.

"Where are you going to be?" she asked.

"At the theater with Nancy. We are to meet Nancy's cousin and the captain."

Marin blinked in surprise. "Nancy's cousin Penny Newsome?"

"Yes. The captain has been a frequent escort of hers."

"But—but she is a widow."

"What difference does that make?" questioned Thomas.

"She is not the captain's type," Marin declared flatly.

"Do say. She is bright, witty, and quite comely. Actually, she much resembles you."

Marin snorted, indignant at the comparison. "Perhaps you should wear your spectacles more often."

Thomas laughed. "Your jealously is showing, cousin."

"Do not be ridiculous," she snapped.

"Come now, Marin, 'tis me to whom you speak. You can deny it all you want, but something happened between you and Reese on that voyage. At last comes a man who can shake your tree. Who would have imagined it to be Captain Thackeray?" Thomas paused upon further reflection. "Actually, it makes perfect sense that he—"

"Oh be quiet, Thomas!"

Thomas chuckled, then sobered again. "Marin, declare Nathaniel and reclaim your life."

Marin's shoulders drooped dejectedly. "I cannot."

"Yes, you can. You cannot betray a dead man."

"But what if Nathaniel is alive?"

"You were in Algiers. Did you find any news of him? Do not you think that in three years' time Nathaniel would have found some way to let you know he was alive if that were the case? If 'tis a life with Reese that you want—"

Marin gave a huff of annoyance. "Why do you persist in that notion?"

"Because you are a poor liar, dear cousin. My advice to you is to tell Reese now or risk losing him and being miserable the rest of your years."

"Perhaps he does not feel so inclined."

"I have it on good authority that he does. He waits on you, but he won't wait forever. You have no more excuses, Marin. The choice is yours to make, and the first step is to declare Nathaniel deceased." Thomas kissed her on the cheek. "I must be off to the courthouse now. Think about what I have said."

Over the next several days, the voices of reason became louder and more persistent, just as Reese had warned her they do when one tries to outrun the truth. She had joined her father at the counting house, hoping to escape them, but they only followed.

The clerk was mystified to find her frequently gazing out the window scanning the wharf. Finally, he asked her one day, "Do you search for someone, madam?"

She turned and looked at him. "No, Mr. Phineas...not anymore. Tell my father that I am going out for awhile."

"Yes, madam."

Marin took a hired carriage across town.

When she walked into Thomas' office, he leaned back in his chair and smiled. "And just when I thought my day was going to be dull. To what do I owe your visit, dear cousin?"

As Marin stated her business, he regarded her with surprise.

"Are you certain about this?" he asked when she had finished. "It could ultimately mean that you must leave your position at the counting house."

Marin nodded. "You will see to the matter?"

"I will straightaway," Thomas assured her.

CHAPTER THIRTY-TWO

Moment of Truth

"Mr. Duncan, may I come aboard?" Marin called up from the wharf.

The second mate hesitated, unsure of what the captain might say.

"I have business with Captain Thackeray—serious business," she emphasized, when Duncan remained hesitant.

"Come aboard then, Mistress."

Marin climbed the gangplank to the deck. "Is the captain in his quarters?"

"Aye, but ye best have a care. He ain't been in a temperate mood."

"Thank you, Mr. Duncan. I shall keep that in mind."

Reese was bent over the table in the workroom plotting the route of his next voyage, when there came a knock on his door.

"Enter," he commanded.

The door quietly opened and closed, uncharacteristic of any of his officers, and he looked up in surprise to find Marin standing at the entrance to the room. He slowly straightened to his full height and came from around the table. "To what do I owe the honor, madam?" he inquired guardedly.

Marin took a deep breath. "I seek to open a new chapter in my book."

His brow furrowed in bewilderment. "I beg your pardon?"

"I have decided to declare Nathaniel deceased," she said. "Thomas is drawing up the document and filing it forthwith. I cannot say if you care now or not…"

Reese made no response and Marin searched his face for a sign that it mattered. When he looked away, her heart dropped; she was too late. Disheartened, she started to leave.

"Marin, wait. I do care," he said. "But you have been so resistant to this course of action. Why now do you seek it?"

Marin turned back to him. "Because you were right. I cannot outrun the truth. I want to move on with my life, and I want to do it with you," she replied, softly.

"Are you certain now? I gave my heart once to a woman to no happy end. I will not commit it again without assurance that the specter of Nathaniel does not stand between us."

Marin took off her coat and let it drop to the floor. Steadily meeting his gaze, she walked over to him, put her arms around his neck, and raised herself up on her toes. "Is this assurance enough?" she asked, pressing her lips to his.

He drew her close and answered her with a kiss of unrestrained passion.

"If the captain has done with his duties now…" she murmured breathlessly.

"The captain has just had done with his duties," he replied, lifting her up in his arms and carrying her across the parlor to the sleeping room. He set her down beside the bed. "Are you sure you do not need more time to think about this?"

"I have thought about it for too long," she replied, pulling off her dress.

"As have I," he murmured, his deep voice husky with desire.

He pulled off his shirt, and Marin gave him an impish grin. "You are not unfamiliar to me, you know."

He gave a snort. "It would appear, madam, that you have the advantage then, and I would seek to remedy that."

She laughed and sat down on the bed to take off her shoes and stockings, then discarded her corset and petticoat, watching as Reese finished undressing, her eyes taking in every inch of his virile appearance. When he came and pressed her back against the mattress, she felt a shiver of desire go through her.

As he began to lift up her shift, she suddenly tensed.

"Have you a change of heart?" he asked, concerned.

Marin shook her head. "It is just that it has been a long time since…since I have engaged in this way," she replied. "I fear that I may disappoint you."

Reese chuckled. "I assure you, madam, 'tis not something that one forgets how to do. There is no right or wrong way, only nuances. You will not disappoint."

Just the same, Marin was still reticent. Her husband had never been much for foreplay, and it sometimes made her question her desirability. And she was moved to ask Reese: "Is a man stirred by a woman or is it just a stirring caused by the nature of a man?"

"A man's need can be impersonal, but I dare say that most times it is stirred by desire for a certain woman," he replied, continuing to apply light, feathery kisses along her neck.

"Then, when it is the first case, it must be the woman who is at cause, is it not?" she asked.

Reese raised his head and looked at her. "Not necessarily. Marin, what occasions these questions? Do you doubt that I love you, that I desire you?"

"No," she said.

"Then what troubles you?"

Marin was silent for a moment before confessing: "During our courtship and in the beginning of our marriage, Nathaniel displayed a most passionate nature. But over time, it seemed to wane and the act to become more an exercise of nature. I can only deduce that it was due to an inadequacy on my part that led him to lose interest…and to wander."

"You would be wrong then," Reese assured her. "The fault was your husband's, not yours, Marin. With some men, the chase is the thrill. It has nothing to do with the woman per se. It is about the challenge she may present and the excitement and ego of prevailing. And having come to know you, I suspect it was a merry challenge indeed that you presented Nathaniel," he added lightly.

But Marin was not convinced. "How can you say?"

"I have known plenty of men like Nathaniel," replied Reese. "They are not capable of fidelity."

He put a hand beneath her chin to raise her gaze to his. "I do not deny that I have been with other women, but I am not as Nathaniel. I promise you, Marin, my passion for you shall never wane. Quite the opposite, it grows every day because you are the one who has captured my heart, who fulfills me, and it is to you that I will always remain true."

Tears welled up in Marin's eyes, and he lowered his head to seal his pledge with a gentle caress, his lips moving seductively over hers with increasing intimacy. He broke off to trail kisses from her neck to her shoulders and to lightly run a hand across her stomach and down her thigh, ultimately coming to play between her legs.

When she caught her breath at the heady sensation, he teased her a little longer before stopping to raise the shift over her head, and, at long last, view the shapely curves and the firm, rounded breasts he had imagined many a time through her dress. Her skin was soft and flawless, save the small mark on her right thigh that strangely resembled the shape of a heart.

"What is this mark on your thigh?" he asked curiously.

"I have had it since birth," replied Marin. "My mother always told me that it was from the kiss of an angel and would afford me protection. After our adventure in Algiers, I am inclined to give her story more credence," she added with a light laugh.

"Indeed," murmured Reese. He pressed his lips to the heart-shaped symbol in his own vow to always protect her.

Marin gasped, then, as he continued on a trail that found erogenous zones she had never imagined. He took possession of her and she allowed it, placing her complete trust in him. It was a cold November day, but neither noticed the chill in the air.

She ran her hands over the corded muscles in his arms, across his shoulders, and down his back thrilling at his strength. The urgency mounted, and she touched him until he needed no further inducement. They seemed to be in tune with each other's needs and desires. When he raised himself over top of her, without hesitancy, Marin opened herself to him.

She gasped again as he filled her. When Reese began to move on her, she fell into rhythm with him, in sync all the way. This was the moment both had thought about often and now eagerly embraced. It fed their hunger, sending currents of electricity pulsing through their bodies, exciting nerve endings to a degree neither thought possible.

When at last they came to rest, their passion spent, they continued to lie quietly together for a few minutes, reveling in the experience, feeling the energy ebb from their bodies. Reese kissed her and rolled off of her. As both began to feel the chill, he pulled covers over them, and Marin snuggled up against his chest.

"You do realize that we are related now," she said, on a teasing note.

Reese chuckled. "My aunt and your father did manage to complicate things."

"Indeed. I was quite beside myself at the thought of us being in the same family," confessed Marin.

"Suffice it to say there was a time that I did not relish the idea any more than you, my dear."

Marin laughed. "I thought you quite arrogant you know."

"And I thought you a pain in the—"

"Yes, I was quite aware, Captain."

"Perhaps now, Aunt Caroline can know some peace at her family dinners. What made you decide to declare your husband?" asked Reese.

"Thomas convinced me," replied Marin.

"My thanks to your cousin. What did he say?"

"Among other things that you have been escorting Penny Newsome about."

Reese turned his head to her. "Thomas mentioned me by name?"

"Not exactly. He made reference to you as captain."

Reese laughed. "So you were moved by jealously then?"

"No…well…perhaps just a touch. Penny isn't really your type," she said with a sniff.

"Woe be it to the man who gets between two women," he chuckled. "But to be clear, it is Peter who is escorting Miss Newsome about, not I. He is rather taken with the lady I do believe."

Marin lifted herself up on one arm and looked at him. "Thomas lied to me?"

"Not necessarily. My brother just received his captain's license."

"O-o-oh, that Thomas! I shall take him to task. He deliberately led me to assume it was you."

"The employment of half truths and assumptions seems to be a talent that runs in your family," quipped Reese. "In any case, do not take Thomas too much to task. You would not be here in my bed otherwise."

Marin shivered but in anticipation as he pressed her back against the mattress and mounted a seductive offense in a renewed campaign of pleasure.

"Reese, I must go," she moaned. "I have been here overlong as it is. Mr. Duncan may take notice. We must be discreet."

"I suppose I shall have to marry you then," he said, raining kisses over her body.

"I heard Mr. Duncan and Mr. White say that you are not the marrying type."

"No man thinks he is until he meets the right woman."

"Must it be a smock wedding?" she asked impishly.

"No, I shall insist upon a naked wedding," he replied.

"Reese Thackeray, I do not care what some silly tradition says. I will not take my nuptials unclothed to signify that I carry no debts from my husband. You shall have to take my word for it."

"There are ways to shield you," countered Reese. "I heard of one woman who stood inside a closet with her arm thrust through a hole made in the door. Another stood on a ladder outside the window for the ceremony."

Marin glared at him. "As I said, you shall have to take me at my word."

Reese laughed. "And your cousin thinks you are a conformist at heart. Tell Thomas to make haste with that document for I will not hold myself long from you."

Marin giggled. "However shall you survive?"

"I put the same question to you, madam," he said, a gleam coming into his eye as he pulled her on top of him.

Up on deck, White approached Duncan. "Is the captain in his quarters? I have a need to speak with him."

"I wouldna bother him right now," advised Duncan. "Mistress Marin is in there. Been there better part of an hour."

White let out a low whistle. "That does not bode well as ill tempered as he hath been. Why is she here?"

"She said it was about business."

"'Tis even worse. Did you hear shoutin'?"

"Ain't heard nary a word."

"Might be one of them is dead then," said the bosun half joking.

Just then the door to the captain's quarters opened and Marin stepped on deck. As she passed by them, she gave them a dazzling smile. "Good day, gentlemen."

Duncan and White stared after her as she practically floated across the deck and down the gangplank.

"If she is gladdened, 'tis for certain the captain ain't," murmured Duncan.

White nodded. "I think I shall speak with the captain later."

"Too late," said Duncan. "He's on deck and comin' our way."

Both men braced themselves.

"Timothy...Andrew, I have some business to attend," said Reese.

"Is all well, sir?" asked the bosun with some hesitancy.

"Aye, Andrew. Why do you make inquiry?"

"What with the way things are between you and Mistress Marin and her bein' here to see you about business..."

"Oh. Yes, well, there was a matter to clear up," replied Reese. "I should warn you that Mrs. Sutton may come by from time to time."

"Should we refuse to permit her to board?" asked Duncan.

"No, let her pass. There may be other matters to discuss. By way of my aunt and her father, she and I have family ties now."

"Our sympathies, sir," commented White soberly.

Amusement tweaked the corners of Reese's mouth. "Indeed."

CHAPTER THIRTY-THREE

A Matter of Peace

Thomas stared across the desk at Reese in disbelief. "You are certain that it was Nathaniel who Marin saw in Algiers?"

Reese nodded. "James Cathcart confirmed it. We convinced her that she was mistaken."

"Nathaniel a corsair…" Thomas shook his head. "Even given my low opinion of him, I cannot credit the thought." He rose from his desk and went to stare out the window. After a few moments' deliberation, he turned to Reese. "I cannot file to declare Nathaniel deceased now."

"Why not? As far as Marin knows, he is dead. He will not return, Thomas."

"How can you be sure of that?"

"Sutton knows he could be tried for piracy if he returns, and—" Reese paused. "And he has taken a wife in Algiers, a Moorish woman."

Thomas looked at him, stunned. "Nathaniel is a bigamist, too?! My God." He rifled a hand through his reddish brown hair, trying to think. "Nathaniel will argue that he was forced into piracy and into marriage with this Moorish woman—and, trust me, he will be convincing. Americans think these people are barbarians. Neither the public nor the government is likely to hold him accountable."

Thomas regarded Reese with a disturbing thought. "You and Marin haven't…" But he could see by the captain's expression that they had. "God's teeth, Reese, what were you thinking?"

"It was just this once, and we were discreet."

"You do intend to marry her?"

"Of course…as soon as possible." Thackeray gave a snort of annoyance. "I am not a cad, Thomas."

"Just the same I am very fond of my cousin, Captain. Marin has known one unhappy marriage. I will not stand by while she makes another."

"It will not be the case. I love her," Reese assured him soberly.

"Well, you certainly put on a good show," continued Thomas. "To all appearances, the two of you are quite averse to each other."

Reese smiled. "Suffice it to say we do not always know our minds until circumstances demand it. I dare say you had a hand in it."

Thomas looked at him in surprise. "Me? How so?"

"You led Marin to believe that it was I who was escorting Mrs. Newsome to the theater."

"Oh…that. Well, I suspected Marin had feelings for you. I was just giving her a nudge. Most certainly, I did not expect you to fall into bed together before matters were resolved."

He paced the floor of his office, thinking aloud. "Though the court has wide discretion in declaring a man dead, it is reluctant to do so inside of seven years and tends to drag its feet in granting the decree. I can make good argument, but, under these circumstances, it will be more to Marin's interest to file for a divorce."

"Will that be a problem?" asked Reese.

Thomas sighed. "She is certain to question it," he admitted. "I will tell her it is the faster course. Now that we are no longer bound by the strictures of the Church of England, it is easier for a woman to obtain a divorce, particularly if charges of adultery, bigamy, and criminal misdeeds are brought to bear."

"Marin will never consent to that course of action—not without being told the truth," said Reese. "It would be very hurtful to her, and even then, there is no telling what she would do."

Thomas thought for a minute. "Perhaps she will not have to know these charges were brought."

"Come again?"

"Given the circumstances, I can prevail upon the court to keep the charges secret," replied Thomas. "I know a judge to whom I can make such an appeal.

"Of course, it may not go well with the public that Marin is divorcing her husband while he still might be held a prisoner," he continued, working through the scenario. "We shall have to put it about that after exhausting all efforts, there is no proof that Nathaniel is dead or a prisoner. Heretofore, if he is alive, he has made no effort to reveal himself in these three years, and, thus, it is in Marin's best interests to declare abandonment as a protection in the event that she remarries and Nathaniel should return."

Reese was skeptical. "It sounds rather convoluted."

"Such an event is not without precedent, particularly in the maritime profession," said Thomas. "Bloody hell, Reese, could you not have given me more notice? If it becomes known that Marin is engaged in an illicit affair with you before this matter is settled, she could be the one charged with adultery."

"I would hardly call it an affair. As I said, it happened just once. Neither of us planned for it, Thomas."

"Clearly, neither of you were thinking either. Once is all it takes to declare an infidelity. Leave me now. I have work to do. In the meantime, you and Marin keep a distance from one another," he warned sternly. "She is on thin ice."

"When can we marry?" asked Reese.

"Not for at least six months after the divorce decree is granted for the sake of appearances."

* * * * *

Caroline was not one to give up and strived to make the family supper a weekly event. She was determined to bring everyone together in harmony one way or another. Even so, all were braced for the contentious sparring between Marin and Reese this night. To the surprise of everyone but Thomas, however, Marin and Reese were in good humor. While the turnabout was bewildering to the other diners, it made for a pleasant time, at last, that no one wanted to question.

The evening had gone so well Caroline couldn't stop thinking about it. She sat propped up in bed braiding her hair. "Did not you find it strange, Benjamin?" she questioned.

"What?" he asked climbing into bed beside her.

"Marin and Reese's behavior at dinner."

"I found it most welcoming."

"Odd would be more the word."

Benjamin laughed. "Has it not been your efforts to unite this family? And now that your campaign has borne fruit, still you are not satisfied."

"Last week, those two were sharpening their tongues on each other. And now the daggers are gone? 'Tis not likely."

"Perhaps Thomas talked some sense into them. Or perhaps Marin feels relieved of a burden now that she has taken steps to resolve her marital status. In any case, she and Reese appear to have called a truce." Benjamin kissed his wife on the cheek. "Good night, dearest. Let sleeping dogs lie and enjoy the peace."

Her husband turned over and went to sleep, but Caroline continued to think about the matter. Her eyes suddenly widened with a thought. *Could there be an attraction between her nephew and stepdaughter?* "No, it wasn't possible," she murmured to herself. They were both too headstrong.

Over the next month, the hours and days seemed to drag by for Marin and Reese. Their only physical contact came at Caroline's family suppers, which they now embraced rather than decried, and the gatherings helped to calm the waters. With each passing day, however, their patience was wearing thin, and their frustration was beginning to adversely affect their more amiable mood.

Caroline was baffled by the seesawing emotions of her stepdaughter and nephew. There was something different about the tenseness between them now that she simply couldn't figure.

"Benjamin, there is something afoot with Marin and Reese," she said, once again raising the subject with him. "It is difficult to know what mood they will bring to the family gatherings anymore. I must insist that you talk to Thomas and find out what bedevils Marin. I shall confer with Peter about Reese."

"What makes you think that Thomas and Peter are any the wiser?"

"Young people confide in their peers," replied Caroline.

Her husband sighed and gave her a smile of forbearance. "My dear, I would counsel you to stay out of the matter. Reese and Marin have had a complicated relationship from the beginning. Now that they are family, it appears to be doubly so. In time, I am certain they will come to terms." At the skeptical glare from his wife, he added: "But I will talk to Thomas."

* * * * *

It was a cold December morning, a fortnight before the holidays, but the sun was warm and bright, and the air was more invigorating than bone-chilling.

Marin chafed at Thomas' insistence that she accompany him on a ride to check on some property he was overseeing. She was still grousing when she climbed into the sleigh.

"A drive in the country will do you good," said Thomas, ignoring her grumblings.

He handed her a fur throw for warmth, then clicked the reins and turned the sleigh in the direction of Roxbury.

"'Tis been a month, Thomas. How much longer am I to wait before the divorce decree is granted?" she questioned moodily. "You counseled me that this would be the faster route, though I am somewhat discomfited by it."

"I cannot say how much longer," said Thomas. "Since the end of the War of Independence, the courts are awash in divorce requests—mostly by women, I might add. But even with the decree in hand, you and Reese must still keep your distance for a measured time before courting," he warned. "In the meantime, I must prevail upon you both to show a more even nature. You are creating strife in the family and raising questions."

"I am sorely pressed to do better, Thomas."

"Try harder, cousin. Uncle Ben has come to see me about the matter, and Peter has been approached by Caroline. The poor woman is quite fretful. She has labored hard to bring the family together and fears that the divide between you and Reese may cause a divide between her and Uncle Ben."

Framed in those terms, Marin felt contrite. Once again, she had been focused only on herself. "You are right, Thomas. I shall offer my apologies to Caroline and promise to be more accommodating."

"Good. Peter is having this same conversation with Reese."

The bucolic, snow-covered countryside gave way to large hills as they came into Roxbury. They passed through the town to the southern end where a huge pond surrounded by wooded hills came into view. Here, gentlemen's estates dotted the landscape in a one-mile area known as Jamaica Plains.

Thomas drove up to an impressive Georgian style home that overlooked the pond and stopped. "Here we are," he said. "It was built by a Tory who fled to England after Cornwallis' surrender. My client bought it for a pittance and is looking to sell for a modest profit. I am thinking of buying it."

Marin looked at her cousin in surprise. "A country estate…I would not have thought it of you. But I fear you may not qualify."

"How so?" asked Thomas in bewilderment.

"It requires a gentleman," she replied with a teasing twinkle in her eye.

"Ha, ha. I am heartened to see that your humor is returning, sharp though it is."

"The house is beautiful, Thomas. But what occasions this decision? I thought you were not partial to the quiet life."

"I am going to ask Nancy to marry me," he confessed shyly.

Marin's eyes widened in further surprise. "Are you really my cousin? You said you thought Nancy too dull."

"Let us say that I have come to appreciate the calm that surrounds her—especially now with your return," he added wryly.

Marin stuck her tongue out at him.

"Do you think Nancy will accept my proposal?"

"Yes, I fear so," said Marin with mock concern. "I shall have to give her some counsel."

"Do not you dare," warned Thomas. "I already have a rebellious cousin on my hands. I do not need a rebellious wife, too. Besides, you are hardly one to give counsel."

Marin laughed and hugged her cousin. "I am happy for you, Thomas. Nancy is proving to be a good influence. I dare say you have grown up in my absence."

"Perhaps," he said with a mischievous grin.

Thomas handed her out of the sleigh, and they walked up to the front door. He unlocked it and opened it for her to pass through.

Marin gazed into the large rooms off the foyer. The furniture was covered in cloths, but she was agog at what elegance she saw in the drapes, moldings, and paneling.

"Oh, Thomas, it is quite lovely," she said. "I think you should buy it. Nancy will adore it."

As she continued to explore the house, Thomas built a fire in the fireplace in the drawing room. When she returned, the room was warm and cozy.

A short while later, she heard a rider approach. "Are you expecting a visitor?" she asked, annoyed. "You know that I am not well disposed towards company this day."

"I seek the opinion of another," replied Thomas. "But do not fret. I promise that you will not be put upon. You may remain by the fire if you wish."

Marin did wish. She stayed behind in the drawing room while Thomas went to greet his visitor. When she heard the men conversing, she went still. She well knew that voice, and she rushed into the foyer to see Reese.

He was just as surprised to see her. When he smiled, she let out a cry of delight and ran into his arms.

"How did you know I was here?" she asked.

"I did not know. Thomas requested that I meet him here."

Marin looked at her cousin, her face aglow. "Thank you, Thomas."

"'Tis in the interest of helping to restore peace in the family," he said. "You have two hours to mend your sore moods. I shall be down at the tavern. Try not to get into an argument and break anything."

He had barely closed the door on them before Reese and Marin became locked in a passionate embrace that sought the release of weeks of pent up sexual tension and frustration.

It wasn't enough and Reese led Marin to a shrouded sofa in the drawing room. She needed no coaxing to assume the pose, and she gave him a come-hither smile as she raised her skirts. He needed no further invitation. He answered her with a seductive half smile, quickly pulled off his coat and vest, and unbuttoned the fly front of his breeches.

As they feverishly engaged, their excitement and pleasure rose to a level that exceeded their first coupling. And if Marin had any lingering doubts about herself or Reese, they were forever dispelled.

When they had finished, their energy expended, Marin lay spooned in his arms, satiated and at peace. She shivered with delight as Reese ran a hand under her skirt and lightly up her thigh, and she turned to face him. When she raised a hand to stroke his cheek, his lips captured hers in a renewed rush of passion. They broke away to disrobe completely, this time feeling the need to come together flesh against flesh—soft curves against hard muscle—in a more deliberative climb to ecstasy.

When Thomas returned, Reese was putting on his coat and Marin was re-pinning her hair. Her cheeks were rosy and both wore smiles of satisfaction.

"I trust you vented your frustrations and came to terms," he commented.

Marin and Reese looked at each other and grinned. "We did," they said.

That evening, peace reigned over Caroline's family gathering once again, and she leaned over to whisper to Thomas: "I know not what you and Peter said to Marin and Reese, but the transformation is most miraculous. How ever did you achieve it?"

Thomas smiled. "You have no idea, dear lady."

"Well, whatever you did, let us hope for lasting success," replied Caroline.

"And speed on the part of the courts," Thomas murmured to himself, wondering how long this transformation was going to last.

When Thomas and Marin arrived home after the family supper, he went to the parlor for a night cap. Marin was about to start up the stairs to her room, when there came a heavy knock on the door.

"I will answer it," she called to Thomas.

She walked back to the front door. When she opened it, she let out a cry and collapsed on the floor in a dead faint.

Upon hearing Marin's cry, Thomas rushed into the foyer to see a man bending over her and froze.

"My God," he breathed. "Nathaniel."

CHAPTER THIRTY-FOUR

Jeopardy

The storm that followed Nathaniel's return was nothing short of cataclysmic.

The community embraced him as a returning hero; Marin's father didn't know which emotion to favor in the interest of his daughter; Marin had taken to her bed in shock; and Reese exhibited exceedingly poor humor. While Thomas was frantically trying to figure out how this was going to play out when Nathaniel learned of the divorce action, Caroline struggled to grasp hold of the upheaval that rippled through her family.

On the morning of the fourth day, Thomas stood at the end of his cousin's bed at his wit's end.

"Nathaniel is downstairs, Marin. This is the third time he has come. You can't put off facing him any longer."

Marin pulled the covers up to her chin. "I cannot, Thomas. What am I to say to him? That I have fallen in love with another man and filed for divorce while he was being held prisoner?"

"He can't have been suffering too much if he was the man you saw in Algiers, cousin."

"Oh, Thomas, I am in such a muddle," she cried.

"Well, it is not going to get sorted out hiding away in your room. Nathaniel is running out of patience, and I have run out of excuses for you. I shall expect you downstairs forthwith."

Thomas started to leave the room when he turned to her with words of advice. "Nathaniel has more to answer for than you, Marin.

Do not let some misguided sense of guilt weaken your hand. Control the story."

The clock struck the hour.

Marin stood uncertainly in the hall outside the parlor. Now that she had given herself permission to move on with Reese, she wondered what she would feel at seeing her husband after all this time. Taking a deep breath, she squared her shoulders and walked into the room.

Nathaniel rose from his chair and gave her a warm smile. "Marin, dearest. How long I have waited for this moment."

He stood a half foot taller than she, lean but well-built. He was dressed in a fine suit of clothes, clean-shaven, and his hair had re-grown and was trimmed to fashion. She had forgotten how pleasing an appearance he presented.

"I shall take my leave," said Thomas.

"No, I want you to stay," responded Marin levelly.

Thomas hesitated. "As you wish."

Nathaniel had expected to have a private meeting with his wife, but said nothing. Instead, he moved to take Marin in his arms. When she sidestepped him, his brows knit in bewilderment.

"You look very well," he said, endeavoring to gloss over the awkward moment.

"And you look quite fit for being a prisoner for nearly four years," she returned.

"Uh, yes, officers were given more leniency," he replied smoothly. "Just the same, there was an emotional toll. Have no doubt that I have been sorely tried these years apart from you, my love." His words dripped from his mouth like honey, and she was reminded of how disarmingly guileful he could be. "I have thought of nothing else than returning to your loving embrace and—" Nathaniel suddenly felt the crack of her hand against the side of his face.

Thomas jumped, startled, and both men regarded her with astonishment.

"Marin, I realize that my sudden reappearance may have caught you unprepared," said Nathaniel recovering himself, "but I must confess I envisioned a far different welcome."

Marin was unapologetic. "I looked for you, Nathaniel. I paid merchant captains to inquire after you. I questioned every seaman who traveled that route, but no one seemed to know of you—an officer no less. Why do you suppose that was? Finally, I hired a buccaneer to take me to Algiers when no other ship's captain would. I saw a man who looked like you at the dey's palace and on the street, and he saw me."

"Marin—"

She put up a hand to silence him.

"Everyone told me it could not have been you because the man I saw was a pirate, a Musselman with a different name," she went on, her voice quivering with anger. "But it *was* you, Nathaniel, wasn't it?"

"Marin, I can explain—"

Marin gave a satiric laugh. "How silly of me to think that I could have gathered word of you—a pirate, a Musselman."

"Dearest, please try to understand. I had no choice. I was pressed into piracy and forced to become a Musselman upon point of death," he rushed to explain. "I heard of your status with the dey. I could not acknowledge you in Algiers for both our safety."

"In all these years, you could have found some way to get word to me," she retorted. "Have you any idea what it was like not to know if I was widow or wife…hope one day, despair the next. I could have ransomed you."

"It was not possible, my love. To renounce the Musselman faith carries a penalty of death. I escaped on a raid at first opportunity and came straightaway to Boston to look for you. You cannot imagine how heartened I was to find you living at the home of your cousin. I feared the American pirate to be holding you a prisoner."

He tried to take her into his arms again, but she walked away from him.

"I had finally resigned myself to the fact that you were gone, never to return, Nathaniel. I need more time."

Nathaniel frowned. He had imagined her falling into his arms, moved to tears at his return, not this anger and estrangement.

"Of course, dear heart…if that be your wish," he replied, sensing that he could not charm his way around her this time. "Meanwhile, I shall search for lodgings for us, as you appear to have sold the house."

"Yes, to raise money for a ransom for you," she responded shortly.

Nathaniel faltered. "I meant no criticism, Marin." When she made no response, he picked up his hat. "Well then, as I have much to do, I shall take my leave. We will talk again, dearest, when you have had time to…adjust." He hesitated, hoping for some encouragement, but Marin remained stiff and unyielding.

Thomas saw him to the door and returned to the parlor.

"When I said to control the story, cousin, I did not mean for you to beat Nathaniel over the head with it," he quipped. "I'm not sure slapping him was the right course of action, but I dare say you got your point across. What are you going to do?"

Marin looked at him with tears in her eyes. "I cannot say," she replied.

* * * * *

Reese was not faring any better. Marin was constantly on his mind, and he desperately wanted to see her. But Thomas held him at bay, pointing out the complications it would cause Marin were his relationship with her be suspected.

He sat brooding in the Bunch of Grapes tavern in the company of his brother and a tankard of ale.

"Look on the bright side," said Peter. "It has been three weeks and Marin hasn't withdrawn the divorce decree."

"'Tis small comfort," responded Reese. "She is still Sutton's wife, and Thomas said that Nathaniel is pressing her to move into the lodgings he has secured for them."

"Why does she not tell Sutton that she filed for divorce?"

"Why indeed?" murmured Reese.

That was a question that had been gnawing at him. Why hadn't she—unless she was having second thoughts. Maybe she fancied that she was still in love with Nathaniel or had guilt reared its ugly head to seize hold of her again?

"The man tells a convincing story," commented Peter.

"He is smart," said Reese. "He is protecting himself against a charge of piracy by bringing it to the fore himself. What he doesn't say is the real reason he became a renegade and a corsair."

"He said he was forced to the life as a slave."

"Peter, during your imprisonment, did you ever hear of a captured officer being forced to the Musselman faith and the life of a corsair?"

Peter shook his head. "No. Even a captured sailor is given the choice. I thought there was something strange about Sutton's story. But why would he convert and turn to piracy?"

"According to Cathcart, he was caught bedding an Algerine woman—"

"Which is punishable by death unless the offender embraces the Musselman faith," continued Peter. "Now it makes sense."

"And from everything I have heard about Sutton," said Reese, "I have no doubt that he saw an opportunity to enrich himself into the bargain by becoming a corsair."

"Once a rogue always a rogue," quipped Peter.

Reese let out a short, mirthless laugh. "That is an understatement. He married the Algerine woman."

Peter looked at his brother, incredulous. "I understand now why you did not want to tell Marin the truth about her husband."

Reese was thoughtful for a moment. "The question is why, after all this time, does he now choose to come back?"

"'Tis hard to imagine that he could not have affected an escape before this had he wanted to," agreed Peter. "Perhaps he tired of the life and seeing Marin in Algiers triggered a desire in him to return to her."

"Perhaps, but, according to Thomas, Sutton always has a play that advantages him."

"Whatever it is, I am sure you will figure it out," said Peter. "I must leave you now. I shall keep an ear open for any news of interest to you." He stood up and laid a hand of support on Reese's shoulder. "Keep heart, brother."

When Peter left the tavern, Reese ordered another tankard of ale and continued to wonder about Nathaniel's angle. A shadow crossed his table then, and he looked up to see an older man of medium height and stocky build.

"Are you Reese Thackeray, captain of the *Sea Nymph*?" the man asked.

"I am," replied Reese guardedly. "Who might you be?"

"Samuel Hayes, captain of the *Grand Fortune* just into port from France. Your first mate told me where to find you. I was directed by the American Minister to commit this letter to your hand only."

Reese took the sealed missive from him. "A drink for your trouble, Captain?"

The mariner hesitated, then sat down. "I could do with a spot of ale. Thank ye kindly."

Reese signaled the barkeep who brought another tankard.

Hayes took a gulp of his beer. "I've heard of ye, Captain Thackeray. Ye be somethin' of a legend with seamen hereabouts…somethin' about havin' the protection of a sea nymph."

Reese laughed. "As a captain yourself, you know that sailors are given to exaggeration. How goes France?"

Captain Hayes shook his head. "Gettin' more dangerous, I fear. What with the pirates in the Caribbean and in the Mediterranean, the revolution in France, and the wars in Europe, 'tis hard to find a safe route to sail these days."

"Take heart, sir. I have it on good authority that the United States government has begun the construction of a navy," said Reese.

"Good news, indeed. I wish them speed." The captain quaffed the rest of his ale. "I must return to the business of my cargo now. Thank ye for the drink, kind sir."

"One good turn deserves another," responded Reese.

When the captain left, Reese picked up the letter and regarded it curiously for a minute. Why would the American Minister to France be sending him a missive? He wasn't sure he really wanted to know, and it was with some hesitation that he broke the Minister's wax seal and opened the letter. It was two sheets, the first a note of introduction:

My good Captain Thackeray, this notice comes to you from James Cathcart by way of Captain O'Bryen. I have placed it under my seal to insure its arrival as it was relayed to me that the contents deserve your most serious attention. (signed) James Monroe, Minister to the First Republic of France.

Reese read Cathcart's letter then with a deepening sense of alarm. When he was finished, he paid for the drinks and strode quickly out of the tavern.

Thomas Langford was not having a good day. When Reese walked into his office, the look on the captain's face told him that the day was about to get worse.

"Thomas—"

"Wait," said Langford. He reached for the decanter of whiskey on his desk, splashed some into a glass and took a fortifying gulp. "Now, you may say. What is the nature of your urgency, Captain?"

"I just received a letter from James Cathcart," said Reese.

"Your friend in Algiers?"

"Aye. The dey feels that he has been cursed with bad luck since Marin was 'kidnapped' from his palace. He is offering a handsome reward for her return."

Thomas stared at him, then let out a short laugh. "Surely, you jest."

Reese dropped the missive on the desk. "Read for yourself."

Langford picked up the communique and scanned it, the dubious expression on his face changing to one of concern. "The dey's arm cannot possibly reach this far."

"I fear it already has," said Reese.

"How do you mean?"

"Think about it, Thomas. Nathaniel is the only one who would know to look for Marin in Boston. And as her husband, he is free to take her away with him whenever and wherever he chooses without question."

"Dear God," murmured Thomas. "I think low of Nathaniel, but I cannot believe the man would be so despicable." He looked at Reese. "If 'tis true what he intends, the situation is more serious than you know, my friend."

"How so?"

Langford poured another drink and pushed it toward the captain. "You will need this one."

"What is it? Just tell me, Thomas."

"Marin is with child. She told me this morning."

Reese looked at him, dumbstruck, then reached for the glass and downed the whiskey in a single gulp. "Is she certain?"

"She went to see your Dr. Pennyman for a stomach upset, and he gave her the news." Thomas snorted. "I cannot imagine why you are surprised."

"Marin was under the impression that she was not able to conceive," said Reese.

"Well, apparently with you she can. Premarital creation raises no eyebrows these days as long as the couple marries, but a child begotten outside of one's marriage most certainly does. Nathaniel can use the knowledge for leverage by threatening to have her charged with adultery, and the baby will be the proof."

"How is she?" asked Reese.

"Shocked—same as you—and worried."

"I need to see her."

"Absolutely not. We have to get the divorce decree before Nathaniel gets wind of it and realizes the leverage he has to stop the action." Thomas regarded Reese soberly. "Marin is going to know that we lied to her about Nathaniel. Have you thought about how she will react to that?"

"I will deal with it later. For now, we need to break Sutton's legal control over her. Get that bloody divorce decree, Thomas. I cannot say how long Nathaniel means to carry on this ruse before forcing Marin to leave with him." Reese turned on his heel and headed for the door.

"Where are you going?" asked Thomas.

"To check on Nathaniel's story…to find out how he got here and how he is leaving."

Reese lost no time calling Peter, Duncan, and White together in his quarters. He told them of Nathaniel Sutton's return and of his suspicions that Nathaniel was in Boston to take Marin back to Algiers.

Reese's long-time officers were shocked, finding it difficult to digest that Marin's husband had returned, let alone that he intended to deliver her back into the hands of the Algerine ruler.

"Why would he do that?" asked Duncan, appalled.

"James Cathcart has written me that the dey is offering a large ransom for her return," explained Reese.

"But how would Sutton know of it?" questioned White, still in a state of confusion.

"Because he was a renegade and a corsair for the dey," said Reese, further stunning them.

"The devil you say!" exclaimed White.

"He says that he was forced to it after being imprisoned and escaped Algerine pirates to return home, but knowing what I do of the man, I find his claims suspect. I believe him to be still in the employ of the dey."

"We will do whatever you need us to do to keep Mistress Marin safe, Captain," said Duncan.

"Aye, that we will," echoed White soberly. "We have a great fondness for the mistress. What would you have us do, Captain?"

"I want you and Timothy to check the manifests at the Customs House. Discover on which ship Sutton came to port. Then talk to the captain and any crew members you can find to learn the details of his passage."

"What can I do?" asked Peter.

"Talk to the harbor master to see what other ships arrived over the past month," replied Reese. "Look for one from southern Europe that is docked in the harbor away from the wharf. It most likely will be of a smaller size for speed and will have a crew of Musselmen."

As Duncan and White departed to do their tasks, Peter hung back.

"Has Marin been warned of your suspicions?" he asked.

Reese shook his head. "She has enough to consider. Peter, I need for you and Thomas to stay close to her. I cannot be seen with her now."

"Why not? Because of her husband? We are family now," pointed out Peter. "It would not be untoward for you to be seen in her presence."

"It would create more complications. Remember, Sutton still thinks me a pirate. If he sees me, he might assume that I am here for the same purpose as he and feel forced to act sooner than expected."

Peter nodded. "Anything else?"

"Yes, tell Aunt Caroline and Benjamin to make no mention of me when in Sutton's presence. I think it best if you stay clear of him as well. You and I do bear a resemblance, and I do not want him to make any connections."

"Reese, we know not yet that it is Sutton's purpose to take Marin back to Algiers."

"*I* am certain of it," snapped Reese. "His return at this time is too convenient. God's blood, Peter, why do you give that man the benefit of the doubt!"

"Easy, brother, I am on your side." Peter eyed Reese curiously. "I have never seen you this on edge."

"Do not the circumstances warrant it?"

"I know you, brother. There is something else that weighs heavily on your mind."

Reese glanced away for a moment. "Thomas informed me that Marin is with child."

"Oh," murmured Peter, surprised. "I had not heard that she went back to her husband. I am sorry, Reese. I had hoped that you and she would—"

"Peter, Marin is carrying my child, not Sutton's."

Peter stared at his brother in disbelief. "How the bloody hell—does Sutton know?"

Reese shook his head. "And he cannot learn of it or of Marin filing for the divorce."

"I can understand why," remarked Peter. "God's teeth, Reese—"

"You can save the lecture. I have already had it from Thomas. After Marin filed for the divorce, matters progressed a little faster than either of us had anticipated."

Peter snorted. "No doubt. You've been in tight corners before, but this…this is a box, Reese. Soon, Sutton will become aware of Marin's condition one way or the other."

Reese felt the knot tighten in his stomach. "I do not need to be reminded, Peter.

CHAPTER THIRTY-FIVE

The Devil You Don't Know

Peter, Duncan, and White gathered in Reese's quarters to report their findings.

"Sutton's account rings true, sir," said Duncan. "According to the captain of a Russian merchant ship, they encountered Barbary pirates. In the course of the battle, Sutton gave himself up and re-counted his story of being forced into piracy. They took him to France where he got passage on a ship to Boston."

Reese looked at his second officer. "Was the name of the ship the *Grand Fortune* by any chance?"

"Aye. How did you know?" asked Duncan.

"Coincidence," murmured Reese, struck by the obscure and not-so-obscure workings of fate. He turned to his bosun. "What did the harbor master say, Andrew?"

"There are no ships in port of your description, sir. Perhaps Sutton is telling the truth."

Reese was silent for a few minutes as he considered the matter. "Or mayhap Sutton's ship has not yet arrived. Keep a watch for such a ship on the horizon."

"Yes, sir," responded the officers.

Reese dismissed them and all but Peter filed out.

"Nathaniel is going to hear that Marin filed for divorce at some point, if she hasn't already told him, Reese. He will have to be given the chance to respond. The matter could get ugly and public, and Marin and the child will be the ones to bear the stigma.

"Even if the divorce came through without Sutton's knowledge and you quietly married her," continued Peter, once everything became known, Sutton would look the victim and neither you nor Marin would be held in high regard. Think how it would affect the standing of her father and Aunt Caroline."

Reese glared at his brother. "Do you not think I know all of this, Peter? It is tearing me apart. I can only imagine what this is doing to Marin. I cannot even see her."

"And you should not," said Peter. "If Sutton's story cannot be discredited, Marin needs to have a clear head to figure the best course for her and the child at whatever sacrifice to the heart."

Reese looked sharply at his brother, realizing what he was saying. "As God is my witness, Sutton will never parent my child, Peter."

* * * * *

Christmas had come and gone with little celebration or joy. Everyone except Nathaniel felt the strain—none more so than Marin and Reese.

Marin stared morosely out the window as the rain pelted the panes and turned the snow to slush. She was running out of time in more ways than one. Nathaniel had rented a house and gave her to know that, upon his return from a business trip, he was expecting her to take up residence with him. He was patient, caring, charming—the man she had first married—but experience told her not to trust him. And she feared how he would react to learning that she had filed for a divorce and was carrying another man's child.

Thomas arrived home. He peeled off his wet Macintosh and hung it on the coat tree in the hall, then went to find Marin in the parlor.

"'Tis raining cats and dogs out there," he said, pouring himself a glass of whiskey. "Has Nathaniel returned?"

Marin turned to him. "No."

"He most likely won't for a few days," continued Thomas. "The roads are nearly impassable with this rain."

Marin closed her eyes with a sigh of relief. A few more days' reprieve. "What am I to do, Thomas?" she asked dismally.

"It will not be easy whichever road you choose to travel," he acknowledged. "I would suggest that you follow your heart."

"I am not sure I have that luxury," she said, turning to stare out the window again.

A heavy silence fell over the room with only the sounds of the steadily falling rain and the ticking of the grandfather clock in the hall.

"Thomas, why did you change your mind and have me file for a divorce instead of declaring Nathaniel deceased?" Marin suddenly asked.

The question caught her cousin by surprise, and he nearly choked on his drink. "I-I told you. It was easier and faster without proof of death. And since you and Reese were in a hurry to marry…"

Marin turned back to him. "You have to give grounds for a divorce, do you not?"

"Yes."

"What argument did you put forth?"

Thomas knew this moment would come but was still unprepared for it and shifted uncomfortably beneath her unyielding gaze.

"Marin, what does it matter—"

"What argument, Thomas?"

"Abandonment," he replied lowly.

"You knew Nathaniel was alive." She gave a short, humorless laugh. "You knew it when you told me that Nathaniel had more to answer for than I…when you advised me not to let misguided guilt weaken my position. How? How did you know?"

Thomas hesitated. "Reese told me."

"Reese! How did he know?"

"Marin—"

"How did he know, Thomas?"

Thomas quaffed the rest of his drink. "James Cathcart told him. You were so insistent that you saw Nathaniel at the palace that day

Cathcart made some inquiries and discovered that the man you saw was indeed Nathaniel."

Marin slowly sat down in a chair, staggered. "And Reese did not tell me."

"If you remember, he had his hands full at the time getting you and Marsden's family out of Algiers," said Thomas. "Later, he—we—decided it served no purpose to tell you."

Marin looked at him, her eyes flashing with anger. "You had no right to make that determination."

"We were only trying to protect you, Marin. Given that Nathaniel had turned Musselman and a pirate, we had not expected him to ever return."

"But he did return, and now I am damned and my child as well."

Thomas raked a hand through his hair in frustration. "Perhaps if you and Reese had waited until your situation was settled before—" he broke off at the pained look on her face. "Apologies, Marin, I should not have said that."

"You are right," she said. "I am to blame."

"You are human, Marin. You made a decision based upon human emotion."

She lifted her eyes to him. "No, Thomas, I made a decision based upon an omission of truth. I realize now how wide and devastating the consequences of that can be."

* * * * *

Reese came on deck and asked the same question he asked every afternoon. "Anything to report, Timothy?"

"No, sir. No ship of interest to us has come to port."

Reese took Duncan's spyglass and scanned the wharf and piers, examining the ships in port and in dry dock. He frowned. There had to be a ship coming for him. He knew that he was right about Sutton. He felt it in his gut. There were too many coincidences.

"Keep watching," he said. "I will be at the tavern."

As Reese strode down the wharf to the tavern, he heard his name called. He stopped and turned to see Thomas hurrying up to him clearly disturbed.

"What's amiss? Is Marin well?" he asked anxiously.

"I cannot say," replied Thomas, breathless from running.

"What the bloody hell does that mean?"

"Marin is gone."

Reese felt the air being sucked out of his body. "You left her alone?"

"I had to leave town on business for a few days," replied Thomas defensively.

"Where was Peter?"

"Keeping an eye on Sutton. Marin went to stay with Uncle Ben and Caroline while she makes ready to move in with Nathaniel. We thought her safe enough there."

Reese looked at him in surprise. "She is moving in with Sutton?"

"He is still her husband, Reese. She has no choice."

"Where is she then? Does Sutton have her?"

"No…at least, we do not think so."

"God's teeth, Thomas, get to the point!"

"Marin set sail on the *Olympia*. She left Uncle Ben a letter saying that she was going to London to stay for a time with Susannah," he hurriedly explained.

"That is not possible. I or one of my men would have seen her on the wharf," said Reese. "We canvas the ships in port every day."

"You know Marin. If she wants to escape notice, she will escape notice."

"Why would she do this?"

Thomas hesitated. "She knows that we were not forthcoming about Nathaniel, and she is very angry."

Thackeray uttered an expletive. "How did she find out?"

"She intuited it. You know she does that, Reese."

"What about Sutton?"

"She said in her letter that she told Nathaniel about the divorce, and he encouraged her to make the trip to take some time to think about the matter." Thomas paused. "Perhaps it is good for Marin to spend time away with Susannah. She has much to consider. She can quietly give birth with Nathaniel being none the wiser until she sorts this out."

Reese ran a hand anxiously across his face. "Thomas, does it make sense for a man who returns after missing for three years to invite his wife to take a months' long absence?"

"Admittedly not, but perhaps Nathaniel is trying to show more consideration to win her back."

"One does not erase time with more absence, Thomas."

"Mayhap he intends to meet her there."

"Where is Sutton now?"

"I cannot say."

"Check his lodgings," said Reese. "I am going to the Customs House to look at the passenger and crew logs of the *Olympia*. Meet me on board my ship then. And get that bloody divorce decree!"

Thomas nodded and grabbed a carriage for hire, while Thackeray hurried to the Custom's House.

Reese returned to the ship an hour later, the expression on his face grim. Marin's name was among the four passengers, and it had an effect on him that was at once disheartening and concerning. She had left Boston without a word to him. And she had no idea of the danger she was in.

"Has Thomas returned?" he asked.

Duncan nodded. "He waits for you in your quarters."

When Thackeray entered his cabin, Thomas was pouring himself a drink. "What did you find?" asked Reese.

"Nathaniel's landlady said he went to Salem for a few days," replied Thomas, pouring another dram of whiskey and handing it to Reese. "He left yesterday morning. Maybe Nathaniel has been telling the truth, Reese. Maybe he isn't here to kidnap Marin and return her to the dey. Maybe he has turned over a new leaf."

Reese threw back his drink and looked at Thomas, skeptical. "A snake sheds its skin, but it is still a snake." A thought suddenly came to him. "Did Sutton leave by horse or by stagecoach?"

"By horse," said Thomas.

Reese set down his glass and bolted from the cabin.

On deck, he called for Duncan and White. "How seaworthy is the ship, Andrew?"

"There be some paintin' and repairs left to do, but she be sound enough for a journey of short duration," replied the bosun.

"Good. Collect me a crew—double pay. I want men who can fight. Timothy, prepare the ship to sail and tell Pots to provision it."

Duncan and White looked at each other in bewilderment.

"When are we to depart?" asked White.

"Two days."

White blinked in surprise. "Captain, that is short notice to—"

"Do it, Andrew."

"Reese, hold on," said Duncan. "Even if Andrew can raise a crew, Pots cannot collect enough provisions by then."

"He can for a week."

"What is the port-of-call?" asked White.

"We are intercepting the *Olympia* on her stop in Halifax."

Again, Duncan and White exchanged looks of confusion.

"Why? Reese, what is amiss?" asked his second mate.

"I will explain when I return from Salem, Timothy."

As Thackeray rushed down the gangplank, Duncan and White stared after him in wonder. It wasn't the first time the captain asked them to do something seemingly beyond the bounds of possibility without explanation. With a shrug of acceptance, they once again, scrambled to accomplish the near impossible task.

Meanwhile, Reese obtained a horse from the livery stable and was speeding across the Charlestown bridge and along Old Bay Road to

Salem pushing the horse as hard as he could, stopping only long enough to refresh himself and the horse at intervals.

The road seemed to wind interminably from town to town, at times muddy and slushy, at times snow-packed. The towns were responsible for the upkeep of the road as it passed through their boundaries, and he made good time in those areas where the towns rose to their responsibility. Where they did not, he cursed precious minutes lost to picking his way around patches of ice, roots, stones, and refuse in the path that made speed foolhardy.

When he finally rode into Salem, he went directly to the wharf and the Custom's House to search the manifests of ships that had recently departed. If he was right, Sutton had directed his ship to dock in Salem Harbor and had come to Salem to meet it.

The harbor was an extremely busy port, more so than Boston, and a fierce competitor of the China and East India trade. It wasn't unusual to see foreign, dark skinned sailors wearing turbans. A crew of Musselmen would not seem out of place.

Reese went through a dozen manifests of ships that had recently left port before one caught his eye. Armed with what he needed to know, he tore out of the Custom's House. It was getting late in the day, and he chaffed at the need to stop for the night in a tavern along the way. But the roads were too dangerous to travel in the dark, and he couldn't risk laming the horse now.

The *Sea Nymph* was a beehive of activity as the ship was being prepared to set sail once again.

Reese returned from Salem and called his second mate and bosun to his quarters for a report. "How do we stand for departure?" he asked.

"Pots is still collecting provisions but says that he will be ready," said Duncan.

"Mr. White?"

"The ship is sound enough. Crew is in place, sir. But Seaton has signed on to another ship. We need a first mate," replied the bosun.

"I will talk to my brother about taking on the position," said Reese. "I want Dr. Pennyman with us as well."

"Captain, what are we about?" asked Duncan.

"Sutton had a ship waiting in Salem for him—the *Triad*. He sailed yesterday morning for Halifax," explained Reese.

White scratched his head in confusion. "Ain't that good news, sir?"

"It would be if Marin were not a passenger on the *Olympia*," replied Reese soberly.

Duncan frowned, immediately grasping the situation. "Sutton is planning to kidnap her in Halifax. We may be too late, Captain."

"Aye, but by the chop of the water, there be a bit of a storm out there," interjected White. "That should slow them some."

"Andrew is right," said Reese. "If we can weigh anchor in the morn and have the luck of wind and fair weather, we will be one day behind Sutton. The *Olympia* has cargo to turn over and will remain in port for awhile."

"But Sutton will not, Captain, and he will have time to get to Mistress Marin before we arrive," pointed out Duncan.

"Hope that he does not, Timothy, or we will be chasing them to Algiers," Reese replied resolutely.

"Have no fear, Captain. We will track Sutton and his ship to the ends of the earth to get Mistress Marin back if needs be," declared White.

Reese laid a hand on the bosun's shoulder, moved by his loyalty. "With a little luck, my friend, that will not be necessary. Sutton does not know we are coming. Hopefully, he will think he has the leisure of time. Now, let us to our tasks. We have not that advantage."

The next morning, Peter and Dr. Pennyman stood on deck with Reese waiting for the wind. Among the crew, only they knew the full scope of what was at stake.

Peter was remorseful. "I am sorry, brother. I never imagined it was in Marin's mind to leave Boston."

"Now you know with what I contend," replied Reese with a wry smile. "No one knows what is in Marin's mind most of the time."

"I can attest to that," remarked Pennyman. "But how did Sutton know that she had sailed on the *Olympia*?"

"I would imagine that after planting the idea of going to England in her mind, he probably kept a check on the manifests," surmised Reese.

It was an hour before they felt the air stir enough to turn the ship to sea. Sails were unfurled, and the call went out: "Weigh anchors."

Thackeray chafed at the time that would be lost in navigating the vessel out of the busy harbor. Every minute counted now.

"Do not ye worry, brother. We shall make up the time once we are in open water," said Peter.

The ship began to pull away from the port.

"Captain," yelled Duncan. "Mr. Langford is on the wharf shoutin' for you."

Thackeray walked over to the port side to see Thomas excitedly waving a rolled document in his hand.

"I have it," he shouted. "…petition…granted."

Langford's words were buffeted by the wind, but Reese heard enough to know that Marin was legally free. Nathaniel no longer held all the cards. He waved back.

Luck, wind, and weather were with them. The *Sea Nymph* glided into Halifax Harbor 12 hours ahead of schedule and dropped anchor where there was less congestion.

It was mid afternoon, and Reese stood on the quarterdeck peering through his spyglass. "The *Olympia* is being unloaded at the end of the second pier," he said.

"Any sign of the *Triad*?" asked Peter.

Halifax was a bustling port. Just as many ships were moored at the causeway as along the wharf and piers, and Reese intently scanned the scene. He suddenly came to a stop. "There," he said, "at the causeway at the end of the pier near where the *Olympia* is anchored." He handed the spyglass to Peter. "What say you?"

"The ship has no markings, but there are seamen about wearing turbans. I would say that is the *Triad*," agreed Peter. "I will confirm it with the harbor master."

Reese nodded. "Have a care you are not spotted by Sutton. I am going to the *Olympia* to get Marin."

The men departed the ship and went their separate ways.

Reese hurried down the causeway to the end of pier and encountered the captain of the *Olympia* coming down the gangplank.

"Captain Thackeray, yes, I have heard of you," said the seaman when Reese introduced himself. "How might I be of service to you?"

"You have a passenger on board by name of Marin Sutton. I would like a word with her, sir."

"I am afraid that I cannot accommodate you, Captain. Mrs. Sutton is not on board at this time. We encountered a small storm and some turbulent waters and the poor lady has been rather indisposed. As this was the first day that she was feeling better, she decided to visit some shops."

"When did she leave?" asked Reese.

The captain thought for a moment. "About an hour ago. Lovely woman. What might I ask is your business with her?"

"I have reason to believe that she is in danger from an acquaintance. I am here to give her safe escort."

"The devil you say. A man was just here inquiring after her. He said he was her husband. I told him the same as I told you. I hope I have not caused her harm."

Reese's heart sank. "Should she return, please send word to an officer on my ship—the *Sea Nymph* docked on the quay to the west," he instructed.

The captain nodded. "Most assuredly, sir."

When Reese returned to the causeway from the pier, he ran into Peter.

"'Tis as you suspected. The ship is the *Triad*," his brother reported.

Reese quickly relayed what the captain of the *Olympia* had told him. "Start at the Parade and work your way down to the harbor."

"What are you going to do?" asked Peter.

"Find a net."

Peter had no idea what his brother meant by that but knew better than to waste time with questions, and he started off moving quickly through the streets, checking each and every shop along the way.

Reese met up with him an hour later.

"I haven't seen her," Peter reported worriedly.

Reese uttered an oath. "We may have missed her. Go to the quay. If she has returned to the *Olympia*, take her to the *Sea Nymph*," he directed. "If not, post Timothy, Andrew, and some of the crew at the *Triad's* gangplank. Sutton must not be allowed to take Marin on board that ship. I will keep searching the streets."

"What if Marin is already aboard the *Triad*?" asked Peter.

"Tell the harbor master that a woman has been kidnapped and insist the ship be detained."

Peter nodded and rushed off.

Reese was moving down George Street, when he saw Marin come out of the apothecary shop and walk toward the quay. Reese called out to her, but the noise from the street and the wharf drowned out his voice. Out of the corner of his eye, he saw another figure emerge from a nearby shop, and Reese frantically wended his way through the crowded street to reach her.

Marin heard her name called and turned, her eyes widening in surprise. "Nathaniel, what are you doing here? If you have come to persuade me to return to Boston—"

"No, I have come in the interest of trade," he replied. "I must confess to being surprised at finding you here. I would have thought you to apprise me of your travel plans."

"It was at your suggestion, Nathaniel."

"Yes, I know, but I would have thought to merit a farewell, dearest."

"I am sorry, Nathaniel. It…it was last minute."

He gave her a disarming smile. "No matter. How coincidental that we should meet here. Perhaps it was fated."

"Perhaps," she replied, feeling a little uneasy. "Well, I must get back to the ship now."

"Wait, Marin. Cannot we share a cup of hot chocolate before you go? There is a cafe around the corner. After all, it will be some time until you are able to enjoy the luxury again and I your company."

Seeing that she was reluctant, Nathaniel sighed. "You must admit I am being most magnanimous given the circumstances in which we find ourselves, my dear."

He injected a note of pain in his voice, and it found the bit of guilt Marin still harbored.

"I suppose a cup of hot chocolate would not hurt," she said.

She took his arm, and they started off."

"Marin, stop!"

The urgency with which the command punctuated the air, brought her to an abrupt halt, and she and Nathaniel turned to see Reese.

"What are you doing here?" she asked in surprise and bewilderment.

She was further nonplussed when Reese quickly pulled her away from an equally surprised Nathaniel.

"Captain, I scarce recognized you without the beard. I would have thought you to be out pirating somewhere," said Nathaniel, not bothering to hide his displeasure. "If you have come to collect the prize, I am afraid you are too late."

Marin looked at her husband. "What is this about? Why are you both here? Nathaniel, if this is about the divorce—"

Nathaniel smiled. "No, dear heart, it is not. It seems that the dey imagines he has experienced ill fortune since you were whisked away from Algiers by the captain, and he is paying handsomely for your return. Luckily, I had the advantage of knowing where to find you. But it would seem that the good captain has the idea of collecting the reward as well."

Marin turned to Reese, thunderstruck. "You knew about this?"

"Yes, but, Marin, I am not part of the deceit," said Reese. "I came here to stop him."

Nathaniel laughed. "Is that so, Captain? Why, then, did you not tell her of the dey's ransom, unless you intended to collect it yourself?"

Why indeed? Marin emotions were in such a jumble she wasn't thinking clearly, and she felt as though the ground was crumbling beneath her feet. Why did everyone lie to her?

When she looked up at Reese, he could see it in her face that Nathaniel had successfully planted seeds of distrust.

"Marin, listen to me. When I received word of the dey's ransom for you and Sutton suddenly appeared, I figured it was his purpose to kidnap you. Until I was certain about it, I did not wish to burden you further. You were under enough strain," said Reese.

Marin gave no indication if she believed him. She turned her attention back to Nathaniel. "If you take me back to the dey, you will never be able to return to America. Your deeds will become known."

"He does not intend to return," interjected Reese. "He has a wife in Algiers."

Marin had experienced enough shock today, but this was the clincher. She looked at her husband in disbelief. "Is this true, Nathaniel?" When he evaded her eye, she knew that it was. "Why?" she cried.

"He was caught bedding an Algerine woman and was facing death unless he conformed to the faith. He went a step further and married her," explained Reese, depriving Nathaniel of the chance to twist the truth.

Nathaniel gave her a faint smile. "It was nothing personal, Marin. She was a means to an end. And, if one knows how to keep on the right side of whatever dey is in power, it is a good life there."

Marin's eyes flashed with anger. "How could you? I searched for you…worried about how circumstances might find you."

"Until you decided to file for divorce," he retorted snidely.

"Do not try to place guilt on me, Nathaniel."

"Careful, my dear, we are drawing attention."

Marin felt her stomach flip over, and, for a minute, she thought she was going to be sick. "I am going back to my ship. I am not feeling well."

"A change of plans, Marin. You are taking passage on the *Triad*," said Nathaniel.

A man suddenly appeared behind them who was obviously an Algerine corsair.

Nathaniel looked at Reese. "I can imagine that the dey would pay even more for you, Captain. He is still raging at your many transgressions." Sutton cocked his head. "The government must have paid you handsomely for the return of Mrs. Marsden and her son."

As though reading Reese's mind, he added. "I wouldn't try anything heroic, Captain. You must know corsairs carry weapons in their sashes." He smiled smugly and waved his arm wide. "Shall we proceed before we attract more attention? We have conversed too long on the street as it is."

"Marin balked. "I am not going anywhere with you."

"You have no choice, my dear, I am still your husband."

"No, Sutton, you are not," cut in Reese. "Marin's petition for a divorce was just granted."

Nathaniel laughed. "Your desperation is showing, Captain."

"I have the legal document on my ship," fibbed Reese.

Sutton weighed the possibility, then grunted. "It makes no matter. Now move." He took Marin firmly by the arm and walked her forward, while the Algerine seaman prodded Reese from behind.

As they approached the *Triad*, Reese saw the entire crew of his ship immediately move to block the gangplank, armed and ready to fight.

"What is this?" demanded Nathaniel angrily. "Tell them to step aside, Captain."

"Or what?" countered Reese. "You cannot hurt Marin."

"No, but I do not think the dey cares how I bring you to him. Algerine corsairs know how to paralyze a man with one slice of the knife."

At this, Reese felt the point of a knife against his spine.

"Actually, I dare say you would be much easier to handle in such a condition, Captain."

"Nathaniel, no!" cried Marin. "Do not hurt him. Please," she pleaded.

A smile slowly spread across his face. "Well, well, well. Perhaps the captain is not the pirate he claims to be." Nathaniel looked at Marin. "Could it be, dear heart, that he is the reason for the divorce? How convenient." A hard glint came into his eyes, and he turned his attention back to Thackeray. "Tell your men to step aside, Captain, before you need to be carried aboard."

Again, Reese felt the knife pressed against his back. He saw that the corsairs on board the *Triad* were closely observing the scene and stood ready with scimitars and knives to descend upon his crew at the first signal. He was searching for a way to play for time, when Marin interceded.

She took her husband and Reese completely off guard when she announced: "I am with child, Nathaniel. By the time we reach Algiers, it will be quite obvious, and I shall tell the dey that it was you who defiled me. What reward do you think you will get from him then?" she asked smugly.

Nathaniel smiled, unfazed. "Nice try, Marin. You always did have a few tricks up your sleeve."

"Ask the apothecary if you do not believe me. He recommended ginger root for the morning upset."

Nathaniel eye's narrowed as he searched her face to gauge the veracity of her pronouncement. "I know you," he said. "While you like to challenge social norms, you never cross the line."

"I've changed, Nathaniel. After escaping Algiers with no word of you, I decided it was time to move on, to experience life again."

Nathaniel burst out laughing. "No wonder you were in such a tizzy when I returned to Boston. Oh, the leverage I would have had…" He looked at Reese. "I assume you are the culprit. If 'tis true, there are ways to deal with the matter."

"It is too late for an herbal remedy," replied Marin. "If applied at this stage, it will most likely result in my death, and you will receive no reward or blessing from the dey."

Sutton remained undaunted. "I know of a few islands where I can hold you, my dear, until you give birth. White babies fetch a handsome price on the black market."

Enraged at the very idea of his child being sold, Reese lunged for Nathaniel and was yanked back by the Algerine and a knife put to his throat.

A black scowl crossed Sutton's features. "While I enjoy the thought of returning the captain to the dey, I am done with playing games, Marin." He spoke to the seaman in Arabic, and the man drew the blade across Reese's neck drawing blood.

Marin gasped. "No, stop!"

"Then tell those men to let us pass," said Nathaniel.

Marin called out to Peter. "Please let us pass…. Please," she pleaded when no one moved.

"Are you sound, Mistress?" asked Peter.

"Yes, but they will kill the captain."

Peter looked at his brother. When Reese nodded, Peter motioned for the crewmen to move aside.

"Are you sure, sir?" asked Duncan. "We can take them bastards, and the captain can handle himself."

A smile suddenly spread across Peter's features when he spied a unit of soldiers hurrying down the quay. "I am sure, Mr. Duncan."

"Hold!" shouted the commander. "Take your hands off that lady!"

Nathaniel gaped in disbelief at the soldiers descending on him, and Peter took the opportunity to grab Marin away from him. At the same time, Reese turned on the startled corsair behind him, sending the man sprawling on the ground with a punishing blow to the jaw. Nathaniel backed away as Thackeray advanced on him, then, to deal the same blow with much more feeling.

"Mistress Marin, be ye hurt?" asked the concerned commander, hurrying up to her.

Marin laughed, almost giddy with relief. "I am fine. Commander Teaberry, words cannot express how happy I am to see you."

The commander beamed with pleasure. "Tch tch, 'tis Walter, my dear," he chided her lightly. "I could scarce believe my eyes when Captain Thackeray walked into the Citadel. I dare say it was a surprise to the both of us. When he told me of the danger you were in, there was no question that I would lend the weight of my garrison."

Reese walked up to them, rubbing the bruised knuckles on his hand. "My thanks to you, Commander. I must say I was getting a bit worried."

"Apologies, sir. There was a bit of a skirmish on the way that delayed me."

"What are you doing here, Walter?" asked Marin, still amazed at finding him there.

"I have you to thank for it, dear lady," he said. "Your kind words of praise found their way to the British Minister at the time this fort was in need of a commander. I only arrived a fortnight ago."

"I was only too happy to commend you," replied Marin, neglecting to tell him that her act of kindness was really born from an act of guilt at having drugged him that evening in Gibraltar. "You are happy with the transfer then?" she asked.

"Decidedly so, mistress."

Nathaniel staggered to his feet massaging his jaw. "Commander, I am this woman's husband, and you are interfering in a domestic matter," he said with as much indignation as he could muster.

Teaberry turned an unsympathetic ear to him. "Yes, the captain said you would say that. Mistress Marin does not have a husband. And you, sir, are a pirate in the employ of the dey of Algiers. You and your crew shall suffer the punishment of your crimes against England."

As Nathaniel was led away loudly protesting, soldiers rounded up the rest of the corsairs and moved to impound the ship.

"What will happen to Nathaniel?" asked Marin.

"Why do you care? He was ready to sell our baby to God knows who and you to the dey, not to mention the fact that he is a pirate and a bigamist," Reese reminded her. "He is no longer your husband and hasn't been for a long time. You owe him nothing."

"You really do have the divorce decree?"

"Thomas has it. Come, it is time for us to go home and begin a life together," said Reese.

She nodded and took his arm, and they walked down the quay to the *Sea Nymph.*

"I do not appreciate the risk you took telling Sutton of your condition, madam. It could have turned out badly," Reese was moved to comment.

Marin stopped and dropped his arm. "I do not appreciate you making me think that Nathaniel was dead when you knew to the contrary, and I do not appreciate you withholding news of the dey's reward for me. That *did* nearly turn out badly," she retorted.

"I sought to spare you worry."

"And I sought to spare our lives."

"For which Sutton had a solution—imprisonment on an island until you gave birth. Besides, I had the situation well in hand with Teaberry."

"Again, which you saw no need to tell me about. How was I to know?" shot back Marin as they moved up the gangplank.

They stepped on deck, continuing to argue.

"Maybe if you didn't meddle so much," charged Reese.

"I don't meddle," rejoined Marin. "Maybe if you weren't so arrogant and pigheaded…"

Suddenly conscious that they were drawing attention, Reese took her by the arm. "We shall finish this in my quarters."

Once inside his cabin, he kicked the door shut behind them. Their argument continued, emotions heightened, and Reese suddenly pulled her to him and crushed his lips against hers in a kiss that spiraled beyond seduction to a need to release the pent up energy from the danger they had narrowly escaped.

As his kisses became more feverish, she flung her arms around his neck, ardently responding. He placed his hands under her buttocks, lifted her up, and carried her to the bed. Aside from the fact that they had been held apart for far too long, the near loss of each other brought a driving need to touch, to feel, to conjoin. Reese set her down, and they quickly pulled off their clothes and fell onto the bed.

Outside, Duncan, White, Dr. Pennyman, and Peter lingered around the bulwark door, listening to the debate rage. When suddenly it stopped and everything became quiet, the men exchanged glances.

"You don't s'pose they killed each other?" quipped White.

Peter smiled. "I dare say they are just coming to terms."

"Whatever that means," remarked Duncan dryly. "Those two ain't seen eye to eye for the length of the Atlantic."

An hour later, the cabin door opened, and Reese strode purposefully on deck. "Peter, fetch a magistrate," he ordered tersely, then returned to his quarters.

Duncan and White ceased their work and looked at each other.

"He cannot be meanin' to have Mistress Marin arrested, can he?" asked White.

Duncan shrugged, concerned. "She can certainly excite his temper."

When Peter returned with a magistrate in hand and escorted him to Reese's quarters, the officers exchanged uneasy glances.

Word that a magistrate had arrived to arrest Mistress Marin, brought Pots rushing up to the main deck. "Has the Captain lost his mind?" he asked Duncan and White in astonishment.

"Can't say," said White. "He for sure was angered."

"What's happening?" asked Pennyman joining them.

"The magistrate was fetched to arrest Mistress Marin," said Pots.

"A magistrate, ay." The doctor smiled to himself.

The sailors had no inkling of what was going on, not having sailed on the last voyage, but they began to gather sensing that something was in the wind.

Twenty minutes later, Reese and Marin came on deck, followed by Peter and the magistrate, their features grim.

Pots and White pushed Duncan forward as their spokesperson.

"Is…is something amiss, Captain?" he asked haltingly.

"Amiss, Mr. Duncan?"

The second mate took a deep breath. "Aye, sir. Be ye fixin' to have Mistress Marin arrested?"

"No, Mr. Duncan, I was fixin' to marry her."

There was stunned silence among the officers. It was the last thing they had expected to hear. Neither did the captain's stern demeanor seem to support such a declaration, and they wondered if they had heard correctly. The rest of the crew exchanged mystified looks, not sure how to react. Only Pennyman seemed not surprised.

Reese smiled and took Marin's hand. "I wish to announce that Mistress Marin and I were just wed, and we want for all of you to partake in our celebration of it. Mr. Potter, bring out food and drink for everyone."

Still no one moved.

"Do ye jest, Captain?" asked White uncertainly.

"No, Mr. White. You should know by now that I do not jest."

They all looked to Marin then.

She smiled. "'Tis true. The captain and I have wed."

Cheers broke out, the crewmen taking their cues from the officers. Pots hurried back to the galley with his assistant in hand to bring out kegs of rum and foodstuff. Musicians brought out their instruments and began to play a merry jig.

"Heh, ye had us wonderin', sir," said White. "What with Peter fetching the magistrate and the argument and all—well, none of us was expectin' this turn."

Reese regarded his bosun keenly. "I hope your loss was not consequential, Mr. White."

"Beg your pardon, sir?"

"In the future, perhaps you and the others should find another subject for your wagers than your captain and his lady."

The bosun became sheepish. "Aye, sir."

Marin giggled as Reese tucked her arm in his and led her away. "How did you know about the wagers on us?"

"A good captain knows everything that happens on board his ship," replied Reese.

"I dare say not everything," commented Marin with a teasing twinkle in her eye. "There was the matter of Henry Shaw."

Reese raised a brow at that. "My crew members are not so devious as you, madam, but rest assured I have recalibrated."

Marin gave him a saucy smile. "We shall see, Captain."

"Indeed, madam." He paused with a thought. "It occurs to me that I shall have much to teach our son about women."

"On the contrary, sir, I shall have much to teach our *daughter* about men," Marin corrected him.

"Madam, if the child is a lass and is anything like her mother," said Reese, "woe be it to the man whose eye she catches. But no matter, his salvation shall be the feel of my sword first should he dare to call."

Marin laughed. "You, sir, are being a hypocrite."

"No, my dear, I am being a father."

White walked over to Duncan and Pennyman smiling broadly. "Well, mates, I dare say you owe me some coin," he said, jerking his thumb toward Reese and Marin.

Pennyman laughed. "Not so fast, Andrew. The wager was on who would tame whom? I dare say it is a draw. What say you, Timothy?"

Duncan nodded absently, still trying to figure out how this union could have possibly come about.

"Any new bets going forward, mates?" asked the incorrigible bosun.

Duncan looked up to see Reese and Marin standing together on the quarter deck hand-in-hand, strong and sure watching protectively over their ship and crew. "Nay. Any bet against them two is a fool's bet," he replied soberly.

They raised their tankards of rum in salute to the captain and the lady of the sea. "Smooth sailing and Godspeed," they shouted out.

They could not know what the future held, but none of them doubted for a minute that whatever Reese and Marin's journeys might be, they were sure to be eventful.

Other Books by Kathy Keller

The Homeward Heart
A Love Too Proud
Destiny's Shadow
Millionaire's Row (Book 1 of the Douglas Saga)—co-authored with A.J. Billman
Millionaire's Row: The Legacy (Book 2 of the Douglas Saga)—co-authored with A.J. Billman
The Paradox
A Little Gentle Persuasion

Visit author's website at **www.kathykeller.com**

ABOUT THE AUTHOR

Kathy Keller is the author of several fiction books that encompass the genres of historical, historical romance, and time travel. She is a graduate of the American University, Washington, D.C., with a degree in journalism. A native of north central Pennsylvania, she currently resides on the east coast of Florida with her husband.